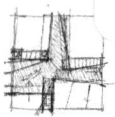

Secret Paths Editions presents

The Reaches

The Storyteller's Quest - Book One

Alan McCluskey

First published in April 2011
Second Edition August 2011
Hardcover edition December 2021

Secret Paths Editions, Mureta 2, CH-Saint-Blaise

ISBN: 978-2-9700756-8-4

Other books by the author

Bursting with Life!
The Cloud Catcher
Chimera

Stories People Tell
Local Voices

The Boy & Girl Saga
Boy & Girl - Book One
In Search of Lost Girls - Book Two
We Girls - Book Three

The Storyteller's Quest
The Keeper's Daughter - Book Two
The Starless Square - Book Three

Coming soon
The Boy in the Book

Thanks

Thanks go to my early readers, Tony, Michele, Annelie and Paul for taking the time to read earlier versions of this book and for making comments. Thanks also to the members of the Writers Circle for our talks about writing. Thanks to my children, Zoé and Iannis, for their suggestions and encouragement. And above all, my gratitude goes to my wife, Huguette, for putting up with me when inspiration came and there was no other choice but to write even when it was in the middle of the night.

Table of Contents

Prologue   7

Chapter 1 - Awakenings   9

Chapter 2 - Propositions   34

Chapter 3 - The Circle   54

Chapter 4 - The Guide   73

Chapter 5 - The Machine   94

Chapter 6 - The Wanderer   118

Chapter 7 - The Lessons   142

Chapter 8 - The Black Castle   173

Chapter 9 - The Mansion   197

Chapter 10 - The Littl' People   214

Chapter 11 - The Shaman   242

Chapter 12 - Virtual Realities   267

Chapter 13 - Oran Mor   295

Chapter 14 - The Threads Unravel   318

Alan McCluskey

Prologue

"Are you sure this is right?" Jake asked.

Nala hesitated at the unfamiliar ring of his voice, then nodded, her green eyes radiant. They stepped inside, bolting the door firmly behind them. Wooden benches lined the wall opposite the ticket desk. A large poster proclaimed in bold, red gothic letters: *Make way for the future!*

Tickets in hand, they squeezed through a narrow gate in a metal barrier and moved towards the stairs that wound down to the Deeper Reaches. Above the roof arched upwards, darkened with time and soot. The place smelt of steam trains. Traces of old stories. Their footsteps echoed softly off the brick walls left and right like a hushed crowd under way.

A violent crash broke the peace. Horrified, they spun round to look. A second crash followed. Someone was trying to ram down the door to the ticket office. The door flew off its hinges and smashed into the ticket counter, shattering at the impact. Light from outside streamed into the office through the broken door as a hoard of burly thugs erupted into the tight space.

"You go. I'll lock the gate," Jake shouted.

Not waiting to see if she'd gone, he moved quickly back to the gateway and fished the key from his pocket: the one they'd found earlier. He fumbled with it for a moment and then it slid into the lock with ease. He turned it and the lock clicked closed. As he stepped back, his relief was short lived.

Roaring. Swearing. Clambering over each other to get at him. A seething mass, all shiny black leather and studs and acrid sweat, twisted hands, hobnailed feet, bared teeth, clawing, pushing, shoving their way towards the high metal barrier that separated them from him.

"That's the blighter wot did it."

"Grab 'im!"

"'Es the one wot 'urt our young Tom."

"Grab the bugger."

They threw themselves at the gate in the barrier like a raging sea. But it didn't give. Furious, some smashed their fists against the metal, sending blood squirting over the floor beyond. Others ransacked the office. Anything they could lift was hurled against the barrier. He shrank back into shadows, edging closer to the steps that led down to the Reaches.

He didn't get far. A heavy paperweight hit him on the shoulder. He gasped and staggered. The pain was excruciating. When he collapsed to his knees, an unearthly roar rose from beyond the barrier, throaty, sickening, like beasts foaming at the mouth, out for the kill.

"Blood!"

A new wave of savages flung themselves against the weakening barrier. A second flying object bowled Jake over, sending him rolling down the stairs until he came to halt against a wall at the bottom. Silence came now and with it a bitter blackness.

Chapter 1 - Awakenings

6.10

Her earrings and necklace shook as the alarm in her phone went off on the bedside table. Vibrating gold on emeralds. Sally lent over to silence the ringing. She caught sight of her abandoned nightdress lying on the rug next to the bed. Pale green silk, laced with mixed fragrances. Shame Keira hadn't been able to stay. Next time they'd have to plan things better.

She pushed back the eiderdown and sat on the edge of her double bed pulling her nightdress over her head. It was cold in the bedroom with only her panties on. What had Keira whispered with her goodnight kiss?

"Dream of me, my love, and I'll be with you all night."

Sally smiled as she stood, running her hands through her shoulder length auburn hair. People said it went with the green of her eyes and the slightly tanned colour of her skin. If she'd been a bit shorter, she might have been taken for an elf. The idea appealed to her.

6.45

The journalist on the radio was explaining that German scientists had recently managed to grow immature sperm cells from human bone marrow samples. Sally had to laugh. Would men ever be mature? Jokes apart, the prospect of developing fully-fledge sperm cells was worth exploring. The idea of a world without men scampered through her mind, only to be discarded. Well at least a world without that obnoxious assistant, Tyrell. Scowling, she vigorously cut the thick slices of hot toast in half with a large carving knife.

A scientist was explaining that it was still early days, but there were hopes of curing some male infertility. Not that she didn't like men. Just that she preferred Keira's firm rounded buttocks and her impudent little nipples to male sweat and swollen pricks and hairy chests. And sperm was such a messy business. Better not think of that. It was Monday, a day of work, well study. And her singing lesson with Naniu.

7.05

Birds were greeting the rising sun from the bushes and treetops along the seaside avenue as she walked to the station. The familiar paperboy cycled past wishing her the top of the morning. An early breeze blew off the sea, ruffling the folds of her blouse sending shivers of expectation down her spine. The salty tang of the sea smelt good. It would be a beautiful day.

7.55

Drat! The spotty schoolboy sprawled on the seat opposite couldn't take his eyes off her. His grossly enlarged eyes, magnified by thick spectacles, had a glazed, absent look to them. May he roast in hell! No matter where he tried to look, his attention always snapped back to her. Curse him. She shouldn't let it get under her skin. But it did.

Strange how men thought they could stare at you unnoticed. As if you weren't really there, like a picture that could be abused at will, without material consequences. But she wasn't an image. She was nobody's plaything. It disturbed her to be abused in such a way. Goodness knows what was oozing along the muddy backwaters of his mind. Nothing that concerned her, that was for sure.

She smoothed her pale green cotton skirt over her legs, it

was one of her summer favourites that went well with her beige blouse, and folded her hands demurely in her lap.

She looked out of the train window at the passing shoreline. Gulls were rising in noisy clusters over the waves. Fish. She could almost smell them. Why did males smell like that when in heat? Sally tried to turn her mind to other things, but she was still being watched, obstinately. She could feel his eyes boring into her.

Aggressive? No. That wasn't the right word. More like spineless: a retreat rather than an advance. Then the ticket in her hand reminded her of her dream. And she slipped gently away. Tantalising fragments of her night floated just out of reach, calling to her: tendrils of wistful longing curled round her and bore her away…

8.10

Brent sat up reluctantly, swinging his long legs out of bed onto the shiny wooden floorboards. It was early by his standards. There was almost time to squeeze in a few more dreams. Well, maybe not.

He stretched his arms and shoulders, surprised that he ached all over, as if he'd been roughed up. He'd done nothing to deserve that. He wasn't the athletic type, but he loved to walk and prided himself on being fit. It was rare that his muscles ached so much.

Pulling the eiderdown around his shoulders - it was a chilly morning - he picked up a notepad from the bedside table and began to write. Coordination between brain and fingers was always sluggish so soon after sleep.

Fragments came surging back though, faster than he could write, making his handwriting all but illegible: a shining knee lying in the mud. He crossed out 'knee', wrote 'key' laughing at the silliness of it and continued: a winding path along the riverbank; and had there not been a brawl with the police? No wonder he felt bruised.

Brent was delighted at the heap of short stories he'd amassed from his dreams. Although they could be acutely embarrassing or frightening or unpleasant, he was no longer terrified of them as he'd been as a child. There was no more guilty blood smeared on the walls or houses that crumbled life-threateningly around him.

He lay down his scribblings on a growing pile of similar dream fragments by his bedside, where they awaited reworking into longer stories. Had not someone stolen his dreambook, he would have had a lot more. He imagined himself flipping through the pages.

The fragments retained much of the magic and excitement of the original dream. It was as if they were charged with some form of living energy that hung in the air. They were glimpses into another world; one that was as real, if not more so, than the world he lived in the rest of the time.

Massaging his painful shoulders, he wondered if actions in the dream realm had any impact on the real world. Jotting down the thought for later, he stood and went for a shower and a late breakfast.

Laid out on a chair in the bathroom his clothes were prepared for the day: light brown cotton trousers and a red and green chequered shirt - comfortable and practical, as always. He found it difficult to choose clothes that suited him, especially as he was quite tall but slim. As a child he'd been redheaded which didn't help but now he was more light brown.

8.45

Amid the eggs and toast and tea, a newspaper article reported on the latest findings about drug addiction. Odd word that, he thought. Drug. Droge Vat. Dried substance in a vat. A powdery white cloud gently settled over the idea, obscuring the substance of it.

Apparently, the radio continued, a doctor at a congress in Milwaukee had explained that drug addiction was a misplaced strategy to solve a personal problem. Once the problem had been unearthed, the way was open to more suitable solutions. *What nonsense!* thought Brent, *As if knowing the problem was enough to solve it.*

He rose from the kitchen table, slipped into his trekking shoes and donned his jacket to go out. Today he was to see a shaman. Maybe the magician could help him solve a persistent problem with his dreams. Contrary to the learned, radio doctor's theory, his problem was quite familiar to him but, despite that, it continued to resist his attempts to solve it.

9.15

Naniu reached up to greet Sally with a kiss on each cheek, her hands firmly placed on Sally's shoulders. She was a little shorter than Sally. Naniu wore an ample long-sleeved, large-lapelled cotton blouse embroidered with the dragon and phoenix motif that was fastened with a series of buttons and loops.

She preferred not to wear the skirt that most Chinese women wore, but rather a Ku, loose-fitting trousers, knotted around her waist with a thick silk sash. She wore her long black hair tied up in a knot. Her feet were bare, her skin tanned, and her features relaxed. If it weren't for something quietly powerful about her, you'd never know she was world-renown for her work on singing.

"Lie down on your back and breath deeply, Sally," she said as she lay down on the carpet herself. "As you breathe out, let the air make a sound."

Sally was always self-conscious to begin with. And the more she sought to let go, the tenser she felt. As she explored the limits of the sounds she could make, however, something relaxed and she sank imperceptibly deeper into the sway of the sounds: deep, throaty growls; tiny high-pitched calls; and glissandi that cascaded from one to the other.

9.30

So this was the shaman. It was difficult to tell the man's age. Forty, maybe. He had an infectious smile that lit up his round face and sparkling blue eyes, inspiring confidence. Clean-shaven and balding, his weather-beaten features continued to reflect something of the sun gathered in times passed.

"Hi. My name is Alo. I am a dreamweaver. I walk between the worlds. But I think you know that because you have come to see me."

The man's voice was surprisingly deep and rich, full of a mass of colours and nuances. Brent felt it resonate in his own body. So Alo was a weaver of dreams, Brent thought. His mind reached back to the origins of the word "weaver" and felt the fine strands of a Sanskrit spider that wove sense through space: a subtle sense-maker that could catch you in its web if you were not careful. Word traps.

"I'm Brent."

He realised he'd imagined someone older and more Indian-like. Although the man had the build of an Indian, Brent thought: tall, well built, muscular. Sitting down on a vacant cushion opposite Alo, Brent glanced around the sparsely decorated room and said, "I would have expected something more exotic: snake skins, eagle feathers, dark corners, wafts of incense, ..."

"I don't seek to confuse this world with the dream world" was Alo's reply. "Now tell me, why do you seek my help?"

Brent leant forward on his cushion and thought for a moment. "It's my dreams. I'm convinced that I have to go somewhere ... but I no longer know where ... or why. I keep getting lost. I spend hours crossing interminable landscapes or wending my way through towns that stretch like labyrinths before me..."

9.40

"Grrrrooouuusssseeeeeeeeiiiiiiiiiiiiiaaaaaahhh…"   Sally slithered over the up-turned curves of the vowels and rocketed downwards into the depths till her toes and fingertips vibrated with pleasure.

"Stand up … when you're ready."

Naniu's voice called her back from the world of breathing and sounds in which she was engrossed. She slowly opened her eyes, peered at Naniu through half closed eyes and stood reluctantly.

"I'll sing a couple of notes, and then you imitate them. Try to keep the same feeling you had when lying on the floor, as if the sound is singing you."

Naniu sang and Sally responded. Naniu shook her head and repeated the first note. Sally tried again.

"You're too low, Sally."

Try as she would, Sally couldn't get it right. In fact, the more she tried the worse it got. She just couldn't hear the difference. She began to fear she was tone-deaf.

"Wait a moment before you sing, Sally," Naniu suggested. "Take a breath. Let the sounds resonate in you in silence. Then let them sing themselves, without thinking."

Naniu sang. Sally breathed in and hung suspended for a moment, as if waiting on the threshold before stepping out. Then she sang.

Naniu broke into a broad grin. "Good."

Sally still couldn't hear the difference, but somehow she felt the harmony of it and it felt good. And she knew that feeling would guide her in the future. She just had to trust herself and let go.

"It will probably be of no consolation to you, but most people don't even know they are on a quest, let alone what the goal of it might be! Whereas you are tormented by the idea. That's a good sign." Alo said, grinning impishly. "It's a bit paradoxical really. Many people's lives are plagued with short-term goals and objectives. They're convinced that their little efforts will change the world. They know nothing of the power of effortless doing! What you seek is to be the purposeless wanderer, but you can't get there using force." He paused, as if he were giving it some silent thought.

Brent felt lost and confused as Alo's words moved beyond his reach. He was about to say something, but Alo changed subjects.

"Practically speaking, though, you should keep a dreambook in which you jot down your dreams."

"But I do, or rather I did," retorted Brent, "only someone stole my dreambook. I left it in my bag on the table in a pub the other day as I went to get a drink from the bar. When I returned, it was gone. Nothing else had been touched."

Alo remained silent for quite a while, pursing his lips. Brent had the impression he was struggling for the right words.

"We need to talk more of this, but not now and not here." Alo spoke so quietly that Brent had to strain to hear his words.

The shaman's reaction seemed grossly exaggerated, reminding him of amateur dramatics from his school days. He was tempted to burst out laughing.

"I'll let you know where and when." Speaking louder, Alo went on: "In the mean time, you might try using white stones."

Brent looked perplexed. He had the odd feeling that Alo might be trying to cast a spell on him.

"Imagine a small set of white pebbles. They need to be

small, very small, very, very small, to cross the barrier between the worlds. As you travel, hold the stones in your mind. Touch them. Feel them cool against your fingers. See them bright white. The important thing is to remember them in your dream, not so much to have them guide you on your way."

10.30

After her hour with Naniu, Sally longed for time alone. She sauntered through Hoyt Park, delighting in the colours and fragrances of the many flowers that graced her path. She stood still for a moment and closed her eyes. A slight breeze blew over her sandaled feet, around her bare ankles and billowed her skirt.

Being in the dark. It was one of her secret pleasures: sensing the world around her otherwise than with her eyes. Irises. Heavenly. How could she put words to such a complex feeling: an aroma deep in colour and rich in harmonies that went straight to the crown of your head? She thought back over her songtime with Naniu. She relived the instant she'd hung suspended over the void, discovering how silence and stillness brought knowledge that movement and effort held at a distance.

Satisfied, she opened her eyes and turned in the direction of Avan University, which was situated at the far end of Hoyt Park. The buildings lay scattered close to one side of the River Bree, not far from where it joined Erinsea. The founders of the university couldn't have chosen a better place for experimentation and learning in such a seafaring town.

She traversed the length of the campus, making her way to the Theosophy department. Like all the other buildings, the Theosophy department was made of the local grey-green stone, but its distinctive shape singled it out for attention. The design was from Madame Blavatsky herself.

Built on an oval-shaped island, separated from the riverbank by a narrow channel, the department curved sensuously with the water that flowed around it. The building was topped with a number of turrets and glass domes for observation purposes.

Sally crossed the bridge that spanned the narrow branch of the Bree and pushed open the massive oak door.

Professor Tangwyn Outman's lecture was due in five minutes. Theosophy, her teachers had told her when she began her studies, was the science of knowledge achieved through spiritual ecstasy, direct intuition, or special individual relations to God. So what was a mathematician like Professor Outman doing giving a lecture in the Theosophy department, you might ask? Chaos Theory was the answer.

10.35

Alo received his clients in a large detached mansion at the top of a small hill overlooking Avan. The extensive gardens that surrounded the property offered some welcome seclusion. Brent bent down to pick up a couple of small white pebbles that lay amongst the weeds beside the path. Slipping them into his jacket pocket, he was surprised at how cold they felt.

The wrought-iron gate closed behind him with a decisive click and he set off down the hill towards the town. The houses in this part of Avan reclined confidently in their well-tended gardens, keeping their distance from the road and from each other. Brent walked on the grass verge that lined the road. It was soft beneath his feet. Across a hedge he spied a young women on her knees, planting flowers in a rock garden. Her hair was a striking blond mass of curls that cascaded over her shoulders and flowed almost down to her breasts. She looked up, caught his eye and smiled at him.

"Good morning" he called out.

She waved a muddy hand at him. Her smile stirred in him all the way down the hill. He toyed with the stones in his pocket. He could feel their calming whiteness. As the road turned and widened at the bottom of the hill, the houses changed: shrinking, they drew closer to each other and to the road. A gravel path replaced the soft verge. The tiny stones slipped slightly with each step, giving way almost imperceptibly under his weight.

Some order must have reigned here at one time for there was an air of family about the houses. With time, however, each had grown a distinctive mark to single it out: here a bay window had sprouted; there a patio had swallowed up most of the small garden.

The closer Brent came to the town, the more the houses huddled together for comfort. Each resembled its neighbour until they stood identical in long lines of redbrick, door after door opening directly onto the street. The pavement here was narrow and made of cement blocks that rang hard beneath his feet.

They should have called him Brent the Wanderer. He delighted in walking: the thrill of each step as his feet met the ground, exploring the feel of the many surfaces that rose to meet him. What was the Gaelic blessing? He sang softly to himself:

"May the road rise to meet you. May the wind be always at your back. May the sun shine on your face ..."

The old station was not just old because it had been there for a long time, but also because there was a new one and the new one, as is often the case, had done its best to replace the old one. Only a couple of trains made the detour to call there on weekdays. If it weren't for the stationery shop, not even Brent would go there. The shop was excellent. It was there he bought his dreambook. Not red this time, though. Blue, he thought, pale blue. He also bought a large felt pen.

The toilets at the old station were relegated to the far end of the platform. Standing in front of the two doors, Brent cursed Lacan. Wasn't it the French psychoanalyst who had condemned young people to hesitate over the choice between Gents and Ladies? Humanity's first trauma, he'd called it. Glancing around to see if anybody was watching, Brent chose the Ladies. He opened the door of the first cubicle, went in, closed the door, lowered his trousers and pants and sat down to piss. Drawing the felt pen from his pocket, he scrawled across the door, just above a hole someone had bored there:

Lacan was here. Signed Confused.

Sally took one of the few remaining free seats near the front of the crowded amphitheatre, nodding greetings to those she recognised. It seemed that the entire faculty had turned out for the occasion. Tense expectation hung in the air. Professor Outman was world-renowned and rarely gave lectures since his illness and his retirement to India.

The lights in the auditorium dimmed perceptibly and the chatter of the audience hushed as a tall, slender young woman entered pushing an equally tall old man in a wheelchair. Their passage across the podium was like a fresco unfolding. From where she sat, Sally could smell the wafts of Masala incense that hung in the air and imagined she could hear the strains of a Morning Raga accompanying them.

Professor Outman's granddaughter, Anju, was dressed in traditional Indian style with an ivory-coloured Lehenga embroidered with a Persian floral motif that reached to her sandaled feet. The skirt was topped with a tight-fitting, short-sleeved ivory-coloured Choli that left a good part of her tanned belly visible. A sparkling jewel embellished her navel. The sight of her made Sally's mouth water.

The Professor wore a traditional Kurta, a loose-fitting collarless shirt made of silk that was discretely embroidered with mystical figures, white on white. Typical, Sally thought. He was always walking the limit between science and mysticism. His cotton Paijama trousers barely concealed his wasted legs. Most striking of all was his face, which seemed lit up by the oriental sun, his eyes bright and attentive behind his metal-rimmed spectacles. His forehead was pronounced and culminated in a shock of wild, greying hair that matched his equally unruly beard.

"Good morning to you all," he said, breaking into a radiant smile. "I haven't been in this building for many years." He paused as if looking back over time, before moving on.

"If you'll excuse me beginning with what might seem like a rather tasteless play on words, I'd like to rewrite the beginning of The Gospel According to John: 'In the beginning was Chaos.

And Chaos was with God and Chaos was God.' That was how the ancients understood Chaos: a dark, deep and undivided godhead that was profoundly feminine. Not a sinister black hole, in the cosmological sense, that sucks all matter into its unending cold embrace, but rather a sensual, throbbing womb that gives birth to all that is to follow."

Sally sensed the people around her collectively letting out their in-held breaths. An intense ripple of pleasure flowed through her.

"The modern notion of chaos is quite inadequate and totally unsatisfying in comparison. Mayhem. Pandemonium. Bedlam. Havoc. So many negative images of disorder, lawlessness and anarchy, when in fact the principal of order and differentiation was born spontaneously out of chaos. Modern mathematics puts chaos back in its rightful place, at the heart of all things."

"Imagine an infinite collection of potential futures brought together in one extremely complex and beautiful curve suspended in exquisite balance above a dark and silent expectancy. Time and movement have yet to exist. All is suspended like a breath held. Then something slips, imperceptibly, more like a faint whisper than a movement. And the time has come. The curve arches upwards and folds over abruptly. Thousands of possibilities collapse to nothing, leaving those that remain to shift and shunt in an urgent need to find a new balance. The cataclysmic shudder produces multiple waves that bring shape and form as the resulting tsunami rolls outwards."

11.10

"Fish. Fresh fish. Straight from the boat! Come on ladies. Take yer pick!"

On the sloping boards of the fishmonger's stall lay rows of neatly aligned fish of all sorts, their eyes bulging in horror at the recognition of their fate. Brent walked on, ignoring their icy screams. He passed by the runny French cheeses that noisily competed with each other to attract the largest number of flies in the Market Place. He avoided the sacrificial salami awaiting the butcher's knife.

He skipped yesterday's dried-up cakes spotted with wrinkled raisins, guaranteed to break a tooth or two. He ignored the shoddily made clothes imported from some poor country where children laboured hours for a pittance. Work no longer made proud, Brent thought.

He passed over the cheap CDs of potted music, the crinkled paperbacks promising love and fulfilment and the herbal teas that worked wonders if you were a true believer. So much flotsam and jetsam left stranded by the receding tide: a truly disgusting and disturbing sight. Hopefully the rising tide would wipe clean this patent evidence of man's decline.

One gem did catch his attention amongst the collective rubbish: a small stand of used postcards. Brent had always been struck by how postcards shaped our way of seeing the world. Coach loads of tourists repeatedly sought to recreate the magical postcard feeling. How did we see the world before postcards, he wondered? Difficult to imagine. But these were not just postcards. No. They had been used. Handwritten greetings added a distinctly personal flavour to the slick, production-line images. There was the inevitable *Wish you were here...* or the *Having a lovely time...* in a lazy, sunlit scrawl next to the official postoffice stamp: Brighton, Torquay, Blackpool, Yarmouth,...

Not all memories were banal though. Brent remembered that time down by the pier on holiday when he'd caught sight of a couple fondling each other behind the deserted dodgem car attraction. The ripples of that had sent him diving for cover. Or when Granny had sprained her ankle trying to stop the girls chasing him across the beach. Kiss chase: how he hated it.

So many delightful memories that had mellowed with time. Things were no longer like that now he was grown up. Despite his childhood belief that becoming adult would open worlds to him, possibilities seemed to have shrunk as he grew older. He paid for an old card of Avan showing the station as it once had been when there were still steam trains and slipped it into his jacket pocket.

11.20

Anju leant forward and offered her grandfather a glass of water from which he drank deeply. The girl's appearance was surprising. She had pitch-black hair like many Indians, but she'd had it cut very short more like a boy than a girl.

The Professor sat silent for a moment. "I am talking about change and how it comes about. There are two key notions in complex change. The first is the way change emerges apparently spontaneously from the field of all possibilities. And the second are the discontinuities that occur in change when the fabric of what is possible folds."

He ran his hand through his beard, tugging at it gently; a frown on his face. "Before I go any further, you have to understand that the perspective of chaos is not to everybody's liking. The main reason for this understandable aversion lies in how institutions are organised and how they handle change. They concentrate power in discrete pockets from which they seek to influence the way people work. For those in power, change is a product of their policies. Their vision is essentially mechanistic: they apply a force to the system and that brings about a pre-determined change. Seeing change in terms of emergence and discontinuities is threatening. It questions the belief that they can manage change and undermines their identity as leaders. Of course, we have to be careful about what we mean by the words 'manage' and 'leader', but that is another discussion."

For all the Theosophy Department's work on the direct experience of knowledge of the transcendent, Sally imagined that the Chaos perspective would ruffle Department sensitivities, but surely the Professor was aware of that.

11.30

A traffic warden was making her way systematically up the crowded high-street. Brent slowed to watch her at work. He liked the way she bent forward short-sightedly to note the car's number. The movement pulled her skirt delightfully taught over her buttocks and pointed her breasts forward pushing out her uniform jacket. She constantly shook her pen to get it to work as she scratched down the details. In her hurry, her hair had tumbled out from under her hat and was getting in her eyes. She brushed it absent-mindedly aside.

Some urgency was pressing her to get on. Maybe she had an appointment for lunch or she had a quota to keep up with. She walked with a slight limp, stooping to rub her ankle from time to time. For all her quaintness, Brent wondered why her boss had chosen someone so apparently inept for the work. She certainly had a lot of work to do. Car owners in Avan must have signed a pact with the devil because they parked haphazardly without the slightest concern for order or safety. The warden limped on. Now it was the turn of a Bentley parked on a yellow line in front of the hat shop. An elegant lady came bustling out, loaded down with hatboxes. She looked as if she'd come straight from the hairdresser's as her hat was delicately balanced in an elaborate new hair-do.

"Sorry love. Just had to pick these up," she told the traffic warden.

The warden handed her the parking ticket and moved on. Brent wondered how the women would react. Anger? Self-justification? Persuasion? Family connections? None of them. She opened her car, placed the boxes in it and then went over to the next car where she slid the fine under the windscreen wiper. A short distance off, the warden stood watching her. She retraced her steps and picked up the fine. Noting some additional information on the paper, she handed it back to the woman whose mouth had fallen open. No words were exchanged. Well maybe the boss had not made such a bad choice after all.

11.35

"Professor, isn't a world governed by chaos a highly unpredictable place to live in?"

Outman asked Anju to shift his wheelchair slightly so he could get a better view of the young woman asking the question.

"It is hard to escape the underlying connotations that words convey. The word 'chaos' is no exception. Complex as it is, it imposes meanings on us that we might not welcome. As I said in my introduction, mathematical chaos is not anarchy. It is centred on stability. When a system shifts from one state to another it does so because it seeks stability. In complex systems stability does not come at a particular point or time, but rather resides in a whole set of points or times. This set we call an attractor. Within the field of the attractor, minor disturbances will not shift the system out of the zone of influence of the attractor. That doesn't mean there is no change, but it remains within the field of the attractor. The name "attractor" is misleading. It inevitably evokes the picture of a force that attracts. Whereas an attractor is not a force, but a set of closely related states in which the system remains relatively stable. Coming as it did from topology, Chaos Theory was more interested in the exquisite shapes of attractors than in the underlying forces at play."

"I'm not sure I understand the notion of attractor," the woman admitted.

"Think of sleep," the Professor replied. "It is a state we are all familiar with. But that state can have myriad forms. It can be peaceful and apparently dreamless, leaving us refreshed when we awake. Or it can be agitated, full of dark nightmares or deep longing that continue to haunt our wakening hours. We can lie still in our sleep or toss and turn, knotting the sheets about us. Sleep is full of diversity. It is a state, like being awake is a state. Although it can be hard sometimes to fall asleep, once the moment is come you generally flip from one to the other. And while you are asleep, most noises and movements will not break the hold of sleep on you, though they may affect your dreams. So you see, sleep is an attractor: a complex set of quite different states we recognise under the name of 'sleep' that is distinguishable and quite separate from a whole set of other states we call being awake."

Just off Market Street, in a narrow alley that served as a shortcut to St. Bride's Cathedral, stood one of those shabby shops that sold second-hand clothes for charity. Through the dusty window Brent could see a room littered with bric-a-brac: unwanted trinkets; clumsy odds and ends; and rows and rows of cast off clothes. Brent tried to trick himself into walking passed, but he didn't manage. The pull was too strong. He was at the door before he knew it.

Opening it set a small bell ringing. How discreet! He nodded to the elderly woman behind the counter who quickly returned to reading her magazine. Judging from the hopeful look he'd seen fleetingly cross her face, he was probably her first customer of the day. The place smelt of mothballs with a faint trace of damp and a much stronger smell of a sticky perfume whose best-by date was long gone. He was reminded of his Grandmother's house. What a confusing chaos that had been for a small kid. Chaos: now there was a word of power! The vast chasm of the Greeks or was it the void?

Walking between the rows of hangers, he ran his fingers over the clothes. A small grey tweed jacket, pulled in at the waist, with a high collar. The girl must have been barely a slip of a thing. Died of tuberculosis no doubt, like his Grandmother. A dark velvet waistcoat that smelt of cigars. Small pleasures after dinner out on the back porch by the privy, but only when it wasn't raining. A pleated school skirt. Girls rarely wore the like today. It's owner driving the neighbours' boy mad. He spent hours at his bedroom window watching her doing handstands against the garden wall. To think his mother believed he was doing his homework.

Ignoring the rows of dungarees and overalls that gave off an unpleasant odour of grease and sweat, Brent halted at a silk bodice. Lace trimmings. She must have felt pretty in that. Early twenties, probably. Got her really worked up when she walked out in it. She could feel his eyes following her, her nipples hard against the cool silk at the thought of it.

26   Alan McCluskey

This kind of shop didn't go in for underwear. Not hygienic. Shame. Lots of stories there for the telling. He stopped one last time close to the door, his attention caught by a bunch of rusty keys held together by a small chain. Someone had put them on display, splayed out on a small piece of velvet: a deliciously sensual offering. They beckoned to him. A rich potential lay waiting to be tapped. What doors would these keys unlock? He enquired about the price, paid and left hurriedly with the dark treasure heavy in his pocket.

11.50

"What about understanding the forces at work?" The question came from an elderly gentleman seated at the back of the room. "Has Science made any progress on that?"

Professor Outman made a quick note in a small notebook. "A very good question. Our friends from Fundamental Physics have a different way of looking at things than us Topologists. They have borrowed the idea of self-organising systems from the Life Sciences and have been exploring what they call 'emergence' in an attempt to describe how new states come into being. That's not my field. I suggest you read Prigogine or Bohm or Varela or Lovelock or Capra."

12.00

The young librarian turned to look at him and nodded in recognition as Brent strode into the library; he was a frequent visitor. Few readers were present: an old man hunched over a newspaper; a teenager seated cross-legged on the floor flicking through a comic book; a smartly dressed women studiously taking notes from an encyclopaedia.

Standing in the middle of the room, Brent closed his eyes, turned thrice clockwise and headed in a straight line to the nearest bookshelf, picking out a book at random without looking at the cover. Letting the book fall open in his hands, he read the first sentence that caught his attention:

Opening these doors is often like a surgical operation, where the doctor, with knife poised, must be prepared for anything the moment the incision is made.

The words sent a shiver down his spine. The slightest ill-chosen incision could open floodgates with devastating results, overwhelming all around as it unleashed bloody horrors. He bowed his head and closed the book, hurriedly sliding it back in the space on the shelf. Returning to the centre once more, he closed his eyes and turned again.

If you are going on a journey, see that you take with you all that you may need.

How odd. Brent could imagine the head of the order instructing his young novice with those words as the boy set out on his quest. Far from travelling light! How could you possibly anticipate what would be needed in a future full of so many unexpected twists and turns? Turning one final time he uncovered a third book.

So singing blessings then for my soul's sake,
As I silent, round me thrice did go
The apostolic light which bid me speak...

He recognised the words immediately. A silent prayer rose unbidden from his heart, intercede for me that I can partake of such a joy!

12.25

Sally carried the tray of drinks and sandwiches from the bar to a table in a quiet backroom that looked out over a garden. She'd deliberately chosen a more secluded spot so they could talk undisturbed. She hadn't seen Tangwyn or Anju since she had visited them in India several years before, so she was pleased they had managed to escape the clutches of the Faculty. Tyrell, one of the assistants, had been almost obnoxious in insisting he join them. Sally had had to make it quite plain to him that he was not welcome, on the pretext that the Professor was tired after the effort of his travel and the conference. No doubt he'd get her back for that.

Handing the Professor his beer, she voiced a current preoccupation: "As I was listening to your conference, Tangwyn, I was wondering how dreams fit in."

He laughed. "The dream world is the realm of chaos, par excellence. It is full of the most outrageous discontinuities that don't bother us in the slightest. I have an untested theory that chaos is so apparent in dreams because our relationship to time and space is not the same there as in the real world."

Shifting closer to Sally, Anju added: "You are right. In that respect, time and space are more like fluids in dreams and they have nothing to contain them."

The Professor took a notebook from his bag and scribbled down a few words. "We describe change in chaos theory using topologies that categorise families of form and shape but give no promise as to their size or duration. In dreams the notion of measurement of time and space is in some ways suspended."

"Have you written anything about it?" Sally asked.

"No. But Dr. Jakob Leuchtli has been working on some applications of Chaos Theory to the dream world, though he is more interested in the release of energy in the discontinuities when the dream fabric folds. He hopes to be able to harness that energy to replace existing power sources. Dangerous ideas, if you ask me. Very dangerous and ill thought out. Smacks of black magic."

13.00

Brent followed the disused railway line along the wharves. It came to a halt at a buffer by a promontory that stretched out into the harbour. The place was abandoned. No doubt the port staff were at lunch. He had the whole world to himself.

He walked out onto the promontory and sat down on the furthermost bollard, from where he had a clear view over the harbour and the sea beyond. He stayed still for a long moment, his hands folded in his lap, relaxing and breathing gently, sinking down inside himself, enjoying the warmth of the midday sun and a refreshing breeze from the sea.

Gradually he let his senses drift out, feeling first the immense mass of water beneath him. There was so much of it and it was so full of raw energy. It threatened to overwhelm him. He let his spirit rise, skimming along in the wake of a flock of gulls. He loved the feeling of spreading his wings and flying, his feathers ruffled in the breeze. He plunged close to the waves looking for fish then banked back upwards and away towards the harbour wall awaiting the incoming trawlers.

Brent shifted his attention to the air, feeling the lazy eddies of warm currents that spiralled up above the darkened roofs of the wharves, curling their way around the girders that supported the cranes. Tiny insects were letting themselves be borne upwards in the rising current before plunging back down through cooler air.

A sharp noise brought Brent back to himself with a rush. A small van had pulled up along the wharf where it stood stationary, its motor still running. Brent resented the intrusion. Exhaust fumes and the stench of overheated metal reached his nose. He wrinkled it in disgust. How dare they enter his world?

The men, for surely it was men in the van, were waiting for a signal from a boat, he imagined. Maybe they had to pick someone up, a wanted criminal, a stowaway, a smuggler. If they saw him, he'd be in for trouble. Stories from books of his childhood came flooding back.

Or maybe they had come to ditch a package in the sea, causing one of the worse bouts of pollution in years. He might be the first to fall ill because of it, having been so near. What a shame to die so soon.

Or perhaps it was the same people who had stolen his dreambook from the pub. His hand went instinctively into his jacket pocket where he had put the new notebook. It was still there, unused as yet. The men were keeping an eye on him. He must be part of some bigger plan of which he knew nothing. Not knowing disturbed him.

In his pocket he could feel the white stones he'd picked up at Alo's place. They had remained surprisingly cold. Cupping them in his hand within his pocket, he stood and walked in the direction of the van. As he pulled alongside, he caught a glimpse of a young couple in each other's arms kissing fervently, oblivious to his presence. Brent hadn't realised how hungry he was. He turned away and set out for home.

13.30

Once Sally had accompanied Tangwyn and Anju to their hotel down by the sea at the limit of Hoyt Park, not far from the University, she planned to return to the Department to sound out reactions to the conference. On the seaward side of the park, not far from the Theosophy Department, the landscape gardeners had planted a complex tangle of rhododendrons through which a number of paths wove maze-like.

A red-coloured object under one of the shrubs caught her attention. Pushing between the branches, she managed to retrieve what turned out to be a small red notebook. She was about to examine it when she heard a familiar voice behind her. Hurriedly concealing the book in her bag, hoping he hadn't noticed, she turned to face Tyrell. Badly dressed as usual - he'd forgotten to iron his shirt. In fact, judging from the smell of sweat, he probably hadn't even washed it

"Having fun in the bushes, Sally?" he smirked.

Was this to be the payback she feared? "Are you coming to the department?" she asked.

"Don't change the subject. What were you doing in the bushes?"

Always so full of unsavoury innuendos. She wished she weren't wearing a skirt. How she hated his arrogant male ways.

"That's none of your business."

She realised that in countering him he'd only feel encouraged. Life was all jousting and combat for him. Sex with him, God forbid, was probably like that too: all poking and prodding, all grasping but not the slightest caress.

"Did Professor Rafter say anything about the conference?"

Rafter was Head of Department, and Tyrell invested a lot of

time and energy getting into his good books. Tyrell was proud of being close to Rafter, as he put it, so Sally hoped he'd rise to the bait.

"He told me he thought it a bit far fetched. He wondered if the Professor's illness and the Indian climate hadn't got the better of the poor man." Tyrell spoke with evident self-satisfaction.

Not only had the Head confided in him, but Tyrell was also able to make fun of Professor Outman knowing he was a close friend of Sally's. She had to resist being drawn into the fight. That was exactly what he wanted. Taking long strides, she headed for the department. He had to hurry to keep up. She was taller than him and a lot fitter. His battles were mainly fought with allusive nods and winks and the occasional well-directed, killer words.

Once within the building, she took refuge in the women's toilets. It aggravated her intensely the way she was when Tyrell was around. Opening her bag, she took out the red notebook and examined it closely. The cover was intact, but many of the inside pages had been torn out. Those that hadn't were struck through with violent pen strokes. Much of it was unreadable. Towards the back, a few sentences had escaped the censor: *Cianala has chosen to go down alone into the Reaches. The parting was most painful. I awoke crying....*

The notebook stirred something deep within her, a strange longing she could not grasp. Turning to the back cover she read: *Brent, the Wanderer* followed by an Avan phone number. She resolved to phone him and take the book back to its owner.

14.10

Stepping into his flat, Brent hung his jacket over the back of a chair, stripped off his trekking shoes and emptied his pockets, laying his treasures on the table: a used postcard of Avan station; a bunch of rusty keys; a few white pebbles; a new dreambook; a large felt pen; and a translation of Dante's Il Paradisio.

He felt exhausted. Every part of him begged for sleep. Moving to his bedroom, he collapsed onto his bed. Despite his fatigue he'd skim dreams for a moment, letting himself rise and fall into the dream realm, surfacing with snatches of words or short sequences of images. He was just drifting deeper into sleep when the phone rang …

"Are you Brent the Wanderer?" a female voice asked. "I've found something of yours."

Sleep shot from him at lightning speed. How could she possibly know he was the Wanderer?

"What have you found?" he managed to ask.

"A red notebook." As he said nothing, she went on: "Why don't we meet tomorrow and I can give it to you."

Chapter 2 - Propositions

The seminar

The midweek seminar with Professor Rafter generally took place in his study, an expansive room on the second floor. It had large bay windows overlooking the river, several of which now stood open, and could seat some twelve people. The study was one of the perks of the Head of the Theosophy Department, a post he'd been awarded some ten years earlier after a brilliant battle of minds and spirits with three other candidates. Rumour had it that Rafter had trained in an earlier life as a shaman, a training which he'd made good use of in gaining the post.

Sally took her place in the armchair that was farthest from Tyrell who was sitting near the Professor's desk. The assistant was on his best behaviour, looking attentively at Rafter. What's more, he'd changed into more presentable clothes and had combed his hair. All the same, Sally noted the way he slouched despite his apparent upright attentiveness.

Thank heavens he was not standing in for Rafter today. When he did, Tyrell always found ways of humiliating her. Feeling her eyes on him, Tyrell glanced her way and pointed meaningfully at his watch. She looked away her face burning and turned her attention to her fellow students who were all busy extracting papers and notebooks from their bags. She wondered what drew them to study theosophy. Tim, for example, looked as if he'd be more at home in a business school than in a department entirely dedicated to the direct experience of the transcendent. Yet for all his appearance of a would-be executive, he was a fervent student.

When everyone was ready, Professor Rafter rose from his desk and walked amongst them, as was his custom, greeting each of them individually. The habit of wearing gowns during lectures had disappeared years ago, but Rafter had revived it, after a sort. He often wore a long black jacket that hung unbuttoned, swaying loosely like a souvenir of a former gown. It would have looked slovenly on many a man but on him it smacked of impeccable elegance as it swirled after him when he moved about the room.

As he'd finished his round, he launched into his subject: "Organised religion generally gets in the way of spiritual experience. Why is that?"

Tim, who was always quick off the mark, suggested: "Religious organisations try to channel contact with the transcendent so as to get control."

Rafter turned to look at him quizzically: "You haven't really answered my question, Tim. But let's follow the path you suggest for a moment. What would they be trying to get control of?"

"The people themselves ... and through them society..." put forward Tim.

Although Sally knew that control over people was one of the unvoiced goals of many religions, she couldn't agree with Tim. Surely, there was something more. She was about to say so when Christina spoke up: "Or the experience itself."

"And how do they control the experience?" Rafter asked.

"By convincing people that they can only reach God through the intermediaries of the religion."

"Is there not also a fear of transcendence on the part of religious organisations?" Sally asked, twining a lock of her hair between her fingers. "Because in its essence, transcendence concerns the individual and cannot be controlled by organisations?"

Tyrell immediately responded: "Fear can hardly be the motivation of such powerful organisations."

Rafter had come to stand near Sally, the beginnings of a smile on his lips.

"Are you really so sure, Tyrell? I think Sally is partly right. It may seem paradoxical, but organised religions, which were initially built around communion with God or the Gods, over time invest heavily in channelling and limiting that communion, which they come to see as a threat. At the same time, we cannot limit the experience of transcendence to the individual; it can also be a collective experience. We have talked of fear and control, let's come back to my initial question and see how these elements contribute to hindering the spiritual experience."

An hour later, Rafter closed the seminar, wishing everyone a good day. As Sally gathered together her notes, Rafter called her over and, once everybody else had left, asked her to come and see him in his office later that day.

"Not now, though. I have to see a scientist from Switzerland: a certain Dr. Leuchtli."

"That's odd," said Sally. "Only yesterday Tangwyn, I mean Prof. Outman, mentioned him."

"Odd indeed," mused Rafter, moving over to his desk.

With a single fluid movement he removed his 'teaching' jacket and hung it up in a cupboard. Extracting a tweed jacket from the same cupboard, he donned it and turned back to her.

"You will have to tell me what he said when we meet later."

A business proposition

Shortly after Sally had left, a sharp knock could be heard at the study door.

"Come in!" called Prof. Rafter as he rose to greet Dr Leuchtli.

Leuchtli was a tall man, almost as tall as Rafter himself, but the doctor was much more solidly built. Noting the powerful presence of his visitor and the intense, almost fanatical look in his eyes, Rafter suspected that the meeting was not going to be easy. Shaking hands, Rafter indicated an armchair near his desk.

"Please, take a seat, Dr Leuchtli. Make yourself at home."

Sitting in an armchair opposite his guest, the professor asked: "To what do I owe the honour of a visit from one of the foremost figures in the field of chaos theory and cosmic energy?"

Leuchtli smiled. "You flatter me Rafter."

The professor noted the potential insult in being thus addressed by someone who did not know him, but decided not to react.

"I have little time, so I will get straight to the point." Leuchtli lent forward, perched on the edge of his chair. "You are the head of the only theosophy department in the country. Your department deals with the experience of transcendence. I am currently working on an experiment involving chaos theory and the dream realm aimed at tapping the endless energy that resides in the infinite folds of the unpredictable. I need someone with experience at accessing the dream realm in a controlled way. I believe you are that man. I propose we set up a joint research project between your department and my company, Energos. I can provide the necessary funds to pay for one of your assistants as well as contribute generously to the running of your department. What do you think?"

Rafter schooled his expression, giving no indication of his thoughts. "Sounds like a very interesting proposition. Let's have lunch together and you can tell me more about your work and what you expect from us."

Thwarted ambitions

On the floor next to a pile of discarded toilet rolls stood a squat glass jar full of darts. Tyrell bent forward and picked one out. Balancing it between his thumb and forefinger, he surveyed the photos torn from magazines that were pinned on the back of the door. Blast that Sally girl. It was irritating the way Rafter always protected her.

What made it worse was that things came too easily to her. The thought made him want to growl and bare his teeth. He imagined her tied hand and foot to a post, her eyes blindfold, awaiting her execution. Not very imaginative, but it would do.

Whump! The dart impaled itself in the tattered image of a busty film star already profusely pockmarked by earlier darts. He picked up another dart. He hadn't made much progress recently on his thesis and now his time was running out, less than a year left as assistant. It shouldn't be that difficult. He'd gathered a great deal of data, but he couldn't pull the ideas together into a coherent whole.

Rafter wasn't helping him as he should. All the professor could do was ask difficult questions. Damn him! And Tyrell didn't have the answers. He let rip with another dart. It bounced off the door and skidded across the floor hitting the base of the sink, chipping off a piece of porcelain. Shit! More costs to add to his bursting budget.

The phone rang in the room next door. He hurriedly finished his business and, holding up his trousers, shuffled to answer.

"Hallo," Tyrell said, not managing to disguise his irritation.

"Dr. Leuchtli, here," the person replied. "I have some more work for you."

Tyrell remembered the last 'job' the Swiss doctor had him do. He eased himself into the armchair next to the phone, his trousers sinking to half-mast around his knees.

"We need to meet this afternoon," Leuchtli was saying. "I don't have much time and I don't know Avan so well. Where do you suggest?"

Tyrell immediately thought of the Cup and Sword. "It's a quiet place at the end of the afternoon," he explained to Leuchtli. "It is just next to the main library," he added.

"OK. Don't be late." And Leuchtli had hung up.

Tyrell sat for a long moment, sprawled in the armchair dazed, not bothering to pull up his trousers. How propitious! It might solve his problem if the doctor was to offer him a solid job. They'd first met at a conference in Hannover. Leuchtli had been interested in his work. He'd asked a lot of questions. He also asked probing questions about the department. Why did people always have to ask him such awkward questions?

The doorbell rang. *"Fuck!"* Could he get no peace? He girded up his trousers, buttoned them at the waist and hurried to the door. It was the postman with a registered letter from Germany. A message from his uncle, of course.

Closing the door unceremoniously in face of the smiling postman, Tyrell tossed the letter onto the table. Nothing important, just his monthly cheque. God knows why the man always used such archaic methods. Well, no. Not so surprising really. If you were a count and lived in a big castle steeped in centuries of tradition, you might not bother with the Internet either. He crossed to the table and retrieved the letter.

Ripping it open, he made sure the sum on the cheque hadn't been cut since last time. It was then that he saw the letter. Well not really a letter, more a note. His uncle didn't like writing. All it said was: *Important family gathering, I expect you to be there.* No signature, just the date of the meeting scrawled across the bottom of the page. No need to ask where. All family reunions always took place in the castle, the family seat.

A new post

When he got back from lunch, Rafter hung up his jacket and sat quietly in a comfortable armchair by one of the windows of his study, looking out over the River Avan. The river was tidal way inland beyond the university, beyond the town too, bringing with it the salty smell of the sea. He closed his eyes and breathed in deeply, gently channelling his attention to his neck and shoulders so as to relax the tension.

The discussion with Leuchtli had left him troubled – the man was not to be trusted – but Rafter would have no time to think about it now. He could sense someone approaching his door. A polite knock confirmed his inner vision.

"Come in, Sally" he said without opening his eyes.

"Sorry. I didn't wish to disturb you. Would you like me to come back later, Professor?" she asked retreating to the door.

"No. Take a seat. Close your eyes. Relax. And I'll be with you in a moment."

With her eyes closed, Sally became aware of the noises rising from the river below. The tide was low and gulls were noisily disputing a prize fish. She could also hear the faint lapping of wavelets breaking against the island on which the department was built, and there was a rowing boat ...

"You can come back in now Sally and open your eyes ... if you wish."

She sighed and opened her eyes to see that Rafter had silently moved to behind his desk.

"I asked you to come because I wanted to congratulate you on your work and to talk to you about your future here at the University, but that will have to wait. Events have happened this morning that force me to set that aside for the moment. I need to talk to you about Leuchli's visit and to make you an offer that may not be to your liking. But first, tell me what Prof. Outman had to say about Leuchtli."

Sally sat up straight, aware of the palpable tension that filled the air. She recalled the discussion very well. Her friend had surprised her by his vehemence.

"He told me Jakob Leuchtli was working on applying chaos theory to the dream realm so as to harness the energy in the discontinuities in the folds of the dream fabric."

She caught her breath, realising that the idea was somehow suffocating.

"Tangwyn said Leuchtli's work was dangerous and ill thought out. I remember what he said very clearly: 'smacks of black magic' he'd said."

"You confirm my worst suspicions, Sally. As I told you after the seminar, Leuchtli came to visit me this morning. He offered the department a contract to work on that project with his company, Energos."

"But why the Theosophy Department?" Sally interrupted, perplexed.

"Because he needs the help of experts in dreams and dream travelling." Rafter paused for a moment, glancing out through the window, across the river to the town beyond. The place seemed dazed as if it had slipped into an early afternoon siesta.

"Like Prof. Outman, I am convinced that our Swiss Doctor is a dangerous man. He's playing at the sorcerer's apprentice. I have come to the difficult conclusion that the only way we can avert a catastrophe of monumental proportions is to join him and seek to limit the impact of what he's about to do. He made it very clear: if we don't work with him, he has other alternatives. I suspect he may already be using someone within my department, but I don't know who."

Sally gasped, as a picture of Tyrell crossed her mind.

"Maybe…" said Rafter, apparently aware of her thoughts, "… but we have no proof as yet."

"Why are you telling me this, Professor?"

"Because I would like to ask you to become one of my assistants and work with me on this project. It's a very dangerous task, but I suspect you're already aware of that, although perhaps not fully so. I think you have the potential to do the job. You are very good, more so than you know, but you'll need special training. I want to surround you with a small team who'll give you all the support you need."

Sally was overwhelmed by the suggestion. She didn't know which was uppermost in her mind: fear or exuberance.

"If you accept, Sally, I want you to enlist the help of your friends Tangwyn and Anju. In fact, I suggest you ask their advice before accepting my offer. I believe they're staying on for a few days."

"Yes. They're spending some time with a friend who lives in a big house in a park just out of town."

"That'll be Alo Marli. He's a good friend. He'll also be helping you. In your courses here in the department you will have learnt something of Shamanism, but you have very little practical experience. Shamanism lies at the limit of what is acceptable to an academic institution, however open-minded it might be. Alo is an accomplished shaman with strong powers in dreamwalking. He'll teach you a lot of what you need to know. But you must not let this be known in the university, especially not to Tyrell. In fact, all of this must remain a secret. When you visit

Alo, people must think your are seeing Prof. Outman."

A worried look crossed her face. "Does that mean nobody will know I am working as your assistant?"

"That is different. The contract with Energos will be official, if discreet. You'll be openly employed as my assistant to work on that project. You'll have to expect some hostility from Tyrell, though." Rafter chuckled. "He seems to think he has a right to me because he's my assistant."

"That won't change much, he's already very unpleasant."

Rafter became serious. "I'll see if I can do something to alleviate that."

Sally had sat down across the desk from Rafter. A pile of books and papers stood close to her elbow. The uppermost brochure caught her attention. It was not so much the title *Energos: the manifold energy solution* under the heading *Top Secret* written in red that intrigued her, but the small logo in the lower corner of the cover. A stylised sun and moon, joined by a horizontal bar, floated above a country divided in two by a river that snaked between them. She'd seen it before. But where?

"Their logo is familiar to you, Sally?" the Professor asked.

"Yes. I've seen it recently, but I can't remember where."

Rafter stood up and came round the desk to stand next to her, towering above her.

"It might be important to remember. Place your left hand on the logo and close your eyes."

She immediately saw Tyrell standing in the rhododendrons near the university, mocking her. Instinctively she put her hand in her pocket and felt the dreambook there: the one she'd found in the park.

"It was in the dreambook," she said to herself.

"Tell me about it."

"I found it in the maze of rhododendrons near the university. Tyrell turned up just at that moment delighted to catch me on my own in the park, but I managed to hide it from him. Almost all of the writings in the notebook had been crossed out with a thick black pen. And these symbols had been drawn inside the back cover in the same ink."

"Let me see."

Sally extracted the notebook from her pocket and handed it hesitantly to Rafter. As he opened it at the first page, he staggered, catching himself at the last moment thanks to her armchair.

"Are you all right, Professor?" Sally asked as she rose to take his arm.

She always saw him as a strong person, someone you could count on even in the most difficult situations. It affected her to see him so afflicted.

"I'll be OK," he muttered, taking a couple of deep breaths. "This is really vicious work. The ritual cancelling of dreams is an evil act."

Sally didn't really understand, but she could imagine the blackness of it.

"I'm meeting the owner of the book later this afternoon. His phone number was written on the last page. His name is Brent."

Some of the colour had come back into Rafter's face as he sat in an armchair opposite her: the very one Leuchtli had been seated in a few hours earlier.

"I'd like to meet your young man, Sally, as soon as possible. He might be in danger. Can you organise that? Somewhere outside the University. Maybe at Alo's place. I'll phone him."

Sally nodded in agreement.

"You need some rest and quiet, Sally. When is your meeting with Brent?"

"Five-thirty."

"Find a safe place where you won't be disturbed and do an hour's depth meditation. When you meet Brent I suggest you don't give him his dreambook, it might be too much of a shock. Rather, ask him to come to Alo's place at seven. I'll have Alo invite us to dinner. Here's the address. We'll be able to talk to Alo, Tangwyn and Anju about this and make some plans."

Standing, Sally took Alo's visiting card that the professor handed her, said goodbye and hurriedly left Rafter's study, the theosophy department and the university. She knew exactly where she'd go to have some peace and security.

Promise of a rest

Sally let herself into Keira's flat with the spare key her friend had given her. Keira was still at the library where she worked. Sally crossed the hall and entered the kitchen. The place was sparkling clean. The cleaning lady must have been in that morning. Rows of spices and dried herbs filled several shelves. She selected a spearmint, nettle and dandelion mixture and made herself herbal tea, then went through into Keira's large bedroom.

Sitting cross-legged on the firm double bed, she drank the tea and prepared to meditate. An hour later, feeling much lighter and more relaxed, she pulled off her jeans and curled up under the covers. The delightful smell of Keira and her perfume surrounded her. Sliding her hands down between her legs, she let herself drift deliciously into sleep.

Sea sick

Tyrell hated the sea. As a child he'd never been near the sea. There weren't even any lakes in the part of Germany were he'd been brought up, only a fast flowing river that was bitterly cold with melted snows and quite unsuitable for a youngster to swim in. In fact, he never did learn to swim, although he didn't let people know it. Most people in Avan were sea folk, at home both on land and on water. They'd never understand.

Here along the sea wall the surging mass of water was only feet away. He should have taken the longer route to the pub where he was to meet Leuchtli. The sight of so much water filled him with panic. He felt an immense weight pressing down on him. Even the air was full of it. There was no escaping: it seeped into your every pore. He broke out into a sweat and hastened his pace.

"Tyrell," a voice called out behind him. "Where are you hurrying to?"

It was Tim, one of Sally's fellow students. He was in Rafter's seminar. Tyrell continued walking. When Tim finally caught up with him, he asked: "Did you know Sally is to be Rafter's new assistant?"

Tyrell prided himself about being one of the first to be aware of department rumours. In fact he started many of them. But this one caught him unawares.

"How could that be? She hasn't even finished her masters."

Tyrell found himself shaking with rage. Tim grinned.

"I dunno. But it looks like you've got company." Tyrell abruptly turned on Tim, grabbing him by the collar.

"Are you making fun of me?" he snarled. Tim went white.

"What's the matter," he stuttered. "I thought you'd like to know."

Tyrell shoved the student away causing Tim to trip and fall heavily on the pavement.

"Well I do not like to know, as you put it." And Tyrell stormed away, not looking back.

Tyrell was still shaking with anger and indignation five minutes later as the road led him away from the sea front. Something needed to be done and quickly. He doubled back to the University. It wasn't far and he had plenty of time before his appointment.

Locking himself in his office, he pulled down the blinds, threw his jacket onto the floor and eased himself onto the meditation mat that was a fixture in many offices of the theosophy department. Riding rough shod over the principals of meditation, he dispensed with all the calming and relaxing preliminaries and plunged wildly forward, fired by his anger as he sank into the deeper spheres.

Once at the familiar crossroads, he reached out seeking the psychic scent of Sally that he knew so well. There she was, unsuspecting, only lightly guarded. No point in wasting time. He drew on all his anger and pounced.

Seconds later, another psychic presence of immense strength bowled him over making him loose his hold on Sally. Whoever it was drove him ever deeper. His defences were stripped away leaving him naked and helpless. His fall came to an abrupt halt, much later, as he plunged into a bitterly cold lake. The water closed over him, pulling him even deeper. Holding his breath he tried desperately to fight off the terror that gripped him.

He struggled to rise to the surface, his arms thrashing, his legs kicking. The water was so cold it burnt his skin. He couldn't hold his breath much longer. His lungs would burst. As water seeped into his nose and found its way between his tightly sealed lips and down into his waiting lungs he thought he heard a man's rich laughter before everything went black.

Deranged

Sally's sleep was abruptly interrupted by the telephone. A deep, male voice spoke: "This is Police Sergeant Rose speaking. Are you Sally Sari?"

Alarmed and worried, Sally replied: "Yes. What can I do for you?"

"We need you to come to your flat as quickly as possible."

"Has something happened?"

"We'll talk about it when you get here."

A policewoman ushered her into her flat when she arrived. The place was in utter chaos. Drawers and cupboards had been emptied indiscriminately on the floor. Clothes and books and food lay in a confused mess. The police had set up floodlights here and there; their stark glare heightened her feeling of disconnectedness. It was unthinkable that this hot, stuffy place could be her home.

The policewoman guided her through the shambles to a burly policeman who stood with his back to her. He turned as they approached.

"Miss Sari. I'm Sergeant Rose. I am sorry about this. I'm obliged to ask you a few questions. But first I'd like you to come this way."

He led her to the bedroom, which was guarded by another policeman who stepped aside and opened the door. Something was terribly wrong. On her bed a twisted form lay covered with a sheet. The Sergeant moved to the bedside and beckoned her over. She didn't want to go. She didn't want to see. Her legs refused to move, but the policewoman took her arm and firmly helped her. The heat of the lamps was oppressive and the smell in the room was obnoxious.

As she came closer, the sergeant abruptly pulled back the sheet revealing the body of a women, her face frozen in pain and fear, her breasts hacked open by a knife that stood impaled in the bloody gash.

"She was raped before she was murdered," he said.

"Keira. Oh Keira." whispered Sally, as the world began to shift heavily about her, spinning more and more slowly.

Waves of darkness flooded over her until she could hold on no more and fell unconscious to the floor. Despite the shock, she fought with all her might against the deathly blackness that gripped her. This could not be. She would not let it happen.

A silent scream rose from far, far away in her deepest depths. Travelling upwards and gathering speed and strength, it forced its way through her lips, and ripped asunder the muted space that imprisoned her, letting in the faint sound of a ringing bell. The telephone.

"Oh no! It's beginning again."

She struggled to be free, but strong hands held her tight.

A distant voice called her name: "Sally. Sally, it's me, Keira."

How could that be? What mockery. She was dead, horribly dead. A violent shudder wracked her body at the thought of the knife.

"Open your eyes. You've had a nightmare."

Like the desperately in-drawn breath of someone who has just escaped drowning, her senses came rushing painfully back. Through tear-filled eyes she saw Keira leaning over her. Sally reached out and pulled Keira into her arms, gripping on to her friend, sobbing violently.

"Oh my love, my love. I thought you were dead!"

Try as hard as she would, Sally couldn't stop trembling, even after a long and comforting moment in Keira's arms and a cup of calming tea. Keira insisted she take a bath with oils of juniper and pine in the water.

"…to cleanse and purify …" she said.

Her friend also lit numerous candles in the bathroom that reflected comforting light off the tiles and mirrors. As she basked in the water, feeling the tension ease out of her, she could hear Keira moving around the flat clapping her hands to drive away any remaining bad spirits.

When Keira returned to help Sally out of the bath she'd changed out of her work clothes. She dressed rather soberly for the library. Now she was wearing a brightly coloured tee shirt, an outrageously short skirt and striped tights. The two girls were about the same height and could have been sisters if it weren't for their hair and eyes: while Sally had auburn hair and green eyes, Keira was blond with blue eyes. Sally was happy to let Keira rub her down and help her get dressed.

Sally hadn't wanted to tell Keira about her dream, but she had to tell her something. She was about to tell her of the talk with Rafter when she remembered Brent and his book.

"Blast. I'm going to be late."

"But you can't go out like that."

Sally had to agree with her friend. Despite Keira's efforts, she felt unable to go out and meet someone she didn't know. She explained briefly about Brent's dreambook and described her talk with Rafter. Keira was astonished at all that had happened to her friend since she left her late the evening before. But there was no time to talk of that.

They tried phoning Brent but he didn't answer. Keira offered to meet Brent herself and invite him to Alo Marli's place that evening. The idea of letting Keira out of her sight alarmed Sally, but she could think of no alternative.

A welcome request

When Tyrell came to himself he was sprawled on his office

floor. His brain felt as if it had been put through one of those old-fashioned clothes mangles and wrung dry. His grandmother had had one. As a kid, he liked to squeeze living mice though the machine when no one was around. He'd found the high-pitched squeals delicious. When they discovered the blood on the rollers, he'd been beaten severely.

To his disgust, coming back to the present, he realised he'd wet himself and his shirt was ripped. Luckily he had spare clothes in his cupboard. He tried not to think of what had happened when he'd attacked Sally, but the horror of drowning clung to him.

Glancing at his watch he saw he had only ten minutes to get to his appointment with Leuchtli. Taking a small flask of Schnapps from his desk drawer he took a swig to calm his nerves and set off at a run for his bright future with Leuchtli.

The Cup and Sword had got its name from a long-told story about the beautiful daughter of the Bailiff of the town and a knight imprisoned for the theft of a golden cup. Tyrell didn't know the details. To be honest, he wasn't interested. He didn't like stories. He found them either frankly silly or strangely frightening: you could so easily get lost in them.

He made it to the Cup before Leuchtli, giving him time to calm his frayed nerves and collect his thoughts over a pint. But his thoughts remained blurred. Maybe it was the residual effect of the meditation and the vicious psychic attack he'd been the victim of. Or was it the Schnapps? Had he drunk too much? He shovelled a handful of peanuts into his mouth and chewed vigorously, hoping food would quell the effects of the alcohol.

When Leuchtli entered, Tyrell recognised the tall, well-built man immediately. He rose to greet him. The Swiss doctor didn't return his greetings, but promptly sat at Tyrell's table.

"So you still work for Rafter?" Leuchtli asked without the slightest introduction.

As a German, Tyrell was not so shocked by the Swiss German as an Englishman might have been. His uncle went about things with much the same abrupt disregard for convention. He nodded in reply.

"Good. I have some work for you. But first I'd like to know what you think of Rafter," Leuchtli asked, calling over the bartender with a wave of his hand to order a drink. He seemed impervious to the fact that things weren't done like that in England. Even Tyrell knew that.

Making the most of the distraction, as the waiter explained he had to come up to the bar, Tyrell thought over his opinion about Rafter. He had long admired the Professor, but the idea that he would employ Sally as assistant, possibly to replace him, irked Tyrell. And there was the business about drowning. The thought of it made him shudder. So much strength! It might have been Rafter. That would make sense. He was always quick to defend the girl.

Tyrell suddenly realised that Leuchtli had got his way and the bartender had brought him a drink. Now the Doctor was scrutinizing him closely.

"He's an intelligent, you might even say dangerous man," Tyrell replied. "But he has made a number of wrong judgements. That is his weakness."

Tyrell sat back, pleased with his answer. It must have suited Leuchtli because the Doctor continued: "I want someone to keep an active eye on what Rafter does. Someone close to Rafter, someone Rafter trusts. Someone who can replace Rafter in my plans if the Professor fails to deliver the goods."

The idea of replacing Rafter delighted Tyrell. He imagined himself Head of the Department...

"Are you that person, Tyrell?" Leuchtli asked.

Without hesitation, Tyrell replied: "Yes."

Leuchtli rose to leave. "Good, but not a word to anyone. I'll be in contact."

Tyrell rose too, astonished at what had happened. It was then that he realised that Leuchtli hadn't paid for his drink. Digging deep into his pocket, Tyrell pulled out the last of his change, went to the bar, paid up and followed the illustrious doctor out of the pub.

Replacement

As a librarian in the largest library of Avan University, Keira knew and was known by many people, and the Cup and Sword was right next to where she worked. What's more, she sang in a popular folk band. Being inconspicuous was a challenge for her. Even her clothes marked her as out of the ordinary. Sally had told her about the art of inconspicuousness.

"Your eyes are important," she'd said. "Do away with any intention in the way you look at the world. Let your regard brush lightly over things; unheard, unseen, unfelt."

Thoughts were important too, she remembered. Noisy thoughts drew attention. You needed to melt into your surroundings. The weeping willow under which she sat hung down around her, offering some measure of cover, if not security.

She tried to calm her thoughts and imagine she was part of the tree against which she leaned. It wasn't easy. The shock of holding Sally sobbing in her arms, inconsolable, was fresh in her mind. Across the road, the Cup and Sword was not yet busy. A couple of people leaned against the wall next to the door, chattering amiably, a pint in their hands.

Sharp laughter cut through her thoughts. She tensed, all pretence of relaxation gone. Tyrell and a tall, well-dressed foreigner just stepped out of the pub. The foreigner turned and set off at a brisk pace in the direction of the university. He'd only taken a few steps when he almost collided with a young man coming fast round the corner. Fortunately the young man sidestepped into the road, avoiding a collision. The foreigner swore in German, but continued on his way.

Ignoring the insult, the young man looked up at the sign of the Cup and Sword swinging over the entrance to the pub. As his face caught in the light of the streetlamps Keira gasped. Brent. She knew him from the library. He was only a few steps from Tyrell. What a disaster.

Tyrell greeted him, hand outstretched. They knew each other. Clasping hands, they disappeared into the pub, the door swinging closed behind them. Blast. What should she do? She couldn't go into the pub after them. Too obvious. Think fast before Brent told Tyrell he was meeting Sally. Reaching into her bag, Keira pulled out her phone. Dialled her friend John, the barman from the Cup and Sword.

"Hi John. It's Keira. Can you do me a favour? Call Brent to the phone. He's in the Cup with Tyrell. Don't tell him who is phoning. It's a secret. Tell him the person didn't give a name. Say it is urgent. Just get him away from Tyrell and have him come to the phone out back. You're great. Thanks."

Keira ducked out from under the tree, crossed the road and ran to the alley by the side of the pub. It reeked of beer and piss. Ugh. Taking a deep breath she pushed her way through the side gate and slipped in the back entrance to the Cup. Brent was already standing in the corridor, pacing up and down near the phone, a confused look on his face. Letting out her breath she signalled to him not to speak. Beckoning him to follow, she pushed open the door to the garden. The place was deserted and shrouded in heavy shadows.

"What's going on, Keira?" he hissed between his teeth.

"Welcome to you too, Brent!"

Hesitating, he lent forward and gave her a brief kiss on her cheek. "Why all the secrecy?"

"Listen. We have very little time." She whispered. "You were supposed to meet Sally this afternoon."

He seemed surprised that Keira knew.

"She's had a problem and couldn't come. It is complicated. She sent me to ask you to meet her at Alo Marli's place this evening. Do you know him?"

Brent nodded.

"You must tell nobody, especially not Tyrell. It may be a question of life or death."

He grinned. "Dramatic!"

"No dangerous."

He looked doubtful. "What am I supposed to say to Tyrell?"

"Tell him your mother's ill."

"Yeah that would probably do it."

"You OK for seven-thirty at Alo's place? Sally will explain. Make sure nobody follows you."

He nodded.

"Good," she said as she turned to go.

Chapter 3 - The Circle

First encounters

The sitting room was warm and welcoming. A fire blazed in the hearth. A faint smell of flowers or was it perfume graced the air. Brent took a step inside, admiring the dark oak beams that supported the ceiling. The walls were lined with bookshelves. He resisted the temptation to browse. The title on one larger volume did catch his attention, though: Isis Unveiled. Blavatsky. Of course!

Ample armchairs were ranged in a wide circle around the fireplace. As he glanced around the room, he noticed a pair of bare legs dangling over the padded arm of one of the chairs. Freckled, suntanned feet, fingernails painted pale pink: a young woman. The graceful bird-like curves made his heart flutter.

He halted, hesitant. He felt like an intruder. When Alo had invited him in and bid him go through into the sitting room for a while, he'd said nothing of there being somebody already there. Brent coughed quietly, but the legs didn't move. A thin gold chain hung attached around one of the ankles, catching the glimmer of the firelight.

Brent took a step forward, curiosity getting the better of him. The thick Persian carpet muffled his footsteps. Keep your distance, he thought. Don't startle her. Rounding one of the armchairs on the other side of the fire, he caught sight of the young woman asleep, her head reclined on her folded hands. Shoulder-length auburn hair partly covered her face. He'd met her somewhere before, but he couldn't remember where or when. Her emerald green dress had ridden a way up her legs, exposing a length of tanned thigh. The sight of her sent desire coursing through his veins.

"So you've finally found Sally, Brent."

Startled, he spun round to find Keira standing in the doorway, her hands on her hips, her blue eyes flashing. Since he met her that afternoon she'd put gel in her hair making it stand up in blond spikes on her head. So challenged, he had to laugh despite his embarrassment.

"Greetings to you too, Keira! Are you getting me back for earlier at the pub?" he replied, making an exaggerated bow in her direction.

His clowning didn't bring the smile he expected. Instead a worried frown clouded her face. He'd never seen her look so preoccupied. Next to her stood Alo accompanied by an elegantly-dressed elderly gentleman who towered head and shoulders above Keira. Behind them came a young girl pushing a smiling old man in a wheel chair. The girl was dressed in a colourful sari that contrasted sharply with her black hair that was cropped short. There was something impish about her, he thought. The elderly man stepped forward, holding out his hand.

"Welcome to our little circle, Brent. I'm Prof. Rafter."

As they moved into the room, Rafter placed his hand on Keira's shoulder

"Keira and Alo you know already. This is Prof. Tangwyn Outman and his granddaughter Anju from India."

"Pleased to meet you all," Brent replied.

"And I am Sally." said a musical voice behind him.

He spun round to find Sally standing in front of the fire, one hand leaning on the mantlepiece, her bright green eyes sizing him up.

"So we meet at last," she added, bowing slightly in imitation of his earlier bow to Keira.

Charming, despite her mockery. The smell of flowers came from her, Brent realised. Irises.

"Are you all right?" he asked, taking a step towards her. "I heard you were ill."

"Just a little shaken-up" she smiled weakly sitting back down in the armchair.

Odd, he thought, how the effort of standing seemed to have strained her. Anju and Alo were helping Prof. Outman to an armchair. Sally indicated that Brent should sit next to her. Keira came forward and sat on the arm of Sally's chair, her arm around her friend's neck stroking her hair. Well, that was clear enough, Brent thought. Rafter remained standing near the fireplace. Once everyone was seated all eyes turned to him.

"I reckon we owe Brent an explanation" Rafter began.

Sally nodded in agreement. Rafter turned to Brent, extracting a small red notebook from his jacket pocket. Brent recognised it immediately. Relieved, he bent forward, stretching out his hand to retrieve it, but the Professor made no move to return it to him.

"I'll give it to you later."

Brent sat back, a look of annoyance darkening his face. Was it not his book? Dreams were a very personal thing. He felt vulnerable. Were they playing with him? Sally must have sensed his irritation because she lent over and placed her hand on his.

"You'll understand," she whispered.

Brent relaxed back into his armchair, looking at her hand that lingered a moment on his. Strange how he continued to feel her touch long after she'd withdrawn her hand. Fairytales again, he thought, as his heart skipped a beat. Couldn't keep out of them.

"Let's begin with this dreambook of yours and see if we can figure out where it fits in the wider story that brings us all together. Can you tell us how you came to lose it, Brent?" the Professor asked.

"As I told Alo, I left it in my bag on the table in a pub the other day. I went to get a drink from the bar and when I returned, it was gone. Nothing else had been touched."

"Did anybody know about it?"

"Funny you should ask. I was thinking about that. I did talk about it to a guy I met the other day in a pub. He was telling me about work he was doing on dreams. A bit complicated. Something to do with the way dreams flip from one context to another. He seemed very interested in my dreambook, but I didn't show it to him. I bumped into him again this afternoon at the Cup and Sword when I was waiting to meet Sally."

"Tyrell" groaned Sally.

He turned to look at her, surprised. She looked concerned. "How did you know?"

"He has his place in the story we are to tell you" added Rafter, cutting across Sally who was about to add something.

"Then you'd better tell me your story," Brent replied somewhat impatiently.

Half an hour later, Rafter had told him of Leuchtli's experiment and the job he'd given Sally. Prof. Outman had explained something of the theory of dreams and chaos and Alo spoke of dream weaving.

"But I still don't understand the connection with my dreambook," Brent said.

"Your dreambook looks intact from the outside, Brent, but it is not." Rafter said grimly. "It has been deliberately tampered with. Someone has ritually deleted all your dreams."

Shocked, Brent asked: "Why would anyone do that?"

"That we don't know" Alo replied.

"We do suspect that Tyrell was involved in taking your dreambook, though," added Sally as Rafter gave her a warning look.

Alo stood up. "May I invite you into the dining room for dinner. We can make plans after we've eaten," he said.

As they all moved towards the door, Rafter came over to Brent and handed him his dreambook. Brent opened it at random to discover that large sections of text had been crossed out with a thick felt pen. Looking closer, he discovered tiny markings next to some of the paragraphs.

"Do you think Alo has a magnifying glass?" Brent asked

Sally.

"I saw one on the mantlepiece," she replied. "What have you discovered?" she asked, coming to stand next to him.

He held out the notebook turned towards her for her to see: "Look at these little markings at the end of some paragraphs."

She took down the magnifying glass and handed it to Brent who examined the markings closely.

"Doesn't make any sense to me," he said handing her the book and the magnifying glass.

She too shook her head. "Me neither."

Alo called from the doorway "You two coming? The food will get cold."

Two left feet

A pungent odour of creosote wound its lazy way around the empty flowerpots that lay scattered across the wooden floor, inched its way up the beanpoles piled slantwise against the woodshed wall and seeped into every nook and cranny of his lungs. Tyrell clamped his hand over his mouth to stop himself coughing.

Rafter, influential head of the theosophy department, Marli the local shaman and therapist, the renowned Professor Outman in town to give a much acclaimed conference, his exotic daughter from India, that young singer who worked in Avan library and Sally, Rafter's newly promoted assistant. He'd watched them all arrive. Fitting them together like a giant meaningful puzzle.

One person didn't fit: Brent. What was he doing there? They'd met that very afternoon at the Cup, just after Leuchtli had left. Had Brent been spying on them? Maybe that was why he left the pub so abruptly with some absurd excuse about his mother being ill. Or did they know he'd stolen Brent's dreambook? He hadn't been able to find it when he went back along the path near the university where he'd lost it. Thank heavens he'd been able to conceal that from Leuchtli.

The teeth of the garden rake were digging insistently into

the small of his back. Tyrell shifted to try to find a more comfortable position, setting the perforated cap of the watering can rolling in widening spirals across the sloping surface of a small workbench.

He took a small step sideways in the confined space and caught it just as it was about to fall over the edge and onto a set of empty watering cans below. Bending to set the cap safely on the floor, he realised he'd stepped into the tray of half-dried creosote.

Hopping to the door, he pushed it open, slipped on the threshold and fell flat on his face in Alo's lush grass. There he lay prone for a long while, not knowing whether to burst out laughing or to break into sobs. Finally it was a nervous giggle that got the upper hand. Poor Tyrell, the laughable victim, he thought. Shaking as if to get rid of the idea, he rolled over into a sitting position and gingerly took off his stinking shoe and began to clean it on the grass.

Clues

Alo had decorated his dining room with a number of large, colourful oil paintings that were neither abstract nor figurative but rather suggestive. Yes, Brent thought, that was the right word. Quite suited to a specialist in dreams. He'd never seen these rooms before. Alo always received clients in his study that had a separate entrance.

Everyone was seated when Sally and Brent stepped up to the table. Keira looked up and gave Sally a questioning look, before turning back to her neighbour and continuing her discussion. Places had been left for them opposite each other in the middle of the table. Taking his seat, Brent placed his dreambook next to his plate and looked around.

Once the first course had been served by Alo's butler, Brent raised his voice and addressed the whole group: "I think Sally and I have found a clue in my dream book. At the end of certain paragraphs there are strange hieroglyphs. But we weren't able to decipher them."

Alo asked to see, but shook his head as he failed to decode them. The book passed around the table without success until it reached Tangwyn. Anju handed him the magnifying glass and the Professor took a long time holding the book up to the light and turning it in various directions. When he finally looked up all eyes were turned to him. "These are symbols we use in chaos theory to indicate different types of events," he told them.

"What do you mean by events?" Sally asked.

"You could say: moments when the system is unstable and it changes from one configuration to another."

Rafter looked excited: "Is there any correlation with the dreams themselves? Can you read any of them Brent?"

Anju rose from the table and walked round to Brent and handed him the notebook. A faint aura of incense surrounded her and some of it had been transferred to his notebook. Now all eyes rested on him.

"It is almost impossible to read. And I'm not sure that I can remember all the details," he said.

"Take your time," Rafter suggested. "We only need a couple of examples."

The butler brought in and served a pungent smelling vegetable curry with rice and chapattis, while Brent flicked through his notebook again more slowly this time, stopping to examine one page more closely.

"This one I do remember," he said holding up the book. "It was so strange," he laughed. "We are travelling in an old-fashioned motorised coach with varnished wooden benches running the length of the vehicle. There is no glass in the windows and wafts of hot air carry a multitude of scents in through the openings. We move along a street crowded with noisy, colourful people. As the street becomes narrower, the coach almost imperceptibly flows into and becomes the street and we are no longer being carried forward but are walking... The transition was so smooth I hardly noticed it."

"Is there a mark opposite that extract?" Tangwyn asked.

"Yes!" and Brent rose to show him.

The Professor lent forward in his wheel chair to examine the sign.

Spotted

Night had fallen and the only light in the garden flooded from the dining room windows. Tyrell crawled across the lawn on his hands and knees, edging closer to those windows, trailing his creosoted shoe behind him. Nobody had bothered to pull the curtains when the light had faded. They must be confident they were alone.

From a distance, he'd seen them change rooms. Annoyingly, no windows were open. If he could get closer, he might just hear something. He'd set up a shield, just in case. It was this shield that lightly brushed the shield surrounding the room. He pulled back immediately. If the person who'd set up that shield was paying attention, he'd know Tyrell was there.

Easing away, Tyrell stood up slowly and pulled on his second shoe. His hands were spotted now with dark stains of creosote. Would he ever be able to get them clean again? Like the time his aunt had locked him in the coal shed: a punishment of course. It had taken him days to get his hands white again and the smell of coal had lingered in his nose for weeks.

There was nothing more he could learn by waiting there. He turned to go when he heard footsteps on the gravel coming up the drive to the house. Who else could be coming now? He hesitated: should he run for it or try to hide? Curiosity got the better of him as he slipped behind a bush and held his breath.

The footsteps didn't stop at the front door but rounded the house and strode resolutely towards him. He was seized with fright. This was no ordinary person. At that moment, clouds shifted and the moon came out revealing that it was a woman. He could feel the power emanating from her, despite her small size. Tyrell bolted across the lawn in a straight line for the gate. The person called out, but he was long gone.

A stifled cry from outside the window startled everyone into abrupt silence.

"It's Naniu!" said Rafter standing and moving towards the French windows.

Brent and Alo rose to join him. As Brent moved alongside the Professor, he whispered "Is it safe to go out like this?"

"We are quite safe and Naniu is unhurt."

Brent wondered how Rafter could know. All three men stepped out of the warmth of the house and into the shadows of the garden to be greeted by Naniu who appeared from between the bushes. Her cloak was muddy as if she'd fallen, but judging from the smile on her face she had indeed not been hurt, as the Professor had predicted.

"I didn't sense the man at first, he was warding" she said.

"Come inside," the Professor suggested, "so we can talk about this amongst ourselves."

Naniu was ushered in and offered a chair at the table. Alo shut the French windows and brought her a drink as people moved back to their places and settled around the table looking intently at the new arrival. Only Sally remained standing. She moved around the table to behind Naniu's chair to greet her with a kiss.

Rafter presented Naniu to those who didn't know her. Brent had heard of her and had even seen her about town but this was the first time he met the famous singing teacher. So Sally was one of her students, he guessed.

Naniu put down her glass and began her tale. "As I walked up the drive I heard movement in the bushes. Clearly someone was near the dinning room windows, but I couldn't sense his presence. Whoever it was must have been warding quite competently. I strongly warded myself and headed directly for him. That startled him. Obviously he didn't want to be seen. He made a run for it. As I followed in pursuit I slipped on the wet grass and fell. That's why my cloak is so muddy."

Brent was perplexed by all this talk of 'warding'. Surely

that kind of thing only happened in books about magicians and witches. He glanced around at the people present. They looked normal enough. But as he looked further, he could have sworn he caught a glimpse of threads of light weaving lines of force pulling the people closer together. As soon as he realised what he was seeing, the vision slipped from his grasp. Now wasn't the time to wonder about such things. The atmosphere in the room was tense. Someone had spied on their meeting and escaped.

"Did you get to see the man?" Alo asked, but Naniu shook her head.

In the ensuing silence Rafter pushed away his plate and rose. "So somebody with some powers has been listening in on our conversation. I didn't feel anybody's presence either."

"Nor did I" said both Alo and Sally together.

Brent, feeling increasingly uncomfortable, asked half jokingly, "Excuse me asking such a silly question, but have I just stumbled into a story about a circle of magicians?"

Naniu laughed. It was like waves of music breaking over him. Brent could take no offence at such a laugh, even if he wasn't sure if she was laughing at him or not.

"You could put it like that, I suppose," she said smiling at her friends around the table. "Some of us have powers that we have learnt to wield. But we find it better to be discreet about it. You too have that power, Brent, even if you don't know it."

Brent felt her voice resonate deep within him making something in him relax: as if he'd always been tense in a way he hadn't noticed and her words had soothed him.

"Naniu is right," Rafter affirmed. "Providence has brought you to us just at the right moment. I was looking for someone to assist Sally in her mission in the dream world."

Brent had no time to ask questions because Naniu brought them back to what had just happened. "Despite our care, though, it would seem that our secret is out" she pointed out. "Someone knows about our little group."

Rafter was pacing solemnly around the table. Brent, his imagination fired by the strange circumstances, wondered if he was drawing up a circle of protection around them. But look as he would, he couldn't see any sign of it. The professor stopped and said: "We're going to have to be much more careful."

Resuming his pacing he added: "We'll have to move faster than planned. We need to be ready when the time comes." He seemed to hesitate a moment. Brent could feel something powerful hanging in the air above them.

"None of us can afford to be away for long. But a couple of days should be enough. Preparation of Brent and Sally will begin tomorrow morning. Naniu, Alo and myself will take care of that."

Now Brent really did feel confused.

"Why me?"

Rafter smiled at him. "Because you are the only one who can guide Sally back from her journey in the dream realm and beyond."

Alo and Naniu both nodded, speaking in chorus "He's right."

Me too!

Keira looked from Brent to Sally and was shocked at what she saw. She rubbed her eyes hoping to wipe away the vision, to no avail. Invisible forces were already twining bonds between the two, pulling them closer together. If she wanted to play any part at all in the adventure the two were embarking on she had to act immediately.

"Can't I come too? After all, I'm closest to Sally. That should count for something."

Rafter glanced at Naniu. Keira didn't miss Naniu's smile and the almost imperceptible nod as she agreed.

"If you must. We'll be going somewhere not so far from here, in a place where no one can reach us. Can you get off work for a short while, Keira?"

How could they know she'd planned to take a few days off to spend time with Sally? She couldn't help herself smiling as she replied, "Sure."

Rafter looked dubious, but Sally spoke up, "If my nightmare

this afternoon is anything to go on, Keira will not be safe if they know I'm involved."

Keira blew her friend an imaginary kiss of thanks, reassured by her support.

Rafter shrugged his shoulders: "You may well be right, although Tyrell is unlikely to do that again," he added, chuckling to himself. "Which reminds me, we need to teach you three to ward your dreams. Ok. Let's go."

Keira stilled her desire to move to Sally's side and lay a proprietary hand on her friend's shoulder. Instead, she smiled at Brent across the table, offering him one of the chocolates scattered between the plates. She felt something else stirring deep in her as she watched him unwrap the sweet with his long fingers and slip it into his full mouth, licking his lips as he did so. If Sally was watching her now, it should be her turn to worry, Keira thought.

Rafter turned to Prof. Tangwyn and his daughter. "I'm sorry we have to rush off like this. We'll catch up on news tomorrow. Alo's butler will drive you to a hotel, a different one, just for tonight, and he'll see you get your things. Tomorrow morning someone will come and fetch you so you can join us in the country for a while."

Naniu said she would join them in the morning and took her leave. Everyone had stood up, so Brent did too, wondering what would happen next. He couldn't rid himself of the feeling that he was standing on the verge of a novel, and if he took one step forward, he'd walk straight into it. For all his love of stories and storytelling, he preferred not to be the subject of the story.

Lost in his thoughts he only noticed Keira had joined him when she took his arm and led him out into the hall where the butler was handing everybody their coats and hats. Taking leave of Tangwyn and Anju, Alo ushered the rest of them down some steps into the basement.

"Follow me" he said quietly, picking up and lighting an oil lamp.

The small group crossed what resembled an underground

garage and entered a low door on the far side. It led to a corridor that sloped down quite steeply. The air reeked of damp and mould. They walked for a long time, one behind another, lit only by a lamp held up by Alo.

Sally and Keira were walking hand in hand just in front of Brent, whispering softly to each other. Brent could not make out what they said. After a while he gave up trying and retreated into his own thoughts. Resurfacing some time later, he realised he could hear water lapping nearby. It was then that the light abruptly went out.

Food for thought

"Yes. I'm sure. All of them. Including the owner of that dreambook we used."

Tyrell sprawled in an armchair with his feet soaking in a large bowl of warm water, errant soapsuds escaping onto the kitchen floor. He was alternately rubbing cream into his hands and then wiping it off onto a wad of toilet paper as he spoke. The phone, which was on "speaker", was propped up against an empty tin of biscuits near the edge of the table. The sight of it reminded him he was famished.

"I haven't got time to talk now. I've got to catch my flight to Zurich. In the mean time, find out what they're up to."

Leuchtli hung up. Tyrell tossed another wad of blackened toilet paper onto the floor where it joined a growing heap. Scrutinising his hands to see if they were any less spotted, he snorted with disgust and squeezed the remains of the cream onto his fingers and rubbed furiously.

Sausages and curried beans! Down on his hands and knees, he found the can half concealed behind a batch of jars of curry paste and packets of other Indian spices on a floor-level shelf as he searched for something reasonable to eat in the local Indian delicatessen. It was the only food shop nearby that stayed open late at night.

He might appreciate good food, but he tended to neglect it, living alone as he did. He turned the tin over to check the best-by-date. It was OK. Just. There was no bread left, so he bought a packet of chapattis and some butter. Given what he was about to eat, he wondered if he shouldn't buy some Alka-Seltzer, but remedies against indigestion were not the fare to be found in such a shop.

The tin rattled nosily in the saucepan as the water boiled furiously around it. He slid a chapatti under the grill and toasted one side. That ought to be enough. Taking one of the dirty plates piled up by the sink, trying not to get his hands dirty, he scoured the dried food stuck on it with a well-used scouring pad. Life in the castle was decidedly more luxurious and far more convenient.

Using a dishcloth to hold the scalding can, he up-ended it over the hot buttered chapatti and shook it sharply, hoping to empty the contents onto the plate. The curried beans offered no resistance, but the sausages slurped threateningly as he tried to shake them out of the tin. Wary that they'd fall out in a rush, splashing curried beans over some of his few remaining clean clothes, he prised them gently out with a fork and sat down to eat.

Belching, he pushed away the empty plate and pondered how he could uncover what Rafter was scheming. Weekends were rarely propitious for investigation. People retreated to unreachable spots or stayed in bed. Tyrell mentally lined up each person present at the shaman's house and studied them in turn.

When he reached the end of the row, there stood Professor Outman grinning. Of course! He was staying at a hotel close to the university with his daughter. If he kept an eye on them, they'd surely lead him to Rafter and his gang. Tyrell could even meet the professor to discuss his conference. Pleased with himself, he burped in celebration. Rubbing his complaining stomach, he undressed for bed.

Flight

In the dark behind her, Sally could hear Brent asking: "Is

everything OK?" as she and Keira stopped to take stock of the situation.

"Alo says we've reached the end of the tunnel," she passed the message quietly back over her shoulder in reply, "so we need to be careful."

Turning towards him, she stretched out her hand in his direction, and finding his arm in the dark, she ran her hand down his sleeve until she could grasp his hand. He seemed tense. At the same time, Keira took hold of her other hand so all three moved forward somewhat awkwardly in single file but hand-in-hand towards the exit; a slightly lighter patch in the pitch darkness.

The three emerged from the tunnel and joined Rafter and Alo who were standing on a raised jetty in a spacious wooden construction, the centre of which was full of lapping water.

"We can use my boat to move up river," Alo was explaining in hushed tones to Rafter. "We'll row a while so as not to attract too much attention. Can you row?" he asked, turning to Brent.

Brent, who let go of Sally's hand, said he could. Alo helped each person into the boat moored to the jetty and then untying the craft he climbed in pushing the boat forward towards the exit. Sally sat in the stern with Keira, laying a nonchalant arm around her friend's shoulders.

Behind them there was a small outboard motor, silent for the moment. Rafter and Brent took the oars in the middle of the boat exchanging a few quiet words and Alo made his way forward, balancing carefully so as not to rock the boat. Once in the prow, he reached forward and undid the gates that opened onto the river.

The three men took it in turns to row. The tide was rising, making it easier for them to row against the current, but it was still hard work. Nobody spoke, but for Alo's brief instructions about where to head around the small islands that were dotted along the waterway. The only sound to be heard was the lapping water and the occasional night beast on the prowl or on the wing. They'd been startled by the screech of an owl a while back. Now bats flitted here and there, hunting along the river-banks. Sally absent-mindedly played with Keira's hair as the girl had fallen asleep with her head in Sally's lap.

Her friend had acted out of character earlier, the way she'd played with Brent at table. Could Keira be jealous? There was no reason. She hardly knew Brent. They'd met for the first time that very evening. She looked forward to where his dark figure curved over an oar, muscles straining, breathing hard with the effort. She caught herself thinking that things were perhaps not quite so simple, when Alo announced that they could now use the motor.

"I can manage," Sally told Alo as she woke Keira. "Go sit midship, Keira, my love," she whispered. "I need room to steer."

Turning her back on the others, she lowered the outboard into the water and got it ready in no time. It was an electric model so it wouldn't make much noise but they wouldn't go very fast. Both her step-father and step-mother had been skilled boatpeople and she had learnt from then. Grasping the tiller in one hand, she stood in the stern looking out over the river ahead and switched on the motor. Alo came to sit near her, offering advice from time to time about which route to take.

Rafter had shifted to the prow where he sat upright, seem-ingly in meditation. That left a rather sleepy Keira sitting next to Brent, or rather leaning heavily on him, her head on his shoul-der. Sally watched him pull out a blanket from a cupboard be-neath their seat and wrap it around Keira and himself. Well, yes. She had to admit there could be cause for jealousy. But who was jealous of whom? Warned by Alo to avoid a small island bare-ly breaking the surface of the water, Sally turned her attention back to navigating.

The moon was rising over the wooded downs, casting a cool silvery light across fields and forest alike. The moon was nearly full. Stars retreated before its halo. The sight of the star-lit night sky always filled Sally with a feeling of awe and belonging. She sought out the constellation of Orion, the Hunter. It was reclined above the horizon about to set, Rigel and Betelgeuse still clearly visible. The bright Lady of the Moon was a hunter too. The ancient Greeks called her Artemis, goddess of the hills and forests, striding with her bow and arrows followed by a herd of faithful deer.

Looking back at the sky after a tricky passage between a number of small islands, Sally saw that the east was faintly tinged red. Day was breaking. Birds awoke, here one then another further away, serenading the new day. Rafter stretched in the prow, his arms splayed out and upwards, fingers spread, in greeting to the new day.

Shaken by deep-seated joy, Sally broke into a wordless song that rose and fell in trills and glissandi mingling with the growing dawn chorus. Alo and Rafter joined her in an improvised choir, tenor and bass with her soprano. A startled cormorant rose from the waters near the riverbank, an eel in its beak. All three singers stopped and spontaneously burst into laughter. Unaware Brent and Keira slept on.

Brent was awoken by someone or something nibbling his ear. It didn't make sense. He was reminded of the drunkard's nightmare, waking in the arms of a woman he didn't know, wondering how he got there and, above all, what he'd done. Then he remembered Keira and the boat. Opening his eyes, some distance away he saw Sally standing in the prow, the tiller in her hand, her hair streaming out behind her as she surveyed the river ahead.

Alo sat at her feet pointing to the bank. She nodded to him and shifted the tiller to bring the boat round in the direction he indicated. Then she glanced down and looked straight at him. Their eyes met, only very briefly, but they said so much that he could barely understand: pain, disappointment, longing, anger and something much deeper. Embarrassed, he moved his head to stop Keira getting at his ear. She complained wordlessly, but slept on. Unwrapping that part of the blanket that was around his shoulders, he gently laid Keira on the bench warmly bundled in the blanket and moved forward to sit near Rafter.

The sun was rising with a fresh wind that whipped up tiny

wavelets on the river surface and stole into his clothes stinging his sleepy body.

"Good morning," Rafter greeted him. "Sleep well?"

Brent groaned, at which Rafter chuckled. These people missed nothing Brent realised, feeling abashed.

"We're navigating up a tributary of the Avan. We'll arrive shortly." Rafter informed him.

On the jetty he could see a plump lady waving to them.

"That's Mrs. Martin, my housekeeper," Alo told them.

Sally cut the motor and glided the boat skilfully towards the landing place. Mrs. Martin tossed them a rope that Alo caught. Leaving Alo to pull the boat in the remaining distance, Sally knelt next to Keira and awoke her friend with a kiss. Both of them looked a little embarrassed, Brent thought, but maybe it was only his imagination. He certainly felt embarrassed. Once moored, Alo stepped out of the boat, greeted Mrs. Martin and helped each person alight.

"Follow me," Mrs. Martin invited. "Breakfast is ready."

Mrs. Martin was a laugh, a true storyteller. Brent liked her immediately. She had a stock of anecdotes about Alo and his family and his dog and the house and the boat and the countryside nearby that she told with brio. As she bustled about the dining table carrying the coffee pot and warm croissants and all manner of preserves, she delighted her sleepy listeners with her tales.

"… We searched from the attic to the cellar, but we couldn't find him anywhere," she said as she handed Brent the butter. "It was his dog that finally tracked him down. Young Alo had climbed an old oak tree on the hill up behind the house, and couldn't get back down…"

Brent glanced at Alo who was smiling at the memory. Despite the worries about Leuchtli and yesterday's intruder, they were happy to make merry this morning, as all manner of chuckles and laughter rippled around the cosy room.

"There are several free rooms on the second floor," Alo said to Sally, Keira and Brent as they stepped out into the entrance hall. "Pick the ones that suit you." Adding, as he left for his own room: "We'll meet for lunch at around one."

Brent couldn't face the idea of the three of them choosing rooms. It was likely to be a rather embarrassing moment, at least for him. So he said, not untruthfully: "I'm too worked up with all that has happened, I don't think I could sleep straight away. I'll go for a walk first."

Chapter 4 - The Guide

Unexpected meetings

Nala had barely taken a few steps down the broad stairs into the growing gloom when she was enveloped in a cloud of vanilla scent. How embarrassing! The smell had her completely aroused. She tried to quell the excitement but didn't succeed. Her skin tingled and her nipples were erect. Luckily there was no one around.

It was then she caught sight of a schoolgirl climbing the remaining steps towards her. A schoolgirl? Yes! Complete with patent-leather court shoes, blue knee-length socks, pleated navy blue skirt, white blouse, blue and white striped tie and regulation navy blazer with school crest! The whole works. How could such a seemingly ordinary sight be so alarmingly out-of-place?

"Welcome, Cianala. Do not be afraid, I am here to guide you," the schoolgirl said as if it were self-evident, pushing her shoulder-length, blond hair out of her eyes.

She must have been about fifteen. Her voice was soft, but firm, more self-possessed than Nala would have expected from a person that age and unbearably seductive. The girl held out her hand to Nala.

"Take my hand. It will reassure you."

Nala hesitated, not trusting the girl but above all not trusting her own emotions. The schoolgirl smiled knowingly and took Nala's hand. The girl was right, like her voice, her hand was firm and confident.

"What's your name?" Nala asked.

"I have been given many names: An, Anah, Aine, Emily, Hannah, Helen, Hena, Tanya, ..."

Nala felt her head begin to spin. The girl spoke more like a benevolent grandmother than a schoolgirl.

"In the Reaches everything is manifold." Or a university professor! "And just as I have many names, so I have many forms. At the moment, you see me as a young girl. That's my favourite form."

Nala laughed nervously.

"Later I may look different. If you like, you can call me An."

The girl turned and pulled Nala gently by the hand. Nala resisted, jerking her hand free as she looked back up towards the station she'd just left.

"Hold on a moment!" she exclaimed, causing An to stop abruptly.

"What am I thinking!" How could she possibly have forgotten! Her mind was playing tricks on her. "What about Jake? I should go back for him. He might be in trouble."

An gave her a searching look and then smiled, her eyes sparkling. "Don't worry about him, he's got other things to do before you meet again. He's got his own journey to go on. The best thing you can do for both of you is to continue yours."

Nala stood there for a long moment, undecided. Could she trust the girl? She glanced out of the corner of her eye to see the girl waiting patiently for her a few steps away, hands clasped demurely in front of her. What a picture of innocence! Yet Nala feelings were in turmoil as she tried to resist the unseen force that attracted her to the girl. Finally giving in, she sighed, turned back to the girl and took a step in her direction. Linking hands again, the two started down the stairs.

"You are going to find it difficult coping with the complexity of the Reaches to begin with," An said, although her rational discourse did nothing to allay the strangeness of the place. "Things are quite different here compared to your world."

To Nala's surprise the stairs broadened and faded until they were walking on a sloping surface. She almost tripped and fell as her feet misjudged the lay of the changing land.

"From the way you entered this place, you might think it is at the frontier between the Realm and the Reaches," An continued to expound like a professor giving a guided tour to undergraduates. "But there is no real boundary between the two. They are, in fact, the same place. Let's say, for the sake of simplicity, that it is a question of dimension or frequency."

Nala couldn't help giggling quite uncharacteristically. How could the girl talk of simplicity?

"You are more familiar with the dimensions of the dream world, even if that too seems strange to you. Do you hear that sound?"

Nala did: a faint vibration she hadn't noticed before. What was the girl going to spring on her now?

"Listen carefully," An said, drawing a small circle in the air with her hand.

Nala felt like a circus animal being taken through it paces. Jump, she thought, but instead she concentrated. The humming slowed. Loosing its machine-like timbre, it stretched itself out as parts faded and it became intermittent. The crests of sound strengthened and it beat faster. Heartbeats, of course!

"Now, go with it." An urged her, cracking her whip and shaking the tails of her dress coat.

Nala surged forward, feeling it beating in her own chest. Her own heart! What was this, a science lesson or a circus performance? She let go and blended with the sound, riding on its steady waves. The beating became more complex, dividing into parts, each taking its own course, each moving in a complex counterpart.

Each part in turn filled out and became richer. Nala laughed, astonished to realise she could follow each voice. Yes. Voices they were: an ethereal choir. Coming back to herself with some difficulty, she felt her hand still held in An's.

"How the hell did you do that?" she asked letting go of An's hand and shaking herself, unable to get the strains of music out of her head.

"What are you talking about?" An asked, a picture of innocence. Then she relented and grinned impishly. "All that you heard was already there. I just opened your mind to more possibilities. Each moment, each action, each person, each thing, each thought is manifold."

Nala was fed up with the word. Manifold this, manifold that! It was giving her a headache.

"For some reason, that diversity upsets those who live in the Real."

An picked up one of the many books that were lying in heaps all over the lawn. She tore a page from it, replaced the book on another pile and handed the page to Nala laughing.

"Here. Take a leaf from my book."

Nala was perplexed. Her head was bursting with questions, but the question she asked was not the one she intended.

"How can you have all those different forms and names and still be able to call yourself 'me'?"

An laughed so heartily that tears sprang to her eyes. Wiping them away, she donned her professor's gown again: "What is this continuity you call 'me'? For most people in the Real, it is bounded by their physical body and the duration of their life. Yet even between those artificial limits, their identity is necessarily composed of many differing parts that are often at conflict with each other. In fact, knowing that you are manifold helps you come to terms with some of your less attractive selves."

Nala remained silent and thoughtful for while, trying to get her head round An's words. She couldn't believe she was made up of many independent characters. Maybe she'd misunderstood.

Better change subjects, she thought. But many of the other questions that sprang to mind, the usual conversational gambits, could immediately be classified under the heading of 'senseless' in the Reaches, especially when you didn't even know if you were awake or asleep and you were holding hands with a fifteen year-old schoolgirl genius.

Where do you live? What school do you go to? What do your parents do? What do you plan to do when you are grown up? What do you do during your weekends? Have you got a boyfriend? And then the question came, unbidden.

"Do you have families in the Reaches?"

"Yes. For us, a family is a group of people with whom we have strong ties across the many shapes and forms we take and across the many times and spaces in which we exist. We look forward to meeting each other whenever or wherever that may be. The bond between us flows deeper and stronger than that of blood."

An paused a moment as if she were gathering her thoughts. "Know that when you talk to me, you are talking to all my Family."

"Grrrrrrrrrr!" A deep-throated growl startled them.

An spun round to face an enormous red-brown Bull mastiff that had crept up behind them. She was hampered by Nala's hand that she still held tight.

"Keep away, Connor. She's not for you." An's voice had deepened.

Gone was the schoolgirl. Next to Nala stood a muscular Amazon warrior, a bow and a quiver of arrows on her back, a sword unsheathed in her free hand. Nala would have laughed at what might have seemed a silly caricature if it weren't for the threat that hung in the air. The dog reared up on its hind legs, towering above them, and placed its great paws on An's chest, thrusting her backwards before she could defend herself. Tumbling over, she lost the grip on Nala's hand. Nala stood alone with the dog that promptly sat down and began busily licking its paws. Stretching itself, it rolled over and stood up, a schoolboy.

"I've been looking forward to meeting you for ages, Ciana-la." He smirked. "Maybe you remember me. I was watching you the other day in the train."

Nala managed to utter one strangled word: "You!"

Then, gathering her strength, she clenched her fist and swung it at him with all her force. He dodged nimbly and slapped her face. The blow sent her reeling. She staggered back and fell, though she didn't hit the ground. She continued to fall into darkness and nothingness. She thought she saw Connor dive in after her, but she couldn't be sure.

As she fell, she could hear threatening guttural snarls and ripping noises in the dark around her. She cringed, fearing for her life, but no blow hit her. Suddenly a howl of pain cut through the blackness and silence followed. The smell of blood filled the air leaving a metallic taste on her tongue.

Nala's fall slowed and she came to a halt in a clearing in an ancient oak forest. She took a deep breath, relieved. An old woman stood next to her dressed in what Nala imagined were the robes of a priestess: deep blue, embroidered with fanciful golden moons.

"Why did you not tell me I was Sally?"

"Hush, my child," the woman replied. "It was not yours to know. Not now. It will complicate our task."

Nala held back. She couldn't help seeing this woman as a stranger.

"If it makes things easier for you, you can call me Aine, even if I am still An as well."

Nala pulled herself together and stood up straight. "Tell me Aine, is Connor also Tyrell?"

Now the door was open, she couldn't help enquiring. She thought she saw a resemblance between the dog and the Assistant. Sally would find that funny.

"It is not good for you to speculate about correspondences between the worlds, Cianala."

Nala found the priestess almost haughty. But then the woman relaxed a little. "Let's go get something to eat. After that fight, I'm starving. Yes! Even here we eat."

Nala had never seen such a tall man before. He towered above her, tall and spindly, his head reaching up amongst the lower branches of the surrounding trees. A tree-man, she thought. He turned and bent down towards her smiling and then spoke to her as if returning to a conversation broken off only moments earlier.

"What if the spiritual is down rather than up?"

Nala stopped abruptly. "Do people never greet you normally here?" she asked.

"All our metaphors place the spiritual above," the man pursued, ignoring her question, "but much of our feeling of spirituality is nourished by the energy and the magnetism of the Earth? "

"Stop teasing her, Father. Nala, meet my Father or rather my step-father. He's sometimes known as Vic."

An, the schoolgirl, was back, although dressed for home rather than school, in a blouse and cotton skirt. It was the scent of vanilla that heralded her return.

"Well you came with such a serious question, I thought I'd give a serious answer." He burst out laughing, dancing round and round.

"We noticed" Nala replied, amused by his capers. "But your answer missed the point, because I haven't asked you my questions yet."

"Are you sure?" he said with some difficulty as he continued to dance. "Everything about you is begging the question!"

Nala was perplexed.

"Ah. Now you've multiplied the number of questions and are full of confusion."

He stopped dancing and, as he did, shrank into an old man bent over with age. Pausing to catch his breath, he said in a shaky voice: "Walk me over to the table, my loves, and I'll try to answer some of your questions."

Nala took one arm, An the other, and they walked slowly towards the massive oak table laid out in the shade of the first trees. Something about him reminded her of Prof. Rafter. Maybe it was the way he asked challenging questions out of the blue.

"She needs to understand the richness of the Reaches, Father," An said once they had seated the old man and taken their places opposite him. "And she needs to be able to protect herself from the likes of Connor."

Glancing round, Nala noticed a dishevelled man with a dirty grey beard peering at them from around a tree trunk.

"Who's that?" she asked An.

"Who?" the girl replied, glancing where Nala was indicating.

"The guy behind ..." But when she looked no one was there.

An's father picked up an apple from the fruit bowl and handed it to Nala. "In the Reaches, some of us have a variety of forms and we transform to suit the context. Not the context you're acquainted with in the Real. Your context is all surface and appearances. I mean the web of forces and energies and intentions that swirl around us."

He was interrupted by the arrival of a large black bird that landed on the table squawking rudely. It strutted across the table and started pecking at Nala's apple.

"Could you not do that, Mum." An said, pushing the fluttering bird away from the fruit. "Meet Teresa, my Mother, Nala. She always has to make a spectacular entrance to impress visitors."

Nala gingerly pushed the apple towards the bird: "You can have it."

But the bird preferred to hop onto the chair next to the old man and transformed into an elegant lady in her late forties.

"So what force led you to be a bird at this moment, Madame?" asked Nala, pursuing the earlier conversation.

"My husband has a rather narrow interpretation of the multiplicity of the Reaches" Teresa said patting Vic on his wrinkled hand. "Our own intentions and desires also play a part."

"Like I said, you were showing off" put in An.

"Well it's not everyday someone from the Real comes to visit us," she said, a sad look flitting across her face.

The old man coughed, getting their attention. "When you've finished ladies, we've got some serious questions to answer."

Nala turned to him and laid her hand on his "But I still haven't asked you my questions."

"No need my love, I know what you want."

She felt so at home with them she couldn't help asking, "Are you my family?"

"Well that wasn't the question I had in mind," Vic said smiling roguishly.

He seemed to be getting younger all the time. Gone was the stoop. His skin was less marked and wrinkled and his voice was more firm and full-bodied.

"This place is not just about transformation," he said.

Nala glanced at An questioningly. Could she be family too? The young girl smiled back.

"It's also about integration: owning up to the parts of yourself, however much you might not like them. In the Real there are so many taboos that people are completely fragmented. That's the joke of it. They cling rigidly to the idea that they are one unique person, while they are busy hiding parts of themselves they can't accept."

An leaned over to Nala and laid her head in Nala's lap, snuggling up close. An's breath caught.

"Just take An, for example."

An wiggled her head in Nala's lap at the mention of her name, sending shivers deep between Nala's legs.

"Can't you feel the excitement mounting? She attracts you, but you can't admit it. You deny that part of yourself."

Vic turned to his wife who was standing up. "Come. It's time for a flight through the woods, Teresa."

As they rose into the air and flew away, An put her arms around Nala's waist and nuzzled her nose against her breasts. Nala closed her eyes and tried to resist. She knew An wasn't really the age she appeared to be. She might even be hundreds of years old for all she knew. But a voice in her head insisted that what they were doing was wrong.

Waves of vanilla fragrance wafted around her as An gently undid the buttons of her blouse and slipped her hands over Nala's breasts. Leaning forward, An softly sucked them one after another nibbling gently as Nala stroked her hair...

When she awoke, Nala felt the warmth of An cuddled up

naked in her arms. They were lying on a bed in the shade of the trees. Kissing her blond hair, Nala gently shifted away and rose to pull her clothes on. A movement caught her attention across the clearing. The same bedraggled man she'd seen earlier was staring at them from the cover of a bush. He thrust his hand through his hair making it stand even more on end.

Had he seen them make love? Aware that she was naked, she quickly pulled on her skirt and slipped her blouse over her head. When she looked back defiantly in his direction, he'd disappeared. The thought that those eyes had pried between their bodies as they pleasured each other left her feeling soiled. But she refused to let him take away the joy of the moment.

An was looking up at her when she returned to the bed. "How does it feel?" the girl asked.

"I feel like I'm coming home for the first time." Nala grinned.

"Welcome back." An held out her hand to Nala who took it and, pulling on it, rose, laying her arms around Nala's neck.

"Why do you say 'welcome back'?" Nala asked, troubled. To the best of her knowledge she had never been there before.

An chuckled. "Mainly because you've only just now arrived."

Sally was perplexed. That wasn't what she meant. "But I've been here for a while already," she protested.

"In fact you've been hovering at the limits of the Dream Realm with one timid foot in the Reaches."

Sally had great difficulties getting her head around the idea. "So the schoolgirl was a figment of my imagination and our love-making...?" she asked, disappointed.

"The schoolgirl was my mother's idea. She told me girls of my age dress like that in your world. I thought it might reassure you to see something familiar."

Nala spluttered remembering her surprise at seeing a schoolgirl in such a place.

"Much of the rest you will no doubt remember in some strange and distorted form, as often happens with dreams."

Nala couldn't help looking regretful.

"As for the love-making, well ... that was delicious." And An kissed her fervently on the lips.

"Anyone for breakfast?" a male voice called out.

The two girls, still enlaced in each other's arms, turned to see who was disturbing them.

"Nala, meet my stepbrother, Jim" An said.

"Hello Jim" said Nala "I'm starving."

Their arms around each other's waists, they joined him at the table. He offered them piping hot tea and fresh granary bread full of little seeds and creamy golden butter and tart bitter orange marmalade and the smoothest of honey and delicious home-made apricot jam. An licked her fingers. As did Nala.

For all the delight of it, something had shifted with the arrival of Jim. Not just the usual stuff about no longer being in a cosy tête-à-tête. Something deeper, as if the ring of the place had changed. Nala couldn't quite put a name on it.

"So you want to fight Connor?" the young man said turning to Nala.

"Don't be silly, Jim," An said, prodding him playfully in ribs with her index finger. "Defence not offence. Nala needs to be able to protect herself against Connor and his crowd."

Nala studied Jim closely for the first time. Unlike his stepsister, he had black hair that he wore carefully combed. His blue eyes sparkled and he looked quite muscular. But try as she would, she couldn't feel the family in him. Maybe the family had been a part of the dream.

Pushing aside his plate, he said: "First you need to be aware of the fields of force and intention. You can feel them in the Real too, but most of you have turned your backs on them, only to let them work their way under your skin." The idea seemed to amuse him. "Haven't you noticed how some people are unbearable? You don't know why, but can't wait to get away from them. They are literally repulsive."

She immediately thought of Tyrell. The colours drained out of her surroundings as if the world were awash with a grey shadow that chilled her to the bone. Shady. Sinister, more like. Malevolent you might even say. The words were simply not potent enough. An's vanilla scent had been totally eclipsed by a pungent animal smell. Dogs. All wet fur and flees and dirty paws. Ugh!

"Sorry about that." Jim said as he moved to her side and laid his hand on her shoulder. "I hadn't realised how powerful you are - even though you don't know how to control that power."

Colour flowed through her once more, although she was still frozen to the core. "You resonated so strongly with something in your thoughts that you transformed this whole place. What were you thinking about?"

"An assistant at the University who has it in for Sally."

An laughed triumphantly. "I told you it was about Connor, didn't I."

Jim smiled at his sister. "Well at least Nala can still transform things. That's a start."

Watching

He watched her intently, from a distance, half hidden in the branches. Her auburn hair flowed in waves down to her shoulders, each wave catching the sunlight, brilliant and breathtaking. A gentle breeze stirred a lock of hair that came to rest across her face. Absent-mindedly she brushed it aside, tucking her hair behind her ear. She was in animated conversation with a young man and the girl she'd made love to earlier. They were laughing about something, but he could not hear.

Watching her filled him with warmth. He loved her body as much as he hated his own. The constant aches and pains reminded him he had a body however hard he tried to forget it. Otherwise, his body was like an empty husk that he had to carry around with him everywhere he went. It was only when he looked at her that he forgot the pain and began to feel alive: almost as if he could enter her, take possession of her body, lose himself in her, forget and remember all in one … or was it the other way round. He was never quite sure. The divide between them seemed so blurred.

Time and again he felt possessed by her. The sight of her drew him like a giant magnet that held him in its grip and wouldn't let go. The slightest detail of her captivated him: her every move was a delight. It was not so much desire, he told himself, knowing full well that he lied. Of course there was desire. It burnt within him like a red-hot rod. But he didn't want his feelings for her to shrink merely to that. He'd never be able to get close to her by brandishing his desire.

There was more, he was sure. He could feel it. Something deeper. More profound. More worthy. More likeable. It was like a bittersweet yearning for something that was so familiar it hurt. Something he'd lost without ever knowing he'd lost it. Something elusive that floated just beyond his grasp.

She stood now and walked thoughtfully away towards the house between two rows of upright posts. She held her head high. Her arms were stretched out in front of her at shoulder height, her fingers splayed. The young man was encouraging her, gesticulating at the posts. At each step she took, ripples of power flowed out of her sending the posts flying into the forest. He could feel the enormous force she wielded despite the fact that he was so far away.

She stopped suddenly and turned in his direction, as if she'd heard his thoughts. She shouldn't have been able to see him but the force of her look nailed him to the spot. She had him in her grasp. He thought he'd suffocate. A sudden blast of hot air rammed into his chest sending him bowling over in a cloud of dust and dried leaves. More pain, he thought distractedly.

The force of the blow carried him over a great distance. Not surprising really, he weighed next to nothing. When he came to rest at the foot of a large tree, he picked himself up, dusted off his already dirty jacket and trousers and shuffled dejectedly away, disappointed at being so dismissed. So much for devotion, he thought.

An's mother was engrossed in a book when Nala stepped into the sunlit study. Seated in an armchair her head lay against one of the wings of the chair, making the woman's hair fall across half her face.

"Something's troubling me, Teresa," Nala said.

The woman set aside her book and turned to face her. Rather than ask what the problem might be, Teresa just looked intensely at her, waiting for more. Her look left Nala even more troubled. It made her feel uncomfortable. It was almost as if Teresa had been expecting her to come and ask a question.

"In the world I come from I don't have parents. I was an orphan. Despite the fact that I was brought up by a very kind couple, not having parents was a great suffering. So you can imagine how important and troubling it must be for me to hear you call me a member of your family."

She took a deep breath hoping to calm her quivering emotions, but it didn't help. The idea of being part of a family appealed to her immensely but she was afraid it would turn out to be just another fleeting dream that slipped through her fingers.

"I can feel the deep bond that links me to you and An. But that doesn't explain why you should call me 'family'. If there really is a family bond between us you owe it to me to tell me."

Teresa remained silent for a long moment. Nala even wondered if the woman would reply. To her surprise she saw tears welling in Teresa's eyes.

"It is because you really are my daughter," the woman said, clearly moved.

"But I don't understand," Nala said haltingly. "I've never been here before."

Teresa smiled as if some distant memory had crossed her mind.

"Ah, but you have. You were born here and lived here for a short while."

It was Nala's turn to remain silent as she weighed up the implications of what she'd just learnt. "So Vic is my father?"

"No. Your father was another man, someone from your world, someone who was very dear to me. When he was forced to leave he took you with him."

Nala was having some difficulty grasping the change in her situation. "But I was always told I had been abandoned by my parents as a baby. How could my father have done that?" She could feel the anger smouldering in her. "Why did you let him take me away?" Nala asked accusingly.

"It was not possible for him to stay here. I was already married to someone else and our rules are very strict about such things. He was ordered to leave and take you with him."

Tears were now flowing freely down Teresa's cheeks. She tried to wipe them away with the back of her hand, but they continued to flow.

"It broke my heart to let you both go. I hid myself away for a long time. Then I discovered I was pregnant with An and that helped me find my way back to life and the world."

Nala felt less angry now that she realised Teresa had suffered too but she remained indignant. "So who is my father?" she asked.

"I cannot tell you that. It is up to him to reveal."

Nala sank down in an armchair and stared out the window trying to understand. She had a real mother and probably a father. She was grateful that Teresa kept her distance. Nala thought she might have screamed if the woman had moved to console her.

Standing, Nala took her leave saying, "I'm going out for a walk. I need to be alone. To think."

Teresa nodded, adding, "I'm so sorry, my love. I wish it could have been otherwise."

Not wanting to hear more, Nala left for the gardens and walked amongst the trees.

Evening Glory

The conservatory had been converted into a dinning room. Nala was deep in thought when she arrived, but as she stepped over the threshold she came to an abrupt halt, astonished. Never had she seen anything like it. The walls and roof were made of slender, arching metal girders that twisted and twinned like living twigs supporting delicately coloured stained glass panes.

Although a glass door lay open onto a veranda letting in a cool breeze that heralded the setting sun, the room retained much of the day's warmth. Milky white balls of light of differing sizes hung suspended here and there making the black shiny girders glint as if they were more real than real. She could almost taste their texture.

Instead of the usual rows of flowerpots, a wide flowerbed ran the length of the three glass walls making a mockery of the distinction between inside and out. Giant tufts of bamboo pushed upwards in one corner, splaying outwards as they reached the glass roof. The large white moonflowers that climbed up and around the door and across the ceiling were opening to greet the evening, giving off a heady fragrance.

An and her family relaxed in padded armchairs around an imposing table set in the middle of the conservatory which echoed the glass walls with its fine black metal latticework encrusted with slivers of coloured glass. An was laughing at something Jim had just said when she caught sight of Nala and rose to greet her with a kiss.

"Come join us," she said, taking Nala's hand and pulling her to a free chair next to her own. "We were telling our parents what happened when you thought of Tyrell earlier."

Nala grimaced at the memory as she eased herself into the waiting armchair.

"Good evening Nala. Now you have joined us, we can begin," said An's stepfather, Vic.

But there was no food to eat. Instead they bowed their heads and closed their eyes. As she glanced from one to another she saw looks of peaceful concentration. She closed her eyes and imitated them. A wave of peace and wellbeing flowed over her.

Delicious smells of food wafted in her direction. Opening her eyes, she saw that servants were laying numerous small dishes on the table containing a wide assortment of cooked and raw vegetables as well various varieties of beans in colourful sauces. There was fresh crusty brown bread too and all manner of exotic spreads adding splashes of colour to the meal.

Some time later, Vic pushed away his plate, raised his glass and turned to Nala.

"What do you think of the Evening Glory, Nala?" he said, gesturing to the Moonflowers hanging above his head with his outstretched glass.

As she leaned back to look up at them they turned from white to pink, finally becoming pale blue. Surprised, she looked back at him questioningly.

"You need to rediscover how to channel the forces in you so you can weave the world around you," he replied, smiling at her. "You too can do that. No effort is needed. It's a bit like what people call prayer in the Real. You must want it with your whole being and yet, at the same time, be indifferent about the outcome. See if you can change the colour of the glass," he suggested.

Nala surveyed the panes above her. Each had a different shape, a different hue or mix of hues. Change the colours he'd said. She had no idea how. How could you want something so much and yet not want it at the same time?

Perplexed, she studied the glass again. She picked up a faint vibration in the colours: the brick red; the slate blue; the olive green; … She listened to them, feeling them vibrate in her, with her, for a long while. Then she shifted them gently until the colours began to roll slowly forward like a giant wheel moving through the rainbow and beyond. Her concentration was broken by An's squeal of delight.

"Well done, lass," Vic said. "Now try again."

Knowing what it felt like made the second try easier. Instead of starting from the colours of the glass, she let an image float unbidden into her mind. The star-filled night sky, just as she'd seen it from a refuge on the top of a mountain.

All was quiet and peaceful at that height. God-touched, you

might say. A crescent moon crested the horizon and rose majestically into the sky. The Conservatory had gone very quiet. Opening her eyes, she looked around at her family. They were all starring up at the star-studded heavens, transfixed. A shooting star traversed the sky causing everyone to gasp. An clapped her hands and leaned over to Nala to give her a hug.

Vic raised his glass for a toast: "Welcome home, Cianala."

Helpless

Sitting on an up-turned tree stump at the edge of the forest, shroud now in darkness, Vee watched from across the garden as the colours shifted on the Conservatory roof and walls. Such silent pyrotechnics left him indifferent. The whole family was gathered for evening meal, warm and cosy.

He wouldn't sneer at them, though. He would give anything to be with them, to belong somewhere. She was there too. Surrounded by people who loved her. As for him, he was outside, peering in from his uncomfortable hide-away. Despite that, he did get a pleasure from stealing a glance into brightly lit windows at night. He glided through the windows like an incubus, feasting on the inner warmth of the place.

He could smell the food even from his distant vantage point. His mouth watered. He hadn't eaten for ages, lest it be with his eyes. He could see her smiling at the others, unaware he watched her. But he was not alone. Unmoving, he followed the progress of a dark figure that crossed the lawn and neared the Conservatory windows from the right.

The man, he was sure it was a man, came to a halt, hidden from those inside by the spreading bamboo. When the Conservatory roof transformed into a starlight sky, the dark figure snorted in surprise, but no one inside noticed, despite the opened veranda door. Vee smelt danger, the air was rife with it, but he was powerless to do anything. He certainly couldn't fight off the man. He had no strength in his arms or legs.

Then he saw a second figure sidling across the lawn, closing in from the left to hide close to the house wall. Still as the stump on which he sat, Vee watched the men watching. You'd think those inside would feel so much watching, he thought. But they seemed oblivious to all the eyes fixed on them.

The lights winked out in the Conservatory as the family moved into the house. It was late, time for bed. He wondered if the two girls would sleep together. Useless speculation really, even if the evoking of it did arouse him a moment. Now was neither the time nor the place. The two men were still concealed close to the Conservatory. After a while they moved together and exchanged a few whispered words.

"Yer got the stuff?" a worried voice asked.

"Sure!" the other hissed in annoyance. "And no touchin', the merchandise. 'e wants it all for 'imself."

Disgusted the other man spat at his feet and turned to scale the drainpipe to the first floor balcony, while the first man slipped into the Conservatory by the open veranda door.

All was dark in the house. Stillness had settled, were it not for the occasional noise of night beasts scurrying through the forest at his back. Vee continued his silent vigil. An owl hooted mournfully through the dark. He wondered what had disturbed it.

He scrutinised the windows, imagining the two men as they crept along the upstairs corridor towards the room where Nala lay asleep in the arms of An. They probably had some substance that provoked sleep. Once the girls were unconscious, he imagined them silently pulling back the sheets, uncovering the intertwined bodies, smooth skin on smooth skin, their nightdresses riding high up their thighs.

He shivered. One of the men pulled Nala roughly from the bed and slung her limp body over his shoulder. The other girl groaned in her drugged sleep. Nala was not so light. The man staggered under her weight, saved from falling only by the hand of his accomplice steadying him. They moved out into the corridor and onto the landing. Vee saw them as they eased the sleeping girl out of the veranda door. Carrying her between them now, they hastened across the lawn. When they reached the drive, the second man stumbled and almost fell.

"Stop oglin' 'er legs 'nd carry 'er properly, yer bloody fool!"

Standing cautiously, trying not to make a sound, Vee set off in pursuit of the ravishers. Skirting the forest edge, he managed to keep abreast of the men without them noticing him. He was so intent on keeping up that he stumbled on a branch and fell to his knees on the grass making a loud noise.

"Idiot!" he said to himself.

Neither men paid him any attention. It was as if they could neither see nor hear him. He moved closer when the forest crowded thickly around the drive and followed them a few strides away. They really couldn't see him.

Around a sharp bend in the drive, a large horse-drawn cart waited. The men laid Cianala in the back of the cart, covering her with a blanket, before they hauled themselves into the driving seat and prepared to leave. Vee grabbed the side of the cart, intending to clamber inside, when the cart lurched off down the road.

He clung to the side of the cart, his feet dragging on the ground. He didn't have the strength to pull himself up into the cart. He thought his arms would be wrenched from their sockets. The pain was excruciating, but he hung on. One of his shoes flew off when it hit a stone in the road. The stones and roots along the way battered at his shoeless foot. He was afraid he would pass out and relinquish his hold, loosing Cianala for ever. Mercifully the cart ground to a halt while one man got down to open a gate.

"Give us a 'and!" the man called out. "It's stuck."

Swearing coarsely, the other man clambered down and wrenched the gate open. Making the most of the distraction, Vee let go, staggered to the back of the cart and managed to ease himself up next to Nala were he lay nursing his bleeding foot.

Despite the throbbing of his shoulders and the agony of his foot, he couldn't help wondering at his temerity. Here he was inches away from his life's desire. He only had to stretch out a hand and he could caress her hair. How he'd longed to do that. And she could do nothing to stop him. But he didn't. He wouldn't. He couldn't. It wasn't the same. She was not in his power. She was in the power of those two brutes that had drugged her and were spiriting her away under the cover of night.

As the cart lurched on a bump in the road, her unconscious body slid up against him. He shifted away, as if the touch of her would do him harm. How odd. He'd always yearned for that touch, now he shied clear of it.

The cart was gathering speed. The trees had been left behind, but he couldn't see where they were because the sides of the cart blocked his view. All he could see was the road stretching away behind them into the dark forest where Cianala's family lived. He lay on his back trying to fight off sleep, but he must have dozed off because when he opened his eyes it was almost day and the cart was at a halt.

He heaved himself up on a box lying in the cart and saw they were pulled up in front of a massive black castle that towered above. The portcullis was being hauled up as the drawbridge lowered to let them in. He watched unseen as the cart rolled into the inner courtyard and the portcullis shuddered back into place leaving them prisoners in that dismal fortification.

Chapter 5 - The Machine

An interview

The nameplate on the door read "ENERGOS – The Manifold Energy Laboratory" beneath which was the name of the director: Dr. Jakob Leuchtli. It was not so strange to find such a high-tech firm in a tiny village in the Jura Mountains hidden amongst the sprawling farms and the herds of cows. Home of the watch industry and some amazing clockwork inventions, the region had a long history of entrepreneurial brilliance, meticulousness and sheer hard work.

He rang the bell and entered. Inside, a massive guard in uniform blocked the way. Demanding to see his credentials, the guard searched his pockets and bag, confiscating his camera saying that no photos were allowed.

"You'll get it back when you leave, Mr Downes."

The guard then stepped aside, revealing a short hallway that led to a reception area in which a secretary sat behind a large desk. There was a very faint but unpleasant smell in the air that he couldn't quite place. Hot metal maybe. Engrossed, the young woman didn't look up from the two flat-screens she was studying.

"Bonjour. Je suis Tom Downes, journaliste au Temps" he said. "J'ai un rendez-vous avec Dr. Leuchtli."

"Take a seat," she said, pointing to a number of armchairs arranged around a low table. "Dr Leuchtli will be with you in about ten minutes. You do speak English, I suppose?"

He nodded.

Picking up a coloured brochure entitled, *The future lies in manifold energy*, he sat down and began flipping through the pages.

He knew very little about Leuchtli. The short CV on the Internet said Leuchtli got his doctorate from the Federal Polytechnic in Zurich during the 80s writing a thesis on energy related aspects of dissipative structures and indeterminacy. The idea of dissipative structures had first been developed by the Belgian-based Nobel winner Prigogyne in the 70s.

Leuchtli had also got a Masters in cellular biology. The editor had sent him to interview Leuchtli because they were running a series on 'local' personalities. But Tom knew there was another reason: a rumour was going round that strange things were happening in Leuchtli's laboratory. He was supposed to see if he could discreetly unearth something. Tom felt uncomfortable in the role of detective. He was not that kind of journalist. Poking and prying meant running the risk of things turning sour.

The brochure explained that 'manifold energy' was energy potentially released in complex systems when they flipped unexpectedly from one of their possible semi-stable states to another. The challenge of ENERGOS was to find ways to harness that energy in an exploitable way. It crossed his mind that harnessing any source of energy necessarily produced unwanted side effects and he wondered what they could be in this case. Maybe that was the problem he had to uncover.

Dr. Jakob Leuchtli interrupted these thoughts, when he strode into the room, leaving the automatic door to hiss closed behind him. A tall, solidly built man with bright, piercing blue eyes, he didn't look like someone who put up with much nonsense. Sitting opposite the journalist, Leuchtli didn't bother with introductions.

"I don't have much time. What can I do for you?" he asked.

The journalist explained that they were running a series on important personalities and asked about ENERGOS. Ten minutes later Leuchtli had finished with him, leaving him about as knowledgeable as he'd been when he came in. As they rose, Tom tried one final time.

"So when will we be able to see the first concrete results?"

Looking irritated, Leuchtli was about to reply when he was interrupted by a bald little man in a white coat beckoning to the doctor from an opened doorway.

Leuchtli curtly said "Goodbye" without the slightest explanation and headed for the door. As it hissed closed behind him, Tom heard a voice say: "She's dead!"

He could have sworn these words were followed by a grunt of pain and a dull thud.

The secretary interrupted his thoughts: "The exit is over there Mr. Downes. Bonne journée."

Good riddance, Tom translated, smiling grimly. He had a really bad feeling about the place, so much so he was glad to get outside.

Accidents

"Have you got no brains, Trottel, blurting out such things when we have a journalist snooping around" Leuchtli complained, rubbing his fist to ease the pain of the blow he'd given his assistant. "Aufstehen!"

And he set off in the direction of his office with the assistant trotting nose-bloodied after him. Seated behind his desk, the door firmly closed, he turned on the little man.

"What's all this about death?"

The man was a mess. Blood was flowing freely from his nose sending red streaks down his white coat.

"Speak up. I haven't got all day."

"She was gone too long on the other side. We couldn't get her back."

"Didn't you try giving her a shot?"

"That only made things worse. Body rhythms sank as soon as we started increasing the energy, until we finally lost her. Nothing would wake her. Like she gave up."

"Get rid of the body then. Tonight. There's a pothole up near the lake. It's deep and the bottom is full of ice all year round. Throw her down there. Make it look like she lost her way and fell in. Ask Sykes, he'll know where it is."

Leuchtli turned away, dismissing the man. Damn nuisance. They'd have to find another subject: someone who was more resilient but also someone who wouldn't be noticed if something went wrong. He couldn't risk using the people from Avan University yet. It was too soon. The process was still unstable.

Potholes

Tom had been sitting at the wheel of his car in a deserted side street across from the almost empty ENERGOS car park for several hours. In these villages of the Jura most of the farms and houses were strung out along the main road, sometimes spreading for miles. Up front ENERGOS had once been a farm. Out back, new one-storey buildings flowed around the car park and out into the fields beyond.

It was getting late and he was feeling cold and a bit miserable. He hadn't eaten yet. Jenny would be waiting for him. They were to go potholing with Jenny's brother over the weekend. The three of them were to plan it that evening. Tom wondered if he'd been wrong about ENERGOS. Nothing was going to happen.

Just as he moved to start the engine, a movement caught his eye: two men were struggling with a heavy bundle between them. Dumping it with a thud on the ground, one of them opened the boot of a station wagon parked at the back of ENERGOS and they unceremoniously rolled their lumpy object inside. Tom let out his breath with a hiss between his teeth. This didn't look good at all. If they saw him …

"Tiens! Regardes qui est là."

Startled, Tom spun round to face the stocky man peering in his car window. A fist flew in his direction, landing with a dreadful cracking sound on his nose. The pain was excruciating as blood flowed freely down his face.

"That'll teach you not to stick your nose into other people's affairs."

The man opened the car door and roughly pulled him out. Tom stumbled and fell at the man's feet where he was greeted by a vicious kick in his stomach. The blow drove all the air out of him. Gasping, he was dragged to his feet and pushed towards the station wagon. One of the other men opened the boot giving him a brief look at the sack lying there. The stench was unbearable but he didn't have to put up with it very long. A sharp blow on the back of his head sent him collapsing forwards on the sack and blackness and silence embraced him.

Tom drifted in and out of consciousness as the car glided unseen and unheard through the moonless night. Dark dreams of wading through rotting, lifeless bodies gave way to waking nightmares filled with the stench of death and the pain of a broken nose.

In a lucid moment, hearing the men talking gruffly to each other in German, he tried to lift himself away from the sack so he could reach his belt. Easing his hand underneath it, he managed to press the button that set off the GPS alarm. Jenny and Martin would know something was wrong and come looking for him. He immediately realised his mistake. He'd only been thinking of himself. Now he'd put Jenny in danger as well. He sank back onto lumpy sack and gave way to despair.

The car jolted as it drove over an uncovered tree root on the dirt track rolling Tom facedown on the putrid sack. The blow sent a sharp pain shooting through his body as his nose hit the sack, bringing him abruptly back to his senses. The track wove its way through a dense pine forest shifting him violently from side to side. Tom's groans were lost in the roar of the engine as the car climbed a steep rise. After its effort, the vehicle came to a halt near a broken fence where a rusty sign warned of danger.

Tom was dragged out of the car and dumped in a heap on the ground as the two men went back to fetch the body. Tom recognised the place in the lights of the car. It was one of the entrances to an underground cave that was renown for being half-filled with ice all year round. Centuries earlier it had been used as a source of ice for the well-off far and wide. The safe way down was via a slippery metal ladder, a drop of four or five meters, to the cave floor below.

As an experienced explorer of potholes, Tom had been there several times. There were several other ways down, but all of them were through narrow chimneys that dropped vertically so that they could only be scaled with ropes. It was down one of these sheer drops that the men, grunting with the effort, were now shoving the sack with its stinking load. They then turned to Tom who lay still on the ground feigning unconsciousness. Clearly the men were cautious about getting too close to the edge. The fall of the body in the sack had already caused smaller rocks and tufts of earth to break from the edge of the hole and fall clattering into the darkness.

Grabbing him by the arms, they hauled him closer and tried to push him in from as far away as possible. At the last minute Tom gasped their coats trying to drag them in after him. All three rolled in a muddled heap at the verge of the drop, each fighting desperately to get free. Tom held on bitterly, despite the kicks and punches he suffered. One of the men managed to fight free, leaving an empty coat in Tom's grasp. The other man took advantage of Tom being momentarily off balance and shoved him towards the hole.

Tom slipped over the edge, grasping the branches of a bush that grew on the far of the chimney. They slowed him a moment but couldn't completely brake his fall. Unable to hold on any longer he plunged into the dark pit, letting out a terrible scream. He hit the bottom with a sickening crunch of breaking bones. This must be the end, he thought. Yet he didn't feel broken. Tentatively feeling around in the dark he realised he had fallen on the sack with the body in it. It had broken his fall. It wasn't his bones that had cracked but those of the dead body. As he marvelled at his escape, something soft came fluttering down on top of him: the man's coat. As it draped over him, he passed out.

Backers

Arvo Pärt's Te Deum played quietly on the sound system in one corner of the plush office. Voices rose and fell in ever growing waves straining upwards to reach the chorus of violins that rippled above. Heavenly. The Swiss banker leaned back in the leather armchair and sipped delicate mouthfuls of whiskey savouring the taste as Leuchtli paced the room, evidently pleased at being able to explain his plans.

"We first built a device that could capture brain waves at a distance on a frequency that corresponded exactly to the discontinuities in the folds of the dream fabric. Unfortunately the signal was too weak. We needed more energy to amplify it than the signal provided us with."

The banker picked up a large cigar from the desk, clipped the end of it and held it between his teeth as he lit it with Leuchtli's gold lighter.

Blowing out a mouthful of smoke, he said: "I don't suppose that deterred you."

"No, it didn't. You're right."

Leuchtli paused to point to a small black device on display in a glass case in the bookcase.

"We discovered a simple way to echo the waves back to the brain such that a sympathetic resonance was set up producing a much stronger signal."

Leuchtli refilled the banker's glass and, taking some more himself, he pursued: "It was a very tricky business. First of all, the set of frequencies depended on the person, or rather his DNA. We found a way round that by using the person's DNA to generate an initial signal that would home in on the individual. All we needed was a piece of hair or nail clippings or a drop of blood. Our second difficulty was the stability of the signal. If it got off balance and the wave spread beyond the right cluster of frequencies it could severely damage the brain."

The banker put down his glass, placed the unfinished cigar in an ashtray and looked intently at the doctor.

"But you managed to generate the energy, all the same?"

100   Alan McCluskey

Leuchtli grinned. "At first we thought that was what we would be able to do. And we continue to tell people that. But what we discovered is much more important."

He came to sit opposite the banker, leaning forward till he was only a few feet from the man. "And potentially much more lucrative."

"Interesting." The banker was clearly having difficulty concealing his enthusiasm. "Tell me."

"We invented a Machine to lock into the waves and retransmit them to someone else."

The banker looked perplexed. "I'm not sure I understand."

"That was our big breakthrough. It meant we could enter people's dreams and modify them."

Leuchtli sat back in his armchair and swilled down the last of his whiskey.

"And the applications?" the banker asked.

Leuchtli quelled his irritation. These bankers had no imagination, no vision. You had to spell everything out for them. "Hundreds. Therapy but also war, tourism and entertainment, but above all power and control."

A timid grin surfaced on the banker's face, spreading rapidly until he laughed out loud and slapped his hand on his thigh. "You're a real devil aren't you, Leuchtli?" he said appreciatively. "Our bank would be very interested in considerably increasing our backing, but we need proof. Can you organise a demonstration?"

Leuchtli shifted away, turning his head to look at the clock to conceal his discomfort. It wouldn't do to kill someone in front of his backers. "In a week or so. We are currently trying out some new techniques to improve control on the Machine. As soon as that is done I'll organise a full demonstration."

The banker rose to leave, stretching out his hand to say goodbye. Leuchtli took it in his and, pulling the banker abruptly towards him, he yanked out a few strands of banker's hair. Startled the man stepped back rubbing his head.

"Are you crazy? Why did you do that?"

Leuchtli smiled. "You understand, of course, that all that I have said to you about our Machine is top secret. Let's say I have taken some of your hair as a guarantee you don't get too talkative."

The banker looked perplexed, his mouth hanging slightly open. He really is a bit dim, Leuchtli thought.

"So that if I am short of people to experiment on I can always call on you."

The man paled as he realised what Leuchtli meant and hurried to the door.

Rescue

"Tom! Are you down there?" A worried young woman's voice awoke him.

He groaned. Despite the sack beneath him and the coat over his back, he was freezing, as if we were lying on the ice itself.

"Jenny?" he called back feebly.

"Don't move," she said relieved, "we are coming down for you. Everything will be alright."

The block of ice that covered almost all the floor of the cave was particularly treacherous because it curved round and under as it neared the walls of the cave. If you got too close to its edges you could easily slip further down and be trapped under the ice itself. Shivering, Tom tried not to move. He could hear the noise of tackle being set up and the screeching of a pulley as the rope let a weight down towards him. It was Jenny's brother Martin.

"What a mess," Martin exclaimed, shining the lamp on his caver's helmet on Tom. Having checked Tom for broken bones he said, "Let's get this harness round you, so we can get you out of this hell hole."

Inquisition

It was very late in the evening at ENERGOS and most people had gone home. A small group of scientists in white coats sat around a large table talking quietly to their neighbours. The blinds had been pulled down and the lights were dimmed. The atmosphere in the room was suffocating and several people were having some difficulty breathing. The moment the door hissed opened all talking ceased and heads turned like clockwork to watch Dr. Leuchtli march in.

"So what did you do wrong?" he demanded as he sat in his seat at the head of the table.

The scientists glanced nervously at each other, but nobody dared answer.

"Are you telling me that with all the brains I've paid for none of you has an answer?" He spoke quietly, knowing he did not need to raise his voice to make his words threatening.

A little man with a bruised face and swollen nose finally spoke up. "Our supposition is that the brain naturally resists being used as a resonator. There seems to be some sort of automatic mechanism that protects it by lowering the acceptable input frequency threshold. One of the side effects of that is that many of the normal impulses to the body are also cut off and after a while life processes break down."

Leuchtli remained silent, staring at the man for quite a while. Then he licked his lips and smiled viciously: "Well congratulations. You've invented a Machine that kills at a distance. Maybe we should test it on you."

A few people laughed nervously but stopped immediately realising it might not have been a joke.

"Not many of you have a sense of humour this evening, so let's be serious. What evidence do you have for this hypothesis?"

A young woman opened her computer, flicked on the projector and displayed a graph on the screen. Leuchtli had met her at an international congress and had recently invited her to join his team. She was a molecular biologist, specialised in human energy fields.

"We've tested thresholds on several people and in each case we've found the same phenomenon," she said. "There's a marked cusp in the curve."

"Thank you Francine. Is the level too low for us to get under it?"

As discussion moved to science people began to relax a little and more of them ventured to talk. Leuchtli leaned back in his chair and surveyed the animated group that debated solutions. Fran was pointing to a diagram on the screen. Her white coat had slipped open so he could see her blouse that was unbuttoned, revealing the upper part of her firm breasts. He imagined caressing her naked breasts and tying her down, spread-eagled on his desk as she cried for help.

He'd have her tonight, he thought, once the others had gone home. He abruptly awoke from his fantasy to discover the whole group were looking at him awaiting his reaction.

"Good. But remember, whatever solution you find, it's got to be independent of the subject. We need to be able to enter people's heads without wires or drugs! And I need that solution within two weeks."

Not waiting for a reaction he stood up, pushed back his chair and moved towards the door. Stopping in front of it, he turned and said: "Oh, and, Francine, meet me in my study in about twenty minutes, I have something important to talk to you about."

He looked across the room at her and saw her go pale and grip the table for fear of falling. Good. He liked fear.

The boss's study

Leuchtli's study was a converted apartment on the top floor of what used to be the farmhouse. He'd had a large part of the flat converted into a comfortable room where he could receive guests. It had plush armchairs, an open fireplace and low tables.

One door opened to an equally spacious bedroom with a large double bed, another door led to a bathroom and the third door led to a small kitchen. Nobody cooked there, of course. He generally had food brought in by a caterer when he needed it. He liked this place because it was isolated from the rest of the buildings and he could do what he liked there without anybody bothering him.

At a faint knock on the door he called out "Come in!" and went to sit in an armchair. When he looked up he saw Fran standing in the entrance. She was slim and medium height. Her shoulder length hair was blond and her eyes blue. Leuchtli had been waiting for this moment ever since he'd seen her sitting on a table swinging her legs in animated discussion with other young scientists during the international congress where he first met her.

She had taken off her white coat revealing a green blouse now carefully buttoned up at the neck. She was wearing tight jeans.

"Come and sit next to me," he said, feeling the anticipation rise in him. When she continued to hesitate in the doorway, he added: "I want to talk about your promotion."

She moved timidly into the room and came closer. "What do you want me to do?" she asked.

Good girl, he thought, you just do what I want and we'll get along fine. "I want you to replace my assistant who has made too many mistakes recently."

She still wouldn't come any closer. He got up and walked to the bar. Looking over his shoulder, he said: "How about a drink to celebrate?"

"I don't drink alcohol" she replied.

So cautious, he thought. But it won't help you though. "I have a fruit cocktail in the fridge if you like."

When she agreed, he went to the kitchen, leaving her still standing in the main room. He took out a bottle of fruit juice, shook it, poured her a glass and slipped a small amount of a colourless powder in the drink. Stirring the mixture with a spoon he also poured himself a tomato juice. That way they wouldn't get the drinks muddled, he smiled to himself.

Carrying the drinks back into the main room, he offered her hers.

"Thank you," she said.

He loved the sensuous roughness of her voice. It caressed

his skin and made him tingle all over. Strange, he thought. He'd never had such a gut reaction to her before.

"Excuse me. Could you tell me where the toilet is?"

He pointed to the door. Their drinks were standing untouched on the low table by the fire. He didn't really like tomato juice anyway. Moving to the bar, he picked up the whiskey he'd served himself earlier and drained half the glass. It amused him to think of her sitting with her pants down only a door away. For all his desire for her, he hoped it wouldn't take too long. It had been a long day and he was tired. He eased himself into an armchair and closed his eyes.

He awoke with a start as she shook him.

"You forgot your drink, Dr. Leuchtli," she said handing it to him.

Still half asleep he took it and drank a mouthful. Odd. There was something peculiar about this tomato juice. It must have gone off. It tasted more like fruit juice. When what had happened dawned on him, he looked up to see her grinning at him. He struggled to get up but he was weak at the knees. His glass slipped out of his fingers, fell to the floor and smashed.

He felt torn inside. Desire was waging war with sleep. He felt hot all over and started to sweat. His cock was rock hard, protruding embarrassingly through the front of his pants. He shook his head, trying to clear his vision.

"Francine, what have you done to me?" he slurred drunkenly.

He couldn't understand, surely he hadn't drunk that much whiskey. "Help me." He stretched out his arms and tried to grab her but she took a step back, continuing to watch him with caution. He slipped off the chair and rolled onto the ground at her feet. Looking up as she towered over him, he felt himself fading into unconsciousness.

Unpleasant news

When Tom awoke, he was lying on a bed in a chalet with Jenny at his side, one of her hands holding his, the other smear-

106   Alan McCluskey

ing arnica cream on his broken nose. It stung terribly, but he was delighted to see her. He tried to smile, but it hurt terribly.

"Just stay quiet you silly boy and don't move," she said. "There's plenty of time. You can tell us what you've been up to later when Martin gets back. He's gone to the flat to get some things."

At that moment he heard a noise at the door and he felt Jenny's hand tense in his.

"It's me!" he heard Martin call out.

She relaxed a little. Unlike his sister, who was petite, almost elf-like with sparkling green eyes, Martin was more of a giant, tall with strong broad shoulders and massive hands, a deep voice and even deeper brown eyes. He pushed open the door, nodded to Tom and went to lean against the mantle piece, warming his hands in front of the blazing fire. When he turned to face them, Tom saw that his features were set in a worried look.

"I went to your flat," he began, moving away from the warmth of the fire. "After what happened, I was cautious. I didn't immediately go in, but waited across the street watching. I saw two men come out carrying a pile of papers and photos. Once I was sure they'd gone, I went in. I thought something was wrong, because it didn't smell right the moment I opened the door. But I couldn't have imagined what I was going to see. Your flat had been completely ransacked. It looked more like a battlefield than a place where people live. "

For several years, Tom and Jenny had been sharing a large ground floor flat in one of the middle-sized towns that were dotted along the Jura Mountains. Jenny had recently painted a richly coloured fresco in the living room that depicted a wild forest peopled with all manner of mythical forest creatures. It had taken her six months to complete. It was breathtakingly beautiful. Together they had reorganised the furniture around the fresco and bought a new massive oak table, on which they planned many a meal with their friends who could admire her work.

"I'm so sorry Jenny." He was close to tears and his voice trembled as he spoke. "Your fresco is completed ruined…"

Jenny burst into tears. Tom wanted to comfort her, to take her in his arms, to share her grief, but any movement hurt so much all he could do was squeeze her hand that still held his. Her body was racked with sobs, shaking the bed on which Tom was lying.

"Why? Why?" was all she could say.

When she finally quietened, Martin invited Tom to tell them what had happened to him. At the point where the dead body had broken his fall and saved his life and the jacket had fluttered down to land on him, Jenny began crying softly again.

Martin, who had been silent for a long time, ran his fingers through his hair and said: "Your story of the body reminds me of something I heard the other day about a young woman who was found wandering in the woods not far from the village where ENERGOS have their offices. She was half naked and talked gibberish. The police could get no sense out of her. From what I read in the newspaper they put her in a mental home."

Jenny was looking at her brother through her tears. "Maybe she can tell us something that will help us understand what is happening to us."

"If she is still talking nonsense, I'm not so sure she can help us," Tom pointed out.

"There's one more thing you need to know," Martin interrupted. "When I left your flat I slipped out of the back entrance, through the garage. I picked up my car and drove past your flat. I saw two men sitting in a car parked across the road watching the entrance."

"Are we safe here?" Jenny asked, fear in her voice.

"I don't think we are," was Martin's reply. "We need to get far away from here."

"Fast," added Tom.

"I still think we should try to see that woman before we leave," Jenny insisted.

Martin took charge of things. He was a born organiser.

"Do you think you can walk, Tom?" he asked.

Tom tried to get up, but collapsed back onto the bed.

"I'll carry you to the car," Martin said. "I managed to rescue a few things from your place that were still intact: clothes, some food and some medicine. They were locked in a cupboard under the stairs. I also found your address book, Jenny. Lucky they didn't get that." He handed her the small notebook. "The rest is in the car. Maybe we should get you dressed in some clean clothes, Tom, before we leave. That blood will attract too much attention."

While Martin went to fetch a change of clothes for Tom, Jenny flicked through her address book. As Martin came in she stood up and turned to both of them.

"I know where we can go. We'll drive to England and visit my friend Sally in Avan. I haven't seen her for ages and she keeps begging me to go."

Escape

Fran, shocked, stood starring at Leuchtli's unconscious body slumped at her feet. His legs were folded awkwardly under him, making him look stunted, deformed, dwarf-like. His head hung pitifully against his chest, saliva dribbling over his chin. In contrast, his arms were splayed across the floor, spread-eagled as if for a ritual sacrifice. Nearby, a blood-red stain marred the carpet where the drugged fruit juice had spurted, bringing an end to his rampant desires.

Try as she would, she couldn't stop shaking. Her teeth chattered incessantly. She was appalled. What had she done? Maybe he was dead. No. She could hear his ragged breathing. She wrenched herself from her shocked state and picked up a blanket from where it lay on the back of the settee, wrapping it absent-mindedly around her shoulders. An icy cold penetrated her to the marrow. A stiff drink would have helped, but she didn't dare touch anything in case it too was drugged.

She began pacing the room trying to get some order in her thoughts. She had to get away. He would come after her, hot for revenge. That was for sure. And he had the means to get it. He had a hair sample of all the staff. He'd tricked them, hadn't he?

Said it was to avoid any of them being singled out as a mistaken target by the waves of the Machine. With that hair he could use his Machine against any of them.

Maybe if she got far enough away, it would no longer have any effect. It was possible that the impact diminished with distance, but that was only a hypothesis. Magnetic resonance of that sort might be instantaneous and ubiquitous. Not a good perspective, but she congratulated herself, all the same, pleased to see she was beginning to think like a scientist again. Maybe she'd manage to get her hair back before he came round. It was unlikely, though. He'd surely locked up the samples in his safe.

She tugged gently at her hair, wondering what to do. A brilliant idea struck her: she'd get some of his hair. Not that she had a Machine to use on him. But it was precaution. You never knew what might happen.

In the bathroom she found a small pair of nail scissors. For some reason they disgusted her, but not as much as the thought of touching his hair. Using some toilet paper, she gingerly grasped a clump of his hair and hacked it off. He groaned in his sleep, startling her. A part of the hair slipped between her fingers and fell onto his face. Keeping a good grasp on the remaining lock of hair, she wrapped it in the toilet paper and carefully folded the little packet into her back pocket.

She felt suddenly much warmer. Casting off the blanket, she let it fall to the ground. As an after thought, she pulled the blanket over him. Strange! She wondered at her own behaviour. He wouldn't have had so much compassion.

Better wash that whiskey glass, she thought. Don't want to leave evidence lying around. She'd read enough detective stories to be cautious about such things. Not that she was in a habit of poisoning people. She grinned to herself. Come off it Fran, this is serious, she thought. A moment more and she'd be laughing hysterically.

She was about to leave the flat, when she heard faint steps beyond the door; one of the security guards no doubt. Whoever it was probably wouldn't come in; he wouldn't dare disturb the

Doctor. But she couldn't take the risk. She'd do well to find another way out. She looked around the room and caught sight of his jacket where he'd cast it carelessly over the back of a chair. Typical, she thought. Rummaging through his pockets she found a bunch of keys. She also fished out a small black notebook with a large spiral binding.

Crossing to the door, she tried several keys till she found one that fit and locked the door, making as little noise as possible. She left the keys in the lock and, still grasping the notebook, went to the window. There was a small balcony from which she could probably climb onto Leuchtli's garage roof.

Realising she was still holding his notebook, she let it fall open where a bookmark separated the pages. It was the last entry. She read:

... (20:30) Francine: white lab coat, open at the neck, a low-cut green blouse, firm young tits. Stick out when she leans over the computer ... Good strong legs too. I'll ride her tonight.

Fran could hardly believe what she was reading. Her breath caught in her throat. Opening the notebook elsewhere at random, she read further:

... (22:15) Donna: shame she has gone mad. The Machine got her. She had such strong fingers. Gave me so much pleasure. And pretty too ...

She slapped the book closed with a grunt of disgust and was about to throw it across the room to get it as far away from her as possible. She felt soiled by the touch of it. But something made her hesitate. Opening it once more, as if to confirm what she couldn't believe or possibly compelled by morbid curiosity. She discovered a page of names, addresses and phone numbers, all girls and women. Hers was amongst them. Leuchtli had written a title in bold capitals: MACHINE FODDER.

This would require more time and thought, she realised. She slipped the book into her pocket and stepped out onto the balcony, pulling the window closed behind her. Straddling the balustrade, she made her way gingerly across the garage roof and jumped down onto the grass beyond. The night would have been peaceful, were it not for a biting wind that blew from the North. 'La Bise' the locals called it: the kiss. She shivered as she skirted the ENERGOS buildings to fetch her car from the almost empty car park.

Donna

The mental hospital was quite small. It was one of the few escapees of a wave of so-called rationalisation that had swept away nearly all the small clinics in the area. Built on a hill over-looking a minor town, the hospital was surrounded by pine-woods. Martin drove along the narrow, winding lane through the trees and parked the Land Rover in the car park that lay in front of the main entrance. They had agreed that Jenny would question the woman and Martin would accompany her, just in case there was any trouble.

Tom was to stay locked in the vehicle and try to rest. They all had miniature walky-talkies if ever anything happened. Tom shifted in his seat trying to find a more comfortable position from which to watch the entrance as well as the drive up which anybody would have to come if they wanted to enter the hospital.

They had stopped off at the library on the way to check on the Internet for the name of the woman they wanted to see. Donna Martinez. She'd been a nursery school teacher for a while, but had lost her job a few months earlier. There were hints of some form of scandal, but nothing concrete. The newspaper report said she had no known relatives.

As Jenny stepped out of the car and headed for the main entrance she felt apprehensive. She didn't like mental hospitals. They made her nervous. She wondered if the others felt uncomfortable too. At a quick glance Martin seemed relaxed enough. He was even whistling softly to himself. She had good reasons to fear such institutions. As a little girl she had heard voices and could see people that her parents said were not really there.

At first they'd thought it was just a game she played. But with time they'd become more and more worried and finally they'd taken her first to their family doctor and then to a specialist in just such a hospital. The specialist, she remembered him well, was very unpleasant and didn't smell very nice. What's more, he seemed quite unaware that his office was full of noisy, complaining people. They made so much noise she could hardly hear what the man was saying.

After several appointments, the specialist had suggested they take her in for a few weeks of observation. She was about ten at the time. But her parents, who were as horrified about the place as she was, refused. Luckily a friend of her mother's had suggested they visit an old man who lived in a nearby village. He had a reputation for curing all sorts of problems. There were many such people in the Jura Mountains. They called their healing ability the 'secret'.

Jenny had liked the man immediately. He'd taken her seriously and believed in the voices and the people she saw. He'd told her so when her mother was out of the way. He'd explained what these people were and how to shut them out if she didn't want to be disturbed by them. He'd also suggested she didn't talk about them to people like her parents and teachers and even her friends at school. She would have liked to spend more time with him, there were so many questions left unanswered, but she never saw him again.

"So you want to see, Donna?" the nurse at the reception asked them, bringing Jenny back to the present with a jolt. "It might be a bit difficult. She's been rather disturbed."

The nurse was obviously concerned about her patient and, judging from the sceptical look on her face, she was going to refuse them access.

"I'm an art therapist." Jenny said. "So I'm used to handling difficult cases."

As if to prove her point, Jenny pulled a large drawing block from her bag and a box of pastels. It was hardly convincing, but it might work. The nurse glanced at the block and then looked from Jenny to Martin and back to Jenny.

"Ok. I'll show you the way."

They followed her to the lift.

"I'm Martina," she said as they all stepped inside.

Pressing the button for the third floor, she turned to them and smiled. "Donna really needs someone she can trust, a good friend. She must have had a terrible shock to spark off such an episode."

Jenny wanted to know more, but the lift doors slid open.

"Follow me," the nurse said pulling out a large bunch of keys from her pocket.

Every door in the building seemed to need a key. When she'd unlocked it they went through into a large corridor that stretched the length of the building. Donna's room was at the end. Looking through the solid glass window that separated the room from the corridor, Jenny could see Donna curled up in a ball on her bed.

"You wait here, Martin. I'll go on my own." She was convinced it would be better if she went alone, but she also hoped the nurse would take the hint and stay outside as well. She needed time alone with Donna.

Apprehension gripped her. Maybe this wasn't such a good idea. If they were to talk of Leuchtli that might drive the woman to take refuge even deeper within herself. Martin placed a reassuring hand on his sister's shoulder.

"Where can we find you if we need you?" Jenny asked the nurse.

"I'll be with the duty nurse whose office is just down the corridor."

Jenny nodded, turned the handle and stepped into the room. The woman on the bed paid no attention to her. She continued rocking gently backwards and forwards, whimpering softly. Jenny was acutely aware of the dark shadows swirling around the girl. They made her shiver. She'd shut such things out of her life for years.

Jenny's instinct was to run away as fast as possible, but she couldn't do that. This was important. Their lives might depend on the answers she could get from the woman. So she steeled herself and moved closer, saying: "Hallo Donna. My name is Jenny. I am an artist. I want to draw you a picture. Would you like that?"

She went over to the bed, sat down a way away from the woman and took out her colours and the drawing block. Laying the block on the bed, she began to draw a brightly coloured bird that flew through lush tropical trees. As she drew she sang quietly, improvising a bird-like melody that soared and fluttered and hung in the air.

When she finished, Donna had stopped moaning. Leaning on her elbows, her head resting on her folded hands, she stared at Jenny's bird through terrified eyes. Her pupils were completely dilated. Drugs, Jenny thought. She detached the sheet and placed the drawing on the bed, deliberately leaving the block open in front of Donna. Donna picked up the black crayon and distractedly played with it between her fingers.

"Would you like to draw something?" Jenny asked.

Donna leaned forward and scratched sharp black lines that crisscrossed the page, filling much of the space. When she stopped, Jenny picked up the blue and handed it to her. Donna drew two round blue spots next to each other in one of the few spaces left between the scored black lines. They looked to Jenny like Donna's wild, trapped eyes. Jenny removed the page and placed it next to her drawing. Donna picked up the black colour again and drew a large blurred, upright shape that filled almost half the page.

She went on to fill out the shape vigorously with the same jagged black lines she'd used before. Jenny thought it might have been a giant or at least a very large man. Donna drew a horizontal line under the giant's feet and across the page till it ran off onto the bed covers. Seeing the black mark on the bed covers, Donna began whimpering again. Jenny took the black colour from her hand and offered her the blue.

"It's all right. Don't worry," she said reassuringly.

Donna looked back at her drawing and added two small round blue blobs side by side at the feet of the giant. Jenny realised she'd started to sweat. She'd never lived anything so intense. She offered Donna another colour, but the woman ignored it. Jenny detached the picture and placed it with the others.

Donna picked up the black again and drew a wavy horizontal line. It could have been hills. The woman added dots here and there on the hillsides then stopped. People, maybe, seen from afar, or animals; although they looked tiny. This time Jenny didn't need to offer the blue. The woman took it of her own accord. She drew the now familiar two blue blobs in the air above the hills and then picked up the brown and drew little squiggles to the right and left of the eyes.

My God! Jenny thought, wings. A bird. She couldn't help giving a startled look at the woman who just starred at her drawing blankly. As Donna didn't continue to draw, Jenny once more removed the sheet of paper and placed it next to the others. Donna immediately picked up the black crayon and drew a low, flat box in the middle of the page. She added the two blue eyes lying on one end of the top of the box and added a single squiggle from the eyes to the farther end of the box.

To Jenny it was obviously Donna's own tortured body laid out on a table. Picking up the black again she added jagged lines like lightening striking the reclined figure from various angles. Donna sat back on her haunches and began keening loudly as she rocked backwards and forwards.

Hearing the door open behind her, Jenny quickly slid the drawings face down into her block of paper leaving just the bird she'd drawn on the bed and rose to face the nurse. She had no idea how long she had been there. It could have been hours. Jenny had been completely absorbed by the woman's silent monologue.

"What a beautiful bird!" the nurse said delighted. "Do you see what your friend has drawn for you, Donna?"

Jenny rose and placed a hand lightly on Donna's shoulder saying: "I hope we meet again soon, my friend."

She walked to the door and out into the corridor clutching her drawing block and her colours in her hands. When she saw

Martin worriedly looking at her she burst into tears. How could anyone do such a thing to that woman? Senseless violence. Martin wrapped his arms around Jenny's shoulder to comfort her.

"Are you all right?" The nurse asked, joining them. "You spent almost two hours with her!"

Jenny was surprised. "I didn't realise. I was so caught up in what was happening."

The nurse offered them tea, but Jenny refused, remembering that Tom had been waiting outside, worrying about them all this time. No need to worry, though, he was fast asleep.

Chapter 6 - The Wanderer

The start

Jake paced up and down the tiny room. He wanted to be off. He'd been stuck there too long. It was the most unwelcome waiting room he had even been in. Devoid of any furniture or decorations or carpets, it had no windows, just two doors, both of which were shut. Jake had entered through one. The other, slightly smaller, must be the exit, he supposed. Nobody entered. No one came to fetch him. Maybe they'd forgotten him. He could be suspended there forever. Jake the pointless wanderer.

He checked his pockets to be sure that all was there. The little, white pebbles, still as cold as ever. His dreambook and a pen. He wasn't sure he'd be able to use them where he was going. But it reassured him to have something to write his thoughts on. And the old postcard of Avan Station, hopefully to guide him home when the time was right.

He came to a halt before the smaller door. Small indeed, for now he would have to stoop to get through it. Turning the pebbles over and over in his hand he wondered if it was up to him to make the next move. Letting the pebbles fall back noiselessly into his pocket, he grasped the doorknob tentatively, turned it and pulled open the door. The doorway was completely blocked by a haphazard jumble of boxes of varying sizes. Push or pull as he might, he couldn't get them to budge. Frustrated, he sat down cross-legged in front of the entrance.

Effort would get him nowhere. He'd been trying too hard.

Closing his eyes and quietening his breathing, he concentrated on the air flowing in and out of his lungs and the constant pulsing of blood in his veins. An image of the River Bree flowed through his mind on its way down to Erinsea, heavily laden with ships sailing to other lands. He waded in, ever deeper, feeling the river lap up around him. The water tugged gently but insistently, wanting him to cast off and slip away. Forgetting himself, he relaxed his grip and let go, flowing with the tide, buoyed up, away and beyond.

The water abruptly receded leaving in its wake a feeling of loss. Strong gusts of wind blew wildly around him, carrying with them an acrid smell of burning that stung his nose and throat. Wracked with inexplicable grief that shook him to the core, Jake opened his eyes. Tears were streaming down his cheeks. The pile of boxes stood still before him, but he was no longer in the room.

Shuddering, he wiped the tears from his eyes and glanced about. A landscape of desolation awaited him. Houses had crumbled in a confusion of charred ruins. Roads, cracked asunder as if by an earthquake, were littered with broken tables and chairs and all manner of household objects. The sun, which hung close to the horizon, cast a ruddy glow over the gloomy scene. Jake pulled himself up, his hand held protectively over his aching heart. His slightest move sent ripples undulating out through the air in ever growing waves. The house he'd just left - the only one still standing - promptly collapsed. Only the pile of boxes lay stubbornly intact. There would be no returning by that route.

He set out cautiously along the road. His every move caused the landscape to shift and slide about him. Stepping over the cracks in the tarmac that continued to grow, he wove his way amongst the discarded objects that littered his path. Some objects scampered out of the way, others cowered, trying to disappear in the cracks, while yet others rose up as if to challenge him. The grandfather clock, for example, towered above him.

"Where you think you're goin'?" Its voice more of a groan than a chime.

"Down the road" Jake replied evasively. In truth, he had no idea. "Nowhere special" he added, trying to be polite.

"Doubt you'll get there. Whole place is in chaos. Too many contradictions"

On which the pendulum shuddered erratically, which Jake took to be a laugh, causing the whole clock to wobble dangerously before rocking back into place.

"Good luck" Jake thought he heard it mumble.

As he made his way painstakingly along the road, he experimented. How could he move without unwittingly shattering all that lay near him? The trick was to consciously calm the energy of his movements. Here much less effort was required. With time, moving effortlessly became natural and he was able to think of other things.

His attention was drawn to the dusty remains of a train halt slouching along beyond a line of trees, keeping pace with him. Through the leaves, he glimpsed a familiar female figure stepping up onto the platform. Forgetting himself, he sprinted after her, his efforts sending the countryside splintering in every direction. Vaulting over cracks and crevasses, he reached the halt as a train drew in, but Nala was nowhere to be seen. As he searched for her, the train began to puff laboriously out of the station, gathering speed noisily.

He ran alongside, struggling to haul himself into one of the carriages. When he thought he could go no further, a helping hand pulled him on board. Bent over double, fighting to get back his breath, he fumed at the train driver for not waiting. Heavy smoke from the loco swirled around him bathing him in its sooty smell. Looking around to thank the person who'd helped him, he found he was alone. All the other passengers were huddled together in a shocked group beyond the carriage on a grassy bank. Joining them, he shared their concern. Large sections of the bank had split off and threatened to collapse across the road and tracks. Jake jumped down and moved away from the imminent landslide.

He felt a deep urge to put some order in this chaos. Leaning against a large standing-stone by the wayside, he drew out his dreambook and began to write. What he wrote however bore no relationship to what he'd intended to write. Instead of writing backwards over what had happened, giving structure and meaning to his story, he wrote forwards, slipping into troubling futures. The young man he wrote about was shorter than him and slimmer too. However, his scraggy beard was the same ginger.

As the youth drew alongside, he turned to Jake and asked: "You're Brent, aren't you?"

There was something unpleasant about his voice. 'Cloying' was maybe the word, thought Jake, too sweet for comfort.

"No. My name is Jake" he replied politely.

"But you could be Brent, couldn't you?"

What a stupid thing to say. The conversation was beginning to annoy him. He had more important things to do, although at that moment he couldn't remember what.

"Jake. Not Brent. They are not at all alike."

"Why does it upset you that I call you Brent. It's the sort of name I'd like to take to bed."

Jake cast a dubious glance at the youth. His hair needed a wash and his clothes were tattered and teeming with tiny insects.

"Don't be silly. You can't take a name to bed."

"Why not! I'd willingly bed you."

This was getting out of hand. It was then that Jake noticed the smell of fish in the air. Was it the young man who smelt so bad?

"No it's your desire awakening." Retorted the young man, as if he could read Brent's thoughts.

"I don't want you" Jake spluttered.

"Oh but you do and you will" he said in his sickly, seductive voice, moving closer to Jake. The fishy smell got stronger. "Imagine my hand cupped over you crutch and your desire growing to fill me."

Jake pulled away.

"Why do you deny what you've always wanted, Brent?"

"For the last time, I'm not Brent and I don't want you."

"Then why do you have a hard-on, Brent? Why don't you just give in?"

Jake spun round, thrusting his hand deep in his jacket pocket. Contact! Pulling out his pen with a flourish, he brought it down abruptly to put a full stop to the sentence. Ink spluttered across the page at his clumsy gesture. He closed the dreambook with a snap and looked up determined. He was alone.

Taking a step off the road, he wondered if his imagination had conjured up such a cloying presence. He took a deep breath. Beware the story that tells itself! Then he remembered what had been troubling him. Something just beyond his grasp. He had to look for Nala. How could he have forgotten? It would seem that intentions were hard to hold on to in the Realm. Or was there more to it? Could someone be meddling with his dreams? He'd have to be more careful. But what must he watch out for in such an undecided place. Short moments of lucidity?

He looked around. The road was nowhere to be seen. He was walking on the pock-marked remains of a lava flow long since cooled. Andreas ran on ahead at break-neck speed. Surely he'd slip on the wet rock. But he seemed to be enjoying himself. Jake set off after him at a trot till he was stopped by a creek. The path went via a yacht moored there, but once on board the other shore was too far off. Without stopping, Andreas shouted back over his shoulder

"Jump!"

At that moment the wind rose billowing the canvases, the stern of the boat swung round and Jake jumped as the bank moved within reach. In the distance he could see Andreas enter an isolated grove of trees. What they used to call a holt. Probably from the German. But the decor was more like Greece. And he disappeared through the open doors of a derelict tavern. Scarred remains of the war.

Gilles was there, dressed in black and white, a smart waiter for the summer holidays. And there was Martin and Peter, both older than he remembered. So many people gathered around small tables ranged along the walls. Talking discreetly. Drinking. Watching each other warily. Some he recognised. Many not.

He sat down next to Tricia who lay back in his arms and tongue kissed him. As if it had only been yesterday. Teresa smiled at him from across the room. She really shouldn't have been there. Tricia was fumbling with his zip, trying to open his flies but he managed to extricate himself and followed Teresa outside. Stepping into the night, she was nowhere to be seen.

"This could go on for ever" he said to himself. "I need a guide or a map."

Maps galore

"I've got plenty of maps, Ducky, a whole shop full of 'em, just over the way."

He spun round to find a plump lady standing close behind him. He instinctively moved away.

"Where exactly would you be wanting to go?" she asked, taking a step closer.

He shuddered. She made his skin crawl. Pretending to be in a hurry, he set off briskly across the road.

"That's the problem. I don't know where I am going," he called out to her over his shoulder.

No point in telling her the whole story. You never knew whom you could trust in this place She waddled after him, waving her arms a bit like stunted wings.

"Oh! I've got some of 'em too. You know, maps wot show yer where to go afore yer even know yerself."

He stopped to look at her, astounded. She didn't look so dangerous as she squinted at him from behind her glasses. Maybe she was just a map seller.

"Don't be afraid, youngster. I won't bite yer. Not yet anyroad."

She cackled, showing her blackened teeth. Inexplicable fear gripped his stomach. He was inches away from turning and running for his life. He took another couple of steps backwards as she inched closer and he tumbled over a doorstep, falling into a shop.

"Don't yer go breakin' nothing, yer ragamuffin. My maps are worth a pretty penny."

She shambled into the shop, shutting the door behind her and locking it, setting a tiny bell ringing.

"Wot yer doin' on the floor? Let me give yer a 'and."

As she leant towards him he could smell stale memories of onions and cabbage. Declining her offer, he scuttled to his feet and moved round a table piled up with maps that stood in the middle of the room. Ignoring the slight, she picked up one of the maps and began unfolding it.

"'ere. Take a peek at this 'un."

From where he was standing he could see the page was blank.

"There's nothing on it," he pointed out.

"I know that yer dimwit. Gotta pick it up in yer own 'ands, ain't yer."

And she flung it at him. More to protect himself than to catch it, he put up his hands and caught it.

"Go on, 'ave a look-see!"

Blurred images were beginning to form on the page. He watched fascinated, riveted to the spot.

Her rugby tackle caught him completely by surprise. He was down before he had time to blink. She clung to his legs as they rolled over and over under the table, maps spilling on top of them. They ended up against the bookshelves on the other side. She was surprisingly strong. Heaving herself up with the help of the bookshelf, she straddled him, her plump backside firmly planted on his chest. All the air went out of him. Her knees locked his arms so he could only move his legs, but to no avail. He felt he was going to be sick, but only bile came up.

"Let me go, you lump."

She rubbed her meaty fist in his face, saying "Let's 'ave a bit a' respect, yer guttersnipe."

It was then that the back door opened and a young girl stepped in.

"What are you doing to that nice young man, Auntie?"

124   Alan McCluskey

The woman shifted her weight to get a look at her niece, crushing his lungs even more. He thought he would suffocate if she didn't get off him immediately.

"Help!" he wheezed.

"Don't yer pay no attention to 'im, Mia. Get me them 'andcuffs wot are in the draw in my desk."

While Mia noisily searched the desk, the woman rolled Jake over onto his stomach and jerked his hands behind his back. He felt the cold steel of the handcuffs close round his wrists.

""'elp me get 'im in the storeroom, girl. I ain't got all day."

The two women bundled him into the storeroom and closed the door leaving him alone in the dark.

In the dark

He was awoken by a light touch on his lips. The room was pitch black. The finger, for he was sure it was a finger, continued to caress his lips. Getting more adventurous the finger tried to push its way between his lips. He resisted, but the person was insistent. He could hear laboured breathing close by. A faint smell of sweat mixed with a delicate deodorant wafted past his nose. The finger withdrew, to his relief. Then he heard someone spitting copiously … and the finger was back, dripping wet with saliva. The finger slithered back and forth trying to prise a way between his pursed lips.

"Ouie!" he cried out as a nail scratched his lower lip.

That was a serious mistake, he realised. The girl, he was sure it must be Mia, had seized the occasion to slip several fingers into his open mouth. He clenched his teeth around her fingers. He could have bitten harder but he was torn between rising desire and latent disgust. She moaned as his teeth tightened. Her fingers were far from clean, he realised, as he unwillingly tasted their sweet-and-sourness mixed with spittle. He tightened his hold with his teeth. The response was immediate: her free hand grasped his balls and squeezed tight.

"Aaaiiieeee!"

He immediately stopped biting her and, after a while, she

relaxed her hold on his balls although she kept them cupped in her hand. Freed from his teeth, her fingers continued to explore as they slithered around his tongue. Clasping it between thumb and forefinger, she pulled gently on it, shifting it from side to side. As her fingers moved further back into his mouth, he was more and more alarmed at what she might do. When her fingers reached his throat, he gagged violently. She withdrew and was gone. He sat shuddering in the dark, disappointed.

She came back repeatedly. Once she nibbled on his earlobes and licked the folds of his ear for what seemed like hours. Another time, she licked his eyes, poking her wet finger repeatedly into his nose. She never said a word … and neither did he, lest it be to protest if she hurt him. It was as if they had a tacit agreement about remaining silent. Maybe it was to stop her aunt from hearing.

She was careful about what she did, he realised, so he didn't think she wanted to hurt him. One time she undid his shirt and began on his nipples. He was surprised how erotic it was. He hadn't realised. All the same, he felt like her object. Each time she used him in one way or another for her own pleasure only to leave him after a while.

As time went on, her visits were more and more given over to sucking and nibbling his rock hard prick and rubbing it between her fingers. She seemed to know what she was doing because she never let him come, even though he was bursting to do so. On one such occasion, she straddled his rigid member and raising her skirts, sank down on him little by little. She gasped as she drove him deeper inside her and then she began rocking backwards and forwards until she came, sinking her nails into his back as she moaned with pleasure. She rose immediately and left him breathless, sitting in the dark.

Five more times she came back and took her pleasure at his expense. He was painfully sore and exhausted. What's more, at no time did she bring him food or water. The sixth time she straddled him, he broke the silence.

"If you don't give me food and water, I'll die. And your little games will be over," he whispered.

She continued her business, paying no attention to his pleas. Maybe she was deaf and dumb. He groaned at the thought. He was wrong. The next time she came, she brought a pitcher of water, some bread and cheese and a strong smelling unguent. She took mouthfuls of water, and squirted it into his mouth as she kissed him. Then she fed his with pieces of bread and cheese that she had first chewed. She even licked his lips clean. Finally she gently rubbed the unguent all over his limp cock. It stung dreadfully, but her insistent touch began to arouse him again.

To his surprise, she hissed "Naughty boy!" as she gently patted his prick and left.

The Monk

Mia's aunt left the shop often during the day as she went about her business in the village. She was never gone more than thirty minutes at a time. Mia had no idea what the woman did while she was away, but she did know she had to keep an eye on her aunt's shop till she came back. If her aunt caught her playing with the man out back she'd get severely beaten. Her aunt was expecting an important man, she'd told Mia, and she couldn't afford to miss him.

As she stepped out of the darkened storeroom, the tube of unguent in one hand, the empty pitcher in the other, the shop doorbell rang. Hastily hiding her guilt in a curtained alcove, she turned to face the man. She saw first his long curved nose, prominent in his weather beaten face. His hair was concealed by a hood. He was dressed in a monk's habit.

She knew what that was. She'd met monks before. Her father had been one. They weren't always very kind. She wanted him to go away so she could continue playing with the pretty young man tied up out back. Then she caught sight of his piercing blue eyes. They droved her back against the wall making her knock a pile of maps onto the floor.

"Well girl, what have you got to say to me?" His voice was razor sharp. He terrified her.

"My aunt will be back shortly," she stuttered, trying hard not to show her fear.

He pushed a pile of maps from an armchair sending them cascading onto the floor and sat down putting his feet up on the table.

"Fetch me a glass of your best wine, girl, and some fresh bread and cheese."

She hurried into the small kitchen and came back with a tray of food and drink. Seeing her coming, he tipped the maps off the table to make room for the tray. She balanced her way over the map littered floor with difficulty before putting down her precarious load in front of him. He grabbed her wrist as she was about to escape to the far side of the room. Pulling her closer, he peered deep into her eyes for what seemed like an eternity. His giant nose was inches from her face. She could see the bush of black hairs growing out of his nostrils.

He terrified her. She was sure he'd rip her apart with his teeth if she couldn't get away immediately. It was the doorbell ringing that broke the spell. He shoved her brutally away. She collided with a bookcase that crashed onto table. Maps flew everywhere, mingled now with wine, cheese and bread. The monk paid her no further attention. He turned to her aunt who stood silently looking at the chaos in her shop.

"Always so charming, Markus, I see. Let's go, you're late."

To Mia's surprise the big man followed her aunt docilely out. Pausing on the doorstep her aunt bared her teeth and growled, "Clean up this mess, or I'll roast you for breakfast when I get back the day after tomorrow."

The door slammed and Mia was alone. Her legs gave way and she sank limply to the floor, curled up on a heap of maps.

Chaos

Jake had heard what had happened next door from the dark of the storeroom where he lay half naked, his hands handcuffed behind his back to a metal bar. He heard the dull thumps and the crashing of wood. He heard the angry voice of a man and what he supposed was the terrified voice of Mia. He heard the aunt's threats and he learnt that she would be away for several days. Hope at last, he thought.

"Mia!" he called out, "Mia?"

Maybe she was unconscious. He called and called, but she didn't come. He sank back down onto the floor, a wave of helplessness rolling over him. Could she be dead? He was just drifting off to uncomfortable sleep when he felt her hands on his hair, tugging gently. She whimpered and snivelled as she pressed her shaking body against him.

"Mia," he said, "we need to get away from here before your aunt returns. You and me. Together."

He badly needed her to reply. She had to talk to him if he were to convince her to free him. He couldn't convince a mute, especially in the dark. He felt her stagger up and move away. Desperate, he called out to her

"Don't go, Mia. I need you."

To no avail. He heard the door close behind her. He burst into tears.

Several minutes later she returned. She carried a lantern and a bunch of key.

"Don't cry," she whispered as she pushed her way behind his back to undo the handcuffs.

Freed at last he sank forward, laying his head on the ground in front of him. He ached all over. He wasn't even sure he would be able to walk.

"Help me stand, Mia."

She did, her arm around his waist. He felt her hand slip to his prick.

"Not now, Mia. Later. First we have to get out of here."

She didn't seem to want to let go of her prize. She finally relinquished her hold when he shuffled to the storeroom door.

Despite all he'd heard from his storeroom prison, he wasn't prepared for the chaos awaiting him in the shop. Maps lay scattered all over the floor. The table was upturned and a bookcase had fallen across the table. He sat in the armchair and looked up at Mia. She looked so young and fragile. He could hardly connect this person to the woman who had played so shamelessly with him in the dark.

She stepped forward and sat on his lap, put her arms around his neck and began to cry. He stroked her hair, muttering sweet words to calm her.

"We need to think how we can get away, Mia," he said after a while. "I need clothes. We need food and drink and if possible some means of transport."

She stood up and went into the kitchen, coming back with a monk's habit.

"This was my father's," she said handing it to him. She insisted on undressing him and putting more unguent on his prick before he pulled the rough monastic habit over his head. He went with her to the kitchen and helped her load food and drink into two satchels. She spoke very little.

"Does your aunt have ponies, or a cart, Mia?"

Mia was cuddling on his lap again as he sat in the armchair. They had enjoyed a filling meal together in case they didn't get time to eat once they left.

"There's a horse and cart, if she hasn't taken it with her," Mia replied, nibbling his ear lobe.

They went out back to see if the cart and horse were still there. It was night so nobody could see them. Jake wasn't so sure about riding out in the dark, but Mia said she knew the first part of the road well. So they fixed the horse to the cart, loaded their food and, with blankets wrapped around their shoulders, they set off down the road with Mia showing the way.

On the road

As the sun rose over the horizon, bright yellow, welcoming the new day, they pulled the cart off the track and came to a halt on a small rise that afforded a panoramic view over the brilliant patchwork that surrounded them. The fields were neatly laid out in squares and oblongs, each with its hedge or ditch or dry stone wall. Here were deep greens of clover; there the bright yellow of rape plants used for the pungent oil of their seeds. The occasional field of lavender, its bluish-purple standing out against the sea of green and yellow. They stood under the only tree in the whole scene, a twisted oak, dwarf-like, gnarled, no doubt a victim of the winds.

They had met no one on the way, but Jake preferred to be cautious. He'd parked the cart within a cluster of boulders so it could be seen neither from the track nor from the countryside around. Mia had slept most of the night cuddled up against him as he drove the cart along the winding ways. In many ways she was like a child, although when it came to sex there was nothing childlike about her. Now she prepared them breakfast. She had brought a small stove on which she heated water for the coffee. She broke off a hunk of bread and handed it to him with a pot of jam and a knife.

Between bites into her bread, she rummaged in her satchel.

"I've brought one of my aunt's precious maps."

She handed him a cup of coffee and returned to searching through her bag.

"It should show us the country here abouts... Ah! Here it is."

She pulled out a small folded piece of paper and gave it to Jake. It would be good to know where he was going, for once, he laughed.

"What's so funny," she asked, looking a little worried.

"Since I've been in the Realm, I have had no idea where I was going. I don't even know my destination. I have a mission, but I'm damned if I can remember what it is"

She looked at him, perplexed. "Why ever should you want to know where you are going?"

He laughed again. Her way of looking at things was so different from his. Seeing her face cloud over, he added: "I'm not laughing at you. I'm laughing at myself. I've always wanted to know where I was going."

She smiled, now, and held his hand.

"Silly boy. What funny ideas have got into your head! Let

me flush them out." And she began nibbling at his ear lob, giggling.

Not letting himself be distracted, he unfolded the map and proceeded to examine it, much to her annoyance.

"That can wait," she protested, trying half-heartedly to push the map away. "Let's do it right now, to celebrate the rising sun."

He kissed her fingers then turned back to the map.

"Look, here are the boulders behind us. This map is extraordinary. There is even our cart standing there." He continued to study the map closely. "What's this eye, up here in the corner, Mia."

She lent forward to look … and screamed. Snatching the map from him, she held it over the stove. It burst into flames that crackled and sparked, producing black smoke that rose in a column in the sky.

"Why did you do that?" he asked, deeply disappointed to see their chance of finding their way go up in smoke.

"It's her. My aunt. She was watching us through the map."

He rose and began packing things into the cart. "We need to leave immediately. That smoke could be seen for miles around. And if that was her in the map, she'll know where we are."

A short way down the track, a new track led off across the fields. He turned the cart in that direction and encouraged the horse to go quicker. They rode in silence for a long while.

Something troubled him. What if she was unwittingly carrying something else that linked her to her aunt? He tried to push the idea away as absurd, but he couldn't get it out of his mind. He pulled the cart to a halt in a dip in the ground and ordered her off the cart. She looked frightened.

"I've got to check you've not carrying something else from your aunt that she can use to track us."

He emptied out their bags on the grass and searched through the contents as she stood watching him, pouting. Nothing. There was nothing concealed in the blankets either. He checked the cart and the horse. But there was nothing there. He turned to her.

"I have to search you too. It is for our own good."

He took her shoes and examined them closely. He pulled her dress off over her head and searched the linings. Nothing. She was standing there, naked in front of him, her head hanging down, her knees together, her feet apart. Round her neck she wore a small chain with a blue stone hanging from it. Looking closely, he saw there was a small eye engraved on it. Bursting open the clasp, he pulled the necklace from her neck. She shouted out with pain.

"You bastard!" she swore.

He laid the blue stone on a rock and hammered it with another rock over and over again till it shattered into pieces, letting off a foul smell of rotten eggs. Coughing, he moved away.

Mia, still naked, was stepping backwards towards the horse and cart.

"No you don't!" Jake hissed grasping her by the wrist. "You knew, didn't you? You knew she could track us through that stone."

He was shaking with anger. He had trusted the girl, thinking she was being mistreated like him. What a fool he was. She'd being playing with him all along.

"Put your dress back on!" he barked as he took a rope from the back of the cart. He tied her hands together and then tied her to the cart.

"I swear I didn't know," she snivelled.

He hardened himself to her words. Suddenly, a nasty thought crossed his mind. He pulled the monk's habit over his head and stood naked by the roadside searching through it for possible charms or evil eyes. To his relief there was nothing. He climbed back up onto the cart and drove the horse along the track at full speed.

After two days of riding westward, they still had met nobody. No houses. No farms. No villages. No animals even. Nothing. Just endless rolling hills and the colourful patchwork of fields. The breeze was fresh, as if it rolled in from the sea, but they never reached the sea.

They rode in silence most of the time. When they stopped,

he gave her food and drink, but otherwise ignored her. They had enough to eat and drink for another couple of days but they'd have to replenish their stocks.

Jake thought back over what had happened. The more he puzzled things over, the more he came to the conclusion that Mia probably didn't know about the watching eyes. Hadn't she destroyed the first one herself? He remembered her scream. He found it difficult to think she could have faked it. He was still angry though, more at himself than her. He disliked feeling gullible. He hated feeling a fool. And he felt twice a fool at the moment.

The knife

When the cart stopped, the lack of movement awoke Mia. She opened her eyes. It was early evening; the sun was low on the horizon. The rope around her wrists had cut into her skin leaving a painful weal. She saw him get off the cart and come to her. It was then she saw the knife in his hand. She cringed, whimpering with fear. He was surely going to slit her throat. Then he wouldn't need to feed her. She knew supplies must be getting low. As he took hold of her wrist, she bent forward and bit him.

"Aaaiieeee! Idiot. I'm not going to hurt you. I was just going to cut the ropes."

Nursing his bleeding hand, he stood several steps away, breathing hard. She licked her lips, tasting his blood.

"OK. You have good reasons to be angry. I was probably wrong about you. I'm sorry. I apologise."

She could see it cost him a lot to say so. He seemed somehow deflated

"Now let me cut your ropes."

She still wasn't sure she could trust him. Could it be a ruse to get closer and knife her? Then again she'd like to have her pretty boy back so she could play with him. She missed the taste of his body; the feel of him deep inside her. She held out her hands, gritting her teeth. The knife slid cold along her wrists,

134   Alan McCluskey

blade outwards, slicing through the rope. Once her hands were freed, he handed her the unguent to rub into the wounds.

"Aren't you going to heal it for me?" she asked looking hopefully at him even if she knew he wouldn't.

"I have to prepare a meal. You do it this time." And he stomped away.

Once they'd finished eating, he stood up and started pacing up and down the deserted track.

"I don't understand," he said, thinking out loud.

Mia couldn't fathom him. He was always thinking about complicated things. It seemed such a waste of time. It certainly didn't get them anywhere.

"We've been travelling for days and we seem to be stuck in the same place all the time."

You see, even he agreed with her, she thought. But he didn't understand all the same.

"Quit worrying about getting somewhere. Why bother? You don't even know where you're going."

He gave her the kind of look designed to wither even the strongest of mortals, but she was impervious. He lacked trust. That was his problem. Now he'd got her thinking. Damn it, if it wasn't catching!

"Let's fuck," she suggested, "it's the only thing that's worth doing in this place."

He laughed again. She never could decide if she should enjoy his laughter or fear it. Whatever. He'd obviously made up his mind at last as he grabbed her round the waist, pressed his lips against hers and forced his tongue into her willing mouth.

"Mmm. Good," she said as she plucked blades of dried grass from her hair. Pearls of sweat ran over her belly in discreet rivulets plunging between her legs to join other sources. She watched him as he lay back on the grass, his hands behind his head. He looked relaxed. Maybe he'd stopped worrying about the road.

"That's better isn't it?"

He nodded in reply. With the sun just below the horizon, the evening breeze began to blow. She saw him shiver.

"Come back in my arms," she told him. "I'll keep you warm."

Instead he rose and pulled on his monk's habit. She wasn't surprised. She was beginning to know how he reacted. He didn't seem to want sex as much as her. She had some difficulty understanding how he could resist. Odd as it seemed, he was so different from her.

"Let me tell you a story," he said as he began pacing again.

"Only if you stop walking up and down like a caged animal and lie down in my arms."

He did stop. Maybe he was seeing sense. But, no, he took up his round again.

"I need to move. Do you know, where I come from, they call me the Wanderer."

"That was a short story," she said teasing him as she slipped her dress over her head. It was getting colder. She rose to fetch a blanket and wrapping it around her shoulders, she joined him as he walked up and down the track. Arm in arm, she leaned gently against him.

"So where's this story then?"

Off for a ride

He liked her when she was like that. Under her obsession with sex, she had a delightful sense of humour. He warmed to her.

"In the world where I come from they begin stories by the words 'once upon a time'. That doesn't seem quite right here in the Realm."

"You use too many words," she said.

He laughed once again. Hadn't he heard that so often from Professors at university?

"OK. Off we go."

The chalet was perched on a ridge surrounded by snow-covered mountains. It must have been summer time because there was no snow on the ground around the chalet itself. Edelweiss grew in clumps of white stars scattered across the prairie. Deep blue gentians were pushing their way upwards here and there. Jake and Mia sat next to each other on a wooden bench outside the chalet watching the setting sun reflect on the mountaintops.

Behind them they could hear the laughter from the crowd within the chalet. Jake found it difficult to understand why people would want to be shut inside when they could be out in such beautiful scenery. All of a sudden, an inexplicable wave of anxiety rode rough shod through his body. He stood hastily, pulling Mia to her feet.

Moving away from the chalet, he looked back from a distance. Beyond the chalet he saw a massive shape cresting the ridge. A jumbo jet laboured noiselessly higher into the sky. He was utterly convinced it would not make it. To his horror, he realised it was going to crash right on top of the chalet. Frozen on the spot, he watched the plane inch its way forward towards the unsuspecting chalet. Mia screamed, bringing him back to his senses.

"Run to the bridge suspended over the ravine and wait there to help people across."

Not waiting to see if she had obeyed, he ran in the direction of the chalet. Bursting inside, he hustled people out. They didn't want to go. They didn't believe him. But once outside they saw the Jumbo suspended over the chalet only tens of feet away. Stricken with panic they scattered in every direction.

He herded them towards the bridge as best he could. As the last person to cross the shaky bridge, he hurried over himself to Mia waiting for him on the other side, her arms wide open.

"We must go further. This might not be enough," he said.

He hustled the people on down the goats' track, away from the ravine. As they reached a bend in the track, he turned back to see the fat belly of aeroplane glide majestically over the top of the chalet, flattening it to nothing. The plane continued on its path towards them, moving slower and slower till it came to a silent halt at the edge of the ravine, snapping the cables holding the bridge. Set free, the planks of the bridge plunged nosily into the river deep below.

All around him, the revellers he'd saved from the chalet pushed and shoved each other to get a better look at the giant nose of the airplane as it towered above them. One of the most rowdy of the revellers, cheered loudly and others began to cheer with him.

Jake turned on them, raising his fist threateningly and hissed: "Silence. You'll set off an avalanche."

They stopped immediately. But the damaged was done. A deep rumbling announced the avalanche as the rocks began to gather speed and the body of the plane shifted closer.

"Run!" he called out.

Pointless really. The avalanche would inevitably drive its way through the pass. He stood for a moment watching the wings of the plane snap off as the weight of rocks forced the plane in front of them.

He was shaken from his shock when Mia yanked his arm, pulling him to one side.

"Here," she shouted out, trying to be heard over the din. "There's a cave. Get in."

He scrambled in after her and, taking her hand, moved back into the growing gloom. Boulders roared passed the entrance, some finding their way inside, heralding a cloud of dust and a strong smell of kerosene. Both of them instinctively covered their mouth and nose with their clothes, but the dust got in everywhere making them cough violently. Abruptly the noise stopped. The dust took longer to settle. The stink of kerosene lingered longest.

Sitting in the dark, Mia spoke up: "Wow. You tell a gripping story!"

He laughed but his laughter turned to coughing as some of the dust lingering in the air tickled his nose.

When he quietened, Mia continued: "Now you'll have to tell us another story to get us out of here."

"I'm not sure I can do that to order. Let me think for a while."

He sat down on a flat rock while Mia felt her way around in

search of a way out. He'd always seen himself as a storyteller. He had a passion for stories. But what stories could do in the Realm frightened him beyond measure. He felt weighed down by the responsibility. If he got it wrong they could be literally projected into a nightmare.

Once upon a time

"Well?" Mia asked "How does it go: 'Once upon a time…'?"

"Don't poke fun at me, Mia."

"I'm not making fun. I'm deadly serious. There's no way out of here and we've got neither food nor drink."

He sighed. He wasn't even sure how he'd got them there. That first time he had no expectations, no ambitions. It was totally unpremeditated. Now they wanted it, they needed it. Everything depended on it. How could he forget what he had experienced? The innocence was lost forever. What a strange form of knowledge where knowing what you could do implied you could not longer do it.

Mia stood beside him, her fingers playing gently with his hair.

"Let me help you," she suggested in her most sensual voice.

She could feel he was resisting. His muscles were tense. He had convinced himself it was not possible. Well stories could do that too. He shifted impatiently as if he wanted to shrug her off.

"Let me help … and when you feel yourself slipping away, tell the story that flows into your head."

She began humming a wordless lullaby, casting musical circles about him in the dark. She let one of her hands slide slowly down his back, making gentle circular movements as she descended. Her feet firmly planted on the earth, she shifted from humming to quietly singing long vowel sounds that rose and fell. The sound vibrated off the cave walls, echoing back like an earthy chorus accompanying her.

She placed her free hand on his chest, letting it lay there, communicating its warmth to him. She could feel the beating of his heart: slow and insistent; strong and beautiful. She aligned her hands, her voice, her whole being with that beat and lifted him gently, very gently upwards...

"... It was raining. It had been raining for hours. The rain fell on the trees, on the rocks, on the rounded cobblestones. And it fell on us, our footsteps splashing as we trod wearily along the way..."

Jake looked around. There was not much to see for rain mingled with thick mist shrouded all from view. Sea mist. He could hear the waves breaking on the rocks, The sea was nearby. In the distance, but fast coming close, he could hear the rattling of a carriage on the road and the sound of hooves.

Instinctively, he pulled Mia to one side, sliding between the rocks as the vehicle lurched by. A figure dressed in black, coat tails flying in the wind, stood balanced at the font of the carriage, whipping the horses to spur them on. In a blink, he was past and gone. Following in the same direction the carriage had taken, they spied a brown satchel open in the middle of the track, its contents splayed across the way. Mia ran forward.

"Careful," he said. "It may be a trap."

"No, no. It is your way of providing us with food."

He laughed at the thought and helped her gather up the goods and push them back into the satchel.

"Now all we need is some shelter," she added. "Can you manage that too?"

Jake groaned theatrically at the faith she showed in his abilities, and took a few steps further down the road. The rain seemed to ease off slightly and the mist began to lift. By the road side some fifty feet beyond where they stood lay a small croft, apparently abandoned but still in good shape.

As he wondered if he'd created the welcome shelter or if it had just happened that way, Mia ran forward, pushed open the one and only door and moved in out of the rain.

"Let's eat," she suggested when he joined here. "Then we can fuck as much as we like ..."

"And after that?" he asked, with a broad grin.

"We go visit my mother who lives in a large mansion not far

from here."

Taking a seat at the rough table in the middle of the single room, Jake pondered how he'd unwittingly brought them to a place where her mother lived. She must also be influencing his stories.

Seeing him hesitate over the dried meat, bread and apples she had laid out before him, she asked: "Would you prefer we do it before we eat?"

He burst out laughing and pulled her to him, tasting her delicious lips once more.

Chapter 7 - The Lessons

Under the oak tree

The narrow path away from the kitchen door wound its way through the well-stocked vegetable garden, round a spacious lawn dotted with wicker chairs and a matching table and across a wide meadow full of wild flowers and tall grasses that swayed gracefully in the early morning breeze. A wooden gate in the fence marked the end of the meadow and the beginning of the arable land that covered the gentle flank of the hill. The farmer had planted oats in neat narrow rows. Brent closed the gate quietly behind him and looked up at the oak that rose in the distance on the crest of the hill. He took the path that ran along the edge of a field up in the direction of the venerable tree.

He would return in an hour when Sally and Keira were tucked up in bed, probably together, and he'd be able to slip into one of the unused rooms. Keira excited him. There was an animal side to her that set off deep instincts that he preferred not to awaken. Sally was different. Something about her fascinated him. She didn't set him on fire like Keira, but he resonated with her in a way that he didn't understand. She troubled him at the same time she reassured him. It was as if they already had a long story together. It would be so easy to step into it and get completely lost.

Reaching the top of the rise, Brent took the time to walk slowly round the oak on a carpet of last year's acorns studying it from all sides. The trunk was massive. Quite a few people would have to join hand in hand to encircle it. On one side the boughs curved down almost to the ground making a shaded place close to the trunk that was almost hidden from view. Brent slipped under the branches, laid his jacket at the foot of the tree, sat down and leaned his back against the timeless trunk. Closing his eyes he fell asleep almost immediately.

Keira tip-toed down to the deserted kitchen, slipped on her walking shoes at the back door and stepped out into the garden. Grasping one of the larger tops from a row of carrots in the vegetable patch, she pulled it out and went to wash the carrot at a nearby tap. Munching on the carrot she strode across the lawn, weaving her way amongst the chairs, whistling a song to herself between mouthfuls. As she reached the meadow she broke into a jog.

Avoiding the path, she zigzagged through the tall grass, enjoying its touch on her bare legs. She'd changed into flowery shorts and a black t-shirt on which the name of her folk band had been printed. Not bothering to open the gate, she climbed over the dry-stone wall setting a few of the looser stones rolling. If the oats had been ripe, she'd have rubbed their heads between her fingers till the soft grains came free and eaten them. Instead she broke off the head of a plant and held it between her teeth.

She slowed her pace as the path steepened up the hill. From where she stood she could see crows circling the crown of the old oak, settling suddenly then rising again noisily into the air. She thought of Brent. She'd waited for him to come up to bed, but he'd stayed away. She couldn't understand his behaviour. She'd already felt his discomfort at breakfast. She sighed. He made her deeply hungry. She wanted to feast on his body, nibbling his fingers, sucking his toes, licking his nose, biting his thighs, ... Being with him was nothing like lying in Sally's arms. Sally was different. Sally was soft and satisfying. Sally made her feel content and complete.

The tree was much bigger than she had thought. From close up, it was rather intimidating as it towered above her. On her side of the oak, the branches formed a low archway that opened an avenue to the aged trunk. They seemed to invite her and she willingly accepted. Moving forward, she put her arms around the trunk, well, a small part of it, and pressed her lips against the bark, tasting its earthy bitterness. She let herself slip downwards to the ground and curled up amongst its roots where she fell asleep.

Finding neither Keira nor Brent anywhere on the second floor, Sally was troubled. She made her way down to the ground floor and looked out of the kitchen window. The garden seemed deserted. Pushing open the door, she followed a cat out. The animal headed knowingly for the garden, where it nosed amongst the flowers that bordered the vegetable patch. Attracted by the smell of irises, Sally moved closer to admire them. One flower had broken off. She picked it up and carried it to the wicker table that stood on the lawn where she found a small vase. Filling it with water at the garden tap she set the fragrant iris in the middle of the table. Sitting for a moment in one of the chairs, she studied the skyline. Across a patch of fallow land dotted with wild flowers she saw a rounded hill rather like an ancient barrow standing out against the cloudless sky. Planted in the very middle of the barrow stood an age-old oak, serene and majestic. It made a very symbolic tableau she thought.

The cat was making its way across the meadow, so she decided to follow it, humming quietly to herself. The animal stopped in front of the gate waiting for her to open it, which she did. When the cat set off up the hill, Sally was hesitant. She didn't feel comfortable walking on a barrow, if that was what it was. But something was drawing her on, so she followed her feline companion.

She realised that she had been so engrossed in the scenery that she had forgotten she was looking for Keira and Brent. To hell with them! She liked them both. She loved Keira and she felt a strange communion with Brent, but at that moment, standing in front of the magnificent oak whose roots reached deep into the place of their ancestors, she really couldn't be bothered with personal quarrels and petty jealousies.

Getting down on her hands and knees she crawled under the low branches of the oak and made her way to the trunk. She ran her hands over its pockmarked bark, sensing the history of the place. Then, turning her back to the tree she sat down cross-legged and prepared to meditate but the mists of the past swirled up around her carrying her off into sleep.

Brent, Keira and Sally, unaware of each other, awoke to the sound of song. People were walking ceremoniously round the oak, clapping their hands from time to time. Deep male voices chanted a wordless drone while a brilliant soprano sang in a language unknown to any of them. It was breathtaking. None of them dared move, not wishing to disturb the music, not wishing to reveal themselves either. Finally the footsteps stopped and the voices fell silent. If you listened carefully, you could almost hear the oak breathing out a sigh of pleasure.

"Come out you three. The lesson is over."

It was Rafter's voice that broke the spell. Emerging sheepishly from beneath the cover of the oak branches they discovered not just Rafter but Alo and Naniu as well, not to mention their embarrassed selves.

"Let's go have lunch," Rafter suggested smiling mischievously, without a word of explanation.

An appointment

"Is that Jenny Tay?"

"Yes. Who's calling?"

"My name is Fran. I used to work for a man called Leuchtli."

She heard a sharply in-drawn breath. The woman was going to hang up. She was sure of it.

"Please don't hang up. I need to talk to you. It is extremely important. I'm in a lot of trouble. And so maybe are you."

The hesitation at the other end was palpable.

"How can I trust you?" came the answer.

"I don't want to say much over the phone. Yesterday evening Leuchtli tried to drug me. But I managed to escape."

Tears brimmed over and began rolling down her cheeks. Fran was forced to pull over by the roadside and stop talking as the memories of the previous evening overtook her.

"I'm sorry," she said between her sobs. "It's all too much for me. You're the first person I've talked to about it."

"Where are you now, Fran?" Jenny asked.

"I'm driving North-East … towards Germany and my home town. I can't stay anywhere near the Jura. He'll find me. He'll drive me mad like he did poor Donna."

Fran heard Jenny gasp.

"Are you alright?" she asked.

"We went to see Donna only yesterday. She's in a really bad state, although she's in good hands."

Fran wondered at the coincidence. A worrying thought flitted through her mind: could she trust Jenny? Maybe she was in league with Leuchtli.

The woman must have sensed her concerns because she added: "Leuchtli's henchmen tried to kill my Tom. They've ransacked our apartment and carried away a lot of papers. We're running like you, Fran."

Fran refused to let herself be overwhelmed by the feeling of helplessness that surged unbidden.

"Where can we go?" she asked out loud.

"I think you should avoid Germany. Leuchtli might know that's where you come from." Jenny replied. "We are heading to a friend's place where we reckon we'll be safe. Why don't we meet somewhere and then you can come with us."

"Where do you suggest?"

Jenny didn't reply however. She seemed to be following her own train of thoughts. "You need to change cars. Leuchtli might be keeping tabs on your car."

"You're right. I hadn't thought of that."

"Once we get together, you can come in ours. Where are you now?"

"Not far from Basel."

"OK," said Jenny taking control of the situation. "Drive

146   Alan McCluskey

across into France and meet us in Montbéliard. We can be there in two hours. There's a café across from the station. It's part of a hotel. We'll meet there."

Jenny went on to ask Fran to describe how she was dressed so she could recognise her when they met and then hung up.

Jenny put down the phone and turned to Tom and Martin. They were sitting in narrow armchairs around a low table in a hotel room. On the table lay a map of Europe. Fully unfolded, it overflowed onto the floor at their feet.

"Why did you say we'd be in Montbéliard in two hours when we are already there?" Martin asked.

"A precaution," she replied, examining the roadmap. "If she's bringing Leuchtli or his henchmen we'll be able to see them coming."

Tom stood and limped backwards and forwards in the small space left between the double bed and the table where the others were sitting.

"I wonder how she knew about you, Jenny."

"That's one of the things that worries me." Jenny replied, gesturing to Tom to sit back down and spare his leg.

"I trust her," was Martin's only comment.

"Well, we'll know in a short while. She should be here in about an hour, so we should plan what we are going to do, and get into place for her arrival." Jenny concluded.

Out of the muddle

When do two and two make five? It all depends on the way you look at things. Evidence points to the contrary, though. And history may not be right …

The voices chattered on and on through the muddle in his head. He wanted to shift his legs that hung somewhere nearby, uncomfortable, but he didn't know in which direction to send the message. Instead, he opened his eyes. And shut them again immediately. What was he doing lying on the floor? With an effort he managed to coordinate his movements, lifting a hand to scratch his head. Something strange was tickling his eye. He made a clumsy grasp at it. Hair! A lock of hair! His hair.

In one crisp movement he was sitting bolt upright, his eyes wide open, his brain crystal sharp with fear. Who had cut off a lock of his hair? Fran, of course. Memory flooded back. Rolling over onto his hands and knees he pulled himself into the armchair, and slumped against the armrest.

Glancing at his watch he saw it was passed nine. He'd been out all night. Looking round he saw nobody, just a window slightly ajar. His brain was fitting bits and pieces together at a frantic rate forming an alarming picture that drove him to his feet. His keys were in the lock of the study door. His jacket had slid from the armchair onto the floor. As he bent to pick it up, he spotted the blood red stain on the carpet and a broken glass. Other thoughts rushed up, screaming to a halt right in front of him. Oh no!

He hurriedly slid his hand into his jacket pocket and found nothing. The notebook had gone. He checked the other pocket, just in case. Nothing there either. Flinging the jacket onto the floor, he paced to the window and looked out. Nobody of course! Picking up the phone from the table he dialled an in-house number: "Sykes. Meet me in my office in ten minutes." And he hung up.

Striding to the bar he poured himself a whiskey and was about to drink it when he halted abruptly. Fool! He tossed the liquid down the sink in the bathroom. Glancing at the mirror, he looked ghastly. He ran the cold water, scooped up a handful and splashed it on his face, scooped up a second handful and swilled out his mouth. Yesterday evening had left a bitter taste.

"Sykes. Fran has stolen a confidential document from my study: a small black notebook. I want you to get it back. It's absolutely urgent. Then dispose of her once you've got what you want." Leuchtli spoke from the little shelter his desk offered.

Across from him Sykes stood massive but hesitant. "And how am I supposed to find her?" he asked cowering as if he expected to get hit.

"Phone her. Tell her we are going to use the Machine on her.

We've got a sample of her hair. Get my assistant to help you set it up."

Once Sykes had left, Leuchtli pulled open the draw in which he kept his personal whiskey flask, poured himself a glass, but couldn't bring himself to drink it. Blast her! She'd poisoned his existence. He picked up his phone and strode around the office while he waited for the person to answer.

"Tyrell? What news of Rafter and his gang?"

He stopped in front of the glass cabinet in which earlier versions of the Machine were on display. These petty people weren't going to get in the way of his grand scheme.

"What do you mean you haven't found them yet? Find them quickly or I'll work with someone else."

And he slammed down the receiver, knocking the untouched glass onto the floor where it shattered.

On the trail

The hotel reception was empty. Tyrell rang the bell energetically. Not that he felt very energetic. Yesterday evening's meal still lay heavy in his stomach. As did his short conversation with Leuchtli.

"Yes sir. Can I help you?" the young receptionist asked.

He turned on what he hoped was his most winning smile. "I'm looking for a friend of mine: Professor Outman."

She looked troubled. "They left in a hurry yesterday evening."

He cursed mentally. His clumsiness in the shaman's garden had made them cautious. "Have you got any idea where he's gone?"

"They didn't say. But a man came to pick up their cases this morning and I heard him say they were at the Star."

Tyrell turned and hurried for the door. "Thanks," he called back over his shoulder. An afterthought.

The Star was quite a step down after the other hotel. There was a pub on the ground floor, which was where he found the receptionist cum barmaid tidying up after the previous evening's festivities.

"We're not open yet," she told him, mistaking him for a customer.

Concealing his growing irritation, Tyrell enquired politely about the Professor.

"He and his daughter left early this morning taking all their things with them. I have no idea where they went," was all she'd say.

What more could he do? He was a scientist, not a detective.

Deep in thought, Tyrell didn't notice the long ladder propped up against the wall by the hotel entrance. If he'd noticed it, he would have poked fun at the idiot for putting it right in the middle of the path. He didn't even feel the ladder as he bumped into it sending it toppling.

As it was, he only became aware that something was wrong when he was drenched with cold soapy water as the window cleaner's bucket emptied over his head and he heard the screams of the owner of the bucket hitting the pavement at bone-breaking speed in front of him. Tyrell stood frozen to the spot, looking at the scene, uncomprehending as the receptionist rushed back into the hotel to call an ambulance.

Accompanying the unfortunate man to the hospital – the ambulance driver and the hotel receptionist had both insisted – Tyrell shivered despite the blanket they'd laid around his shoulders. The man's groaning had stopped thanks to the painkillers, but he continued moaning about his wife and four children and the cost of new ladders.

Tyrell tried mentally plugging his ears, but to no avail. Finding that attack was the best form of defence, Tyrell began telling the man at great length and in much detail about the goldfish he'd eaten as a child. The tactic seemed to work because the whining ceased and the man and the nurse turned to look at him aghast.

The doctor who examined Tyrell at the hospital pronounced him in a state of shock and prescribed a sedative that was administered by a delightful nurse who happened to be passing by. Tyrell managed to slip the pill into his pocket rather than swallow it. The nurse hurried off to her other duties, leaving him to sit down on one of the hard benches in the corridor. He closed his eyes and pretended to sleep. Maybe people would leave him in peace so he could slip away.

"Yes... several weekend courses ... the shaman."

Now there was a conversation to spark his interest...

"... very ... for the work."

The two nurses were too far away for him to hear all, but the fragments were enough.

"... his country house..."

When she said the name of the place, he could have jumped up and hugged her. Instead, he shuffled in the direction of the toilets only to continue down the corridor towards the side entrance and escape. There could only be one well-known shaman in Avan!

Dream travelling

A faint sound of breathing was all that could be heard.

"Make your way back," Alo called out softly, breaking the silence as he stroked the chimes with his hand.

In the distance a church bell struck two. A steamboat chugged laboriously up the river, wearily sounding its horn in the early afternoon heat. Unconcerned by the sounds around them, Sally, Keira and Brent sat cross-legged, eyes closed on the thick carpet of the first floor study. With a fluttering of eyelashes, they opened their eyes and looked intently at Alo who sat opposite them.

"Good. Now I want you to go to a place I'm going to indicate and let's see if you can meet there."

He picked up a large picture from the pile of books and documents that lay next to him on the floor and showed it to them.

"Study this door carefully. Then memorise it."

Alo glanced out of the window and across the field to the oak on the hill where they'd been earlier that morning. He smiled to himself as he remembered the surprise of the young ones finding themselves asleep under the tree together. Rafter's idea of bonding them through the oak was brilliant. All three had been very receptive, despite their differing levels of training.

"OK. Now return to the dream realm and imagine that door in front of you."

He gave them time to return and then he said: "Now open the door and step through."

As Sally turned the handle, the door swung open with ease. She looked out cautiously before stepping into the garden that lay beyond. She sensed no threat. On the contrary, the place was welcoming, intoxicating even. She wandered along the alleys, engrossed in admiring the flowers and shrubs. There were many sorts she'd never seen before. The place was a riot of colours and heady fragrances that made her giddy.

A noise behind her reminded her that she had come there with a purpose: to meet the others. Turning she saw Keira striding through the garden. She looked younger, more girlish, her movements sending shivers of expectation down Sally's back. As Keira approached, she noticed that her friend was surrounded with a bluish light. Sally wondered if she appeared the same to Keira.

"You do indeed," Keira said in her head.

"So you can hear my thoughts. I'll have to be careful what I think."

Keira grinned and kissed Sally generously on her lips.

"I love you too!" Keira said somewhat breathlessly.

Pulling back, self-conscious as she'd never been before with Keira, she asked or rather thought: "Where's Brent?"

"No idea. Maybe he's got lost."

"Or maybe he can't join us for some reason. Maybe we're keeping him out."

Keira laughed, catching the drift of Sally's thoughts. Moving away, Sally headed for the door.

"Come on. Let's invite him in."

They broke into a run, weaving their way along the flowered

alleys. It was Keira who got there first.

Pulling open the door, she bowed with a flourish and welcomed Brent in.

"My Lord," she said theatrically.

He seemed a little uncertain and hesitated about crossing the threshold.

"Are you shy?" Sally asked as she arrived. Pushing passed Keira, she leaned forward and took his hand in hers, leading him out into the garden. Not to be outdone, Keira took his other hand and the two young women gave him a guided tour of the gardens, rivalling each other in inventing the most outrageous explanations of where the exotic flowers came from.

For all their laughter, Sally sensed that Brent was uncomfortable holding hands between the two of them, but she tried not to think it too loud for fear the others would hear. She searched for a way to put him at ease.

"Let's sit on that bench," she thought out loud.

Brent was startled that she could speak directly into his head.

"Yes. You have to be careful what you think here!" Sally said.

Brent blushed and pulled his hands free.

All three sat in silence on the bench, thoughtful. A safe space separated Keira from Brent and a similar space stood between him and Sally. The situation was hilarious Sally thought and she burst out laughing. Keira must have thought the same because she laughed too. Brent, however, looked troubled. No doubt he wondered if they were laughing at him. Sally sent him a picture of the three sitting rigidly upright on the bench, all shifting uncomfortably, each sitting on their hands, blushing furiously. He could no longer keep a serious face, and he finally gave way, joining them in their laughter.

"What a hilarious trio you make!" a new voice hooted.

Startled, all three looked up. Opposite them, on the armrest of the bench across the path, perched a tawny owl. Hopping down onto the seat of bench, the bird strutted a few steps before continuing to address them: "You've done well. Although we need to talk about why you girls stopped Brent getting in."

Sally saw that Keira felt as ashamed as she did. She also noticed that Brent didn't seem to understand.

"Alo," for she had realised it was him. "You'll have to teach us how to shapeshift like that, it could be very useful."

The owl hooted. It might have been his way of laughing, she thought. "That'll have to wait for another lesson. Now is time to go back and get something to eat."

Reception committee

From her vantage point in an armchair in the reception of the hotel, Jenny had a good view of the comings and goings in the next-door bistro without being seen herself. She recognised Fran the moment the woman walked in, setting the bell over the entrance ringing as she did. She watched her look nervously around the place then thread her way to a table by the window. Few customers were there at the time.

Fran ordered a coffee and took out a small notebook from her bag which she began reading once she'd made sure nobody could read over her shoulder. She seemed completely absorbed in her reading, only occasionally putting her hand to her mouth as if in shock or alarm. Whatever she was reading, it left her agitated. Through the window, Jenny saw Martin saunter across the road from the station and give her a nod. He'd checked to see that Fran was alone. She glanced at Tom who was sunk in an armchair on the other side of the reception.

"OK?" she signalled.

He too nodded. All three converged unnoticed on Fran.

Discovered

Closing Leuchtli's little notebook with a sigh, Fran zipped it away in a special hidden pocket in her bag and, preoccupied, looked unseeingly around the bistro. The situation was worse than she'd thought. Unknown to her, and to many of her colleagues at Energos, Leuchtli had secretly tested the Machine

154   Alan McCluskey

on a number of unsuspecting young women most of whom had paid for it with their lives or their sanity. She shuddered to think that he'd tried to drug her intending to rape her and that he'd planned to use his Machine on her. She wished she'd poisoned him instead of just administering a sleeping draught.

A strong hand took hold of her shoulder making her jump in alarm. Keeping her back to the person threatening her, she reached for the small gun she now kept handy in her bag.

"You won't be needing that!" a tall, solidly-built man said as he stepped forward and took possession of her bag.

She turned to run, but the way was blocked by another man whose face bore sinister cuts across it. The hand on her shoulder tightened its grip.

"Sit down Fran, we need to talk."

It was the young woman holding her shoulder that spoke. Pushing Fran back down onto the bench from which she'd risen, the women slid in next to her. The two men sat on the bench opposite, one of them still grasping her bag in his big hands.

"My name is Jenny," the woman revealed. "This is my boyfriend Tom," she said pointing to the man with the cuts on his face "… and this is my brother Martin."

Fran broke down for the second time that day. "Oh my god!" she managed to say between her sobs. "I thought you were from Leuchtli."

The big man grasping her bag offered her a handkerchief. Taking it gratefully, she wiped her eyes and blew her nose.

"Why did you want to meet me?" Jenny asked.

"I wanted to warn you about Leuchtli and to see if you could help me escape."

Jenny glanced at both men before reacting. "We can't talk here. Where is your car? Can you leave it there for a while?"

Fran indicated that she could.

"Then I suggest we drive out to the hotel we are staying in. We'll be safe there for a while. And you can tell us what you know and we'll do the same."

Martin placed some coins on the table to cover the price

of the coffee and all three stood up and accompanied her out through the back door.

The hotel room was too small to accommodate four people comfortably. Tom lay down on the bed, Martin opened the window and leaned against the window frame while Jenny offered Fran a seat in the armchair opposite her.

"What happened to your boyfriend?" Fran asked.

Jenny told her how Leuchtli's henchmen had disposed of the woman's body and tried to kill Tom. Shocked by these revelations, despite all she knew already, Fran told them how Leuchtli had tried to drug her and how she managed to escape. The idea of the doctor caught in his own trap made Tom and Martin laugh. But Jenny remained unsmiling.

"Do you still have that notebook?" she asked.

"It's in my bag," Fran replied pointing to the bag Martin was holding.

As he handed it to her, they were all startled by her phone ringing. They looked at each other questioningly.

"Go ahead," Jenny said.

Fran rose to take her bag and fumbling nervously in it, she pulled out her phone and answered: "Fran speaking."

It was Sykes. Her legs buckled under her and she collapsed into the armchair.

"The Doctor is very upset you took his notebook. He wants it back immediately."

She wanted to protest, plead her innocence, but her mouth had gone dry and she couldn't find her voice.

Sykes broke the silence. "We're setting up the Machine for a new experiment using a sample of your hair for the test."

Fran gasped as blood drained from her face. She felt weak and dizzy and cold.

"It'll take us about two hours to calibrate the Machine. That's all the time you've got to bring back the notebook."

"But I'm too far away to get back in two hours," Fran pleaded in a strangled voice.

"Tough luck!" Sykes laughed as he hung up.

Fran slumped forward, her head resting on her arms that were laid on the table and all went very quiet and dreadfully dark.

Jenny was terrified at the young woman's behaviour. As Fran dropped the telephone, her face went almost green and her eyes rolled back into her head so that only the whites could be seen. A ghastly snoring forced its way out of her mouth as her head collapsed onto her arms. Martin helped Jenny carry the limp form to the bed while Tom looked for something akin to smelling salts.

"I've got some essence of lavender in my bag. That might help," Jenny told him as she rubbed Fran's hands between hers trying to warm them. "Help me get her into my arms," Jenny asked Martin. "She desperately needs human warmth and attention."

Cradling the unconscious girl in her arms, Jenny rocked her back and forth, humming a soft tune and whispering soothing words. It must have been having an effect because some of the colour had come back into the girl's face. She looked so young and helpless. As Jenny studied Fran's sleeping features her eyelids fluttered and her eyes opened, looking directly at Jenny.

"Please help me," was all the girl said.

"Rest now. We can talk later."

"There's no time," Fran replied, agitated again.

"Then tell us what's wrong. We don't understand."

Fran leaned back in Jenny's arms and told them briefly about the Machine.

"So they threaten to use it on you?" Martin asked.

Fran nodded.

"Is there no way to block it or get away?" Tom asked, his voice full of concern.

"I'm not sure. We might try to get as far away as possible. The effect may diminish with distance, but there is no guarantee. Or I could try to stay awake. I'm not sure what the impact of the Machine on a waking person would be. As far as I know it has never been used like that."

Jenny stroked Fran's hair, feeling the full force of the girl's despair.

"Whatever you do, you can't go back. They'll probably use the Machine on you anyway," Tom added pessimistically.

Jenny knew he was right and she suspected Fran knew it too.

"Ok," Jenny said decisively, helping Fran to stand. "Let's get going and put as much distance between us and them. We'll talk about what else we can do on the way."

Warding

"I once heard of a would-be master in psychic defence who threw ethereal knives and axes at his students. They were supposed to ward them off as best they could, but it didn't work. They had no idea what they were doing and, what's more, they were terrified. As he was the only one amongst them who could see the weapons, he delighted in giving a running commentary on how deep they cut into their auras."

Rafter laughed at the memory.

Seeing the alarm in Keira and Brent's faces, he added: "But don't worry. I won't be subjecting you to such a cowardly assault."

He was pleased to see Sally grinning. She at least had got the joke. "We'll concentrate on warding in dreams. That is to say, how to protect yourself against hostile forces directed at you in the dream realm."

Alo had told him of their trip into the dream garden earlier, so he planned to build on that.

"Your imagination is both your best defence and your worst enemy. Let me explain."

Pleased at their attentiveness and the effort the three put into carrying out his instructions, he wondered if he shouldn't restructure his future courses at the University around a specific mission and work with smaller groups.

"If you doubt, if you imagine you are weak or vulnerable, that's exactly what you'll be, even if you are psychically much

158   Alan McCluskey

stronger than those attacking you."

"Think strong," Sally said parodying the idea of thinking positively.

"Doubt and anxiety and fear work like gapping holes in your psychic defence," Rafter added.

A troubled look crossed Brent's face. It wasn't going to be fear so much as doubt that would plague Brent, Rafter thought. And most of that doubt would stem from the women he met.

"But how do you protect yourself?" Brent asked, making the girls laugh.

He saw the young man flinch. "It may seem funny…" Rafter said glancing at Sally and Keira. Their close relationship could well turn out to be the barrier he'd suspected it might. "… but yours is the key question for a would-be shaman, Brent. We won't have enough time to go into much depth. Training normally takes years. But I will give you some hints."

The doubting man is always the first on the path to discovery, Rafter thought. He liked Brent and he didn't want him to get lost. He decided he'd have a private talk with him later.

"But I also said imagination could be your best defence. And it is where we'll start. Using your imagination to weave protection around you."

Two hours later, Rafter called a break. He could see their concentration was on the wane.

"Brent. Can you stay on a moment? I want to look at something in particular with you."

Brent looked a bit surprised, but not as much as Sally and Keira, who didn't seem in any hurry to leave. Rafter smiled to himself at their behaviour.

"Come Brent. Let's go for a walk. Just between men."

He could have sworn he heard Keira scoff, but he ignored her as he swept out of the room and down the stairs.

Stepping out into the garden, Brent wondered what Rafter wanted with him. The Professor turned to him and asked if he'd already discovered Alo's well. Brent hadn't. Apart from his trip to the oak, he'd hardly left the house.

"Let me show you where it is," Rafter said.

They walked round the house in silence and headed towards a part of the garden that was densely planted with rhododendrons. He had to admit that the Professor intimidated him. This was the first time he'd been alone with Rafter and he felt a little tongue-tied. The path wound its way between the shrubs that weren't yet in flower.

"It's not easy for you with Keira and Sally." Rafter said, startling Brent.

So that was it. Well it might be good to talk about it although he wouldn't have chosen the Professor as his confidant.

"Er ... Yes. They make me uncomfortable."

"Let me guess. They both attract you, but in different ways. At the same time the closeness between the two keeps you at a distance."

Brent blushed. Rafter would never make a good therapist, Brent thought. But Rafter surprised him again.

"You're very good, Brent. I can see it in all you are doing. You have talent and you understand fast. If you have time later, I'd willingly accept you in my seminar."

Brent wondered why everyone kept making him blush. Was it a conspiracy?

"My real vocation is story-telling," Brent said, feeling much surer.

"Yes. That is your greatest force. You are right. Remember that next time the girls make you doubt. Know also that you are a match for them if you want to be."

Astonished, Brent wanted to make a comment but he couldn't make up his mind whether to contradict or clarify or complain. Rafter cut his thoughts short: "So here is the well. Beautiful isn't it."

A small fountain played quietly beside the raised stonewall that surrounded the well, above which an arc of wrought iron spiralled gracefully from one side to the other. Moonflowers had twinned their way around the iron creating a flowered archway. A robin sat on the wall chirping at them.

"I suggest you sit here for a while and talk to the robin about storytelling and the girls and listen to what he has to say to you."

Rafter didn't wait for an answer; he turned on his heals and headed back towards the house. When Brent looked up he could have sworn that the robin cocked its head on one side as if waiting for him to begin.

A close shave

"I don't understand," Tom said from the back of the car, breaking an uncomfortable silence.

They'd been driving for nearly an hour and a half non-stop along French motorways and were nearing Troyes.

"I thought their infernal Machine was designed to generate energy."

Fran caught the warning look that Jenny gave him.

"No. It's alright Jenny. It is better if I tell you as much as I know."

Yes, she thought to herself, especially if I will soon be unable to say anything coherent.

"That was Leuchtli first brainwave. It was an attractive idea, but it proved flawed."

She went on to explain why and how the Doctor had pretended to continue his explorations so no one would guess his real intentions. Thinking about it now, she wondered his behaviour hadn't struck her as odd at the time. She'd been caught up in the intricacies of her work and had lost sight of the wider picture.

"If you can explain how the thing works, maybe we can dream up a solution."

Fran laughed nervously at his unconscious choice of words. Realising what he'd said, Tom apologised.

"Dream is the key word," Fran said laying a reassuring hand on Tom's shoulder to let him know it was OK.

In such a short time, she'd come to like all three of them very much. It would be a shame to lose them so soon.

"In trying to strengthen the signal, Leuchtli discovered how to set up a resonant signal between the Machine and the brain.

In a way you could say that the brain and the Machine communicated with each other. The signal was extremely complex and different for each person. The first masterstroke was modulating the signal with information from the DNA of the person. Doing so guaranteed that communication was focussed on only one person using a sample of their hair, for example."

Tom looked perplexed. "But why would that be dangerous for the receiver?"

Fran glanced at her watch. There were another twenty minutes before the deadline expired. She could feel beads of sweat rolling freely down her back. Forcing herself to be the scientist she'd so long trained to be, she went on: "If the person has nowhere or no way to channel the energy as resonance increases, the brain automatically protects itself against such interference by reducing its tolerance to incoming signals, not only from outside but also from the body itself. In a way, you could say it progressively shuts down communication within the body until life finally stops …"

Seeing the tears brimming up in Martin's eyes she saw that he had grasped what she meant.

"Is there nothing we can do to protect you?" Tom asked, clearly as stricken as Martin. "Like Superman and kryptonite and lead: a metal that could act as a shield?"

Fran smiled at the reference.

"That would be pointless; the Machine works with quantum resonance. There is no transmission in the usual sense."

It was Jenny that broke the weighty silence that ensued. "So, if I understand correctly, it is not so much the DNA code that is used as the quantum resonance of near identical material?"

Fran looked up, puzzled. "Yes. You are right."

"And Leuchtli has some of your hair?" Fran nodded.

"So if we shave off all you hair, the Machine might not be able to resonate with you." Jenny added triumphantly.

"Would that work?" Tom asked turning to Fran.

"It might. It might indeed."

Jenny turned to Martin and said urgently: "Take that exit,

Martin. It's a motorway lay-by. We can use the toilets to get you shaved, Fran. I've got a small battery-operated razor with me that I sometimes use for my legs."

Martin pulled the car to a halt opposite the toilets.

"We've got just five minutes left." Jenny said as she slid open the door and searched through her baggage for the razor. "Come on, Fran. We've got work to do."

They set off at a run heading for the toilets as Tom called out after them "Make sure you remove all of the hair!"

Jenny heard Fran groan as she realised what Tom meant. He was right of course, however embarrassing it might be.

"Well that's your head done. I can loan you a hat if you like. What about under your arms?"

"No need. I do it regularly."

"So that leaves between your legs," Jenny said, embarrassed.

"Let's get it over with," Fran said, pulling off her trousers and pants. "To think that Leuchtli has managed to make me take my trousers off, but not for him."

Jenny was amazed at the resilience of the young woman who could still joke in such alarming circumstances.

"I can't understand why some men find hairless women exciting," Fran pursued. "It's damn uncomfortable."

"Sorry. Did I hurt you?" Jenny asked, worried, as she tried to come to terms with the mixed feelings coursing through her veins at what she was doing.

"No. You do that very gently."

Ignoring the tone in Fran's voice, she finished what she was doing and said, "Use this brush to make sure that no cut hairs cling to your skin. And shake out your clothes too."

Jenny cleaned the razor, began gathering up as much of the hair she could and flushed it away down the toilet, while Fran got dressed.

"We've got one minute left. Let's get out of here."

Missed

Leuchtli watched the baldhead of his assistant bobbing up

and down as the man struggled to get a fix on the girl.

"Are you really so incompetent, Johannes?"

He could see pearls of sweat forming on the man's shiny pate. He found the sight disgusting. How could anyone get into bed with that, he wondered, surprised he could even dream up such a question. Johannes was checking the readings on the computer again.

"I've hooked the Machine up to the mainframe to be able to double check the measurements," he said, rubbing a grubby handkerchief across his face. "But it's not reacting right."

"What do you mean by 'not reacting right'"?

Leuchtli was loosing his patience. Damn that girl for messing up his plans. He'd got no time for this. He had to concentrate on the coming demonstration for the backers. He realised that Johannes had been talking but he hadn't heard what he said.

"Say that again!" he barked.

"I'm getting a weak signal back, but it doesn't have the right profile. It's more like a faint echo."

"Could they be using a decoy?" The assistant looked up startled.

"I can't see how."

He ran his fingers nervously over his glistening head.

"It is as if we've got resonance, but the brain is not there to respond."

"Could she be dead?"

"Maybe." Johannes said, crossing himself absent-mindedly.

Nothing irritated Leuchtli more than the withering faith of these Catholics that continued to believe and act out of habit long after all the rest had dried up. The church had to be strong or nothing at all.

Bringing an ENERGOS brochure crashing down on a desk, he swatted a fly that had been buzzing around the workshop for a while, leaving a bloody streak across the words "... Manifold Energy..." There was far too much laisser-aller. Leuchtli tossed the soiled brochure into the wastebasket and crossed the room to examine the sample of hair that lay between the sensors of the Machine.

"Could we have got the wrong sample of hair?"

The assistant shook his head. "The plastic bag clearly had her name on it. The hairs are the right colour too."

Leuchtli drew in a sharp breath. Of course! That's how she's done it. Why hadn't he thought of that before. He had to laugh, even though it was far from funny.

"If she cut off all her hair would that produce the echo you're getting?"

Johannes nodded grinning, relieved that it wasn't his fault. "You're brilliant, Doctor. That must be it."

Leuchtli shifted to the door: "We'll get her, mark my words. Sooner or later she'll let her hair grow and we'll be waiting for her."

Now he really had a good reason to laugh. Two can play at that game, Fräulein Francine, he thought.

"Set up the experiment for this afternoon's test." And he left, whistling to himself.

Oran Mor

"The Celts called it Oran Mor, the Great Song or, you might say, the Great Story. All creation springs from that song, that story. That is why music makers and storytellers alike were revered in their culture."

Naniu sat atop a large flat rock, one amongst many strewn at the foot of the cliffs, a stone's throw from the water's edge. Waves broke noisily amongst rock pools upheaving crabs and all manner of marine life before receding anew. Sally, Keira and Brent each sat perched on similar rocks listening intently.

"The Hindus talk of Nada Brahma. Others have other names. All know sound is at the heart of being."

It was so easy to say that you needed to get people to listen before they could sing. But it wasn't so simple. Listening was a grossly underestimated task.

"I could talk about it for hours, but that wouldn't bring you any closer. Instead, I'm going to stop talking and let you listen for yourselves. Silence is the door to Oran Mor. Close your eyes. Quieten your thoughts. And listen. Listen in particular to the sound of the waves. Let the Great Song sing in you. In an hour I will ring a bell. When you hear it, make a sound that resonates with the waves. Let it flow and develop, calling on all you have heard in the silence."

A flock of gulls dived from the cliff above, skimmed close over their heads and drove out to sea, calling to each other as they went. Naniu closed her eyes, reached out for the water and let herself go with Oran Mor.

Their song came spontaneously to an end. Only the sea's waves rolled on. Sally opened her eyes. Keira and Brent sat heads bowed, no doubt engrossed still in the world of song. Drawing in an unsteady breath, she looked around. The tide had flowed out leaving large expanses of sand, marked with the ripples of the receding water.

Naniu, who was weaving her way barefoot between the tiny puddles that lay dotted here and there, called out: "Come and join me!"

Naniu drew a large circle in the soft wet sand with a stick. Sally watched her preparations, for this was surely no idle activity to pass the time while Keira and Brent crossed the beach to join them. Sally turned to study the two who seemed in no hurry to reach them. Brent was clearly keeping his distance from Keira. There seemed to be a difference in how he acted to both Keira and herself since Rafter had taken him aside. She was intrigued as to know what the two had talked about. Looking back at Naniu she saw that her singing teacher had planted the stick upright in the middle of the circle. Sally remembered one of Rafter's seminars when he'd talked of the circle as the perfect form that both protects and opens the way.

"Now gather round. I want to work for a short while on dance and movement."

Sally loved dancing. She and Keira often went out to dance. But what she liked most was to dance alone in a wild place to the music in her head until she completely lost herself in the movement.

"Take up your positions at equal distances from each other just outside the circle. Good. Now turn slowly, very slowly, clockwise, your arms outstretched."

Naniu sang softly as they danced and shook a rattle, setting up a slow, steady rhythm.

"You can stomp lightly with your feet in time with the rattle, if you like, so you are more aware of the ground beneath you."

Naniu herself began turning on the spot, shaking the rattle above her head.

"Now, as you turn about yourself, begin to turn clockwise around the circle following each other in time with the rattle."

Sally felt herself getting into the rhythm as the dance drew on.

"Keep your arms outstretched, but turn your hands upwards towards the sky."

Energy from her feet was coursing upwards along her spine to the crown of her head. At the same time, she felt tingling in her fingertips that became like lightening rods conducting energy from above down through her to the ground.

"Wonderful! Now as you turn you will notice that the sun in setting into the sea. Each time you see the sun, bend your knees slightly, in reverence, blessing the sun."

Naniu took up her chant again, stronger now as it wove in and out of the rattle beats and the stomping of their feet. Sally had the impression she was rising up above the circle looking down. Their combined movement rippled and whirled around the circle in a way that was so delicious she couldn't find words for it.

The disc of the setting sun had finally sunk below the horizon when Naniu slowed the rhythm till it finally came to a halt and they all came to a halt with her. All three of them had tears streaming down their cheeks as Naniu brought the lesson to an end.

"That is how the world was created. That is how all things are shaped. With music and movement."

Flight

Martin drove the car off the motorway and at the earliest opportunity turned down a narrow lane, stopping at edge of a wood far from all buildings. Jumping out of the car, all four danced around the vehicle, taking it in turns to hug Fran.

"We did it. We beat them." Martin said laughing as he swung Fran in a wild fling.

Fran was surprised at his strength. He seemed such a gentle man. When he finally put her down, she ran her hands over her hairless head, trying to get used to the feeling of the wind on her skin.

"Touch!" she said, spontaneously taking his hand and placing it on her head.

Somewhat embarrassed, he ran his hand slowly over her skin, feeling the form of her skull. His warm touch sent shivers down her spine. She must have made some sound of pleasure because he quickly withdrew his hand.

As their joy quietened, Fran said: "You realise of course that he won't stop at that. He'll wait till I let my hair grow and try again."

It was a sobering thought that brought them back to a sinister reality. It was murder they were talking about and she was to be the next victim.

"We'll just have to keep you shaved," Martin said.

At which they all burst out laughing.

"I like you like that," he protested, blushing when he realise the implications of what he'd said.

"You can shave her next time," Jenny said, teasing him.

This time it was Fran's turn to blush.

Back in the car, Fran prepared herself to rest after the tension of the last hours. Only now could she trust herself to sleep without fearing an attack from Leuchtli or his gang. Thinking of him reminded her of his notebook. She'd promised to let Jenny read it.

"Jenny. If you look in my bag there's a hidden pocket inside it, closed with a zip. In there you'll find Leuchtli's notebook.

Just watch out though. There's also a gun in there too."

Fran was awoken an hour later by Jenny gasping: "*Oh no!*"

The young woman seemed really upset as she waved Leuchtli's black book in front of her.

"What's the matter?" Tom asked.

"It's Sally. She's here in Leuchtli's book."

"Who's Sally?" Fran wanted to know.

"She's the person we're going to see in Avan. She's my friend. It would seem Leuchtli plans to experiment on her."

Fran shuddered. "We can't go there. What if Leuchtli finds me?"

Jenny looked shocked at Fran's reaction. "We must go," she said emphasising the word 'must'. "And you must come with us, Fran. To help us protect Sally like we protected you."

Fran bowed her head, ashamed. "You're right, Jenny. I will help."

Tom, who seemed to have been dozing, had apparently followed their whole conversation because he asked, "Have you managed to phone Sally?"

"No. She's not answering."

"Then the sooner we reach Avan, the better," Tom concluded. "Can we go any faster, Martin?"

"Not without breaking French law," was his reply as he pushed his foot down on the accelerator.

An unexpected guest

Sally sat down next to Rafter and looked around the dinning table at their little group as they settled in. Rafter had just returned from a quick trip to the University, looking more concerned than usual. Department business he'd called it. She'd seen Brent writing in Alo's library, thoughtfully filling the pages of his little book with notes. Did she walk those pages, she wondered. She'd heard Naniu singing in the music room in the attic earlier, distant strains of an unnamed oratorio to the sea.

Alo and Keira had apparently been talking about Indian cuisine in the kitchen and continued to do so now. Keira still had the faintest traces of the sauces she'd tasted on her lips. Tangwyn and Anju had just arrived from visiting nearby Celtic standing stones, a spiritual excursion they were describing to Brent who seemed fascinated. But maybe it was just the animation of Anju as she spoke that held him in rapt attention.

And herself. She'd sat out in the growing dark in the garden thinking over everything that had happened to them in the last few days. Eight people: four men and four women; four younger, four older; a symmetrical group. So why were nine places laid?

In a lull in the before-dinner conversations, she asked Rafter: "Who is the extra place for?"

The professor treated her to one of his enigmatic smiles that always exasperated her. Everyone had turned to hear his reply.

"That is for our mysterious unexpected guest."

She wanted to retort that he wasn't being logical, that the person couldn't be both expected and unexpected, but her experience with Rafter told her that he'd prefer to maintain the enigma. He was fond of using theatrical effects to get over his point.

"How can an unexpected person have a place laid for him or her. It's doesn't make sense," Brent pointed out, somewhat confused.

He must have been reading her thoughts, though he hadn't got the bit about caution.

"I say unexpected, because our guest doesn't know he's coming to dinner yet."

Well that made things clearer, she thought.

"You won't get any more, Brent," she warned him knowingly, playing along with Rafter's game. "We'll just have to wait and see."

At which Rafter made a show of being offended, until he burst out laughing. "Sally is right. You'll just have to wait."

Caught

Thank heavens there were no outhouses full of booby-traps around this house. All the same, Tyrell was sure if he chose to sit on one of the wicker chairs that dotted the lawn, it would be that particular one that had been re-varnished earlier in the day.

His road to Alo's country house had been long and tedious. Having escaped the hospital, he'd needed to change into dry clothes. As he had no clean clothes left he'd had to make a trip to the Laundrette where he'd got ensnarled by what he supposed was the local nymphomaniac. She found all manner of pretexts to touch him as she supposedly helped him do his washing. He detested uninvited physical contact.

When he escaped the Laundrette woman, he'd been trapped by his landlady who wanted to know why his kitchen was flooded with black soapy water. And so it went until he finally managed to find Alo's country mansion, having searched down most of the lanes in the area.

Light streamed out of the dinning room windows across the vegetable garden in front of him, casting weird shadows in its wake. As he approached cautiously, still shrouded in darkness, he noticed they were all sitting down to eat. Tangwyn and his daughter had arrived. Rafter was there with the shaman. And Sally and Keira were also there with that Brent guy. There was even the women he'd bumped into in the dark the other day at Alo's town house. To his surprise and shock, one of the windows was suddenly thrown open and Rafter leaned out.

"Come in Tyrell. You'll hurt yourself walking around in the dark."

A moment of utter indecision and terror held him suspended. He couldn't run. After all, Rafter was his boss. But if he went in he'd get massacred. Sally would surely be delighted to get her own back. Maybe he could dream up an excuse...

"Hurry up, Tyrell. We've been waiting for you. The food is all ready."

Now Rafter had thrown him completely. What was this invitation? They couldn't possibly know he was coming. But they did. As he stepped into the dining room he saw one free place waiting for him. All heads were turned in his direction, many of them frankly hostile. Rafter smiled however, as did the shaman.

"Take a seat, Tyrell."

As he moved to the table he felt like a puppet.

"I believe you know most of the people here. Well you will have seen them all the other night."

Rafter seemed pleased at the allusion. Tyrell could only guess that they knew everything. They might even know he had been working for Leuchtli.

Sally was almost as shocked as Tyrell at his sudden arrival.

"So that's our unexpected guest?" she said, weighting the word 'that' with a heavy dose of disdain, if not disgust.

"Now, now, Sally." Rafter chided her. "We need to be polite to our guest."

Turning towards Tyrell, the Professor added, "He's going to tell us all about it. Aren't you Tyrell? But let's eat first, I'm starving."

From Sally's perspective, Tyrell looked like a fly nailed to a slab of wood awaiting a scalpel. She couldn't imagine how he could possibly eat anything under these conditions. His presence had taken her appetite away. Yet despite his situation, the assistant didn't seem to have any problems with eating as he shovelled food onto his plate. She felt his presence as more than an intrusion, it was like a violation of her space. This was her world, her story and he had no place in it.

Chapter 8 - The Black Castle

Blasted

A giant clock ticked noisily, halting from time to time - suspended momentarily - only to pursue its slow round, the immense cogs engaging and disengaging relentlessly, till a heavy thud finally silenced its racket, shaking her very limbs. It made no sense. Nothing made sense. Her thoughts squirmed in a quagmire, struggling to get free of the mud that clawed at them, pulling them back down. The place stank of damp and piss and rotten cabbage. Maybe she'd fallen into a bog.

Her head ached. Her every joint ached. Where was she? She tried to open her eyes, but they were glued shut. Reaching out with her hands, she had some difficulty finding her eyes. When she finally succeeded, she rubbed her eyelids vigorously. To no avail. Other noises troubled her. The whinnying of a horse, for example. Where did that fit into the black picture? Or the sound of boots on cobble stones. She pulled at her hair as if the pain might bring a light.

"Blasted Dungbats!" she swore, bumping her elbow against something hard and unforgiving.

"Looks like the Princess is awake, Guv." The voice was harsh and crude. "Shall I put her out again? I'd enjoy that."

"I'm sure you would," a younger voice replied making the brute laugh.

The horse neighed, more clearly this time. She managed to open her eyes, slit wise, peering out at the sopping wooden boards on which she was lying. It was daytime, albeit dull and grey and wet. She shut her eyes tight.

"No. Haul her to her feet. I want her to see where she is."

She recognised that voice, young and male, but she couldn't place it. A cloud of sweat and beer approached, rapidly taking the form of a thickset man with huge hands that grabbed hold of her arms, roughly pulled her off the boards she was lying on and yanked her to her feet. She promptly collapsed in the mud only to be dragged up again by the brute.

"Shrivelled midget!" she swore at him.

He slapped her face sending her flying into the mud once more. Why were her legs so wet and cold? Opening her eyes as little as possible she saw she was wearing a mud-spattered nightdress. She closed her eyes immediately. Her thoughts were as blurred as her vision. Was she going crazy? The brute dragged her a third time to her feet. Behind her she felt something solid against which she leaned. Daring to open her eyes, she shook her head to clear her sight.

She was standing in a muddy, cobblestoned courtyard surrounded by high black walls that towered dismally above, finishing in a forest of turrets and spires beyond the battlements. In front of her, leaning against the blackened wall next to the massive entrance, stood Connor, his hands tucked in his trouser pockets, a grin on his face.

"Welcome to the House of Cellerini, Cianala, my former family seat," he said bowing mockingly to her.

To Connor's right, some ten paces away stood the voyeur, as grubby and dishevelled as ever. He'd even lost one of his shoes and his bare foot was flecked with mud and blood. The bloke raised his hand to his mouth, an alarmed look on his face, and begged her silently to be quiet, placing one upright finger in front of his lips. She starred at him, uncomprehending.

"Why do you stare so at a blank wall?" Connor asked as he turned to see what she was looking at.

She couldn't understand their behaviour. It must be some game they were playing together, making fun of her.

"I have to go now," Connor continued, "No one will bother you here," he smirked "This place has been abandoned for years. But the walls are still solid enough to keep out an army or to imprison the likes of you."

His laughter echoed off the walls. She bared her teeth and would have growled, except that would have made her like him. How she hated him. How she hated all men. Concentrating with all her force, she unleashed her power and sent a scorching blast in his direction. It rippled off his shield as he neatly sidestepped. Deflected, the blast sent the bedraggled old man flying. One down, at least, she thought as she looked at the writhing heap of dirty clothes on the muddied cobblestones. Glancing back at Connor, a blinding light flashed from his hands. There was nothing she could do. Jim had not yet taught her shielding. The bright light went on forever. There was no heat, no force, just the bright whiteness. When would it cease?

She slid her hands over her eyes, but the light continued. It didn't make any sense. Then it dawned on her: if all she could see was a bright white light then he must have blinded her. She groaned and sank to her knees, unheeding as her bare knees hit the stones.

"Why have you done this?" She heard him laugh.

"You'll have plenty of time to figure that out as you feel your way through the Black Castle. An appropriate name, don't you think, for the prison of someone who sees only white."

She imagined him gloating at his own ingeniousness, strutting around before her, a proud cock.

Chivalry

Stepping forward, Connor helped her up out of the mud and took her arm as politely as he could.

"Let me guide you to your room," he offered and led her into the front door and up the main staircase.

He was surprised at the softness of her arms. He'd never touched her before. The feel of her skin sent shivers rippling down his spine. He stopped to steady her as she stumbled on the top stair.

"That oil painting above the stairs is my Great Grandfather Thomas Cellerini. He had this place built. A mastermind at strategy. A great man. He had thirteen wives most of whom he strangled with his bare hands."

He enjoyed showing off his family to her, even if she couldn't see. Her head was hanging down, her shoulders rounded and her face smudged with tears; in her muddy nightdress and with her dirty legs she looked like an urchin, abandoned by the world, awaiting to be executed at sunrise. The image pleased him. He wasn't very poetic, but he found the idea movingly beautiful.

"Thomas would have fallen for you, Cianala. He loved tragic women."

He led her across the main reception room, through a service door and up the back stairs that wound their way to the servants' sleeping quarters. Opening one of the doors he led her in.

"This was the room of one of Thomas' favourite servants. He often came to visit her."

He guided her across the small room to the single bed and helped her sit down. She sank into a heap on the bed and began crying, holding her hands over her eyes. It wouldn't do to pity her. If Thomas had been there, he'd have been furious to see his great grandson so weak.

"Down the hall you'll find a kitchen. I think there is some food there. One of my men will come along from time to time to check up on you. We don't want you to die, do we? Otherwise you'll have the Castle to yourself for as long as you like."

He rose, picked up a coarse blanket that lay at the end of the bed and drew it over her.

"Enjoy your stay in Cellerini Castle, Cianala."

Slipping through a hidden door, he stepped out of the servants' quarters onto the main staircase and made his way down to the entrance. Thomas' picture watched him striding down. Was the old man frowning at him, Connor wondered? He'd never noticed that look before. Outside the rain had eased off. His two men were waiting for him next to the cart. He gave them instructions about locking the castle and mounted his horse.

Crossing the drawbridge he halted. Now was certainly the right moment. He pulled the leather thong that hung around his neck over his head and studied the small stone attached to it on which was engraved a small eye. Feeling a mixture of loathing and anger at the sight of it, he flung the thing into the moat. Relieved, he rode away along the muddy highway, his men following slowly with the cart. The drawbridge swung up behind them and the portcullis rattled down into place. A thick mantle of forgetfulness sank over the Black castle.

Alone

All was silent. Nobody stirred. She was alone, completely alone. Abandoned. She felt exhausted, but wondered if she would be able to sleep with such a bright white light shining in her head. She had no idea what time of day it was. At least the blanket kept her warm. Odd gesture that. Why would he bother to cover her with a blanket? So out of character. The blanket was rough: it chaffed her legs and arms. And the bed was hard, the mattress was thin and lumpy. She didn't really care. Life seemed pointless. She cupped her hands over her eyes, as if that could lessen the light. The light shone on. She curled up in a tight ball.

What had gone wrong? She didn't deserve this. She thought of An. She tried to picture her half sister's lovely face, but nothing could defeat the white light. The light weighed on her, pressing her down. If her blindness had been black, like blindness normally was, she might have some room for her imagination, some room in which to exist. But this whiteness filled her, leaving no room for anything else. Why was black always seen as evil? Surely it was white that was evil. It denied all else. It burnt, it crushed and it gave you a headache.

Something very small and furry scuttled by, brushing her face. She chased it away with her hand. Well at least she wasn't completely alone. Humour? How could that be? It sprang up like a tiny living shoot in a desolate wasteland. She closed her eyes - she hadn't realised they were open – and breathed deeply.

The Reaches   177

Her stomach rumbled. She hadn't eaten for a long time. And her mouth was parched. She slid her legs over the side of the bed and felt for the floor.

Easing herself off the bed, she stood up and stretched her arms out in front of her. Tiny step after tiny step, she moved gingerly across the room till she came to a wall. Following it round to the left, she found a door and slipped through the opening. To her disappointment it was only a cupboard filled with boxes: a dead end. Negotiating her way back out, she followed the wall till she reached a second door. It was locked. The doorknob rattled in her impatient hand. The third door was more promising. Something told her she was in a corridor. She felt her way down the corridor, trying each door she came across. On this side of the corridor all the rooms were empty. The air in them was dead, unstirred for years.

A rustling sound behind her made her stop. Mice? Rats? Or someone silently watching her? The noise had ceased, so she moved on. Reaching the end of the corridor she began tracking back in the opposite direction along the other wall, arms still outstretched in front of her. Beyond the second door on that side, a welcome breeze greeted her. Was she outside? No. It was a room with tables and chairs, but a window must be open. She tentatively moved towards the breeze and found it was coming from a smaller room that was cooler than the rest. Along its walls were shelves, laden with what must be food. She picked up what felt like a large carrot and sniffed it. It was covered in dust that made her sneeze.

"I wouldn't eat that," a whisper said.

She spun round to face the voice. "Who are you? What are you doing creeping up on me like that? You scared the life out of me."

So she wasn't alone after all. However, she wasn't sure she welcomed this other presence.

"Don't be afraid," the whisperer replied after a short silence. "I can do you no harm. I have neither the strength nor the will for that."

"Who are you?"

"My name is Vee. I have been watching you for a long time."

She snarled: "You!"

"Don't be angry," he whimpered, "I can't help it. That's how I am."

"What a lame argument. Preying on young women. Prying into their private lives. Nothing is sacred, not even their most intimate moments."

She thought of him watching her making love to An. All her anger burst out in righteous indignation.

"Is it not you who looks all the time, nobody else but you? Is it not you who chooses what you do? Nobody compels you. Do you have no backbone? You coward. Can't you fight against it? Have you given up for ever?..."

She could feel the fight going out of her. What was the point? She was cold. She was dirty. She was hungry and thirsty. She must look pitiful herself. She was hopeless and helpless, struck blind and imprisoned, possibly forever.

"What did you say was your name?" she asked, the edge gone out of her voice.

"Vee," he whispered, relief in his tiny voice.

She felt for a chair and sat down, resting her elbows on the table and her head on her hands.

"How did you get here, Vee?"

He told her of his vigil outside An's house and of the men in the dark that carried her away. He told her of his pursuit and the discovery that Connor's men couldn't see him. He passed quickly over how he got onto the cart with her and described their arrival in the Castle forecourt.

"I thought you were in league with Connor," she sighed, remembering how she'd blasted him, reducing him to a shuddering mass on the muddy ground. "Now I understand why you didn't want him to know about you."

Changes

He remained quiet for a moment, watching her from across

the scullery. She was different somehow. He'd been watching her for so long, but now she seemed unfamiliar. It wasn't just that she was now so fragile, so hurt, so aimless. She was alive in a way he'd never seen before. He too felt different, although he wasn't sure he could explain it. Something was missing, as if he'd lost something important. But then again, he felt more whole than he'd done for ages. He glanced down at his shrivelled hands and then looked up at her.

"Would you like me to prepare you something to eat?" he murmured. "I can't do much with my arms," he explained, "I am very weak. I have no strength in my limbs. But I should manage that for you."

She laid her head on her crossed arms. "I'd appreciate that, Vee," she said softly.

The sound of her saying his name shook him to the core. He turned away, not wanting to linger and went into the larder. The vegetables were in a sorry state, but he managed to wash the carrots at the stone sink and gave her one to chew while he searched for more to eat.

Their frugal meal finished, they both sat in thoughtful silence. After a while, seeing her nod off to sleep, he suggested she go back to her room and rest. She agreed, laying her hand lightly on his arm as he led her back down the corridor to her room.

"There is a window in your room," he told her as she settled on the bed. "I'll open it for a moment. It is so stuffy in here and you'll sleep better with a bit of fresh air."

She'd curled up under the blanket, her eyes closed.

"It is night time," he informed her. "I'll wake you for breakfast tomorrow. If you agree," he added as an after thought.

She nodded. He moved to the door and was about the close it when she called out to him.

"Vee?"

"Yes."

"Thank you," she said quietly.

"Don't mention it. Goodnight." He pulled the door closed.

Vee followed the same path Connor had taken earlier, making his way slowly down the main castle staircase to the ground floor. The carpet on the stairs was worn thin in places, but it must have been beautiful once. He was quite out of breath by the time he reached the bottom. He paused to recover. There were so many things he needed to do, and so little energy to do them with. He had to find her clothes. She'd get ill if she didn't have something warmer to wear. She would also need somewhere to wash properly. He had to find better food too. And he needed to see if there was anyway they could get out of their prison.

He couldn't remember ever having had so many things to do. He smiled. A movement caught his eye as he shuffled across the lobby. An old man dressed in scruffy clothes, bent over, almost hunch-backed, was watching him. He turned to look properly and the man turned to look back.

"Is that me?" he asked out loud when he realised it was his reflection in the mirror. Studying his pitiful state, he thought he too could do with a good bath and a change of clothes.

He'd steeled himself at the idea of having to take a cold bath, but the water was surprisingly warm. There must be hot springs nearby. He stepped naked into the bath and lowered himself slowly into the suds. He'd found a sweet-scented liquid soap that he'd poured generously into the tub. The odour of thyme and rosemary almost masked the smell of sulphur that rose from the water.

He couldn't remember the last time he'd had a bath. It was as if he'd always been dirty. Grime was a part of him. Some of the aches and pains that were his constant companions seeped away into the warm water leaving him more at ease and relaxed. He took the pumice stone he'd found lying on the floor and scrubbed himself all over. Not all of the dirt gave in to his feeble efforts, but he felt and looked much cleaner. He'd even found a set of thick, soft towels. He was sure she'd like those.

In the dressing room next to the bathroom he'd laid out clean hose, leather breeches, a pale blue silk shirt, a blue and silver waistcoat and a very smart dark blue riding jacket. There were even very elegant boots his size. He thought he'd dress in them tomorrow morning but couldn't resist trying them on immediately. They hung loosely on his emaciated body, but he didn't care. He felt good as he set off a little more briskly than usual in search of stocks of food and a way out.

A new day

He knocked gently and opened the door.

"Cianala, the sun has been up for several hours. I have prepared breakfast ... and I've a surprise for you."

He did not enter the room, but stood in the doorway.

"What is that smell of wild flowers, Vee? Have you brought me a bunch? Is that your surprise?"

He laughed, a whispered laugh. "No, Cianala. That's perfume. I found a place to have a hot bath, so I tested it for you."

"Lead me to the hot bath, Vee." Delight sparkled in her voice. "If I could dream, I am sure I would dream of just that."

He took her arm and guided her out of the servants' quarters and down the main staircase.

"I've also found you some clothes. You must be cold dressed like that."

She shivered in response.

"I wasn't sure of your size, but as there is a great selection, I'm certain we'll find something that fits."

Walking and talking still made him breathless, so he halted for a moment.

"You've changed your clothes too, haven't you Vee? I can feel the difference: they are thicker, richer and they smell good. Describe them to me."

So he described what he was wearing and from time to time she asked for more details. He hadn't talked so much for ages. They made their way slowly down, pausing from time to time. She asked him to describe the place they were in. She was thirsty for details. So he did his best, finding that words came more easily the more he called on them.

"... and this is the bathroom. There is a large cast iron bath-

182   Alan McCluskey

tub planted in the middle. It's standing on four squat legs, a bit like a fat lizard. The floor is covered with cream coloured tiles and some of them bear the Cellerini crest: a giant oak tree traversed by a bright red arrow."

He led her to a chair in one corner and helped her sit down.

"You wait here and I'll run the water. It must be a volcanic hot spring because it smells a bit of rotten eggs. I'll add some perfume to the water. That'll make it more bearable."

Then he guided her to the bath's edge and asked her to wait again while he dragged the chair close to the bath.

"Feel," he said, taking her hand, "I've put two large towels here for you. You can dry yourself with them and then you can wrap one of them round you when we go to choose your clothes." He stepped back "I'll leave you then. I'll be in the next room if you need me."

"No peeking though, Vee." And she giggled as she stepped into the bath.

"This tissue is gorgeous," she said later, as she ran the blouse through her fingers. She pressed it against her face. It was so soft and smooth.

"It's emerald green. It goes very well with your auburn hair."

"Turn your back to me then, Vee, while I dress."

She realised that asking him to do so was a bit silly when he had so oft seen her naked. But now they were talking to each other she needed that distance. He seemed to appreciate the fact. She had the feeling he even welcomed it. And she trusted him. He could so easily pretend. He surely would have done so before. As she just couldn't see what he did, there was no way to know. But she felt sure he wouldn't take advantage of her. He'd changed.

"There. How do I look?"

"Like an angel!" he gasped.

"Someone else said I looked like an angel," she said, suddenly feeling sad again.

"You will tell me about that someday. But now, let's go and eat. I'm starving."

Yes. She too was very hungry. How thoughtful of him to seek to distract her.

"Show me the way, Vee."

"That was delicious. I've never enjoyed eggs so much before. Where did you find them?"

She licked her fingers, drying them on a napkin he'd given her. It was difficult to get the knack of eating when you couldn't see what you were doing.

"The main kitchen is one floor down. I found a large store of food. This place really doesn't seem deserted. It is too clean and orderly. The larder is too well stocked. I imagine we won't stay alone for long. It is as if the castle were awaiting the imminent return of the Cellerini family."

She tensed at the thought. Hadn't Connor boasted that his great grandfather had strangled his thirteen wives? Looking nervously around, unseeing, she remembered that she was their prisoner. They could do with her as they wished.

"We need to get out of here before they come back. I don't think they'll take too kindly to us making ourselves at home as if we were privileged guest of the Cellerini family."

He'd gone silent. Had he slipped away, abandoning her? She couldn't believe it.

"Are you still there, Vee?" She could hear the doubt in her voice.

"I wouldn't abandon you, Cianala," he whispered. "I just don't like to see you frightened. It frightens me."

"Silly man," she said warmly. "You mustn't be afraid. I need you to be strong and guide me away from here."

He snorted, apparently amused at the irony of him being called strong.

"I'm sure you can be strong, Vee. You were once and you will be again."

He remained silent.

"Are you smiling, Vee? I imagine you smiling. You must look younger when you smile."

He wouldn't admit it, she thought.

"I explored parts of the castle last night. I've found a place where we may be able to hide if and when they come back. There is an old chapel hidden in a park at back of the castle. I found a passage beneath the chapel that leads to a series of underground rooms. They are dry and healthy. There's even fresh air that blows through the tunnels."

She stood up and clapped her hands. "This is excellent news, Vee. We'll need to take food and clothes. Let's go now. Who knows when they might come back? We need to be settled in before they come charging back."

Vee found a small handcart in a storage room. They piled it up with food and clothes and tools and bedding. She did the pushing while he guided her. There was a hidden door that led to a walkway across a small courtyard. When she bumped into a large empty flowerpot they both burst out laughing.

"If anyone can see us, we must make a hilarious picture," she said when the laughter subsided.

"Let's hope no one can see us," he said, bringing them back to the danger of their situation.

They wove their way through another wing of the castle till they finally stepped out into the park Vee had mentioned. She felt the breeze blow against her skin. It stirred her long dress and ruffled her hair. How good to be outside. She could smell pine trees and mint and thyme.

"This is delightful," she said to him, stopping a moment for him to catch his breath. "With all this exercise, I'm sure you'll get your strength back," she added.

"Not far now," he told her. "Let's hope this cart doesn't leave any marks on the path. That would be like shouting where we are."

She was right about his strength. He did feel better. He had to stop less often to catch his breath.

"We're lucky," he pointed out. "The ground is very hard and the cart leaves no marks."

The park was quite large considering it was inside a castle. At one end there was a large wood of pines. Unlike the castle, it was less well tended. The trees grew close together. Some had fallen, lying at various oblique angles against their neighbours. It was here that the chapel lay hidden. He guided her down a new path that headed for the wood.

"There is a fountain near the chapel if ever we can't find a source of water in the chapel or in the underground passages."

He looked up at the sky. Heavy black clouds were rolling in.

"We need to hurry. It's going to rain," he told her.

They had reached the fountain when the first drops began to fall. He helped her push the cart as they hurried to the chapel. They arrived under the porch when the downpour began.

"Ouf! We made it just in time," he said.

"This is good," she replied. "If ever they have dogs – and I'm sure Connor has dogs – the rain will cover our tracks."

He hadn't thought of that.

"They may not be able to see you, but if they have dogs they may well be able to smell you."

She wiped the wheels of the cart with a cloth before she pushed it down the main aisle. He guided her round the altar, opening a door concealed behind a tapestry. The doorway was just wide enough for the cart to get in.

Closing the door behind them, he lit one of the lanterns he'd taken from the castle store. It smoked a bit, but that couldn't be helped. He fitted the bar in place to block the door.

"There is a bar," he explained. "Looks like this place was used in case of a siege."

She nodded her head to indicate she'd understood.

"We are in a tunnel that winds its way down through the rock till it gets to the secret rooms I told you about."

He stood behind her and put his hand on her shoulder to guide her as she set off with the handcart in front of her.

"How do you feel, Vee?" she asked, turning her head in his direction. "It seems to me you really are getting stronger. I don't hear you gasping so often when you make an effort."

He didn't really want to talk about himself. It disturbed him. He wasn't so important. Instead he said, "We're nearly there."

The tunnel ended in a thick metal door that stood open. Inside was a series of rooms: a kitchen, a bathroom, a number of rooms with small beds in them, even a library. He described the place to her.

"Let's take these things to the kitchen. I'll guide you so you know where to put the food on the shelves while I put the other things in the bedrooms."

They sat around the small wooden table in the kitchen eating the meal he'd prepared.

"I think you should stay here now, Cianala. If ever they arrive suddenly, we could never get you back here in time."

She looked tired, he thought. The colour she'd had regained earlier, had paled again.

"It would be good if you got some rest. I'll make up your bed for you."

Smiling weakly, she mocked him gently: "You are a real mother to me, Vee."

He'd been called many things, but never that. He snorted at her little joke.

The tower

As he stepped out into the park, the rain had stopped although raindrops still splashed from the soaked branches and leaves. He took a roundabout route, hoping to conceal his tracks as he stepped from stone to stone. He stopped suddenly. Smoke. He could smell smoke. Somebody else was in the castle. He shifted back into the shadow of the trees. He'd seen a tower not far from the chapel. If he climbed that, he might be able to spy out the land and see if there were any signs of life.

Tracking back towards the chapel, he turned away along a narrow path that led through brambles till it reached the foot of the tower. The front door was locked, but a service entrance round the back was open. It was a watchtower not a defence work. The stone staircase wound steadily around the inside of the wall. The centre of the tower lay open right up to the roof many tens of feet above.

He set out to climb to the top. The first few steps went well. He felt quite confident, but the higher he got the more the aches in his legs and back returned. He'd almost forgotten them. Apparently they hadn't forgotten him. His breathing came with difficulty. On he went till he thought he would die of suffocation. He just couldn't get enough air into his lungs.

He paused to catch his breath, but it eluded him. He sat down on the stone stairs when black patches danced before his eyes. Was he going to go blind too? Or was he going to snuff out? He willed himself on. He got up on his hands and knees, and battled on, moving upward painfully. The wheezing of his lungs echoed off the circular walls, magnifying his efforts in a grotesque concert of stifling demons. When he finally reached the trap door onto the roof and pushed his way through, he fell forwards with only the parapet stopping him from plunging to the ground below. He lay there panting, trying to quieten his hammering heart.

Night had fallen, but the castle was ablaze with light. A line of carriages crossed the drawbridge slowly, passed under the raised portcullis and came to a halt in the forecourt. Well-dressed gentlemen and elegant ladies alighted and strode up the main stairs in the light of hundreds of fluttering lanterns. Servants in livery were milling everywhere. He could hear the orders being shouted. He swore silently. The whole Cellerini court was returning with their guests. Thanks heavens they got away when they did. He wondered how long before they realised Cianala had gone.

Urgency gripped him by the throat. He had to get back to Cianala before they came looking for her. He stood shakily and began his way down the spiral staircase. Running his hand along the wall, he fought off the giddiness that threatened him. He'd almost made it when he missed his step and tumbled down the remaining few stairs. His shoulder gave an ominous crunch as he hit the ground and pain shot down his arm. He wanted to scream, but he didn't. Instead he hauled himself upright using this good arm and staggered out the door. He lurched along the path towards the chapel, scratching himself on the brambles in the dark.

He finally made it to the porch and pulled the door closed behind him. The light that burnt above the tabernacle over the altar cast an eerie red glow as he staggered down the aisle and round behind the altar. A wave of sheer relief washed over him as he replaced the bar across the door. He sank to his knees behind the door and sobbed. Tears rolled own his cheeks, till he thought he'd be completely dried up.

A good while later he heard a distant voice: "Is that you, Vee?"

He looked up to see Cianala moving along the passage, one hand carrying a lantern, the other outstretched feeling its way along the wall. He rose, ignoring the shooting pain in his shoulder.

"Yes. It is me. Let me hold the lantern and we'll go back to our rooms."

Something was amiss, seriously amiss. She knew it. She could feel the pain emanating from him.

"Are you hurt, Vee?"

He groaned as he sat down at the table opposite her. She rose and made her way cautiously around the table and laid her hands on his shoulders. He flinched.

"It's your shoulder, isn't it?"

He nodded, unwilling to speak. She could feel the movements of his head through her hands still resting lightly on his shoulders.

"Tell me what happened."

And while she listened to his story, she let her energy flow gently into her hands warming his shoulder. The white light stopped her visualising the inside of his shoulder, but her fingers still gave her an idea of what was wrong and where. She felt her hands soothe the tendons and unblock the muscles. By the time he told her how he made it back to their tunnels, his shoulder was much better.

"There," she said, taking her hands off his shoulders and

returning slowly to her seat. "Try moving your shoulder."

She heard a gasp of surprise.

"How did you do that?" "It is one of the things I learnt to do."

"Thank you, Nala." It was the first time he'd used the familiar form of her name.

Changing the subject, she returned to his story: "So the whole Cellerini Clan is upon us?"

"Yes."

"We need to get out of here fast. As soon as they realise I've gone, they'll be swarming over the castle and its grounds, hounds panting ahead of them, searching for us."

She heard him stand and begin pacing the room.

"If we try to flee on foot, we won't get very far. They have horses and hunting dogs."

She agreed, but what else could they do. He stopped pacing and came closer.

"Prepare things for the two of us to take on a journey. There are two backpacks in the kitchen. I'll go and explore beyond these rooms. I know the tunnel goes on but I've never been any further. Maybe I'll find a solution."

He took her hand to lead her to the larder, but she stopped him. She leant forward and aimed a kiss at his cheek, but missed and kissed his ear instead.

She laughed nervously, saying: "Be careful, Vee."

He squeezed her hand. Stepping away, he went into the tunnels that sunk deeper under the ground.

When she finished folding the two small blankets over the top of the food and drink and medical supplies and cutlery and much more, she heard him coming back. His footsteps were much faster than usual. Maybe it wasn't him. She pulled back into the larder wondering where she could hide. But it was him.

"Nala. Are you there?"

She came out of hiding and flung her arms around him, relieved.

"You're all wet," she said. "Were you out in the rain?"

190   Alan McCluskey

"Something much better," was all he would say as he slipped one of the backpacks on her back. Presumably he was taking the other one. "I'll tell you as we walk," he added.

Escape

And as they made their way down the path ever deeper under the rocks, he told her his story.

"... and then I heard a roaring noise. I couldn't figure out what it was. In such a confined place it sounded terrible."

She was walking next to him, her hand in his. He could see her face in the lamplight, intent on what he told her.

"Can you hear it, Nala?"

He knew they were getting closer.

"Yes. What is it?"

"A waterfall. A majestic waterfall that cascades into an underground lake that seems to stretch for miles. And there is a boat tied up along the shore. I thought maybe we could get out that way."

It was risky. Who knew where the lake went and whether they would find a way out? But one thing made him hope.

"There's a line made of stout cord that leads out across the water, suspended from poles sunk into the water. I suspect it is made for people in boats to follow so they don't get lost."

His last words he was obliged to shout, the noise of the waterfall was so loud. Shouting? Yes shouting. There was no end to the changes he was undergoing.

He led her to the water's edge and helped her climb into the waiting boat. The noise of the waterfall was muffled where they sat. She imagined there must be a rock in the way. She could hear the water lapping against the shores of the lake.

"Shall we do it?" he asked her.

She nodded. She felt the boat rock lightly as it moved out into the lake. She let her finger tips brush the water as her hand hung over the side of the boat to get a better idea of their movement. There were no oars, he had explained, so he pulled the boat hand over hand along the cord. As the water flowed through her splayed fingers, she thought of how much he had changed.

"The water is warm," she said surprised.

"You're right. It is beginning to steam a little."

She could hear the continuing noise of his hands on the cord. Worry grew as the warmth of the water increased and the air was increasingly filled with the smell of rotten eggs.

A sudden roar followed by a dense hissing startled her. Vee screamed.

"A hot water spout. Take out your blanket and wrap it around your shoulders and over your head. Protect yourself as much as you can."

"Are you all right?" she asked in return.

"A bit burnt. But nothing you can't heal when we reach the other side."

She could hear him rummaging in his own backpack. The water roared and hissed in several places close by.

"That was a near thing," he told her, clearly shaken. "That last spout barely missed the boat."

She could feel the heat now on her face, despite the blanket. She was beginning to sweat.

"Can you see anything?"

"No. We are in a thick mist. I see just the cord for about an arm's length in front of us."

Some while later, she felt the temperature begin to fall. There had been no more hot water spouts for several minutes. And the air no longer smelt so strongly of rotten eggs.

"Are we clear of it?" she asked.

"Looks like it," he replied. "But I can't see very far with the lantern. It is difficult to tell. We must have been moving forward for almost an hour."

Somewhere ahead she could hear a noise, which grew as they approached.

Suddenly, he shouted out in alarm. "It's a giant waterfall."

She huddled in the middle of the boat, holding on tight to the seat.

"Grab the cord," he shouted. "Help me pull us against the

current. The line cuts across in front of the fall heading for the bank. If we can make it, we'll be fine."

She grasped the cord with both hands and began tugging with all her force. She could feel the pull of the water, a great mass in movement, determined to drag them over the brink into the foaming depths below.

"We are nearly there," he called out.

She could barely hear him over the roar of the crashing water. Her arms ached; her hands were blistered. She didn't know how much longer she could continue.

"Made it," he said as he stepped out of the boat.

Without him putting his weight on the cord, the boat ripped free and moved off towards the fall. She hung on to the cord. Pulled out of the boat, she found herself suspended from the cord, her body buffeted by the water. She felt his hands next to hers on the cord as he came back to fetch her. They eased their way to the shore. Crawling onto the bank, they both collapsed side by side, exhausted.

They couldn't stay there. That was for sure. Clambering first onto all fours then standing, he felt around for the lantern. It had gone out when he set it down on the lakeside earlier in his rush to rescue her. He dried the lighter on his shirt and lit the lamp.

"Are you all right, Nala?"

He became alarmed when she didn't reply. As he bent over her to be sure she was still breathing, she opened her unseeing eyes and smiled at him.

"I'm OK."

He sat down beside her and took off his pack. Fishing out some fruit, he offered her an apple and a piece of cheese.

"There is a path over there. Let's eat, then we'll follow it."

She leaned her back against his knees and bit into the apple.

One of her hands resting on his shoulder to guide her, she followed him slowly along the path. Although she couldn't see where she was going, his description of what he saw in front of him allowed her to know what lay ahead. The path led to a narrow tunnel that finally opened out into a wider cavern.

"It's like a miniature underground railway station," Vee told her, excited at the find. "There are rails and there is a small open carriage big enough for four people. But there is no engine to pull it."

These people are well organised, she thought, they must have had some way of pulling the thing.

"Are we on a slope?" she asked. "Maybe we can free-wheel our way out."

He left her holding on to the carriage as he went to explore along the track.

"The way is flat as far as I can see," he said when he came back. "I'll just have to pull us," he said.

She reached out to take his hand. "We have no idea how far we will have to go, Vee. Even with your new found strength, I doubt if you could pull me for very long."

"Help me into the carriage, Vee, and climb in to join me."

They sat there in silence for quite a while as she puzzled over ways to get them out of there. Maybe she could use her force. Apart from healing Vee, she hadn't called on it since Connor had blinded her. Maybe he hadn't damaged it.

"Have we got all our things onboard, Vee? And is the door closed?"

"Everything is onboard, Nala, but there's no door. If we do get moving, we'll just have to hang on."

She breathed deeply, holding back the ever-present white light that pressed in around her.

"I'm going to use my force to push us down the line. You'll have to continue describing what you see ahead so I can guide us properly."

He shifted to sit next to her, both of them facing down the line, and began telling her what was ahead. She opened her mind and felt out for the walls around. Once she had them in her mind, she pushed gently. The carriage creaked and rolled forward slowly, only to stop a few feet further on.

"Hold on, Vee. I've got to do this differently."

The walls were too far away. She sent her thoughts out to

the rails behind her and pushed again. This time they moved forward and continued moving, gathering speed.

The underground railroad went on for hours. Vee was almost hoarse with his unending commentary, despite the occasional mouthfuls of water he used to moisten his throat. Nala was suffering too. She was shuddering with the continuous effort of propelling them down the tunnel. Vee could feel her every movement as they sat close to each other and what he felt worried him. Her breath was uneven and from time to time she started coughing and could hardly stop.

"Maybe we should stop and rest," he suggested.

"No. I think we are almost there. Give me your hand and send me your energy."

He did as she requested and could feel his energy seeping out of him. If they didn't arrive soon, neither of them would have any energy to go on. They had no idea what awaited them when they arrived. They might walk right into a trap. Shaking himself out of these grim thoughts he peered down the tunnel.

"Slow down, Nala," he whispered urgently. "There is a light up ahead. We need to get our strength back before we affront whatever is waiting for us out there."

She brought the carriage to a halt and sagged into his arms, exhausted.

He shifted her as best he could onto a wide platform that ran beside the track. He folded up his blanket and laid it under her head and spread her own blanket over her.

"Don't go to sleep yet, Nala. Stay with me. You must eat and drink something first."

She groaned. He could see she was shivering despite the blanket. He lay down next to her and put his arms around her trying to warm her up.

"Here, drink," he said after a while, offering her a small flask. "It's schnapps. It's not very good, but at least it will warm you up."

She coughed up the first mouthful.

"It's vile," she whispered.

"Drink a little, all the same."

He helped her sit up with her back leaning on the tunnel wall. He was pleased to see her sip the liquor. After a short time her shivering ceased.

"Now eat some of this bread and cheese."

She nibbled unenthusiastically then lay down under the blanket.

"Don't leave me alone, Vee," she whispered. "Stay with me. I need your warmth. I'm frozen to the marrow."

He lay down next to her, took her in his arms and snuggled up closer, nuzzling his nose into her hair. All was quiet lest it be for the faint sound of her breath that came regularly now. She was asleep. Nothing moved in the dark. And if anybody came, they probably wouldn't see them lying there. He was glad he'd taken the precaution of pushing the carriage away down the track. He relaxed and let sleep settle over him.

Chapter 9 - The Mansion

Ruins?

The late afternoon light was failing when they finally arrived. Somewhere, not so far away, he could hear waves crashing against rocks. Despite the rain, the smell of the sea was in the air. When was the last time it had stopped raining, Jake wondered. Maybe it had always rained.

He was soaked to the skin, they both were, but that was nothing new. Rain splashed into the puddles that lay strewn along the country lane. He should have been cold and miserable, but he wasn't. On the contrary, he was elated and that gave him a wild sort of warmth. He had come to enjoy and appreciate Mia's company, their love-making and her strange way of seeing things that often left him baffled.

They moved along the wall around the property till they came to a place where the stones had crumbled. Mia scrambled over the heap of rubble and jumped down into the grounds. He followed her, almost stumbling on the wet stones but she caught him in her arms, preventing him from falling.

She turned her back to him and rubbed her wet buttocks against his hardness, setting him on fire. He feverishly grabbed her hips and tried to pull her tighter against him seeking release, but his hands slipped hopelessly on the dripping fabric as she swayed from side to side. He had to laugh. And then he shivered. How could he be so hot and cold at the same time? She pulled away, leaving him panting and thirsting for her. Funny how the tables were turned now. It was him that frequently wanted her while she insisted on concentrating on making their way to her mother's place.

Dark, leafless trees huddled together in clumps trying vainly to hold off the rain. Mia shifted further away, hesitated a moment and then set off, avoiding the pathway that wove around the trees. Not so much out of fear of being seen, he realised, but more to avoid the deepening mud that threatened to carry away the path. Heading through the wood after her, he caught a glimpse of the roof of a deserted mansion in the distance as it fought for a place amongst the trees. She turned back to him and nodded.

When they finally reached the building, he was disappointed to see it was a ruin. Rainwater cascaded over blocked gutters leaving dark stains down walls. Shutters hung listlessly, half-open, failing miserably to protect anyone from anything. A dank smell filled the air reminiscent of rotting masonry mixed with fungus.

"Behold, my mother's place", she said leaning close so he could hear her over the driving wind and rain.

Her lips brushed his ear before she pulled away. She made him continually thirsty. He wanted to catch hold of her and crush her body against his as if that would break the spell that gripped him, but she swung gracefully up onto the wooden scaffolding that encased part of the building. He did the same, more cautiously, being careful not to slip on the moss that grew on the planks.

She clambered up a rickety ladder and climbed in through a broken window on the third floor. He set one foot on the ladder, then the other, testing each wooden bar to see if it would bear his weight. As he eased himself through the window he found himself alone in an endless, dark corridor that stretched the whole length of the building. For all its size, the place was stifling. There was no room to breathe. And Mia was nowhere to be seen.

The amphitheatre

Seeking relief, he crossed the corridor and tried the door opposite. Fresh air burst out to meet him followed by a shaft of light that flooded the darkened corridor where he stood. As his eyes adjusted, he saw before him a very large room that sloped steeply away down to a small podium on which an old man with a long beard sat talking.

"The original sin of the Church was exclusivity. It alone knew the one god and its god was the only one."

The spotless fittings and furniture surprised him as much as the light. He was startled by the contrast between the inside and the outside of the building. This amphitheatre didn't fit in the world they'd just come from. Below, a good number of people - many of the men dressed in matching gray suits - were intently listening to the old man's lecture, studiously taking notes.

Strangely however, platforms were scattered here and there amongst the students' benches on which tables were laid out for a candle-lit dinner as in one of the very best restaurants. Here too people sat quietly listening to the bearded man as he sat at his desk on the podium piled high with books and papers that overflowed disorderly onto the floor around him.

"So the church divided up the world, and sent out god's little soldiers to fight against the evil that it had created."

It is amazing how quickly we adapt, Jake thought. Having taken in the scene at a glance, it no longer seemed unusual. He stepped forward into the room, closing the door behind him, and threaded his way downwards, discreetly nodding to familiar faces that he couldn't quite place. Mia was nowhere to be seen. He found a free seat in the front row next to one of the new girls. He vaguely remembered she'd told him she came from an eastern country. Was it Russia or Bulgaria?

"Hi!" she whispered, kissing his lips softly.

He drew back surprised, but she leant towards him and placed her hand on his crutch squeezing his bulging prick between her fingers. What would people think? Jake wondered breathlessly as her hand lingered on his sex. Nobody seemed to be paying them any attention. Should he really be so surprised, after his experience with Mia?

Jake picked up the pen in front of him to continue taking notes. Don't ask how he could possibly continue as he had just arrived. That was just the way it was. Don't ask what the talk was about either. He had no idea. Although the bearded man continued to talk he could no longer hear a word he said. Or maybe he wasn't listening. Jake wasn't sure. The notes in front of him were full of weird hieroglyphs that he couldn't decipher. The amphitheatre and the restaurant were clearly in the same space but somehow they were not quite in the same world. And he seemed to be slipping almost imperceptibly from one to the other.

The scene reminded Jack of a treatise he'd read about the co-existence of multiple realities by Professor Josephina Schmidt. What had she said?

The restaurant with its tables and the circulation of waiters and waitresses between the tables and the kitchen is a distributed model. Whereas the amphitheatre with the attention focussed on the lecturer is a centralised system. The contrast between the two is accentuated by the difference between the sloping floor of the amphitheatre and the flat floor of the restaurant. The cohabitation of these two systems in one space says something about the difficulty of the individual to exist in the institutions he or she and society have created.

Several young waitresses in French maids uniforms serving at the tables caught Jake's eye. Turning, bobbing, bowing, with white laced edges. One of them came and stood close to Jake, her black skirt, amply supported by expansive petticoats, brushing against his hand. He felt like a throbbing dynamo, constantly charged with sexual energy that sought release at any price. One spark would be enough to ignite the whole place.

An elderly Scots lady with a shawl hung over her shoulders, was watching sternly their every movement. From time to time she made them an abrupt sign. A catering school probably, Jake thought. Maybe the woman was Mia's mother. The girl stationed next to him moved away to a table nearby. She seemed embarrassed, inexperienced, clumsy even. She was having a hard time he thought. He was not sure exactly what her difficulty was, something to do with serving. Or was it him.

The matron gave him a sharp look that could have killed and sent the girl to stand by the kitchen door. Wanting to be useful, Jake told himself, he offered to take her place. If he'd been honest, he'd have to admit that his offer wasn't really such a good idea. He was very good at taking notes, but when it came to serving he was really hopeless. The Scots lady, however, accepted his offer willingly. Jake wondered if she would dismiss the girl, but as he was so busy preparing to leave the room he was not to know.

Doing the waitress' job meant that somebody else had to take notes on the discussions for him. Pointless asking him how he knew, he just did. He had a special role: official note keeper of the meeting. Maybe that was why he felt he had already done one good deed that evening. He handed his notes to a tall girl in the back row, showing her what he had already written. Looking at his notes and the hieroglyphs she seemed quite alarmed at having to continue and muttered her discontent. Jake wasn't bothered. He just let her get on with it.

The kitchens

He stepped into the kitchen through the swinging doors next to the podium at the front of the room. Everything was noise and bustle and odours galore. The chopping of vegetables vied with smartly sizzling meat. A hiss as white wine met hot meat. Curry, marjoram, garlic, red peppers, parsley,...

He wondered how none of that overflowed into the quiet, sophisticated atmosphere of the amphitheatre next door. The door opened and the young waitress he was to replace followed him into the kitchen. She began hastily undressing until she was standing opposite him naked with her clothes in a neat pile in her hands. She handed them to him and left without a word. He buried his nose in the pile and inhaled the lingering warmth of her. He was going crazy, he thought, he'd got to get out of there.

As he looked up, he realised that the room had gone completely quiet and everybody was looking at him with disapproval, suspended momentarily in their movements. The spell was broken by a beefy cook who picked up a blood-spattered carving-knife and began edging towards Jake. Others looked around for saucepans, frying pans, ladles, rolling-pins, anything to deal a fatal blow … and moved almost imperceptibly in his direction. A silent wall of hatred aligned against him.

He set the neat pile of clothes down slowly on a table and without turning began inching cautiously backwards into the depths of the kitchen. Sandwiched between shelves piled up with pots and pans and lines of hanging sausages and dried meats, a small door beckoned. Yes! A way out. Before he stepped out, he grabbed the top of one of the shelves pulling the whole set crashing down across his path. Closing the door on the shouts that arose within, relief washed over him.

Now what? A large black Labrador lay sprawled on the marble floor. Both dog and floor were worn and pockmarked with age. Lifting its head wearily off its crossed paws, the dog growled threateningly, as if to say "… and where do you think you'd be going?"

No time to answer. How **do** dogs decide who they are going to bite and who they are going to lick? No time for questions either. Left? Right? Left! Gently does it. No panic, please. There. The foyer. And the lift. Just what he was looking for. Well, it had once been a lift. The doors were open, hanging precariously off the hinges. But the lift itself had gone. All that remained was the empty shaft and water cascading down where the lift had once been. Climbing plants had taken root along the water's edge, punctuated here and there by deep purple flowers. There were even some brightly coloured birds flitting back and forth in the spray that rose from the falling water. A strange sanctuary. He'd have to take the stone stairs up.

As he turned to leave, he collided with Mia who came pelting down the stairs, almost knocking them over. Panting for breath she said: "There ... you ... are."

She'd changed into a long nightdress: eggshell blue, all covered with wild flowers.

"I've been looking for you everywhere," she added, kissing him.

She grasped his hand and pulled him impatiently after her down the corridor.

"I want you to meet my Mum."

After his adventures in the kitchen, he was extremely glad to be back with her. She opened a door and stepped inside ushering him in after her. What struck him first was the great variety of colourful cloth than hung on the walls and covered the bookshelves and furniture, hues of yellow and green dominated, with a smattering of brown and a touch of red. The material rippled as a slight breeze came from the open window causing the place to spring into life. And as the breeze rippled through the cloth, heartfelt laughter mingled with the colours.

"So this is the young man you've told me so much about Mia." The woman's voice was rich and welcoming.

"Meet Elsie, my mother, Jake. Mum, meet Jake."

Jake turned towards the large bed where he saw a woman, who once must have been very beautiful. She was propped up on a copious pile of pillows, smiling at him. Jake was at a loss as to what to call her, to tell the truth he felt shy.

"Good day to you Ma'am."

"You can call me Mum, if you like. Everybody else here does. No? ... Well maybe not..."

She beckoned for him to come and sit in an armchair near her. Mia clambered onto the bed and slithered under the covers next to her mother, snuggling up close.

"I must apologise for the behaviour of Mia's 'Aunt'. Well she's not really an Aunt. Just someone who looks after Mia from time to time when I'm poorly."

Mia's mother had long brown hair that fell in curls across her shoulders, framing her pale face and those deep brown eyes.

"For someone who has a reputation as a storyteller, you don't seem to have much to say."

Mia peered at him from behind her mother, saying: "I do believe he's tongue tied."

"Now, now, Mia. Don't tease Jake. Fetch us some of my favourite eggleberry cordial from the kitchen."

Apparently not so happy about having to get up, Mia rolled off the bed and made her way to the door.

"You too, Jake?"

He had no idea what eggleberries were, but then, "Why not."

An errand

"Now young man, let's not waste any time. Mia will be back in a short while. Get me out of here."

Jake looked at her, astounded.

"I see you don't understand. Well it's normal I suppose. But we have no time for explanations. Suffice it to say that I'm a prisoner here in my own house and I absolutely must get away."

It was true she seemed to be stuck in bed, but she didn't appear to have been mistreated.

"Even if I believed you, I've no idea how."

She made a face as if she couldn't believe how stupid he was, then smiled. "With a story of course."

It might have seemed obvious to her, but Jake wasn't convinced at all.

"But what about Mia. Won't they take it out on her?"

"They might, but she's clever and anyway you are to come back here once you've carried me away."

Elsie pulled out a picture from under one of her many pillows and handed it to him. "Take a good look at this and then tell us a story about you and me in that place."

Jake looked closely at the picture. The thatched cottage was surrounded by a low dry-stone wall that had fallen down in one or two places, but the cottage itself seemed in good repair. Be-

204   Alan McCluskey

yond a forest of pine trees swayed gently in the breeze that blew in off the sea. Glancing behind himself he saw that the building faced out over the sea. Jake turned back to the cottage, opened the gate and took a few steps to the front door.

As he knocked it opened and Elsie greeted him. She seemed much healthier there. Gone was her pale complexion and she seemed to have no difficulty in walking.

"I'm glad you managed to make it Jake. Come inside."

She must have known he was coming because he could smell the scones cooking and the table was laid for two.

"Take a seat. I'll pour some tea. Then we can talk."

As she bustled around the kitchen fetching butter and jam, her transformation astonished him. You would never have thought that only minutes before she was ailing in bed.

"You have a very expressive face, Jake. Did you know that? You don't really need to tell stories, you can just let your face speak for you."

She laughed as she poured them both a cup of tea. In some way she reminded him of Mia. Was it the spontaneity? Or was it the completely physical way she went about life? She seemed to be earthy in an exciting sort of way. She sat down opposite him and offered him a scone.

"You like Mia, don't you?" she began. "And she likes you. A bit like earth and fire attracting each other."

She bit into her scone and munched silently for a moment. Jake thought it better to remain silent too.

"Mia and I are earth souls. People like you need us to balance your fieriness. You talk with words. We talk with our bodies. Much of your energy is channelled to your minds. Ours bursts out of our bodies in riotous pleasure."

She took hold of his hand and licked his fingers, pressing them against her lips. When he pulled his hand gently away she continued: "Making love to Mia must have been a torture to begin with."

It was Jake's turn to laugh. "You have no idea!"

She looked at him questioningly for a moment.

"Coming to terms with you wasn't easy for her either. Your words, your ideas probably hurt her a lot."

Jake couldn't remember Mia being hurt, well yes, when he had thought she was in league with her Aunt. He had betrayed her then.

"I see you remember."

He resisted the urge to get up and pace around the room.

"It makes you restless to realise how much you can hurt a sensitive person."

She leaned closer. He could smell the faint scent of fruit jam on her breath.

"You're OK, Jake. I like you. Mia has re-awakened the earth in you. You're not like those people who've taken over the mansion. They strive to be pure spirits: people of the word. They're hard and cold and deadening. Such people have always hunted down beings like Mia and I. We understand the Earth. We feel it in our bones, in our blood, in our thoughts. We terrify them. They can only think of stamping us out. Remember the witch hunts in the Real."

She paused for a moment looking carefully at his face.

"The people in the Mansion made me ill. Their thoughts made me ill. A little longer and I might have succumbed."

She laid her head on her cupped hands as if the thought of it was too heavy for her. Jake hesitantly put out his hand and ran it through her hair. He imagined her feeding on his caresses. After a while he stopped and she looked up at him, tears streaming down her face. He moved round the table and took her in his arms, feeling her warmth, her softness, her willingness.

Pushing him gently away, she said: "You must go back, Jake. Mia needs you. Take care of her for me. She's a treasure." She kissed him on the forehead and pulled away. "Just think of the room we were in and tell yourself a story…"

Clothes chase

But the room wasn't as he remembered it. Not only was Elsie no longer present, but also the long lengths of colourful material lay in strangled heaps on the floor. At that moment the door swung open and Mia entered carrying a tray of drinks. The instant she saw the cloth on the floor her eyes snapped to the empty bed.

"Where's Mum?" she mouthed.

He had no time to answer as two men in dark suits pushed past Mia into the room sending her tray crashing to the floor. She turned and fled. Thinking fast, Jake beckoned to the two men, pointing to the far side of the bed: "Help! Elsie's fallen out of the bed. I think she's hurt."

As the gray suits moved behind the bed to look, Jake bolted for the door and slammed it after him.

"Mia?" he called out.

But there was no answer. Running back to the lift shaft, he caught sight of someone scampering up the stairs.

The floor above was in a much better state than the area below: wall-to-wall carpets, crisp wallpaper, neat fittings and, above all, unlike the lift shaft, it was dry. A new world again. Pushing his way rapidly through the swinging door to the right he came across a group of young girls lounging on the plush crimson carpet, talking in hushed tones.

Dressed alike, they wore grey pleated skirts, white knee-length socks and crumpled blouses each. A tiny backpack lay open on the floor, its contents scattered in a half-circle: an alarm clock, a chewed pencil, a well-used novel, a notebook, a tube of discarded lipstick, some chewing gum, a packet of condoms, ...

They must have been sleeping there in the corridor, he concluded. Despite the hard floor, they seemed comfortable. It was a living language lesson. German in fact.

One of the girls pushed herself up on her elbow and asked "Shouldn't the word 'Amen' punctuate the end of the sentence in German?"

That struck him as tediously artificial. But an unseen teacher said she was right. "There'll always be an Amen at the end."

Ah learning! That's something to take risks for. Let me try, he thought. He wanted to ask about the missing comma in the sentence, but words failed him in German. How did you even say "Comma"? How silly of him to embark on such a complex task without being sure of the words first.

A girl had drifted apart from the others. She reminded him a lot of Mia.

"You should make an effort and speak English", he said motioning for her to come over, "I know you can."

He wanted to explain something. He picked up the notepad and scribbled down some words in English with the chewed pencil. The words wouldn't come out right. He had to score them through several times, much to his surprise, and try again. As she moved closer and touched his hand, an astonishing shockwave of presence flowed out from her, so strong it transcended the usual dimensions. Like a powerful odour that suddenly penetrates a world made only of colour and movement. Inviting. Invigorating. Inebriating.

It was only then that both of them saw the words he had written on the paper: 'Elsie' and 'OK'. Panicked, she pushed past him and fled down the corridor, running at top speed. It was Mia. She had somehow managed to disguise herself. He took off after her, following the trail of scent she left behind. Vanilla. Screams of laughter and taunting lascivious remarks pursued them down the corridor.

As he rounded the corner, he caught a glimpse of her rushing on ahead. He called after: "Wait, Mia. I need to talk to you!"

But she didn't. Around the next corner he spotted her white plimsolls discarded in front of a door. He picked them up, noted they were still warm and tried the doorknob. All was dark inside. Flicking the switch by the door turned on a weak bulb that cast more shadows than it did light. In the middle stood the only piece of furniture in the room: a double bed with a large bulge hidden under the covers. Moving gently for fear of scaring her, he shifted back the covers.

"It's me, Jake," he said, seeking to reassure her.

Disappointment. There was no beautiful shoeless girl under the covers, just a large, empty duffle bag. Picking it up, he slipped the shoes in the bag and went back out into the corridor.

Drawing the strings together to close it, he shouldered the bag and continued down the corridor leaving the door open behind him. The corridor ended in a short flight of stairs that led up to a further corridor that was narrower. It was lined on both sides by darkened oil paintings. Family portraits, maybe, the light was so bad, he could hardly make them out.

She must have continued here because Jake could still smell her vanilla perfume. He set off at a run down the gallery corridor that came to an abrupt halt when two corridors branched off to the left and the right. Which to chose? He sniffed his way down one, then retraced his steps and sniffed down the second. She'd taken the second.

As the corridor curved round he came across a faded armchair in an alcove under a dim lamp. Laid out neatly on the chair was the girl's blouse, tie and pleated skirt. Her socks, in contrast, had been cast higgledy-piggledy on the floor. Undoing the duffle bag, he slid the clothes carefully inside, bent down and picked up the socks, added them to the clothes and continued after her. He feared what he might find next on this weird vanilla-scented treasure hunt. He was beginning to think he should maybe run slower when an outstretched foot sent him sprawling on the floor.

"What will you be looking for, Master Jake?" a deep male voice asked.

Nursing his bruised elbow, Jake turned to look at the man towering above him. A beefy sort of guy, clean-shaven but certainly strong and muscular, with a toothless grin and the all too familiar gray suit.

"You won't be needing that," the man continued, picking up the duffle bag that had fallen at his feet.

Jake got on his hands and knees then eased himself up until he was standing opposite the man. "Where's Mia gone?" he asked.

The only answer he got was a hefty cuff around the head that sent him flying.

"Now piss off!" the bloke concluded. "You have five minutes. Then I'll come after you and if I catch you I'll stuff you in the bag and hang you out the top floor window."

Jake scrambled up and bolted down the corridor. So much for courage and determination.

Once round the corner, he stopped and listened. Silence. The suit was not following. Not yet, anyway. They must have got Mia, the smell of vanilla had evaporated. Should he double back? He imagined himself searching endless dusty rooms, uninhabited for years. He imagined nosing around long empty meeting rooms, filled only with desolate chairs. He opened cupboards, pulled out draws, pushed aside faded curtains. Nothing. No one.

A great deal later he stopped to catch his breath, leaning against an empty bookcase that had been shunted into one of the darker corners on a deserted landing. There seemed no end to these corridors and no sign of a way out. His feet and legs ached. His elbows hurt from the fall and he was sure the side of his face must be swollen. What's more, he was dreadfully thirsty.

He must have been running for hours, but he'd met nobody. He was stuck in a rut. Strange word that: 'rut'. He had to laugh. It struck him as hilarious. His laughter echoed alarmingly off the silent walls. Glancing around nervously, he hastily moved on.

At one of the frequent turns in the corridor, a narrow passageway led to a steep flight of stone stairs that curved down. Counting the steps as he eased his way down in the dark, he guessed he must have gone down three or four floors. The walls felt cold and damp against his outstretched fingers. After such a long descent, he was surprised at the extended flatness of the landing at the bottom. He stumbled forward pushing open a small door.

In the half-light he could make out a deserted kitchen. It was nothing like the kitchen he'd escaped from earlier. This one was smaller, more homely, but it hadn't been used for years. The floor was laid in large slabs of stone. A wide, wooden working surface filled the centre of the room. A blackened range ran the length of one wall, topped by a massive extractor hood.

Opposite him was a set of windows either side of a small door. It was from here that the light penetrated. The rose brushes outside had gone wild and almost entirely filtered out the sunlight. Under one window stood a sink graced with a single tap. It turned with some difficulty, but the water flowed fresh and clean. He let it flow cold into his mouth and drunk deeply.

His thirst finally slaked, Jake tried the door that opened inwards easily. To his disappointment, rose bushes blocked the path. Turning to look back at the kitchen, he spied a large breadknife abandoned on the work surface. Its serrated edge was still sharp. He picked it up and began sawing at the roses. It took him nearly an hour to break through into the brilliant sunshine. When his eyes were accustomed to the light, he saw he was standing on a large shingled terrace bordered by a stone wall, beyond which he could hear the sea.

Outside, inside and upside down

Exhausted, he sank down on a bench in the sun and took a deep breath. Laying the bread knife under the bench, he looked back at the mansion behind him. He expected to see a vast, sprawling edifice. After all, he'd spent hours in it. Instead he discovered a one-storey cottage. Turning back to look out over the terrace, he sighed with relief. At least he'd managed to get out and away from the clutches of the suits, although he'd lost Mia.

Slipping his hands into his jacket pocket, he felt the small white stones waiting for him. Memory flooded back as he remembered why he was there. Intentions were like water in the Realm. They slipped through your fingers when you tried to keep hold of them. Laying back against the bench and closing his eyes, Jake listened to the twittering of the birds playing in the sun and wondered if he would ever get to the end of his quest and find Nala. A sharp noise behind him in the house jerked him back from his thoughts. Glancing over his shoulder at the house, nothing seemed to be moving, but you could never be sure. He rose hastily and strode across the terrace to the sea wall.

Clambering over the granite blocks, the light shifted abruptly from bright sun yellow to vibrant emerald forest green. The innate sense of greenness was so potent it almost lifted him off his feet. Awareness of that latent power had led many to try to harness the energy of the Realm. Witches, warlocks, magicians, psychics, artists, soothsayers, time travellers, ... Jake thought of Dr. Leuchtli and his wild scheme. Channelling energy released when parts of the Realm folded back on themselves. But the power of the Realm was nothing like electricity or gas or petrol. It was a life-energy that flowed resolutely in the psychic realm.

A rusty ladder led down the side of the wall. All but the first two rungs were long gone. He felt for the other rungs with his foot. Maybe they were there beyond his sight. But he felt nothing. Lowering himself as best he could, he landed in the ruins of a small hut surrounded by trees and bushes. All was green and quiet and peaceful. The heaps of surviving masonry were covered with moss. Grass had forced its way between the tiles of the floor. He bent to examine an abandoned holdall that lay open before him. It gave off a distinct smell of mould that was compellingly familiar. Déja vu?

The bag was full of disused clothes: a printed dress with faded flowers; an old-fashioned bra with stays sticking out of it; a crumpled blouse that looked pale green in the prevailing light; tiny lace gloves; ... He shuddered, remembering Mia and the Mansion he'd just left. There were also crinkled newspaper pages from the war period, much of the print lost with time, and a couple of fashion magazines full of smart celebrities. Nothing that could be of value, he thought, nothing worth getting lost for.

He stepped over the threshold in a low wall beyond the ruins and the light changed again: sinking deeper, a dark brown, almost black, although he could still see dimly. On either side of the corridor that stretched away into the gloom sat silent men. Thoughtful and unmoving. They might have been statues had it not been for their eyes turned expectantly towards him. Some-way down the corridor he saw a brightly coloured stone that sang in the dark. As he set out towards it, the old men keeled over backwards out of sight and the floor began to crumble. Soon, only the squared timbers between the floorboards remained forcing him to tread gingerly from one to the next. As he stretched forward to recover the stone, it slipped off the beam on which it was poised and fell noiselessly into the dark reaches below, pulling him in after it.

Chapter 10 - The Littl' People

Caught in the net

"Twenty-two. Twenty-three. Twenty-four. Twenty-five. Twenty-six." The deep, throaty voice ceased counting.

"That should do it," another male voice answered, echoing off the walls. "'ang the net across the passageway."

A thickset man, not more than four feet high, came into view carrying a lamp and a staff. Tools hung from around his belt.

"The moment anyone touches it, we'll know."

The little man set his lamp down on the ledge not far away from them and began hammering nails into the rock. The blows reverberated around the confined space. Vee prayed Nala wouldn't call out. He didn't dare move with the men so close. Thank heavens they were both covered in grey blankets.

"How much time 'ave we got before she gets 'ere?" The first voice asked.

"Dunno. She was seen a day ago near the lake. Maybe an hour, maybe much more." The hammering stopped.

"OK. Let's get out of 'ere."

Vee slid his hand over Nala's mouth to stop her calling out in fright and whispered urgently: "Are you awake, Nala?"

"What was that noise? It woke me," she asked, alarmed.

He explained briefly. "We need to leave straight away."

"No." Nala disagreed. "If we leave now, we might walk straight into them. Is there no other way out of this tunnel?"

"We can't go back. Their net is blocking the way."

Nala thought for a moment and then said: "Well maybe if they think I'm on the other side of the net they won't be watching the entrance. Let's try. But first you must reconnoitre."

Vee didn't like the idea. So much could go wrong. But he preferred her hope to his own pessimism. He got to his feet, rolled up his blanket, donned his backpack and said: "Get ready to leave." He handed Nala her pack and added: " Stay back on the ledge against the tunnel wall while I go and see what's happening at the entrance."

"Be careful, Vee" was all she said, although he could hear concern and more in her voice.

After a prolonged stay in the dark, the sunlight shone harsh on his eyes. The leaves of a large number of trees that grew around the entrance to the tunnel were not enough to filter out the light. Vee blinked several times trying to focus. A small rustic village had grown up at the edge of a forest a short distance from the tunnel, or rather tunnels, because the village was strategically placed at the mouths of many tunnels into the hillside at the end of what appeared to be a narrow valley.

Close by he could hear the clang of metal on metal from a smithy. A large chimney in the midst of a slate-covered roof carried the smoke up and away from the surrounding houses. A similar chimney had been set up in a neighbouring building that looked like a covered forum open on all sides. Benches and tables were grouped irregularly under its roof around a kitchen fire set up in its middle. These people must form a close-knit community if they all ate together. Women, even smaller than the man he'd seen earlier, were busy around the fire, presumably preparing their next meal.

People were moving back and forth between the buildings and the tunnels. It wasn't going to be easy to escape unnoticed. He was about to turn back into the tunnel when a strident whistle went off behind him setting men running from all over the village in his direction. There was nowhere to hide, so he pressed himself hard against the rough stonewall and hoped some of his former invisibility would save him from detection.

Nala had done as Vee had suggested, she'd crawled back from the edge of the ledge and, thinking it wise to be really sure, she had sought an alcove or small cave in which to hide. None was immediately apparent as she felt her way along the wall. Heavily handicapped by her blindness she found it difficult to judge distances. She knew she was moving away from the tunnel entrance, but she hadn't realised how far she had gone when her hand brushed a thin string strung across the passage. Even such a slight touch had been enough to set off the alarm, filling the air with an ear-piercing whistle.

She could hear people running into the tunnel. Their heavy footsteps and their throaty shouts were loud enough to be heard over the alarm.

"It's 'er. I'll look after 'er." A guttural male voice said. He smelt of sweat and spirits and pipe tobacco.

"'ow come she's 'ere on this side o' the net?" another voice asked.

"We can think on that later." He was clearly the leader, Nala thought, although he sounded as coarse as his smell. "Stop that alarm. And the rest of yer check if anyone else was with 'er."

The leader pulled her off the ledge and slung her over his shoulder in one muscular movement. Nala had decided to keep quiet but, as her stomach hit his shoulder, she let out a gasp as all the wind was knocked out of her.

The other man, who apparently hadn't yet obeyed orders, slapped her exposed buttocks saying: "We'll 'ave some fun tonight."

She squealed and kicked out hitting him in the face. She heard him grunt with pain as he fell to the floor. Steeling herself against the blows she was sure would come, she was surprised when the leader set off at a jog, calling out over his shoulder.

"Serves yer right, yer bloody fool. Get on with what I told yer to do."

She knew they had left the tunnel because the quality of sounds around her changed. No longer so enclosed and stifling, they tended to stretch out, only occasionally coming back from further afield. And then there were the birds and the rustling of the breeze in leaves. Nala heard cries go up from some people nearby and, judging from the jumble of voices both male and female, a crowd had gathered around the man who'd stopped jogging and was setting her upright next to him with great care.

"El'na," he said. "Take 'er down to the stream and get 'er cleaned up. And find 'er new clothes." And as an afterthought he added: "And take care of 'er, she's blind."

Exclamations of shock went up from the crowd. The little man sent them all back to their work. Judging from the way they moved off without further comment or complaint, they all respected or feared him.

A small hand grasped hers. "This way missy," a sweet little voice said, gently pulling her in the direction of the sound of water. "I'm El'na."

The girl kept up her soft chatter all the way to the stream giving Nala a fragmented glance into life in the community. The men worked the mines, mostly extracting gems and some precious metals. They also made arms and jewels. That was what the smithy was for. The women tended the village. They looked after the garden and the hearth, made the food and cared for the ill and wounded. There was a common kitchen and places to store food and wood for the fire. They all ate together. They didn't live in couples. The women moved from man to man as it suited them. D'rick, the man who'd carried her into the village, was their leader. Had been for years.

"And this is where we women wash. The men 'ave another place nearer the mines. Don't worry we're all alone. Just yer and me."

They stopped close to the water and the girl helped her sit down.

"Let's get those clothes off yer. They're filthy."

El'na began undressing her and then helped her into the water. Nala squealed with surprise at how cold it was. El'na laughed.

"Yer'll get used to it," she said handing Nala a cake of lavender soap. "Would yer like me to wash yer?" the girl asked.

Nala was undecided about how she felt at the prospect of being washed by someone she didn't know and couldn't see. It would certainly be easier. So she agreed. The girl was efficient and rigorous in her efforts. When El'na rubbed her dry at the end of the bath, Nala wasn't sure if her skin stung from the coldness of the water or the thoroughness of the washing.

The girl slung a large cloth over Nala's shoulders and led her off in another direction, away from the noise of the stream but also away from the distant clang of the smithy.

"We're goin' to the w'men's 'ouse. That's where we meet from time to time, just us w'men. And that's where we make and keep all our clothes."

Thinking that she might do well to have an ally in this girl, Nala told El'na her name.

"Cian'la!" the girl exclaimed with pleasure. "What a beautiful name."

Nala couldn't help liking the girl. "Most people call me just Nala."

Clearly the girl felt that she was being given a great privilege because she knelt before Nala on the path and asked for her blessing. Not sure how to react, Nala place her hands on the girl's crinkly hair and stroked it ceremoniously for a moment saying: "I grant you my blessing, El'na."

Nala could hear that the girl was softly shedding tears. "Why are you crying, El'na?"

The girl blew her nose as they set off along the path. "Yer so kind to me. I'm nobody special and yet yer bless me."

Nala was beginning to wonder in what role she was being cast. El'na seemed to think Nala was someone very special. Why else would she have asked her to bless her? Why else would she have been so moved? Nala didn't have time to pursue her musings though because they had reached the "w'men's 'ouse" as El'na called it.

"'ere we are."

The place smelt strongly of cloth and dyes and delicate perfumes. Nala could hear the regular clack of a loom at work and the snipping of scissors.

"This is Cian'la!" El'na announced proudly to the women present. "She's the one wot's come to us from under the mountain."

Nala could sense the women gathering round and she felt the more adventurous amongst them touch her hair briefly.

"Keep back!" El'na called out. "We need clothes for 'er."

Two women measured Nala while El'na continued her explanations. Nala hadn't realised they were going to make her clothes. But it made sense, of course. They couldn't possibly have anything to fit her size.

"We w'men wear br'tches and blouses like the men,"

As El'na spoke, the girl stood on a chair so she could brush Nala's hair.

"You do that so well," Nala complimented her.

"Thank yer, Cian'la."

A long, slightly embarrassed silence followed punctuated only by the sound of the loom and the scribblings of the women as they finished taking down her measurements.

After a while El'na stopped her brushing and said: "We'll make yer br'tches and a blouse too, but in a lighter material 'cause we wanna make yer something special: a long gown that yer can wear o'er the rest."

The women had begun whispering amongst themselves as they moved away. Although she couldn't catch what was being said, Nala thought she sensed disagreement.

"Please tell me what's going on, El'na," she pleaded.

"We can't decide what colour'd be best for yer."

"Let me feel the material and I will choose."

The girl took her hand and led her to a low table. "This linen'd be for the br'tches," she said laying Nala's hand on three bundles of cloth.

"This one," she said picking the bundle in the middle because it felt right to her.

"Oh that's lovely. A very pale sandy y'llow."

Nala also chose the same colour for her blouse.

"Now the silk for the gown."

Nala had never realised how soft and sensual silk was. She chose a pale green that El'na said went well with her hair.

While they waited for the material to be cut and sown together for her to try, El'na led her to another table and encouraged Nala to lie down on her back. Nala wondered at the spontaneous trust she had in these people. She tried to figure out how she could accept to lie naked on a table and let herself be massaged by one of these people.

Only a short while earlier she'd been convinced there were going to catch her and hand her over to Connor. El'na's loving and caring attentions had done much to set her at ease. The girl was an excellent masseuse. In another life, in other circumstances, Nala would have been delighted to have her as a lover. But here and now she just let herself relax and enjoyed the sensations as El'na's hands roamed over her body.

When she awoke, she found that El'na had covered her with a blanket. As she stirred, El'na asked softly: "Are yer awake?"

Nala nodded and squeezed the girl's hand.

"Thank you. That was delicious."

Nala couldn't understand why, but she had the impression that her thanks embarrassed the girl.

"Yer clothes're ready. Let's try 'em on."

The fit was excellent and very few adjustments were necessary. When the final stitching had been completed, El'na dressed her and let her turn round and round slowly so the other women could admire the result. She had to hand it to them, the clothes were excellent: so light and comfortable. Running her hands over the cloth she realised it was strong too and would wear well.

As she turned slowly in the middle of the w'men's 'ouse, Nala thanked them all for making her such beautiful clothes. Loosing some of their awe for her, the women drew closer, forming a tight group around her, touching her hair and her shoulders, each whispering her name as if it were a good luck charm or an incantation or perhaps even a blessing.

The men's place

A thick pall of pipe smoke hung over the room, cloaking sight and sound alike. Vee had to get closer. Intuition told him that something important was about to happen. He moved away from the empty space in one corner of the men's haunt from where he'd been watching the Littl' People, as they called themselves, and eased himself closer to the group of men.

Tankards of beer crowded a central table around which the little men congregated, squatting on the ground or perched on small one-legged stools. Vee had been surprised to see that each man was intently working silver into necklaces encrusted with jewels. From time to time one of them would reach for a tiny hammer on his belt and beat the metal into a new shape.

"No. We can't do that," one voice rose above the mass. It was the man who'd carried Nala off earlier that day. D'rick the others called him.

"But we've sent out invitations all over …," someone else said.

"The coming of the Pr'ncess changes everything."

"But I don't understand," the first man pursued. "

"Yer wouldn't would yer. Yer not from 'ere, are yer."

Others muttered their agreement, not bothering to remove their pipes from their mouths.

"We Littl' People knew she'd come. We've bin waitin' for 'er for centuries. Our legends foretell 'er comin'. She's to save all our lives."

The men spontaneously broke into song: a deep chorus that wound as intricately around the solo of the leader as the exquisite jewellery taking shape in their hands. Vee was profoundly moved as the music penetrated deep inside him.

Watching through his tear filled eyes, he noticed the outsider, the one who'd raised questions earlier, was the only one not singing. Vee didn't trust him. He could see the man edging slowly towards the exit only to be stopped as the song came to an end by a solid group of men who dragged him back before the leader.

"Only someone as stupid as yer would dare lay an 'and on the Pr'ncess like yer did in the tunnel," he said with scorn and distaste.

The outsider had given up struggling, though Vee could see he was steeling himself to escape at the first occasion. But the Littl' People weren't to be fooled. The leader stepped forward and, while the others held the man in a vice-like grip, D'rick placed his hand firmly on the man's shoulder causing him to crumble in a heap unconscious at his feet.

"Bind 'im. And shut 'im in an empty cupboard."

When the men came back, D'rick climbed up on the table and addressed them all.

"In two days we 'old the mark't. Ain't no way we can put it off."

He went on to explain that people from all around had been invited months ago to come and buy the jewels they'd made over the past year. They were expecting a large turnout as the Cellerini clan was in residence at the castle not so far away and they were big spenders, despite their long standing feud with the Littl' people.

Vee wanted to turn and run at the mention of the Cellerini Clan. Had they made their journey under the mountain for nothing? He had to warn Nala and get her away as quickly as possible. His attention was drawn back to D'rick who was still talking: "… so we need to keep the Pr'ncess away from them Cellerini people, they're 'orrible with w'men."

Several voices broke out at once but he quickly silenced them.

"We'll call a Meet in two 'ours. We'll greet the Pr'ncess and explain to 'er what's 'appening. And ask 'er advice."

Vee took the opportunity to slip away. Two hours might just give him the time to find Nala and warn her.

"In two 'ours we'll 'old a Meet so we can welcome yer to the Littl' People. Would yer like to wait 'ere in the W'men's 'ouse or go outside?" El'na asked.

"I'd love to be outside. Somewhere I can sit quietly under a tree. I need to be alone to think." That might give Vee a chance to reach her unnoticed.

El'na took her hand and led her amongst the sewing tables to the door.

"There's a giant oak not far from 'ere. And there's a bench yer can sit on, 'though it might be a bit low for yer. We call it the Lover's Nest 'cause it's where some of us w'men like to meet our men folk."

Outside the air was ripe with life. Distant sounds wafted over from the mines: heavy wooden wheels rolling on loose stone paths; picks ringing out against unforgiving stone; deep throaty voices grunting with unseen efforts; ... She could also hear a group of men, farther off, laughing and singing together.

Nearby the fragrances of flowers rivalled with bird song for her attention. She hadn't felt so happy for a long time. Squeezing El'na's hand in gratitude, she began humming a dancing tune. In reply, El'na raised Nala's hand to her mouth and gave it a timid kiss.

"'ere's the Lover's Nest. I'll go 'nd wait for yer over there by another tree. I've got some sewin' to do. Now don't yer go meeting any men," El'na said laughing. "If yer need me, call out."

Nala leaned back against the tree trunk and inhaled deeply. How good it was to feel safe and cared for.

"Nala," a voice whispered right next to her.

It took all her self-control not to jump up startled.

"It's me, Vee."

She felt his hand take hers. Relaxing back against the tree she let out her in-held breath.

"You startled me, you silly man."

"I had to see you. It's urgent. Connor will be here in two

days."

His words shattered her peace and feeling of wellbeing.

"Surely he can't have found us," she whispered.

Vee told her what he'd heard in the Men's Haunt. So they had two days, she thought. Surely that should be enough to get far away. They had no more time to talk because El'na came running over to her.

"Did I 'ear a man's voice?" she asked excitedly.

Nala couldn't understand the girl's reaction.

"Silly girl. You can see there's no one here but me."

She could have burst out laughing at the weirdness of the situation as Vee was still holding her hand.

"That's the point," El'na replied enigmatically.

"Is there something you are not telling me, El'na?" Nala could hear the girl shifting uncomfortably in front of her.

"Tis not for me to say. D'rick'll tell yer all there's to tell."

Greeting the Princess

The forum was packed, El'na told her. All the Littl' People were there. As they waited outside in the shadows, Nala wondered if Vee had been able to follow them.

"When D'rick says, we walk into the middle of the room. I'll be 'ere to guide yer," her little friend told her.

Apparently their leader had made some unseen sign because El'na said: "Tis time."

Although she couldn't see them, Nala felt the pressure of many eyes watching her. The place was electric with expectation. Reaching the middle of the room, D'rick took her hand and turned her round.

"Welcome Cian'la."

She really liked the way the Littl' People pronounced her name and would willingly have had it pronounced that way by her friends.

"My people 'ave been waiting ages for this moment. Our legends tell o' the comin' of a tall w'man from out o' the mountains that will save all our lives."

So that was it. But it couldn't be her.

"How do you know it is me?"

"I'm certain. But there is one test."

Here we go, she thought. Is it going to be walking through fire or living under water, she wondered, mocking herself.

"Our legend says that the w'man will speak both with the voice of a w'man and a man."

"And your legend is quite right!" spoke up a familiar male voice right next to her. It was Vee, she felt him take her hand as they stood together before the assembled Littl' People: one seen but unseeing and the other unseen but seeing.

For Nala the effect was totally unexpected. The whole gathering burst into song, men and women alike taking the lead from D'rick whose bass voice intertwined with El'na's soprano in a heart-rending duo rising above the collected choir. Tears streamed down Nala's face as Vee put his arm around her shoulder to share her joy and sadness.

"Don't doubt yourself, Nala," he whispered in her ear. "You may really be here to do what they say."

Their joy and their faith touched her but, despite that, she had been deeply saddened at first, thinking that the two of them were misleading these trusting Littl' People. But maybe Vee was right, maybe D'rick was right, maybe all the Littl' People were right, maybe she was there to help. Though she didn't know how.

As the sound of singing settled, the electric expectation had given way to tenderness and hope. D'rick addressed her again.

"In two days we 'old our annual Mark't. Tis where we sell our jew'ls. People come from all around. Amongst them there'll be the Cellerini Clan. We feel we 'ave to protect you from 'em, but we wanted yer advice."

Vee replied for her. "They imprisoned us before we came here."

He'd apparently opted for the 'we' instead of the 'me', she noticed. Shocked exclamations burst from the assembly. D'rick quietened them.

"We managed to escape under the mountain. Now we must escape from them again. You must help us."

Mutterings filled the air. Nala was afraid they thought they were going to lose their legendary hero having just found her.

"It was Connor that blinded me," she revealed.

The place was in an uproar. Nala could hear benches being overturned as people stood in anger. She could imagine them waving their clenched fists in the air above their heads.

"For all our anger at what they've done to yer and for all the years that they've tried to drive us away, we can't make war on the Cellerini Clan. They're too powerful. And we can't 'ide yer 'ere."

"Is there no safe place you can take us before they arrive?" Nala asked.

"What about the Lost Meadows?" El'na asked. It was the first time the girl spoke and Nala imagined it had taken courage to do so.

A disturbance had broken out at the back of the room. Vee whispered in her ear that one of the Littl' People was pushing his way through the crowd to the front surrounded by several others. The assembly had gone completely quiet as the man spoke up.

"The outlander's escaped."

D'rick asked for details, handling the situation with calm and efficiency.

"So he was a spy," he concluded.

"We need to get Cian'la to safety," El'na insisted.

"You're right," was all D'rick said as he dismissed the assembly and ushered Nala, closely followed by Vee, into a nearby house. El'na continued to guide Nala.

"The Lost Meadows are a country beyond the mountains full o' rolling 'ills, gentle streams and the occasional tree. Nobody lives there but birds and littl' animals. It can only be reached through our tunnels. The mountains form a wall around the country, protecting it."

The idea sounded good to Nala, but something was troubling her. These people were so open and trusting with her yet she kept Vee a secret.

"D'rick. I want to tell you something important. We have a confession to make. Your legends speak of me as someone with two voices: one male and one female. You have heard those voices and they are real enough, but I feel duty bound to tell you that there are really two of us. The male voice belongs to my friend Vee who accompanies me on my adventures and who saved my life. You think it comes from me, but only because you cannot see him. I'm sorry. I didn't wish to deceive you and I don't want to disappoint you in telling you this."

D'rick remained silent for a while. Nala began to wonder if he was angry but when he spoke there was laughter in his voice.

"That's 'ow yer see things, Cian'la. We see 'em differently. One day, maybe, yer'll realise that yer and Vee, as you call 'im, are one."

She was sure Vee was as confused as she was because he remained as silent as her. El'na broke the silence.

"I'll get yer all something to eat while we discuss 'ow to get yer to the Lost Meadows."

All agreed to her suggestion as it was late and they hadn't eaten for a while.

Escape into the tunnels

"They're coming," she heard a man shout as he ran across the village towards them. "The lookouts 'ave spotted 'em. The whole bloody Clan."

Nala rose in terror, waves of anxiety washing over her, her knees shaking.

"That spy must 'ave told 'em 'ow to get through our defences. El'na, get Cian'la to the tunnel. Take 'er to the Lost Meadows. Watch o'er 'er as best yer can. May yer be blessed g'rl. Do well."

D'rick took Nala's hand and pressed it against his lips.

"May yer be blessed, Cian'la. And may yer watch o'er us and save us when the time comes."

"Will you fight the Clan?" she asked.

"No. We'll take refuge in the tunnels. That's wot we always do when they come against us. They'll ne'er be able to get at us there."

Nala realised she was crying again. It seemed to happen often these days.

"I'm so sorry for the trouble I've caused you."

"You will ne'er be a trouble to us Cian'la."

He moved away shouting orders to the Littl' People as they prepared to flee into the tunnels.

"Maybe you should stay with your people, El'na. You may not be able to get back from where we are going. Although I've been blinded, Vee can see and he can guide me."

They were sitting in a small-wheeled carriage that fit snugly on the rails somewhere near the entrance to one of the tunnels.

"D'rick told me to look after yer. I'll do what 'e said. And anyway, accompanying yer is my life's joy. I would do anything for yer, Cian'la."

Nala kissed her friend's hand and turned to Vee.

"Are you still with us, Vee?"

He was.

"Can you describe our journey to me, Vee, like you did last time? Let me see through your eyes."

So he began describing their journey through the mountain…

"What's that noise I hear behind us, El'na?" Nala asked after they'd been travelling for about an hour.

"I 'ear it too, but I don't understand it. If I didn't know better, I'd say it was 'orses." The girl sounded worried.

"It is horses," Vee confirmed. "We're being followed and they're closing fast. We need to get away quick or find somewhere good to hide."

To Nala's surprise, El'na stopped the carriage and stepped out.

"I need to turn this 'ere wheel. Do yer think yer could 'elp me?" she asked Nala.

"Vee will help."

She could imagine the girl's surprise at being helped by a man she couldn't see. As El'na and Vee clambered back into the carriage they set off again in a different direction for a short distance.

"Vee?" El'na asked, sounding very nervous about speaking to someone she couldn't see. "Could you take this small sack and leave it just before the place where we turned?"

When Vee came back, they set off again.

"What was in the bag?" Vee whispered.

"'orrible smelly smoke," was her gleeful reply. "That should amuse 'em a while," She chuckled.

Indeed, they could hear coughing and spluttering way behind them.

Half an hour later, they could hear the distant noise of horses' hooves behind them again.

"What now?" Nala asked.

"I'm gonna pay 'em back for blinding yer Cian'la. It's more risky though."

She explained what she planned as she worked on the rock face beside the carriage. They moved a short way further down the track and waited.

"Mind yer both keep yer eyes well closed, even yer, Cian'la. Best cover yer eyes with yer 'ands. If this goes wrong I'll be as blind as yer Cian'la," she added grimly.

Minutes later, Nala knew the trap had worked by the screams of horses and men alike. Then she heard El'na's urgent voice.

"'elp me back into the carriage. I can't see a bloody thing."

Vee heaved her on board and they set off again.

"With any luck the effect'll wear off soon. Yer'll have to be the eyes for both of us in the mean time, Vee."

Her friend seemed to be getting used to the presence of Vee. She certainly seemed less disturbed by talking to him and asking him to do things.

"There should be a turnin' to the left soon. We need to take that."

The girl had an extraordinary memory of the tunnels. No wonder D'rick had said the Littl' People would be safe there.

To their great despair, some time later, the clop of hooves resumed its pursuit. At least one of the riders must have been too far back to be blinded by the blast.

"I think there's only one of 'em," El'na whispered. "Can you fight, Vee?" she asked.

"I'm hopeless at it," he admitted. "But I'll try."

Nala tried to put a veto but Vee wouldn't accept.

"Take this big club, Vee," El'na said. "If they can't see yer, maybe yer can club 'em before they know what's 'appening. And 'ere's a little knife. Yer can attach it to yer belt, if yer've got one."

They left the carriage in the middle of the track and Vee helped Nala and El'na hide in a small cave. Then he returned to await the enemy.

The first Vee saw of them was an approaching light. They were being cautious now after so many traps. A horse trotted skittishly into view followed by a second. Two then, he thought. He had to wait till they dismounted. He'd have no chance against them on horseback. They must have known they'd be more vulnerable on foot because they hesitated a long time before dismounting.

He'd have only one chance, so he had to wait till both men had walked past him before hitting the last of them. He pressed himself hard against the rock wall as the two men moved forward, swords drawn. They were so close he could smell the stink of them. As they passed he raised the club and took aim at the second man's head. The blow made a deafening noise in the confined space. The man staggered to his knees and collapsed face down on the tracks.

Vee eased away, hoping the clatter of the man's fall would cover any noise he made in moving across the tunnel. The first man moved to where Vee had been and struck out into nothingness with his sword. The man was getting desperate. He slashed from side to side trying to get in a hit on his invisible prey.

Vee would have no chance of getting close enough to hit him if he continued those wild slashes. The horses were neighing nervously only a stone's throw away.

Now there was a good idea. He bent down carefully and picked up two stones. Waiting till the man's head was turned he threw a stone at the horses head, uttering a silent prayer of excuse to the animal. The horse bolted forward, knocking the man to one side. The second stone had the other horse following the first, kicking the man out of the way. It was all Vee needed. He stepped forward and hit the man as hard as he could with the club. The man doubled over and fell in a heap on the floor.

Relief flooded over Vee. He hated fighting. He'd never been good at it. But he congratulated himself. Raising his club once more he brought down a stunning blow on the man's head, just to make sure. A dreadful muffled cracking sound followed by gruesome gurgling made him think he must have killed the person. He turned to take the same precaution with the other man and then take their horses away, but as he came close to the reclined man a hand shot out and grabbed him by the foot, up-heaving him and throwing him down on the track. The blow knocked the wind out of him. But there was no time to think as the man had crawled on top of him and was grasping Vee's throat with his giant-sized hands.

Vee gasped for air, struggling to push the man off. As he did, his hand brushed the knife in his belt. Pulling it out, he drove it with all his force into the man's chest. The guy collapsed on top of Vee suffocating him even further. With the last of his strength, Vee rolled to the side, relieved when the man slipped off him. He lay there panting desperately for a while before he got up onto his hands and knees and crawled away from the body. It was only then that he realised he was soaking wet. Blood. At first he was terrified that it was his own. But he couldn't feel a wound anywhere. Getting shakily to his feet, he became certain it was the blood of the man he'd killed. Thanks heavens neither of the girls could see him. He must look a terrifying sight.

"Nala. El'na," he called out. When they replied he said,

"Stay where you are. I'll come and get you."

Both wanted to know what had happened.

"There were two of them. I got them both."

They congratulate him. It was Nala who noticed the blood.

"What's that smell? Are you hurt?" she questioned, clearly worried.

"It's blood. But not mine. I had to stab the guy. He was trying to strangle me. The smell's disgusting. El'na, is there any water near here for me to wash?"

The underground lake was much smaller than the one Nala and Vee had crossed earlier but it was more than enough for Vee. El'na had shown them a small cabin full of stores and a change of clothes.

"We 'ave lots of these in the tunnels, if e'er there's a problem."

None of the clothes fit Vee, but a cloak kept him warm while his shirt dried. With Vee's help El'na was able to find the hidden medical supplies so she could smear a balm on her eyes.

"I'm beginnin' to see again, though only vaguely," she announced. "And there was me thinking I could be like Cian'la," she said laughing.

As they sat down to eat, Nala asked the girl how far they were from the Lost Meadows. Several hours was the answer.

"Shouldn't we have taken the horses? They'd come in useful in those meadows." Vee suggested.

"No need," was El'na's reply. "There are tame horses in the Lost Meadows."

The Lost Meadows

Helped by Vee, El'na led them out of the tunnels through a narrow exit just large enough for one person. Then he went back for Nala. Birdsong greeted Nala as she turned to face the sun that must have been midway to the zenith. A slight breeze stirred her hair as Vee placed a hand on her shoulder.

"Tell us what you see, Vee," she asked, knowing that El'na had not yet fully regained her sight.

"We are standing on a small grassy plateau with towering mountains at our backs. Beyond lie gently rolling hills covered with wild grasses and the occasional tree. Here and there horses are feeding on the grass. There's even a cow and some sheep not far off. In the distance, a ring of mountains encircles the meadows."

"Tis like I remembered it," El'na added. "'elp me Vee. We must roll that big stone across the entrance to stop anyone followin'."

El'na led them along a winding path through the meadows. As they walked, she told them stories of her childhood expeditions to the Lost Meadows. Stopping only when all three reached a small shelter half hidden by the tall grasses in a dip in the ground.

"There should be some wood 'ere," she told them as she rummaged behind the shelter.

"Your eyes are getting better then," Vee commented.

"Yes. In a day or two they should be back t' normal."

Nala sat with her back against one of the pillars of the shelter which was open on all sides like the Littl' People's meeting place. She could hear El'na laughing some way off as the girl helped Vee find edible plants. No she wasn't jealous. It was difficult to explain. She hadn't had much time to think of her relationship with him. It was as if Vee was so close to her that she felt no danger in sharing him with El'na, especially as she liked the girl very much. If the two fell in love, it would suit her fine.

"There's a stream nearby," Vee told her as they returned. "We washed the vegetables and collected water to make a soup." He set about building a fire.

"Would yer like me to take yer to the stream to wash, Cian'la?" El'na asked.

It was just what she needed. After the mines, she felt dirty and sticky with sweat and dust. Hand in hand they went to the water's edge where El'na helped her undress. The girl took her hand intending to lead her into the water, but Nala resisted, pulling her close. Putting her arms around the girl's neck she kissed her firmly on her lips. El'na responded with passion, pulling Nala in a tight embrace. Their lovemaking was hasty and maladroit but full of fire, both aware that Vee was nearby.

As Nala thoughtfully caressed the curves of the girl's back, feeling their breasts press firmly together, the situation struck her as familiar. It made her nostalgic for An. How could she possibly have forgotten her half sister?

A delicious smell of cooking vegetables filled the air, and Nala could hear the crackling of the fire as El'na guided her back to the shelter and helped her to a nearby bench.

"It's nigh on ready," Vee informed them.

"I'll dig out the bowls," El'na suggested.

"No need. I've already found them," he replied, ladling generous portions into three large, earthenware bowls.

They ate in silence. Nala found herself wishing she could see again. She hadn't thought of her lost sight for a long while. She'd come to accept the whiteness in which she was imprisoned. All was sound and smell and touch and taste. And, after all, Vee had become her eyes and she saw through his voice.

"Please sit next to me, Vee, and hold my hand," she said breaking their silence.

El'na came and sat on the other side of her, all three hand-in-hand facing the fire.

"I miss not being able to see," she said wistfully.

"Oh look!" exclaimed Vee in a forced whisper. "There's a whole gathering of animals sitting watching us at a safe distance on the other side of the fire."

And as if knowing Nala would want him to describe them, he continued softly.

"There are two large white rabbits sitting quite upright huddled close to each other, their ears pointed in attention. There's also a long slender fox, curled up nearby, licking its great bushy tail. There are several red squirrels darting here and there. Now they've stopped to listen to what I'm saying, as if they knew I was talking of them. I think I see voles and mice too, but they seem to be shy as they are half hidden behind tufts of grass. Oh and there are birds too. Several blackbirds, a thrush, a robin and many whose names I don't know."

"How wonderful," Nala said. Standing, she raised her voice to address them, "You are very, very welcome my friends. Know that no harm will come to you while we are here."

Sitting back down, she said quietly to El'na, "I feel they want something from us."

"Yer right. They do. They want us to gift 'em the music o' the setting sun and the c'ming night." El'na said fetching a collection of drums and rattles and tambourines from within the shelter.

El'na began softly drumming a steady rhythm on a tom-tom with the flats of her hands. For a long time it was the only sound to be heard beside the occasional crackling of the fire. It rang out like the heart beat. The heart of the neighbouring countryside and all the life around. Nala could feel it beating deep within her. Then El'na began singing a wordless ode that rose and fell like a graceful bird on the wing above the drum beat. Taking up the rattle Vee had handed her, Nala accompanied El'na's rhythm. Then, letting her voice join the girl's soaring soprano, the two birds entwined in a heart-rending love song.

Below she could hear the sound of Vee who developed a counterpart to their rhythm on a pair of bongos. And then he burst into song, his voice like a majestic bird gliding through the airs, circling around the two lovers, protecting them, teasing them, thrilling them with his throaty calls. A long, long time later all three came back reluctantly to rest on the ground and one by one the bongos, the rattle and the tom-tom ceased their beating. All was silent and peaceful. Then the animals broke out barking and growling and the birds began singing and chirping, each after their fashion. Nala realised that this was their way of saying thank you and she cheered as did El'na and Vee.

An arrival

After breakfast, El'na announced that she had to return to the entrance of the tunnels as someone was coming. She'd had a dream, she told them. She didn't know who was coming, but she knew it was a friend. She would go on her own as her eyesight was almost back to normal. Once the girl had gone, Nala lay down on her back in the long grasses next to Vee.

"Vee?"

"What, Cian'la?"

She'd noticed he'd adopted the way the Littl' People pronounced her name. She liked to hear him say it that way.

"I wonder if we could ever live separately again?"

He chuckled. "Why would you want to change things?"

"It's just that you've become my eyes and I rely on you to see. And I rely on you for many other things too. But one day I hope I'll get my sight back. I worry that will drive us apart."

Teasing her and poking fun at himself, he said: "If you could see the muscular young man I've become, you would never want to leave me."

She giggled at the thought and snuggled up close. He put his arms around her, holding her close. After a while she felt his lips on hers. It was inevitable really. This moment had been coming for ages. Had she been the one who put it off? She took his hand and laid it on her breasts. He stroked them, his hands surprisingly soft.

Then he gently squeezed her nipples till they stood erect. His kisses became more insistent as the tip of his tongue found its way into her mouth. She ran her hand across his chest, down over his muscular belly until she reached the hairs that surrounded his sex. Grasping his prick firmly, she heard him gasp with pleasure.

Vee was invisible to all except her, wasn't he? So why was she so concerned when she heard El'na return accompanied by a young woman. All the same she blushed at the thought of what they would see if they could see him.

"This is Mia," El'na announced. "She's made a very long journey looking for someone called Jake."

Nala burst out laughing to everyone's surprise but offered no explanation. How could she possibly explain that her journey had begun with Jake?

"Sit down, Mia, make yourself at home and let me introduce myself. My name is Cian'la. El'na you have already met. There is one more person here you should meet although you won't be able to see him, he's called Vee. Only I can see him. He's my eyes and my best friend," she announced.

"Greetings, Mia," he said. "Would you like something to drink or to eat?"

"I think I'd like to have a wash first. I'm filthy after those mines."

"Good, then El'na will show you where you can wash and I will make some soup," Vee said.

After they'd eaten and said hallo to a sheep, several rabbits and a couple of robins that dropped by to keep them company, they sat back and listened to Mia's story. Nala was astonished at all that had happened to Jake, although she suspected that Mia might not be telling the whole story.

"So how did you get away from the people in the Mansion?"

"They were not so interested in me. I was just bait for Jake. When they realised he'd gone, they lost interest. I followed Jake's traces till he entered a dark glade between two rows of sculpted men watching him. I was close behind him. When he fell through the floor, I jumped in after. But apparently we didn't go to the same place. I've no idea where he went, but I ended up in the country of the Littl' People and D'rick sent me after you with a guide."

"Are the Littl' People all right," Nala wanted to know.

"They're fine. The Cellerini Clan drove them into the tunnels and tried to force them through into the Lost Meadows. But the Littl' People know the tunnels too well, so they were able to hide and resist."

Later that afternoon, Nala asked Mia if she would like to go for a walk with her, just the two of them. Arm in arm, the two young women set off towards a nearby hill on which stood a tiny oak not more than four feet high. As they sat with their backs to it, a number of birds flew down from the branches to keep them company.

"Have the birds come?" Nala asked.

"Yes. Are all the animals and birds here so tame?"

"They are not tame, from what El'na told us. They just like being with people."

The two sat in silence for a while listening to the birds singing to them. Nala wondered how she could broach the subject of Jake.

"I wanted to talk to you about Jake," she finally said. "You are his lover, aren't you?" it came out more bluntly than she'd planned.

"Yes," was all Mia replied.

"Are you the jealous type, Mia?" Nala continued tentatively.

"What an odd question coming from a woman," Mia said, laughing. "You know Jake too, don't you? That was why you laughed when I first mentioned his name, isn't it?"

"Yes. I do. I came into the Dream Realm with him and sooner or later we need to meet up again to go home." Mia seemed unperturbed. "And do you love him too?"

Nala hesitated, not so much because of Mia, but because she wasn't sure herself. "I believe I do. Though we were never lovers. I generally prefer women." Nala felt herself blushing at the thought of her lovemaking with Vee earlier.

"Don't be so shy," Mia said misinterpreting her blushes. "I like women too."

The young woman moved closer and ran her hand through Nala's shoulder-length hair. And then she leaned forward and kissed Nala's closed eyes.

"Tell me how you came to be blind."

So Nala snuggled up to Mia and told her of her adventures.

The animals two by two

"I've 'ad another dream message," El'na announced when they arrived back at the shelter.

Nala had never heard El'na so worried before. Once they had settled with their meal spread out on a flat log that served as

238   Alan McCluskey

a table, El'na told them her message.

"I 'ave to leave you. I'm to lead the animals and birds out of the Meadows before nightfall. Something terrible is coming."

"And we're to stay?" Vee asked, surprised.

"Yes. Yer to stay. 'Tis time for Nala to save my people. And the two of yer will 'elp 'er."

Nala told Mia of the Littl' People's legend about her. "So my time has come," Nala concluded. "I thought I would not be called to task. But apparently there's no escaping it."

El'na blew softly into her horn but no sound emerged. All four of them stood atop Oak Hill as they'd come to call it. El'na pressed the horn to her lips and blew again. The sun was on the decline but there were still several hours of daylight left. A third time, El'na raised the horn and blew. Mia looked around for signs of the animals coming, but there was nothing.

"You sure it's working?" she asked El'na.

"'ave faith in me," was all the girl replied.

A robin flew down and landed on El'na's shoulder and chirped loudly in her ear.

"Oh look," Vee exclaimed. "It's the rabbits who came to our night music."

Mia had some difficulty getting used to Vee. You never knew where his voice would come from. Though, to be honest, he was often close to Cian'la. A steady trickle of animals and birds arrived. Could there be so few in the Lost Meadows? Then the horses came, stepping cautiously to avoid the little animals congregating on the ground.

Vee was describing the scene to Nala while El'na helped the little animals into a small handcart. Mia wondered if it would be big enough given the number of animals now arriving. In addition to the mice and the moles, there were also cows and sheep and even a beautiful cock followed by a group of hens.

El'na asked Vee to continue helping the little ones into the cart while she stood before the oak and addressed the gathering.

"My littl' friends," she began. "Yer must all leave the Lost Meadows. Somethin' terrible is comin'. I'm to guide yer thru' the mountains to a safe place."

There was some braying from a donkey that had just arrived and a couple of hens were clucking noisily, but otherwise the gathered animals remained silent. They really do trust her, Mia thought, looking with new eyes at the little woman. Well she wasn't sure how old El'na was. Many of the Littl' People women looked like girls even when older.

El'na had turned to Nala and herself.

"I'll lead 'em to the entrance to the tunnels. Not the one yer came by. Tis too small. Another tunnel."

Mia admired the self-assurance of the girl. She had to keep reminding herself that El'na might really be a grown woman and not the girl she seemed to be.

"I'll pull the 'andcart. Yer to follow at the end and make sure the stragglers get to the entrance. We'll say goodbye there."

As El'na set off down the hill pulling the handcart full of little animals and the occasional bird, the horses, the sheep, the cow and the donkey fell in behind her followed by a procession of smaller animals. A cloud of birds flew noisily here and there above the cavalcade. As she watched them move away, a movement in the grass caught her eye. It was a fox slinking by with a baby rabbit held firmly by the scruff of its neck in the fox's teeth.

"Put that baby down immediately," she said to the fox.

To her surprise, he obeyed. Picking up the little rabbit who was terrified, she realised its paw was bleeding. As she wiped away the blood with her finger to see what damage had been done, she heard Vee describing to Cian'la what she was doing.

"Bring the rabbit here." Nala said to her.

Taking the rabbit in her arms, Nala gently took the paw in her hand and remained still and concentrated for a long moment.

"There you are," she said handing the rabbit back to Mia.

Extraordinary. She'd healed the wound. No blood was left.

"We must go," Vee was saying.

Casting one last glance around the hill for stragglers, the three of them set off to follow the line of animals across the

Meadows towards the base of the mountains.

When they arrived at a small clearing in front of a large cliff, they saw El'na encouraging the remaining animals to enter the tunnel.

"Our journey won't be long. But we must get inside afore nightfall." she was telling them.

She was carrying a staff on which she'd fixed a lantern. Around her waist she wore the tool belt that was so typical of the Littl' People. Breaking off from her talk with the animals, El'na came to greet them.

"Yer must roll 'em rocks 'cross the entrance once we're all inside." Turning to Mia she took her hand and said: "Mia. Good luck. You will need to be patient and to have faith in your friends."

Mia wanted to know why, but El'na had already moved on and was apparently hugging Vee although Mia couldn't see him.

"Goodbye, Vee. What is to happen is for the best. I will always remember you."

Despite herself, El'na seemed to be crying as she turned to Nala.

"Cian'la, my love," she said oblivious to all those watching her. The girl kissed Nala firmly on the lips. "You have made me so happy. I will never forget you."

Nala was stroking her hair as she whispered something in the girl's ear.

"I'm so proud it was me to accompany you, Cian'la," El'na concluded. Taking the rabbit from Mia's arms, El'na stepped into the tunnel and was gone.

Chapter 11 - The Shaman

The sky was overcast and heavy with rain. Weary with walking, Jake trudged along the deserted lane his hands pushed deep in his pockets. The strange house and Mia seemed years away. As for the men in suits, they didn't seem to be pursuing him, at least he'd seen no sign of them.

The line of poplars that bordered the road gave the impression he was in the country, but glimpses beyond revealed stern blocks of high-rise flats that must have escaped from a Soviet nightmare. Stepping through an opening, he picked up a carrier bag of trinkets abandoned by the path and hurried to the closest building that was sorely in need of repair. In the half-light, a group of kids played football noisily on rough ground nearby but no one paid him any attention.

Finding refuge in a single-roomed flat on the ground floor the door of which lay half open, he turned to study his surroundings. The light was so dismal that he had some difficulty. The room was surprisingly large and over twenty feet high. The walls and ceiling were coated with a black rubbery substance that had peeled off in many places, maybe that was why the place smelt distinctly of used tyres. Devoid of all furniture, the room had only one small window that was so low he had to crouch to see out.

A large section of rubber peeled off the ceiling and fell with a dull thud to the floor overturning the bag he'd found. He was about to rummage through its contents when a bell outside caught his attention. Sitting on the floor next to the window, he looked out. It was the post-woman pulling a bright yellow cart packed high with letters and parcels. As she moved between the blocks of flats, a crowd of children ran excitedly around her calling out, each trying to get a look at the packets. A sizeable chunk of black rubber detached itself from the ceiling and fell at his feet, startling him. The post-woman was heading in his direction. He really didn't want to be found there. Standing to head for the door, he slipped on the remains of black rubber and tumbled into darkness.

Jake was confused. Something was not right. Outside firemen were spraying foam on the windows that were spectacularly cracked. He hastily pushed the young girl in a wheelchair down the corridor looking for a lift. The chair must have been coated with a sticky substance because it clung unpleasantly to his hands. Maybe it was the foam from the fire fighters. He had to get the two of them out fast. He found a lift almost immediately, but it was much too small. He had no time to puzzle over how it could have shrunk, but headed in search of another. When he finally found one, he fumbled with the buttons trying to set the thing in motion but he had some difficulty getting hold of them with his sticky fingers.

When he finally succeeded, the lift went nether up nor down, but moved unsteadily horizontally away from the entrance. As it made its way shakily forward, the lift transformed imperceptibly into an open wooden platform. Water cascading from the lift shaft, or should that be the lift tunnel, flooded the platform, forcing Jake to hold onto the guardrails around the platform to stop himself and the girl being swept away. He hoped at least that the water would clean his hands, but they remained stubbornly sticky.

When the contraption finally shuddered to a halt, it was in the middle of a posh restaurant full of distinguished customers eating dinner. To Jake's surprise the girl stood up and walked away leaving him holding the empty wheelchair. He took one step forward, rubbing his hands desperately against his trousers trying to rid them of their stickiness when everything went black, a blackness that must have lasted at least several seconds.

Something was decidedly not right. The flow of life was not moving as it ought. Something was out of joint. What's more, there was a very unpleasant smell in the air. He ran his hands over his belly and down his legs, as if that would bring back a sense of reality. Ugh! An unpleasant object was sticking out of his calf, like the end of a fat piece of string. Increasingly anxious, he tried to pull it out but the string broke leaving part of it inside his leg. In so doing, it had become much thicker.

He squeezed the sides of the wound and the whole thing popped out with a squelching sound followed by some blood. It was like a big, fat worm, almost as big as his thumb. Along its sides were dark marks akin to rotting flesh. The thing stank like a much-neglected sewer. Disgusted, Jake threw the wriggling body into the sink and turned on the water, hoping to flush it away, but the contact with water transformed it into a bright yellow chick. It terrified him. Grabbing a large carving knife from beside the sink, he sliced the chick's head off causing it to become two chicks. Screaming, he turned and ran. It must have been then that he blacked out.

This time the darkness lasted longer. It was an empty, silent sort of darkness he thought. Neither cold nor hot. What a waste, he told himself. You could pack so much in there. And then he was off again.

Several of the groups playing in the pool had no right to be there. Taking justice into his own hands, he hauled one of the young guys out of the bath and was surprised to discover the man was fully dressed and not at all wet. "You have no right to be in there!" Jake shouted.

Letting his irritation get the better of him, he did a judo hold on the astonished young man. But instead of falling to the floor, the man remained suspended in mid air with just one foot on the ground. Jake was impressed when he realised that it was will power alone that was holding the man suspended in such a ridiculous posture.

"You ought to know better, young man! Don't you know

what great works we are doing here?" Having said so, Jake turned and walked away trying to hold himself upright and proud.

And he was back in the darkness again. Laughter filled the darkness startling Jake. He thought he preferred the empty version better.

"How long are you going to keep this up?" a wizened little voice questioned.

Jake ducked to avoid being hit and it started again. He climbed down narrow winding stairs, the walls and floor of which were tiled like a bathroom. He had to be careful not to slip as someone had cleaned the floor recently, apparently forgetting to rinse the tiles after using soap. Reaching the bottom he discovered there was no way out. Slithering to a halt, he took a deep breath and began to climb cautiously back up the way he'd come.

Twice he slipped and almost plunged back down the stairwell. The door he'd used to enter had gone, but another door higher up led out onto a roof that sloped away steeply. No, he thought, too dangerous. Closing the door, he searched for any doors he might have missed. Concealed in a corner behind a fold in the tiles he found another door. He had some difficulty opening it as the handle was also coated in soap. When he finally managed, the door led out onto a rooftop garden that was part of the neighbouring garden centre. Judging from the smell, it had recently been strewn with manure.

Holding his breath, he hastily crossed the garden and was able to climb down into a car park. The main gate, he thought. At least he would be able to get away. It was then that he spotted several mounted guardians trying to head him off. It must have been closing time, he guessed. Jake waved to them, hoping they would interpret it as a friendly gesture.

"We need to question you," they said, riding closer.

They announced that it was to be a formal procedure, whatever that meant. The guardians cut a startling figure with a heavy black veil concealing their faces. Jake stood facing them as one of the horses pissed copiously in his direction. Side stepping to avoid getting sprayed, Jake pulled himself back into the darkness. He'd had enough of that.

"Well that was an improvement", the wizened voice from the darkness told him.

Jake decided to ignore the comment.

"Now that's a clever strategy," the voice said ironically, laughing to itself. "Which is more important to you: what happens in here or what goes on out there?"

Jake wanted to stick his fingers in his ears, but in the darkness he didn't seem to have any fingers or a body either. Well, he thought, I'll just have to go somewhere else.

The beach was deserted. Jake sauntered along the water's edge. The sand was soft and damp between his toes apart from the occasional worm that wriggled across his way. Glancing back landwards he admired the palm trees that grew at the limit of the beach, although he was intrigued by the small wooden cabin leaning precariously against one of the trees.

The only sound he could hear was the lapping of the waves at his feet and the distant rusty grating of the cabin door as it swayed noisily in the breeze. The place was almost idyllic he was thinking when a heavy shadow drew over the landscape and the wind rose sharply. As he had his back to the sea, he was unaware of the giant wave rolling in until it crashed against him knocking him over and soaking his clothes. Running for the shore and safety, he turned back to look at the sea. Great waves were breaking on the beach, driven by the wind, each wave crested with what looked like foaming wild animals. The sun had completely disappeared behind threatening clouds and the place had gone cold. There would be no escaping by boat today so he slipped back into the darkness.

"You're getting quite good at that," his unseen wizened companion told him. "Though you haven't yet managed to control the place you create."

These words gave him cause for thought. Slipping in and out of the darkness was akin to telling a story. And rather like stories, what happened seemed to have a mind of its own. The voice remained silent for once, as if it wanted him to follow his thoughts. Well, let's try again, he decided.

Jake sat in a car being driven through a derelict suburb. A thin, blond-haired girl he didn't know was driving. The fact that she was naked was a little distracting, but he sat on his hands and looked out of the window. There was no way, however, he could politely block out the penetrating smells rising from her warm body. It was amazing how clothes kept body odours in, he told himself, unsuccessfully trying to distract himself with sociological considerations.

All around houses in various state of ruin were shroud in dust. The road turned abruptly as they entered a tower and stopped.

"*We've arrived,*" she shouted.

Stepping out, they gathered their backpacks from the boot and began climbing spiral stairs that rose into the tower. They emerged from the top onto a wide-open terrace laid out with generous alleys and areas of neatly cut grass. He pretended to ignore her and looked around.

Benches, which had been placed here and there, were occupied by groups of children and teenagers. It was apparently a favourite destination for school outings. Jake followed the girl, as she seemed to know where to go. She didn't seem in the slightest bothered that everyone turned to stare at her naked body. They passed under an archway into another area of walkways and grass where groups of young people were seated on the grass picnicking. The girl joined her friends who were also naked and Jake slipped away.

"Well done!" was the comment of the wizened voice as he returned to the darkness. "Do you think we could have some light in here?" the voice asked him politely although Jake detected a trace of irony or was it humour in the question.

"But I'm not responsible for the darkness," he responded angrily, forgetting he'd vowed not to talk to the voice.

"Are you sure?"

There. Now he'd got into a conversation with a disincarnated voice.

"How do you know I have no body, if you can't see me?" the voice replied to his thoughts.

Apparently there was no escaping it.

"I have no idea how to bring back the light," Jake protested.

"That's simple. Do it the same way you tell a story or a dream."

Jake thought of light and found himself in a cheap restaurant that smelled unpleasantly of chips and deep-fried fish. He was armed with a taser, but if anything happened, he thought wearily, the thing wouldn't be quick enough. The waitress, who was leaning against the counter smoking, stubbed out her cigarette in an unfinished plate of spaghetti and sauntered lazily over to take their orders.

"What would you like boys?" she drawled.

Jake could have sworn she was dribbling slightly. It was then that the arms of the plastic chairs started to curl up around him and his colleagues like deadly tentacles embracing them. The waitress laughed insanely, scratching her crutch with one hand while she reached for the cigarette she had perched behind her ear with the other. They were caught in a trap but the more they tried to break their way out, the tighter the arms fastened around them …

Jake was panting when he returned to the dark. "That didn't work so well," he said out loud to nobody in particular.

"Too much effort," the wizened voice replied.

"You sound like one of my teachers," Jake groaned.

"Does that make any difference?" the voice challenged.

"Oh blast you!"

"I'd rather you didn't."

A long silence followed. Jake could feel his frustration growing as he realised he was stuck there.

"So how do I do it?" Jake asked.

"Try a lighter."

Jake thought he'd succeeded because a faint light lit up

the place. From the road where he stood he could just make out a distant bridge spanning the river. He remembered he had an appointment with a woman on the other side. Nearby, grey warehouses towered over the road. No street lights lit the way and the road was dotted with potholes. Through one of these Jake caught a glimpse of water flowing darkly underneath. Of course! He was on a platform that stretched out over the river.

He moved hesitantly forward. In places, all that was left of the road were metal girders that were wet and slippery. Jake balanced his way forward, hampered in his efforts by the growing darkness and the packets he was carrying. Had not the signpost at the beginning said this was a way across? By now the road had completely disappeared leaving only girders that he could just see in the failing light. Even those didn't always provide a suitable path. He found himself having to jump from girder to girder across increasing gaps into the darkness beyond.

"Good try."

Encouragement at last, Jake thought.

"Sarcasm will not help."

"Do you ever let up?"

"No. Not when I have a task to do."

"And am I that task?"

"You could put it like that."

Brent was tempted to return to the dreams or the stories or whatever they were.

"I'm in no hurry," the voice chirped back. "This will take the time it needs."

Jake was at a meeting in Parliament. The large chamber was filled with dark wooden desks and seats set in a semicircle. He was naked and cold. A girl dressed in a thick fur coat sat in his place, studying the papers on his desk. In fact, everybody was dressed in similar winter clothes. Nobody seemed bothered he was naked. Although he remembered having been naked there before, he thought it wise to get dressed, especially as he was beginning to freeze.

"Satisfied?" the voice twittered.

There was still no light in the dark.

"How did God do it?" Jake asked, intending it as a joke.

"With a word," was the learned answer.

Let there be light Jake thought, not intending anything by the phrase. A small candle burst into life on a table in front of him. He was inside a small, windowless hut. Two empty chairs faced each other across the tabletop. Seating himself in one, he noticed that a large tawny owl was perched on the other.

"You see, my patience was rewarded," it said.

Jake rubbed his eyes, as if that would make a difference.

"That was why I thought it better to meet in the dark first," the owl said, teasing him.

Oups! Jake relinquished his hold on the Dark, which was no longer dark, and slipped away. When he finally found out where the next examination was to take place, he was already late. A Bentley drew silently along side him and the driver's window rolled down letting out a cloud of cigar smoke.

"Can I give you a lift?" a man asked.

Throwing caution to the winds, Jake opened the passenger door at the back and climbed in. He had to push aside the magazines of nude men and women that littered the back seat so he had somewhere to sit. Two blocks down the road, he spotted the building, a former cinema.

"There it is," he told the driver, but the man continued to drive on.

That'll teach you not to be cautious, Jake told himself, worrying how he could escape.

"The traffic's too dense here," was the man's reply. "I'll drop you a little further down, unless you want to come back to my place."

Jake explained that he was in a hurry. When they finally pulled to a halt, the man suavely suggested he take any of the magazines that took his fancy.

"Think of me when you read them," the man murmured.

Jake declined saying rather spitefully that he'd heard masturbation was bad for your health. Scrambling to get out of the car as fast as he could, Jake ran back to the one-time cinema entrance and climbed the wide staircase in the foyer two steps at a time. The first floor was crowded with adults come to invigilate the exams. On a rostrum, a man called out names and indicated which room people should be in. No lists of student names hung on the walls.

No fellow students were in sight. Jake had no way to find out where his exam was and time was ticking by. He could ask nobody for help. All were listening intently for their name to be called. The proceedings were interrupted by a procession entering the room. The crowd fell back before dark clothed men who stepped solemnly forward each carrying a long wooden pole on the end of which was perched a lantern. The light, Jake thought.

And he was once more in the Dark.

"Ah! You're back," was all the owl twittered before it returned to preening its wing feathers.

It had not shifted from its perch on the chair-back where Jake had left it. Maybe time was different in the Dark, he conjectured. Jake paced around the tiny space that was left to him on his side of the table, not wanting to get too near the owl.

"Would you agree to sit down, if I invited you to?" the owl asked mocking him.

Jake didn't bother to answer, but sat down setting his elbows on the table and leaning his head wearily on his cupped hands. A long silence ensued. The bird hopped off the back of its chair, strutted across the table till it was within reach of Jake and gave his hand a sharp peck with its beak, before it retreated to its perch, laid its head on one side and stared wide-eyed at him. Jake shifted his hands so he could see the owl and stared back. The staring match lasted quite a moment with the owl finally winning.

"What's your name?" Jake asked, looking back up at the bird.

"Ah! So now we are on naming terms?"

Jake looked away both indignant and somewhat ashamed.

"I'm sorry," he muttered. "I though it would a good idea to

get to know each other."

Jake lowered his head onto his hands and closed his eyes.

"Sharing names is a serious business, young man," the owl told him. "It requires a lot of trust."

Jake kept silent. Where he came from, a long time ago it seemed, people gave their names quite readily.

"That was no great loss. Those names were nigh on powerless," the owl informed him.

Jake felt himself slipping away again.

"You can resist it, if you want," he was told.

A part of him didn't want to resist. That was the part of him that didn't like the feeling that he was being lectured at.

"Why else do you think some schoolboys always fall asleep in class?" the owl continued. "Off you go then, if you must."

The three of them sat in animated discussion, each on his bed. Jake admired the wooden panelled walls that gave a regal air to their bedroom. The panels smelt of bees' wax bringing back fond memories. He leaned against the wall, half withdrawing from the conversation so he could listen to the two others who were making fun of their new English teacher. The unfortunate woman had a tic: she was always pulling her left ear. One of the boys imitated her, making them all laugh.

Jake was restless. Classes had already begun. Missing lessons didn't seem to bother the others. Standing, he bent forward to pick up his books but one of them was far too heavy. He abandoned it on the bed. Out in the corridor he was surprised and worried to discover that the place had been newly renovated and nothing seemed familiar, even the corridors had changed. He did manage to locate the secretary's office.

"There's a timetable pinned on the notice board, young man," the none-too-friendly woman told him, but she refused to give him a copy.

She'd said the board was just down the main corridor but he couldn't find it anywhere. A hoard of younger boys pushed their way passed, each studying a timetable in his hands. Jake turned to watch them jostling their way down the long corridor, wondering what he'd done wrong, till silence fell again.

"Penny for your thoughts," the owl said, greeting him.

Jake sat down heavily. He felt miserable. What he needed was a good laugh, he decided.

"That would be nice." the bird squeaked as it hopped from one end of the chair back to the other.

You bloody fool, Jake told himself. Here you are stuck in a windowless hut with a barmy bird that lectures you when it isn't poking fun at you. Isn't that reason enough to laugh. He could feel the laughter bubbling up from deep in his guts and although something in him tried to resist, the laughter burst out like waves shaking his whole body. He only stopped when tears streamed down his cheeks and he had a stitch. Opening his eyes, he discovered the ridiculous owl was rolling on its back with its legs shaking wildly in the air.

"Is that how you owl's laugh?" he asked.

"You should know," the owl replied managing to roll over onto its claws, setting itself upright.

When he looked perplexed, the bird added: "Well, you're an owl too," as if it were self-evident.

"You really are nuts!" Jake replied.

"Charming. If you don't believe me, look at yourself in the mirror over there."

Hopping over to the mirror, Jake saw a large tawny owl looking back at him. It was too much. He slipped again.

Dramatic, he thought. According to the newspaper a young girl had decided to put an end to the world. There was no mention of how she would snuff them all out, but there was a picture of her on the front page right under the banner heading: PREPARE FOR THE END! She looked young and fragile and quite harmless.

"Has nobody tried to stop her?" Jake asked the others sprawling around the kitchen table next to him.

They shook their heads half-heartedly, saying they thought she couldn't be dissuaded and continued eating their steamed pudding and custard. Jake absent-mindedly raised his feet to get them out of the water that lay ankle-deep in that part of the room. He was determined to do something about the girl. Through the French windows, he could see the lush grass in the courtyard that was already under several feet of water. The difference in level had water seeping continuously in through the walls slowly filling the kitchen.

"I'll call her," he told the others.

"They are sure to have cut the line," one of the faceless others replied.

Dialling the number mentioned in the paper, Jake took a deep breath trying to calm himself and prepare what he would say. A young man answered, announcing that he was the girl's boyfriend.

"We live in the Swiss mountains…." he said, but nothing more as they got cut off.

The others were curious to know what had been said but he ignored them, dialling again. The level of water in the courtyard had risen enough for water to begin cascading into the kitchen through a hole in the upper part of the French windows. Reconnected, the boy told him there was a problem with the girl's family and they didn't have a place to stay in. Jake was offering to find them a place to stay when they were cut off again.

"Feeling better now?" the owl asked. "Nothing like a story of the end of the world to raise your spirits," he said chuckling.

Jake could not look at the bird without thinking that he looked the same. If he was honest, though, he had to admit he'd always liked the idea of being a bird and being able to fly. He stretched his wings tentatively and was surprised at how light they felt.

"Good, hey?" the owl said approvingly.

Jake moved his wings up and down lightly and was startled to find himself rising into the air.

"Take it easy, youngster," the bird warned him. "You need more room to learn to fly."

And he clicked his tongue in his beak and the walls of the hut fell away. Jake swivelled his head.

"Wow," he thought. "That's useful."

Two owls sat on the backs of two chairs facing each other across a tiny table lit only by a candle in the middle of gigantic cavern. Opening his eyes wide he could see into the depths of the cavern and, although his owl's eyes pierced even the farthest shadows, he could see no exit.

"Let's not talk about getting out now," his fellow owl said, "unless of course you want to slip away into the dream realm again."

Jake had an all-consuming urge to fly. It had always been there, he realised, coursing through his veins, but it had never been able to express itself properly before. He spread his wings, taking care to avoid the candle, and brought them down in one sharp movement that projected him up into the air. Oh the joy of it. He let out a quavering hoot of pleasure and beat his wings again as he rose higher in the cave.

Spreading his wings even further, he let himself glide till he'd almost reached the floor of the cavern and then beat strongly pulling back up into the air. He heard a sharp movement amongst the rocks to his left. Turning one eye in that direction he caught sight of a mouse moving rapidly across the floor.

An age-old instinct snapped into place, locking his attention on the little animal. The hunt! Excitement bubbled up inside him as he flew silently towards his prey. His attack was so fast, the mouse hardly realised he was upon it that he killed it with his claws and swallowed it whole. A new noise caught his attention. He swivelled his head to see that the other owl had followed him into the air and flew nearby.

"Follow me," the bird screeched.

The pair returned to the table and resumed their positions facing each other from their respective chairs. Outwardly their situation seemed unchanged, but inwardly no comparison between before and after was possible. Jake felt the overwhelming sameness with the bird opposite him, a deep affinity that knew no words and needed none to be felt and expressed.

"All is not as it seems," the owl said gravely.

Jake swivelled his head nervously in every direction, wondering if an unseen threat had crept up on them. The owl chuckled.

"Even as an owl you have too much imagination."

Indignant, Jake puffed up his feathers and strutted back and forth on the chair back.

"You have no respect," he retorted.

"Oh but I do! Yours is the most important task I have ever had."

Jake was perplexed. Had he not had the impression he was nothing compared to this wizened owl.

"Let's start again. It might be easier," the owl said spreading its wings and then folding them again. "It is true I must talk of danger, but not one that is present here and now." He punctuated his thoughts with a sharp hoot. "In this cavern, the only material beings that might be a threat to us would be large snakes. But once you're outside the situation will be different."

Jake balanced on one leg and stretched out his claws to examine them.

"That will not be enough if an eagle takes a fancy to you."

Jake launched into the air, caught a bat between his claws and offered it to the other owl that promptly swallowed it whole without the slightest comment. Owls must have other rules of politeness, if they had any, Jake thought.

"We've got to get you to your destination safe and sound," the older owl pursued.

"So what should we do?"

"Always travel at night. At the slightest noise head for shelter and, in absolute necessity, change back into your human form."

Jake had been waiting for the subject to come up. Not that he disliked being an owl, on the contrary. But at some time he'd have to return to where he came from.

"How do I do that?"

The owl studied him closely. "When you need to, you'll know how. The experience can be rather troubling at first, but once you've done it several times the feeling will become familiar and it'll be easier."

Feeling pessimistic, Jake wondered what it would be like to be stuck halfway.

"Your're quite impossible," the owl clucked disapprovingly.

"So can we go?" Jake asked, changing the subject as he hopped impatiently onto the arm of the chair.

The older owl scrutinized him for a long moment: "Do you really feel ready?" his voice betraying doubt.

Normally Jake would have given the question careful thought, but the young owl that he'd become was impatient.

"Where is the way out?"

"There is no physical way out. You must fly through the rocks and earth to get out."

If he hadn't been an owl, Jake would have fallen off the chair.

"What?" he shrieked, launching off in angry flight to the confines of the cavern.

As the air ruffled through his feathers flying way above the cave floor, Jake wondered at the impetuousness of the owl he'd become. Did he really need to give in to that way of being? He winged his way back to the table where the old owl sat patiently.

"I apologise," he said settling on his chair back.

"Your behaviour is understandable. This will be one of the biggest challenges you will ever have to face."

"So how do I get through?"

"Some sit quietly and meditate till they are ready. Others try to fly physically against the wall. I advise the former option. It hurts less," he said, chuckling to himself. "It shouldn't be too difficult for you, with your experience as a storyteller and a dream-walker."

Jake glanced at the other owl at the mention of these concepts that he'd almost forgotten. The older owl was staring at him intently.

"One thing I can tell you," the owl said. "Do not let yourself be distracted. There are forces and beings that would be delighted to lead you astray. Ignore them." Shifting closer to Jake, he added: "I would fly with you, but this is something you have to do alone. I'll see you off then I'll wait for you on the other side."

Jake settled comfortably on the back of the chair and closed his eyes. Little noises tugged at his attention, but he brushed them aside. He let darkness roll over him and delved deeper. He sensed a distant force calling him like a minute sound in a vast sea of silence. He flew towards it, guided only by its call. All else was quiet and he was completely alone in the dark. He knew instinctively that he was closing fast on his goal, but when he finally reached it nothing indicated that he'd arrived lest it be a strong feeling of being on a threshold. He halted to get his bearings. Hovering over the imaginary entrance, he cast out his senses in every direction. Ah there it was, off to his right, far, far away. Not sound this time, but light.

He launched off in pursuit of that pinprick of light, only to realise immediately that the darkness on this side of the entrance was far from empty. As he flew forward, he was continually buffeted, not so much by gusts of wind, but rather by something more substantial and troubling and many faced. A pungent smell of sex sent his senses reeling almost making him loose his direction as a naked girl held out her smelly fingers for him to sniff. He flew on, trying his best to ignore her.

"Jake", she called after him, but he continued. "It's me, Mia."

He hesitated at the mention of her name, but she couldn't be there. He'd lost her a while back. He beat his wings strongly and pushed forwards.

A cloud of cigar smoke suddenly surrounded him, threatening to obscure the distant light. An impeccably dressed man beckoned to him.

"Come with me," he said pointing to his luxurious car. "You'll get there quicker."

Jake flew higher, rising above the sickly cloud of smoke. As he winged on, he started to smell burning. There was a fire nearby. He could feel its heat. A girl in a wheelchair called out for help. When he ignored her, she was replaced by a post-woman who offered him a parcel. No danger there, he thought.

She too was replaced by a girl in a fur coat handing him some papers. He ignored them all, fixing his wide eyes on the distance point of light. They'd have to try harder if they wanted to stop him. All the same, he realised he was starting to feel tired. He'd never flown so far. He struggled on, flying lower now.

"Jake" a familiar voice called to him. It was Nala. "I'm all alone and abandoned. Please stay with me."

"I can't stay, Nala," he called out as she ran along side.

"Stop just a moment. You're tired. You're hungry. Eat and rest with me."

It was so delightful to hear her voice again. He longed to fly into her arms and have her comfort him.

"I can't!" he insisted.

She was still running alongside him. In one swift movement she reached out and tried to grab him. Jake screeched and beat his wings with all his remaining strength till he was safely out of her reach. That was not Cianala, he told himself. She would never do such a thing.

His breath was coming with difficulty now. He could hardly keep himself aloft. Landing on the rocky ground he trudged forward, his wings trailing on the ground, his head hanging low, his mouth gone dry. Just a few more steps, he told himself, for the light was very close now.

He dragged himself on in mindless effort. He no longer knew who Jake was or what an owl could be or where he was … all he could do was put one claw in front of another and stagger forward. It was then he saw the wizened little owl standing in front of him waiting, its immense eyes fixed on him. I hope you aren't an illusion, he said to himself, as he collapsed at its feet.

"Jake," the owl said full of concern. "Eat this." And he placed a terrified mouse at Jake's feet.

"Did I make it?" Jake asked having made quick work of the mouse.

"Yes. You did. I'm very proud of you."

Jake pulled himself up onto his claws and looked around. They were in a dense wood surrounded by rocks and towering peaks. It was daytime, but the trees cast deep shadows where the two of them were concealed. Small animals hurried away from the pair of owls while birds darted here and there amongst the branches above.

"Now you must rest. Then we'll travel on," the old owl told him. "We have to reach a large valley beyond the mountains. That's our final destination."

The terrain below was rough and rugged. Trees grew sparsely here and there amongst the rocks. Sheer drops cut deep gorges through the mountainside. Peaks rose majestically above. This was eagle country the old owl told him. They had to be particularly cautious. They had spotted a narrow track that wound tortuously upwards and were following it at a distance.

A faint noise from the road ahead caught Jake's attention. It sounded like a horse. He made a sign to the older owl and the two of them came silently to rest, well hidden within the leaves of a tree.

"There is a horse up ahead," he told the other owl as quietly as he could.

"Several of them," his fellow owl whispered. "Human beings too."

Keeping down wind they flew closer, moving forward in short hops from tree to tree.

"Oh dear!"

Jake acutely felt the fear of the older owl. "What's up?"

"They've got hawks. They must be looking for you."

The two of them launched off from the tree, heading at full speed back the way they'd come.

"We might be able to out fly them," the older owl said as they settled on a branch. "But if they catch us unawares there is no way we can fight them off."

"Can't we hide?" Jake asked.

"They'd probably find us. Hawks have very sharp eyesight.

No. We must travel by night. Hawks don't fly at night."

Jake swivelled his head around to get a better idea of their surroundings. "Down there," he said pointing with his wing. "There's a little cave. We could hide there."

Their luck was in because the cave was home to a colony of bats offering them a welcome lunch. As they sat on the rock preening, Jake suggested he shapeshift so he could roll a rock over the entrance.

"That might disorient you completely," the other owl said. "Shapeshifting is difficult to get used to at first. This is not the moment to have you all muddled."

So the pair of them perched on a rock high above the cave floor and waited for night to fall. As he sat in the dark, a number of things troubled Jake about the story he was involved in: things that seemed to spring from nowhere. Bits of the story were missing he guessed.

"Why did you say those men were looking for me?" Jake asked.

"There's an age-old legend in these parts. The folk that live here, they call themselves the Littl' People, tell that a tall girl will one day walk out of the mountains and save all in this realm from a monumental disaster. But part of the story has been forgotten. A young man in another shape will join forces with the girl in saving the realm."

"And you think I'm that young man?"

"Yes."

"But where do the men with the hawks fit in?"

"The cataclysm that is to hit this realm is the work of people in the world you come from. The men with the hawks are in league with them. And they know of the legend. So they seek both the girl and the young man."

"It must be Nala," Jake said, thinking out loud. "I hope she's alright."

"Who is Nala?" the other owl asked.

"I came into this realm with a girl called Cianala. She had a quest and I was to accompany her. But we got separated and I have been looking for her ever since."

The older bird spread its wing and rose into the air. "It's time to go. Your Nala must be close by."

Rotten luck, Jake thought as they flew out of the cave, it was full moon. If the men let the hawks fly by moonlight, the two of them were in trouble. They flew silently along a gully hoping to find a way up to the pass. The owl had told Jake that they could not fly over the mountains. They were too high. What's more, they'd be easy prey for the eagles that nested high up.

Beyond the end of the ravine, there were few trees to offer shelter. They flew low, zigzagging their way up between the rocks. It was then that they heard the shrill cries of the hawks. Flee or hide, Jake wondered.

"Flee" the other owl replied.

Rising higher to get clear of the rocks, the two flew at top speed. At first the call of the hawks gained ground, getting dangerously close but then it dropped back.

"We've lost them," Jake panted.

"Keep going," was the bird's only response.

A terrible shriek next to him made him look round. A hawk had the owl in its claws. Without thinking, Jake swung round in the air and fell on the hawk, aiming his claws at its face, gouging out its eyes. The bird screamed with pain and let go of the owl that fluttered down to the ground.

Jake circled down to join it, checking that no other hawks were in sight. The owl was lying on its side, blood dripping down its back feathers.

"Get me to the shelter of the rocks," it said weakly.

Jake pushed and pulled until his friend and mentor was out of sight behind some rocks.

"Stand back," the wounded owl said. "I must change shape. It's the only choice. Please look away."

Jake turned to look up the slope. To his surprise, they were almost at the pass. They had almost made it. He was filled with sadness at the thought that the bird might die. Hearing a scuffling sound behind him, Jake turned back to see a white haired old man completely naked leaning against the rock, blood dripping from gashes across his back. At his feet lay a canvas bag that Jake hadn't noticed before.

"There's a salve in my bag. If I rub it on my wounds they will heal in no time," the man reassured Jake.

Jake wanted to help, but there was little he could do in his present shape, so he sat some distance away and watched. The man was quite tall although he walked with a slight stoop. He was weather-beaten as if he was used to walking in the sun and rain,. He had a generous smile. For all his benevolent appearance, Jake was cautious about being close to a human being. How absurd, part of him thought as he was a human himself.

The man had donned a thick shirt and simple cotton trousers.

"That's better," he said pulling bread and cheese out of his bag.

He offered Jake some, but he didn't like the smell of it. So he declined and settled for a mole he caught nearby.

"As you might have guessed, I am the shaman that has been guiding you since you found yourself stuck in the cave."

Jake was impatient to know his name, but his earlier experience with the subject put a check on his curiosity.

"Will you change back into an owl?" Jake ventured.

"No. I don't think so. My idea is to walk through the pass, concealing you in my bag. They are sure to be watching out for you there."

Jake had read enough adventure stories to know that any watchers would be sure to search the bag.

"Won't they search your bag?"

"Not if they can't see it."

"Ah!" said Jake. "Can't you make me invisible?"

"No. That would be beyond my powers."

Jake had to keep a tight rein on his emotions because he felt panicked at being shut in the bag with no room to move and little air to breath. What's more, the bag was full of smells that he found troubling. They'd apparently reached the pass because the shaman was in conversation with another man.

"… I go to gather flowers in the Lost Meadows," the Shaman explained putting on a much older voice.

It was the first time Jake had heard the name of the place they were heading for.

"Doubt if you'll find many flowers this year," the man sniggered. "You'd do better to turn back."

The Shaman insisted and finally he was let through. He walked quite a way, but the Shaman had still not let him out.

"I can't let you out yet," he whispered, apparently reading his thoughts. "Someone is following us."

Sometime later, Jake felt the bag being placed cautiously on the ground and the flap opened.

"Don't fly out," the Shaman whispered. "We are still being followed."

Jake was relieved to have some fresh air. From his hiding place amongst the spare clothes of the man, he looked out at the sky above, blinking because the light was so strong. They must have come down quite a distance because there were more trees around them now. His view was suddenly cut off as the flap was flicked back over the bag. "Someone's coming," the Shaman hissed.

"Greetin's to yer." Jake heard someone say. "We 'eard yer were out walkin' and thought yer might need 'elp."

"Well met," the Shaman replied. And lowering his voice added: "Is there some place nearby we can talk unheard and unseen."

"Follo' me," the newcomer replied with his strange accent.

The Shaman lifted Jake carefully out of the bag and set him down on a rock.

"Jake let me present the Littl' People."

Jake swivelled his head round to see they were in a high-roofed tunnel. A crowd of little men and women had gathered round. The Shaman continued. "This is Jake."

"Pleased to meet you,"

Jake greeted them. The whole crowd took a step back.

264   Alan McCluskey

"Oie! A talkin' bird," one of them said, expressing the wonder of them all.

"This is no real bird. Excuse me for saying so, Jake." The Shaman explained. "He's the companion of Nala come to help her fulfil your legend."

A buzz of excitement rushed through the Littl' People as they gazed in awe at Jake.

A little man stepped forward. "I'm D'rick, leader of the Littl' People," he began. "We've met yer Cian'la. With our 'elp she's gone to the Lost Meadows. But yer can't join 'er there. 'Tis far too dangerous. Yer must wait till she's done 'er task."

The Shaman moved forward. "We need to talk."

"Come with me, then," D'rick said and set off down the tunnel.

Jake hopped onto the Shaman's shoulder and they walked alongside D'rick followed by the crowd of Littl' People.

D'rick told them of Cian'la visit and their legend. He also explained that the Littl' People had been driven into the tunnels by the Cellerini Clan, their warring neighbours who were trying to push them through into the Lost Meadows, but they hadn't succeeded. Jake was astonished about Nala and the man's voice, wondering how she'd done it, but he didn't interrupt to ask questions.

The Shaman told the Littl' People about the lost part of the legend and the role Jake was to play. D'rick was surprised but seemed to accept.

"We must welcome Jake as we welcomed Cian'la. Then Jake can stay with us 'til it is time," he said addressing his people.

And they burst into song. Jake had never heard anything so moving and beautiful. He wanted to sing with them, but he discovered that owl's don't sing. At least not like humans. So he closed his eyes and let himself be absorbed by the sound of it.

When the singing died down, a young woman came forward.

"This is El'na," D'rick said. "She accompanied Cian'la to

the Lost Meadows. She's just r'turned from guiding all the an-im'ls from the Meadows to saf'ty. She'll be yer guide and she'll look after yer till 'tis time to go."

The girl had donned a stout leather glove and held out her hand for him to hop onto it.

"I'm heavy you know," he said to her.

"That's OK."

So he hopped onto her hand and sure enough, she was much stronger than he'd thought. The Shaman came forward to take his leave.

"I have other tasks, Jake. I am proud to have accompanied you on your journey. Know that you can now consider yourself a fully-fledged shaman. May you succeed in what you have to do and may you return safely home."

Jake hooted in reply. "I will miss you old friend," was all he could bring himself to say.

El'na bowed to the Shaman and, turning her back on the others, she walked away with Jake in search of a place to rest.

"Would yer like me to tell yer about Cian'la's journey?" she asked when they were alone.

"I'd love that."

Chapter 12 - Virtual Realities

Confessions

W.B. Yeats, Alister Crowley, Alan Benett, A.E. Waite, Helena Blavatsky, Rudolf Steiner, Anna Kingsford, Annie Wood, Alice Bailey, Dion Fortune, … So many familiar names, Sally thought, as she ran her hand along the spines of the books in Alo's country library. She called on their wisdom and their foresight to guide her in the difficult moments to come. By some strange inversion she had the impression that she was on trial, that the others were there to judge her rather than Tyrell and she couldn't rid herself of the anger and the anguish that caused.

The others had not yet joined her. They were rounding off their meal with a sorbet made of elderberry flowers. She could hear them laughing and chatting together across the corridor in the dining room. She felt excluded even though she knew she had chosen to leave the room in search of peace and quiet. In normal times she'd delight in the delicate taste of elderberry flowers, but this evening her appetite had fled with the arrival of Tyrell. His presence disturbed her profoundly. She felt tainted. He had soured her dream.

Sally moved away from the shelves and slipped into one of the many armchairs dotted around the library, turning her back to the door. Much of the room was in shadows. A lamp inspired by the American glassmaker Tiffany placed on a low table in the middle of the room was the only source of light. She closed her eyes, calmed her thoughts as best she could and began the long climb down the stone stairs in search of her guardian angels ...

She must have fallen asleep because she awoke with a start when the others filed noisily into the library to take their coffee or tea. Mrs. Martin brought in a tray bearing a steaming coffee pot and a teapot topped with its cosy. She set the tray down next to the lamp and offered to serve everyone. Sally was handed a bowl of tiny amaretti, smelling of almonds, but she passed it on, not taking any. Rafter was the last to enter and he remained standing. Once everyone was served, he addressed the company.

"So Tyrell, now is the moment of truth. What do you have to tell us?"

Tyrell looked like he had a bad case of indigestion. She could have sworn he'd gone a slightly green colour. What's more, there were strange dark stains on his hands that she hadn't noticed before. He looked a real mess. His jacket was crumpled and his shirt and trousers un-ironed.

"Stand up, you'll find it easier," Rafter advised.

Sally had some doubt about the advice and so apparently had Tyrell. Hoisting himself unwillingly to his feet with the help of the arm of his chair, Tyrell looked sheepishly around the room.

"I ... er ... have been spying on you," he said with considerable effort.

"Why would you do that?" Brent asked, apparently deciding to do something about Tyrell's discomfort that was making everyone uncomfortable.

"I was paid to," Tyrell managed to say as he studied his shoes, not daring to look at anybody.

Someone let out his breath with a whistle. Sally thought it might have been Tangwyn.

"And who paid you?" Brent pursued.

"Dr. Leuchtli."

Sally glanced around the room. Judging from people's faces, many had not anticipated such a possibility despite the fact that it was coherent with all they knew.

"And what did you tell the Doctor?"

For the first time, something of the Tyrell she knew resurfaced. She could almost see him calculating what to say and what not to.

"I told him you had a meeting. I told him who was present. But I was unable to tell him what you were talking about. I didn't know."

Sally was almost relieved to have Tyrell back to his old scheming self.

"Do you really want us to believe that?" she challenged, unable to keep quiet.

He turned to face her, hatred set firm around his eyes and mouth.

"Ah. Professor Rafter's new assistant has finally spoken," he spat.

"Enough," Rafter interrupted. "I believe what Tyrell has told us is the truth."

Sally was surprised to see the Professor smile to himself.

"Now," he went on, "I suggest we withdraw and leave Sally and Tyrell to sort this out."

"Is that wise?" Brent asked.

"I hope so," Rafter said, chuckling. "But as a precaution, I will ask Mrs. Martin to sit with them. She knows nothing of these things. And she can call us if there's trouble. Though I am sure there'll be none."

Mrs. Martin sat in an armchair near the door, knitting, ostensibly paying no attention. Tyrell was slumped in his armchair, his legs dangling over the armrest staring up at the ceiling, his hand splayed across his face. Nothing had been said for over ten minutes. The steady click of Mrs. Martin's needles and the distant murmur of conversation was all that was to be heard.

Sally rose from her seat her fists clenched, walked over to Tyrell and was about to slap him with all her force when she noticed the tears rolling down his cheeks. The sight was so unexpected and quite shocking that she stood next to him not knowing what to do. He seemed unaware of her presence.

"Do something totally unexpected," a voice whispered in her head.

She leant forward, grasped his hand and, surprising herself, said: "Let's go for a walk."

His head swung in her direction, seeing her for the first time. After a moment in which their eyes locked, he got up without saying a word and followed her towards the door. Sally nodded to Mrs. Martin that all was OK and the woman nodded back.

The Moon was nearly full, casting deep shadows around the garden furniture scattered across the lawn. Sally realised she was still holding Tyrell's hand as they walked in silence around the house. The path led through a tangle of bushes and shrubs, ending up by a little fountain that splashed happily in the moonlight beside a stonewalled well. She sat him down on a bench as he seemed incapable of fending for himself and she sat a little distance away.

"I don't understand," he began, wringing his hands. "Everything has gone wrong." His chest heaved as he drew in a deep breath trying to stave off a sob. "My uncle will kill me when he knows. Leuchtli will kill me too."

He wasn't making much sense, but Sally kept silent.

"Everyone will laugh at me. I've got nowhere to go."

Enough self-pity, Sally thought. "Tell me your story, Tyrell," she suggested talking softly but firmly as if he were a child.

So he began with the beginning, from his young life in the forlorn castle in Germany and the long desolate corridors adorned with empty coats of armour, with his friendless childhood trying to lose himself in imaginary games full of spite and cruelty, and the endless taunting of the local kids because he neither spoke nor dressed like them, and the torturing of little animals he caught in the dungeons and the punishment he'd received as payment for his cruelty, and his battle to get on in school and the short-lived joy at being better than the others, followed by the sorrow of finding himself even more isolated, then came his first exploits with girls, his guilt and his desire, and the relief that he bought with money stolen from his aunt treasure chest, and the discovery of magic and his dreams of being all powerful and finally winning him recognition and affection only to realise it was all hard work and little reward, and clumsiness plagued him, blotching his copy book, making a fool of him in crucial moments, and the hope that had come with his appointment as Rafter's assistant followed by his difficulties to study and complete his thesis, and the frustration he felt with her, Sally, a bit like a sister he hated and desired, who got better results than him and who was happily surrounded by friends and lovers, and Leuchtli's timely offer opening vistas of much wanted power and influence, and the shock of Sally's promotion, and his certitude she would replace him as Rafter's preferred assistant, forcing him to leave the university, his thesis unfinished, his dreams crushed, hopeless and clumsy, and to top it all he was now known as a thief because of Brent's notebook and a vulgar spy unable even to find out what was really going on, and he'd been tried and found guilty by a tribunal leagued against him...

Sally abruptly cut Tyrell's monologue short. "Enough, Tyrell. Stop moaning. You won't get anywhere like that."

Perhaps she should have slapped him earlier, Sally was thinking as her patience ebbed.

"Go run your hands under the fountain and rinse your face."

She expected him to complain or refuse, but he just stood and went to the fountain by the well.

Water dripped off his hair and down his face as he returned.

"Can you forgive me?" he pleaded.

Sally was about to ask Tyrell if she could trust him when nearby birdsong startled them both. Turning to look they saw a robin settled on the moonlit stonewall, its head cocked to one side studying them.

Sally made a slight bow to the bird, saying "Thank you." Then she turned to Tyrell. "I forgive you Tyrell." And she laughed at his look of relief that rapidly turned to distress at the sound of her laughter.

"Come," she said, chuckling, "Let's get back. People will begin to believe we have killed each other." And linking arms with him, she led Tyrell back to the house.

"Let's get down to business, gentlemen."

Leuchtli glanced around the table at each of the four bankers sitting there. They all sat tense with expectation in their smart suits, studying him carefully. A bottle of his best whiskey stood open on the table along side an ice bucket. He'd been wise to oblige some of his own people to be present so he didn't have to face the gnomes alone.

"You've visited the airtight, sound-proof compartment in the basement where we keep the subject."

One or two of them nodded. Pointing to one of the monitors, Leuchtli pursued.

"This screen shows us what is happening in that room. As you can see, my assistant is currently connecting up the subject. The wiring is for monitoring purposes. We don't need it for the Machine. But before we begin the demonstration let me explain one or two things."

He moved to the white board and drew a small red circle in the middle of the surface.

"On certain frequencies, the brain emits signals."

He illustrated the signal with a tiny squiggle leaving the circle, heading horizontally across the board.

"Our Machine picks up these signals," and he added a black square, "… analyses them and sends them back to the brain setting up an increasing resonance between the two."

He sketched in a two-headed arrow between the circle and the square.

"What is more interesting: we've discovered how to initiate that resonance from our Machine rather than wait for the brain to make itself known."

He drew a larger oval around the square.

"Even more interesting and most useful, these signals don't diminish with distance. They stay as strong no matter how far away you are."

He added two vertical lines close to each other with three dots horizontally between the two.

"The base signal is a very complex waveform that is unique to each person but we have found a way to generate it from a sample of the person's DNA."

He added a second small box next to the first representing the Machine and connected the two by a line.

"So we can target whoever we want provided we have the DNA."

He drew a second small circle and connected it to two squares with a new two-way arrow.

"Now comes the master stroke."

He couldn't help grinning at the bankers.

"If we connect two people to the Machine, one of them can enter into communication with the second influencing what he feels."

He completed his diagram with a further circle that he placed next to the squares and connected it to them with a one-way arrow in the direction of the pair of squares.

"For the moment that communication has some limits. You can't simply give orders to the other person but you can influence him or her with moods and emotions."

"What about the applications?" the younger banker asked.

"We anticipate several. In the field of entertainment for example, or in therapy, but also in conflicts and war."

Leuchtli didn't want to launch into a discussion. This had to go quickly. The longer it lasted, the greater the risks.

"Let's see how it works."

He moved away from the white board and poured himself a whiskey. This was the tricky part, the moment when everything could go wrong despite his carefully laid plans.

"I need a volunteer, but before one of you offers let me show you how it works."

He took one of the Machines from his pocket and held it up for them to admire.

"This tiny device, gentlemen, is all it takes."

One of his assistants came forward and threw some switches on the complex apparatus on the table causing two monitors to spring into life and a host of figures to scroll slowly down the screens.

"These screens are purely for monitoring purposes. They are not necessary for the Machine itself."

He passed amongst them pointing out the oval metal button on the back of the Machine.

"Here is where you must place your thumb if you want to send an emotion or an image."

He placed his thumb on the button and burst out laughing. His behaviour startled them, but they understood immediately when they looked at the screen: the subject had also burst out laughing. They were clearly impressed although some still looked sceptical.

"Your turn now," he said.

One of the younger bankers offered and Leuchtli handed him the Machine.

"As it is not easy to generate strong emotions spontaneously I'm going to help you."

The banker had regained his seat when one of the secretaries wearing an outrageously short skirt came and sat on his lap and began tongue kissing him. The other bankers were torn between watching the girl and keeping an eye on the screen.

"Look" one of them called out.

The subject had begun to rub his crotch in a most lewd way.

"Enough," Leuchtli said and the girl left the banker in mid-flight and walked out of the room.

Taking the Machine back, he asked: "Does anyone else want to try?"

All volunteered this time. He handed the Machine to one of the older men when the girl came back in the room carrying a little box. Leuchtli chuckled inwardly at the little joke he'd concocted. Instead of settling on his lap as she had with the younger banker she emptied the contents of her box into his lap: a huge hairy spider that crawled heavily across his crotch heading for his potbelly. The man screamed. And anyone who was paying attention would have noticed that the subject on the monitor was showing signs of terror too. The girl picked up the spider in her hand and replaced it in her box and left once more.

"Does anyone else want to try?"

Nobody seemed in any hurry to volunteer.

"Not to finish on this rather unpleasant note, I have prepared one more example for you that will please you, I'm sure."

Having recuperated the Machine from the man who was still shuddering from the touch of the spider, Leuchtli handed it to the head of the bankers.

"I have here a special perfume from Asia made from rare wild flowers," and he handed a small vial to the banker saying "Smell. They say it is most relieving."

The man was understandably cautious but he took a sniff, he didn't have much choice, and tears immediately began to run down his cheeks.

"The Asians call this perfume Eternal Grief, I believe," Leuchtli added, putting a stopper on the vial and handing it to one of his assistants.

The other bankers were all looking at the screen where the subject, a middle aged man was crying profusely.

Blowing his nose, the head of the bankers turned to Leuchtli and said: "You have impressed us Dr. Leuchtli. I believe you can count on our financial support. We'll have a contract drawn up and will contact you in a couple of days."

Leuchtli concealed his glee, smiling politely and shaking hands with each of the bankers in turn.

"Would you like one last whiskey?" he asked but they declined. All had to rush back to their respective offices. "It goes without saying that all that you have heard here is totally confidential. Your boss knows that," he added, giving the man a meaningful look. He was pleased to see that the guy shuddered slightly before he nodded his understanding.

Setting things straight

"Oui, bonjour. Tom Downes à l'appareil."

All four sat around a wooden table in a lay-by along a road

not far from Calais. Fran and Jenny had their heads together and were whispering about Leuchtli's notebook that they were studying. Martin, his eyes half-closed was watching the two girls with a smile on his lips. Tom was on the phone.

"Yes. I remember you well Mr. Cray. We met at the bank when I was preparing an article about Energos."

Tom waved to the others to catch their attention and indicated that they should stay quiet.

"You sound rather concerned, Mr. Cray. Has something serious happened?"

With his free hand, Tom opened his large block note and wrote: BANKERS MAY BACK ENERGOS for the others to see. Tom listened in silence as the man at the other end told him what had happened. STARTLING DEMO OF NEW INVENTION, he wrote across the page.

"So you were impressed but sceptical," Tom commented, hoping the man would say more. "That's terrible."

MINIATURE WAR MACHINE UNWRAPPED he wrote, glancing at Jenny who had gone rather pale.

"Yes. I plan to go to the office tomorrow or the day after. I'll check it out and let you know."

BANK HESITATES OVER INVESTMENT, Tom added at the bottom of the page.

"Thanks for contacting me. Goodbye."

"Why did you say you were going to the office tomorrow when we are just across the Channel from England?" Martin asked.

"If ever this Mr. Cray is unsure of his allegiances, he'll think I'm near home."

Jenny poured him a coffee from her thermos and asked: "So what have you learnt?"

"This man – he's a banker – was invited to a demonstration of Leuchtli's Machine."

Tom went on to explain what had happened.

When he described the scene with the sexy secretary and the spider, Fran commented: "That's typical of Leuchtli's twisted sense of humour."

Tom ended the story with a brief summary of the theory of the thing.

"That's nonsense!" Fran interrupted. "There's no way he can modulate those signals with emotions or thoughts. I worked on the brain signals. That's my area of expertise. The Machine is still a very crude device that sends and receives the base signal. And that's it."

"So what is Leuchtli playing at?" Tom asked.

"Fudging it to get the money," Jenny answered. "It is easy to imagine how he did it. All the emotions he used were planned in advance. A piece of cake!"

"Can you call the banker back, Tom?" Fran asked.

"Why?"

"So I can explain why what Leuchtli showed them can't be true."

Martin looked worried. "Isn't that risky?" he asked.

"Sure," Fran replied, "but we've got to do what we can to stop him. He's a madman. I wouldn't be surprised if he didn't believe his Machine did what he claims it does."

"Mr Cray? I have someone with me I think you should talk to you." Tom handed the phone to Fran.

"Bonjour M. Cray. I need to tell you some things about the Machine Dr. Leuchtli is building."

There was a pause as she listened to his question, doodling on the pad Tom had left on the table.

"No. I can't tell you who I am. It is far too dangerous. Leuchtli has already threatened me."

She drew two large circles around the word HESITATES and then underlined it several times.

"The best thing, I think, would be for me to explain one or two things about his Machine. Then you can judge for yourself."

She crossed out the word ENERGOS.

"OK. I am an expert in the field and I have inside information about Leuchtli's Machine. It is quite incapable of transmitting emotions, let alone words or orders. All it can do is transmit and receive the base signal he told you about."

She drew an oval around the word DEMO and sketched in a series of tiny lines that looked like hairs growing out of the top of the oval.

"It's quite simple really. As he knew in advance what emotions he was going to create, it was easy to organise the subject's reactions. And you bankers were so caught up by the emotions he'd orchestrated you had no time to be critical about what was going on."

Fran traced a jagged star around the word WAR, nodding her head as she did so.

"Yes. It could be used for war. If the resonance is increased enough the person will go crazy."

She underlined the word OVER and put down the pen.

"I don't think they have ever gone that far yet. But it might cause the person to go crazy or even to explode if he or she can't let the energy out."

She wiped the tears from her eyes as she continued to listen.

"Yes. I'm glad I could be of help. That man absolutely needs to be stopped."

She smiled at something he said and replied,

"Goodbye Mr. Cray."

The Count

"Leuchtli."

"Count."

"Is your Machine ready?"

"We are in the final stages of testing and should be able to …"

"Have you taken it up to full power yet?"

"That will only be feasible when we carry out the experiment for you."

"How do you know it can do what you claim?"

"Extrapolation."

"Speak plain English."

"We measure what it does at 50% and as the effect increases

278   Alan McCluskey

exponentially we can calculate what will happen at 90%."

"And what about 100%?"

"Not a good idea. It might resonate back on this world and cause devastation."

"Hm."

"Remind me what it is that you want to do with the Machine."

"In another world we call The Breaches that can be accessed through the dream realm, our mines have been overrun by a hoard of savages calling themselves the Big Folk. There are so many of them and they are unbelievably violent. We have already lost a lot of our people, gored by their savage attacks on our farms and villages. We need to eliminate them all as fast as possible but without destroying the mines. Those mines are worth a fortune."

"Are these Big Folk all located in the same area?"

"Yes in a large valley between the mountains."

"But how do you suggest we home in on the area. The Machine can only work through the person we are using as a vehicle."

"That's why I asked you to use that young assistant at the University. She has family ties in that area in the Breaches."

"But can we be sure she'll go there?"

"I plan to use my nephew who works with her to ensure she's in the right place at the right time."

"Tyrell, you mean?"

"Yes. The little runt my sister spawned before she died."

"You realise he will probably die doing it."

"That is of no importance. He should have died at birth, not my sister."

"As you see fit."

"I'll go get my nephew this afternoon and pack him off to the Breaches tomorrow. The 'experiment' must take place the day after."

"How can you send him?"

"We are experts in such travel. We do it all the time."

"When will you pay me?"

"As soon as I get news back that your work was completed successfully. So make sure you get things right. And keep that meddling Professor Rafter out of the way."

Double agent

"Good morning, Doctor." Tyrell said into the phone as he glanced at the list of notes scrawled on a paper on the desk in front of him.

"Yes. I have managed to uncover what they are up to."

There was a short pause during which Tyrell ticked off one of the points on his list.

"A rescue team. They plan to send in several people if there's any trouble."

Tyrell glanced up at Rafter who was sitting silently opposite him across the desk.

"No. Not before. After."

Rafter nodded his approval. Tyrell ticked off another point.

"Two. A man and a woman."

Tyrell drummed lightly with his fingers on the desk.

"No. Neither Rafter nor the Shaman."

Tyrell look up alarmed at which Rafter gave him a questioning look.

"What do you mean: you spoke to my uncle, the Count?"

Tyrell felt himself trembling. If his uncle and Leuchtli were working together that really wasn't good news.

"OK. Have a good trip."

Tyrell hung up and put his head in his hands as he leant on the desk.

"What does your uncle have to do with this?" Rafter asked.

"I wish I knew. My uncle is a dangerous man with a cruel imagination, an unpredictable temper and lots of money. If he's in league with Leuchtli, anything could happen."

"Could he have an interest in using this Machine?"

"I have no idea. But Leuchtli said my uncle was coming to see me this afternoon at the University, so maybe I'll find out."

"Something else is troubling you, Tyrell. What is it?"

"In all the time I've been studying here my uncle has never visited me. I can only imagine he wants something urgent and probably unpleasant from me."

"That Leuchtli told you your uncle was coming would seem to indicate they are planning something together and you are involved."

Rafter sat silent for the moment, deep in thought.

"I'm intrigued why Leuchtli insisted on knowing who was going to the rescue and when they were going. It seems to confirm my hypothesis that we should send our people in earlier so they can get in place to help Sally."

"Do you want me to go in too?"

"No you have to play along with your uncle and if you can let us know what he's planning."

Rafter stood up, about to leave, when he turned to Tyrell and added: "Whatever happens, remember you can..."

The door flew open with a loud bang as it flew back against the wall and a tall man dressed in an impeccable suit strolled in. He might have been an attractive man once, but age, over eating and drink had taken their toll. Like many men of his age he had a pronounced potbelly and his face sagged slightly under the wrinkles. But he still had all his hair, a shock of white locks that hung straight around his weather-beaten face.

The man pushed past Rafter without the slightest greeting or apology and dragged Tyrell out of his seat by his ear.

"Come with me. I have things to say to you brat."

Tyrell shook himself free and said with excessive formality: "Professor Rafter, may I present my uncle, the Count. Uncle this is Professor Rafter, the Head of the Department."

The Count turned towards Rafter and stared at him for a moment as if he were examining a laboratory specimen, then nodded and dragged Tyrell out of the office. Rafter stood still for a while as if digesting the Count's lightening passage and then swept up the page of notes that had been lying on Tyrell's desk, folded it into his jacket pocket and left.

Rafter arrived in his office just as the phone rang. He reached across his desk and, picking up the phone, said, "Professor Rafter."

"Good afternoon, Professor. Leuchtli here."

Odd, Rafter thought, Leuchtli is becoming more polite. Maybe it was just in comparison to the Count.

"I wanted to let you know we have completed our preliminary tests and would like to carry out the experiment the day after tomorrow. Will you be ready for then?"

So things were really heating up, what with the visit from the Count and now this call.

"I think we should be ready. Do you need any special equipment?"

"We will bring everything we require. We will just need a quiet room where we will not be disturbed."

"That will be no problem. We have plenty of rooms like that."

Rafter pulled the phone closer and sat down in one of his armchairs in front of his desk.

"You presumably don't object to members of our team observing Sally during the experiment."

Leuchtli coughed. "That won't be possible. The subject must not be disturbed in any way during this delicate phase."

Rafter made a mental note to find a way round that refusal. He already had some ideas how. "But remind me Doctor, what exactly are the stages of the experiment and what are your current expectations about what you hope to achieve by it?"

Leuchtli had already described the experiment to him, but it suddenly struck Rafter as odd that he hadn't insisted on finding out even more about this experiment earlier. He'd been so busy preparing Sally and the others and handling Tyrell. He hoped the mistake wouldn't cost Sally dearly. Then he realised Leuchtli was talking and he hadn't been listening.

"… we use a sample of the subject's hair so that the Machine can lock in on the correct frequency. The subject has to be asleep for the experiment to work. We generally use a sedative."

Rafter interrupted him. "That won't be necessary. Sally is trained in dream walking. It might even hamper her possibility to react in the dream realm."

"And we wire the person up so we can monitor body functions during the experiment, just in case there are any irregularities. The Machine itself doesn't require any physical linking to the subject."

Rafter wondered at Leuchtli's constant refusal to call Sally by her name.

"And what do you expect to happen?"

"As the subject moves through dreams causing a series of discontinuities we will measure the level of resonance and the potential energy output. Once it reaches about 60% we start to be able to harness the energy produced. In this experiment, however, we will not be taking or using that energy. We would like to rise to as much as 80% to check if our calculations are correct."

"And what will Sally feel during this?"

"Most of the people we have already experimented on said they felt next to nothing. We hope to go further this time because the subject masters moving around in dreams."

"Do you need to repeat the experiment several times?"

"Once ought to be enough at this stage. Then we have to work on how we recuperate the energy before we test the Machine again."

Rafter had a very uncomfortable feeling that Leuchtli's story was full of holes and dark corners.

"When do you arrive?"

"Late this evening."

"OK. We can meet with Sally and my people to discuss details tomorrow."

"One more thing," Leuchtli added. "I have to present my work in a Congress in Germany early the next morning so I will have to leave immediately after the experiment. The subject will sleep on for a while. If you could be there when she awakes that would be good. We can do the debriefing later."

The moment Rafter hung up, he phoned Alo.

"Can you get everyone together this evening? Leuchtli wants to carry out his experiment the day after tomorrow. We still have work to do."

Flying home

"Stop snivelling, wretch!"

The Count poured him a glass of schnapps. Tyrell wasn't fond of that particular brand of schnapps, its distasteful smell always reminded him of the Count.

"Here, drink this and listen to me."

Tyrell wiped his nose with the back of his hand, reached for the glass and sipped its contents. If his uncle thought he was a bit simple, he might escape questioning about what Rafter had been doing in his office earlier.

"I have an important task for you."

Here we go.

"Leuchtli is going to send that young assistant on a journey."

So it did have something to do with Sally.

"She is to travel through the Dream Realm and on into the Reaches where she is to visit a village belonging to the Littl' People."

Tyrell knew them well enough: peaceful people who lived across the mountains from the Cellerini castle in the Reaches.

"You must make sure she gets there and that she stays with them."

Why would his uncle want Sally to stay with the Littl' People? It certainly wasn't meant to be a social visit.

"Whatever you do, keep her away from my castle."

It sounded as though Sally was a danger that she needed to be kept at a distance, but that didn't make sense.

"If you need to, you can use some of the men from Cellerini Castle to help you."

His uncle was certainly going to great lengths to get Sally amongst the Littl' People.

"Will the Littl' People be expecting her?" Tyrell asked, hoping his question would be taken for naivety.

The Count laughed. "Oh yes. They have some sort of legend about a woman that comes out of the mountain to save them. Not that it will help them very much."

So there was a threat on the Littl' People.

"You will leave for the Dream Realm and the Reaches as soon as my jet touches down at the castle."

Didn't look like he'd be able to contact Rafter.

"Take this with you," his uncle said, pulling a small stone on a thin leather thong from his pocket. "Attach it around your neck and wear it at all times. It will protect you."

Tyrell took what his uncle handed him and examined it for a moment. He doubted the Count would bother to protect him. The stone had a small eye engraved on it. He'd seen something similar in a seminar with Rafter. What had it been? Ah yes. A device to track people and keep an eye on them. He knotted the leather loosely around his neck and let the stone hang on his chest.

What next?

"Gone!"

"What do you mean gone?"

Rafter and Alo strode into the entrance hall, took off their dripping hats and overcoats and shook them before hanging them up.

"Dragged off by the scruff of his neck by his uncle, the Count…"

It had begun raining seriously that afternoon. The sky was now so heavy with clouds that the hall would have been dark with shadows had Mrs. Martin not lit some candles and an oil lamp.

"… an unbelievably rude and arrogant man. Violent too!"

Sally, Brent and Keira filed out of the lounge to greet them.

"Who's violent?" Keira asked, the last to arrive.

"The Count," Rafter replied, slipping out of his wet shoes,

knowing full well his answer meant nothing to them. When Sally made a face, he added: "Tyrell's uncle."

"You've met him?" Sally asked, surprised.

She was much more interested in news of Tyrell now she'd had her long talk with him, Rafter thought. He congratulated himself on his foresight in bringing the two to settle their differences.

"Not really. He nearly knocked me over before he pulled his nephew forcibly out of the room."

"What could that mean?" Brent asked, stepping aside to make way for everybody to move into the lounge.

Rafter, who remained standing, waited till all were seated before he replied. As theatrical as ever, Sally noted.

"Well we know the Count and Leuchtli are working together. I learnt that listening to Tyrell talking to the Swiss Doctor over the phone earlier today. My guess is that the Count is using Leuchtli's experiment for a purpose of his own and that the Doctor is aware of it. Also Leuchtli knew the Count was coming to see Tyrell this afternoon. Judging from the questions Leuchtli asked he's concerned that we might send someone in to help Sally before the experiment begins. Knowing that Tyrell can travel in the Dream Realm and knowing that Tyrell was antagonistic to Sally, I reckon the Count plans to use Tyrell to make sure Sally does what is planned for her…"

"And what am I supposed to do, do you think?" Sally asked.

The Professor looked troubled which had Sally worrying.

"That we don't know."

"Maybe the answer is to be found in the way the Machine works." Brent suggested.

"Brilliant!" Rafter said, throwing Brent a broad grin.

"We've been told it is supposed to generate energy thanks to folds in the dream world. That seems highly unfeasible to me."

"Far too much like science fiction," Alo put in.

Sally had to agree. She'd always doubted Leuchtli was telling the truth about his Machine.

Rafter continued: "What does seem more likely is that they

have managed to set up the resonance they talked about."

"What would they gain by that?" Brent asked, accepting a cup of tea from Mrs. Martin who was making the rounds.

"The only thing I can think of," Alo chipped in, "is that it would upset the fabric of the Dream Realm causing a disturbance and as a result possibly affect the real world too."

Sally sipped her tea, pondering everything that had been said. Doing so would be like splaying bad dreams in every direction. So she asked: "Surely that would be too indiscriminate to be of use to anyone." Leuchtli may be mad, she thought, but she couldn't believe he'd set out to drive the rest of the world mad with a flood of nightmares.

"Not if the target is beyond the Dream Realm in another world." Alo replied.

Sally was beginning to get worried. Nothing had been said of other worlds so far. She could feel a knot clenching in her stomach that no amount of gentle massage would rid her of.

"So how can I stop them wreaking chaos in another world when I'm probably the vehicle for it?"

An uncomfortable silence followed. Everyone looked embarrassed. It was Brent who responded and she liked him all the more for it.

"I think we should call this off. It is far too dangerous for Sally."

"I agree," Keira added.

Sally glanced from one to the other, her friends and would-be lovers, a pained look on her face.

"No. I must go. If I don't, the madman will send someone else. Alo and you, Professor Rafter, must brief me on how best to channel that energy, if ever our guesses are right."

Rafter smiled sadly: "I admire your determination, Sally, and your courage. I knew you were the right person for this task. But I will not force you to go. I will go myself if necessary."

Sally hurriedly tried to conceal the tears that sprang to her eyes, rubbing her face in her hands.

"Thank you, Professor. But this is my mission. I am the one

destined to save this place, wherever it may be."

A long thoughtful pause followed. Sally accepted another cup of tea from Mrs. Martin who had an uncanny knack of knowing exactly what best to do at any given moment.

It was Rafter who broke the silence: "Good. Then we will send Brent and Keira in an hour ahead of you, Sally." Turning to look at Brent and Keira, he added: "If you still agree, of course."

Both nodded their approval, both looking determined, although Sally could feel how tense and anxious they were.

"Time flows differently in the Dream Realm, so sending you in earlier might not have the expected effect. But, from all we know, it is the best we can do."

It might even be too late, Sally thought, but she wouldn't let pessimism get the better of her.

"And what should we do?" Brent and Keira asked in chorus.

Sally smiled at their speaking together, heartened by their support.

"Brent, you must make your way to join Sally so you can help her when the time for the experiment comes," Rafter said. "Keira you too will help Sally, but first you must help Brent find the way. If I were the Count, I'd try to delay anybody sent to help Sally, so Brent will need your help."

But what happens if Keira is delayed as well, Sally wondered.

Under the old oak

At that moment the door opened and in walked Naniu.

"A strong wind has got up, it's stopped raining … and the moon is out. It's full tonight," she told them.

Her news relieved Rafter as he was wondering how he could carry out the ceremony he now needed to perform.

"You bring good news, Naniu. And you arrive at just the right moment."

Standing up, he offered a helping hand to Sally so she could stand too.

"We must go to the old oak on the hill for one final ceremo-

288   Alan McCluskey

ny before Sally, Brent and Keira head off. It was at the foot of that tree that you symbolically came together and it will be from that tree that just as symbolically you will all set out."

All stood, handing their empty cups to Mrs. Martin who had just arrived to collect them.

"Before we leave, let me explain briefly. During the ceremony each of you three will receive a 'new' name. I say 'new', but you may find it familiar, as if you had often heard it before. It will be your secret, even from each other, at least here in the real world. You will bear this name in the Dream Realm and any other world you may reach. Be careful who you give it to. Your name holds power."

"Will Tyrell have another name?" Sally asked.

"Yes, he will, but I can't tell you what it will be."

It struck him as a good sign that she should ask such a question.

"I believe he may try to help you in the end, Sally. When the time comes, you will have the difficult task of figuring out if you can trust him."

Droplets of rain slipped from the leaves of the oak and splashed to the ground forming small puddles around the tree. Sally, Brent and Keira huddled together in the cool night air while Rafter discussed quietly with Naniu and Alo.

"I'd like my name to be ..." Keira was saying when Rafter called them over.

"We are going to invoke a Name Tree," he announced and turned to Naniu.

"All six of us will thread our way around the tree, a bit like follow-my-leader," Naniu said. "Rafter will lead then Sally, Alo, Keira, Brent, and me. I will give the rhythm."

They set off in a wide circle round the tree. The wind had dropped and the moon was now high in the sky. Only the occasional small cloud laced its way over the moon's surface. Naniu, who beat the rhythm with a rattle, suggested they sway from left to right and back as they danced. The result was a slow rippling movement like a giant snake making its way round the tree.

"Listen to the many names that grow on the tree, pluck the ones that are ripe, roll them on your tongue ..." she instructed. "... and then pitch them into the air with your voice."

Over time, each added his or her strand to the growing thread of names that rose into the air strung out like pearls of sound on a necklace that garnished the tree.

"Martin. Marilyn. Merlin. Erin. Nana. Andrew. Donald. Daniel..."

Naniu launched into a series of names in bird-like trills and warbles that rose above those of the others.

"Freddy. Fanny. Hanna. Aran. Ryan..."

Sally felt herself caught up by the swaying movement and the round of names.

"The Tree will call you when it is your time. Make your way under its branches. When you have received your name, come back to your place in the dance."

The song pursued and developed with Alo joining Naniu in a duo above the syncopated beat of names...

"Berta. Brenda. David. Vero. Roman. Lana..."

"Sally," a deep voice called out in rich tones that were quite distinct from those of her colleagues.

Breaking from the circle, Sally moved under the branches of the Name Tree heading for its trunk. Sheltered from the moonlight, all was dark and almost sinister, making her uneasy. She jumped when the same voice whispered in her ear.

"Place both your hands on my trunk."

Beyond, in the distance, the complex thread of names continued its hypnotic round.

"Are you ready to receive your name?" the voice asked.

"Yes," she whispered, trying to sound convinced despite her doubts.

"Your name is ... Cianala."

The name startled Sally so much she broke contact with the tree. It wasn't at all what she'd expected. It was both foreign and familiar. She repeated the name to herself several times. Nala, she thought, that was her name. Satisfied at last, she left the shelter of the Name Tree, joined the others and, after finding the rhythm, began singing again. It was difficult to resist the temptation to add her new name to the names she sang, but she kept it to herself.

One by one Brent and Keira also received their names and then joined the round no less perplexed than Sally had been.

"Let your arms rise in the air, moving like branches in the wind. You are the Name Tree," Naniu said.

As she waved her branches above her, Sally sensed the knowledge of her name in her like a deep river of sap rising and giving her strength.

"Now break from the circle, turning round and round till the energy quietens and you come to rest. Stand still for a moment listening to your name."

The experiment

Moving towards Sally brandishing a pair of scissors in his hand, Leuchtli demanded a sample of her hair.

"Those scissors won't be necessary," Sally replied pulling out one of the shorter strands of her hair and handing it to Leuchtli.

"I'm not sure that will be enough," he retorted.

"It will do," Sally countered.

He handed the hair to his assistant who took it with obvious dismay. The assistant, a little man with a baldhead, shifted uncomfortably from one foot to another as he waited to be given the Machine. Turning her attention back to Leuchtli, she asked, "Can I see your famous Machine, Doctor?"

He took it out of his pocket, unwrapped the black cloth that protected it and showed it to her. It was about the size of smartphone with a small screen in a black case.

"These buttons help us adjust the level of resonance," he explained.

She had the impression that he swelled with pride as he handed it to his assistant to set the strand of hair in place.

"And what level of resonance do you aim for today?"

"Probably not more than seventy percent."

That wasn't what he'd told Rafter, she noted. Was he just forgetful or was he lying? She preferred not to think about it.

"OK. Lie down on this table," he instructed her.

A number of rooms in the Department were set up for individual massage, this was one of them. At least the massage table was comfortable, she thought.

"My assistant will place this cap over your head. It contains electrodes so we can measure your brain reactions."

Sally could feel the activity of the electrodes as a faint electric vibration on her scalp.

"I still think we should give you a sedative," Leuchtli insisted.

"We have already discussed this, Doctor."

Treating him firmly like a recalcitrant child seemed to work.

"It is not necessary and may even hinder the work I must do."

Sally was reassured to know that Rafter was in the next room and had had hidden closed circuit TV rigged up so he could watch and hear Leuchtli's every movement.

"Now close your eyes and let yourself go to sleep."

It took more courage than she had thought: letting herself slip into the Dream World with only Leuchtli and his nervous assistant hovering around her body. Surely she was the mad one in this story, she realised, as she set off on the path to the Dream World.

"She's in REM. We can begin," the assistant whispered.

Rafter leaned forward to turn up the volume of the speaker so that he could hear better. Leuchtli, who was pacing quietly about the room, had reached the one point that was not visible from the cameras.

"Set up resonance and once it is established increase it to 40%," he said.

Rafter turned to Alo who was sitting next to him: "Is she all right?"

Alo broke his concentration to nod and then closed his eyes.

"We've got 45%," the assistant said, glancing at the dials in front of him. "She's much stronger than the others, but it's still disturbing her brain waves. She'll be out of REM in a moment, do you want to continue or wait?"

"Wait." Leuchtli sat in an armchair and flicked distractedly through a magazine lying on a nearby table.

Sally had begun to sweat as pearls of perspiration formed on her forehead. As he watched her on the monitor, Rafter was filled with misgivings. Despite all his precautions, he was worried that they didn't have enough safeguards if something went seriously wrong. There were too many unknowns. Naniu must have felt his doubts because she lay a reassuring hand on his shoulder. Some while later the assistant looked up from his dials. "She's into the second phase of REM."

Leuchtli rose from his seat and came to look over the assistant's shoulder.

"Good. Up the resonance level progressively to 65%."

The assistant turned to look questioningly at Leuchtli.

"We've never been so high before…"

"Do as I say." Was all the answer he got.

"Should we intervene?" Naniu asked Rafter.

Rafter hesitated. He glanced at Alo who was still deep in concentration his eyes closed and replied. "No. We wait a while longer."

"There are considerable disturbances in the wave forms," the assistant announced, "and there are also the first signs of decreasing nervous system response. I think we should stop. It is getting too dangerous."

Both Naniu and Rafter stood up ready to make for the door.

"You are misinterpreting the data, Johannes. You're such a worrier. Look here." Leuchtli said pointing to one of the monitors. "The overall response rate is quite normal."

"Yes, but…" the little man began to reply.

"Those measures are secondary and unreliable," Leuchtli countered. "Continue to increase the resonance."

The assistant tweaked a knob on the tiny Machine.

"Eighty-five percent," he announced.

Sally had begun to twitch, her arms and legs moving involuntarily.

"There shouldn't normally be any body movement in REM," the assistant pleaded with Leuchtli. "Please, let's stop."

Alo came out of his trance: "I'm loosing her," he said, anxiety in his voice.

Rafter made for the door followed by Naniu and Alo, resolved to stop the experiment immediately. In so doing, they didn't see Leuchtli take the Machine forcibly from his assistant's hand and turn the dial to almost maximum.

"There," he said, satisfied, "… ninety-five percent. You see it works perfectly."

Concentrated on the dials and monitors, Leuchtli didn't see the violent shuddering that was racking Sally's body. Nor did he see the door open as Rafter walked in.

"Enough!" Rafter shouted. "Turn that bloody thing off immediately."

Seeing that Leuchtli didn't react, Rafter strode across the room, took the Machine from his astonished hands, turned it off and extracted the piece of hair from inside it. Livid, Leuchtli turned to face him.

"How dare you interrupt my experiment in my moment of triumph?"

"You are completely mad, Leuchtli. Look what you have done to Sally."

Alo and Naniu were trying to calm Sally with some success but the girl had not regained consciousness. Rafter went to join them. Having reassured himself that her heart was beating normally, he gathered Sally up in his arms and turned to leave the room. It was then that they noticed that both Leuchtli and his assistant had gone.

Chapter 13 - Oran Mor

A tsunami

Dawn hesitated on the horizon as stars retreated, winking out to leave way for the coming day. No birds greeted the sunrise this morn. No cock crowed. All was subdued, apprehensive. Even the wind was still.

"Run!" screamed someone, shattering the silence. "Run!"

Nala was up in an instant. Vee grabbed her hand and the pair ran off down the path as fast as they could, closely followed by Mia. They passed the deserted shelter without stopping and scurried up the hill till they reached the tiny oak at the top. Only then did they halt their headlong pursuit. Bent over double, panting, no one had the breath to talk. The rim of the sun's disk rose massive over the mountains in the east, tingeing their summits blood red.

"What was that?" Mia asked having finally recovered her breath.

"I think ... it's ... starting," Nala replied, still short of breath. "I feel odd... My toes ... and finger tips ... tingle, as if ... I were electric."

"Can you channel it?" Mia asked.

"I hope so," was all Nala could say before she was wracked by a sudden burst of energy. Falling to her hands and knees, she concentrated on her hands and let the energy flow into the soil. She immediately felt better but the earth was beginning to get warm.

"Hey look. The flowers are wilting on the ground around your hands." Mia exclaimed.

"Trace a circle … around the oak," Nala gasped. "To protect yourselves … and the tree."

"We can use all these little white stones scattered around the tree to mark the circle," Vee said, aligning the stones as he spoke.

From Mia's perspective it was like magic as the stones moved seemingly on their own till they formed a circle around the tree.

"Can I help, Vee?" she asked.

"No. See if you can help Nala."

Nala was on all fours, gasping for breath, just outside Vee's circle. Mia moved to place her hand on Nala's shoulder only to remove it immediately when she got a hefty shock.

"I can't touch you, Nala. You're electric."

"Keep … clear," Nala shouted. "Am I … outside … the circle?"

"Yes." Vee replied.

"Whatever … happens … you must … stay inside." Nala told them.

A new wave of energy rolled through her making her shudder violently.

"I … need … to … stand … up," she said to herself as she felt around for something to support her. She felt someone haul her to her feet and put his arm around her waist to support her. "No … Vee … No!"

"What's the matter?" Mia called out.

"Everything is OK," Vee replied. "Whatever you do, do not leave the circle, Mia."

The next wave that hit Nala was much stronger. It almost sent both her and Vee flying. He clung on to her although she could feel his pain. She had to let out more energy if they were to survive. So she channelled it further afield hearing it crackle like lightening as it hit the ground.

In a moment of calm she whispered to Vee: "Tell me …

what … you see."

"The sunrise is magnificent," he said making a supreme effort to talk normally.

"Are … you … telling me … the truth…?"

"My eyes see what is best … my love."

So she clung to him and he to her as wave after wave crashed over them and out into the valley. She could feel the tears rolling down his cheeks, or was it hers. She was no longer sure.

The waves were coming faster now and much stronger. She could do nothing but let them flow through her and out into the valley. Vee spoke no more, but hung limp in her arms.

"Oh Vee," she thought.

It was then that a massive wave blasted Vee away and left her hanging in mid-air for a moment till a much stronger hand grasped her and held her up.

"Channel all the energy to me," the male voice said.

"Connor?" she tried to say, her mouth completely dry.

"Connor, Tyrell, whatever."

She tried to pull away but she had no force left. "Don't hurt … the Littl' People," she managed to plead.

"That energy is going where it belongs: in my uncle's castle."

"No Tyrell. It will hurt you."

A new wave was beginning, far bigger than any before.

"It's now … or never," Tyrell managed to say and he grasped her hand firmly.

Flashes of brightly coloured lights flew off in every direction. They were visible to her, despite her blindness. She couldn't hold on any longer. She sensed she would explode if she continued to resist. She had to decide: trust or not. It was trust that won.

"Thanks … Tyrell."

Opening the sluice gates fully, she let the brute force of the wave flood out through her and into the outstretched hand and beyond. For a brief second she saw the Black Castle as the blast hit and the edifice crumbled in smoking ruins.

She heard Tyrell's distant voice calling out: "Think of me!" And it was done. She collapsed to the floor, and all went black. "Black at last!" she thought with relief.

Recovery

Absolute silence reigned in the valley. No living thing stirred. Mia opened her eyes with difficulty and gingerly moved her limbs to be sure she was not wounded. The circle had held good. She was intact as was the tiny oak tree. The grass inside the circle was still lush and green. But all beyond was black and desolate. Gone were the rolling meadows. Gone were the occasional trees. Gone was their former shelter. The whole valley had been reduced to black rubble. Only the mountains had resisted, and even they were scorched as if a giant flame-thrower had been at work.

A moan a few feet away caught her attention. At first sight she could see nothing. Then something or someone moved almost imperceptibly amongst the ruins just outside the circle. Nala!

"Nala!" she called out as she stepped out of the circle and rushed to the side of her friend.

The ground was still hot, singeing her feet despite her shoes. Nala was still alive. Mia gathered her up as best she could and staggered with her to safety within the circle. Laying her at the foot of the tiny oak, Mia examined her body carefully. Her hands and feet were badly burnt, there were minor burns on her arms and legs, but the rest of her body, although black with dust, seemed remarkably untouched.

Mia had had the foresight to grab her bag as she ran after them earlier. In it she still had the salve she'd used for Jake. She wondered where he was now. No point in yearning for him. All that seemed so far away. She applied the ointment sparingly on Nala's hands and feet.

What she really needed was water to wash her friend, but she couldn't risk leaving her alone to look for some. She heaved herself onto of a rock next to the oak and peered around the valley seeking signs of water. The place looked as dry as a desert. Water was going to be their major problem. She had a small amount in a flask in her bag, but it wouldn't last long.

"Where am I?" a parched voice asked.

Nala had regained consciousness. Jumping down from her perch, Mia knelt next to her friend.

"You are in the Lost Meadows," she told her, "though you wouldn't recognise them."

Nala groaned. "Mia, you survived."

"Yes. Thanks to you and Vee." Nala began crying.

"Oh Vee. Where are you now?" she sobbed.

No answer came. Mia took the young woman in her arms and stroked her hair, rocking her gently back and forth. Deciding that a lullaby was the best medicine, Mia crooned a wordless berceuse. She felt Nala relax and with time her breathing became regular as she slipped into sleep.

"Mia," Nala said when she awoke. "I'm thirsty."

"We don't have much water," Mia replied, pouring a little of their precious water in Nala's welcoming mouth.

It tasted good. Licking her lips, Nala asked, "Can you help me stand?"

Mia slipped a hand around Nala's waist to keep her from falling. It was true she had no strength in her legs. She could feel her knees shaking.

"It's odd, Mia. I no longer see white." She rubbed her hand over her eyes, wondering if she dared hope. "Now that Connor is gone, maybe his spell has gone with him."

Mia kept quiet.

"I need some water to wash my face. I think my eyes are stuck together. Do you think we can find some water?"

"There was a well under our shelter. Maybe it has survived. I'll go and have a look."

"No, Mia. Please don't leave me."

The couple hobbled off down what had once been a path from the little tree to the dip in the ground where their shelter had been hidden. If anybody had been watching they could have been taken for two drunken tramps. Nala had her arm slung over Mia's shoulder for support and the two staggered at every other step. It was slow going.

Nala would have liked to know what the place looked like now, but she couldn't bring herself to ask Mia to describe it. That had been Vee's role. What's more, she didn't really want to know the damage she'd caused to a valley she'd loved so much.

"Oh look. The wellhead has survived." Mia exclaimed with delight. "Let's see if there is still water down there."

Mia set Nala down, her back against a blackened rock, and hauled up a bucket of water.

"The water's fine," Mia announced having tasted it.

Nala splashed water onto her face and rubbed her eyes vigorously. They hurt but she had the impression they were less glued together. She wiped them dry with the inside of her shirt and struggled to open her eyelids. After some effort, they sprang open revealing Mia standing opposite her, a concerned look on her grubby face.

"Mia!" she said startled. "It's you."

And she flung her arms around her friend's shoulders and burst into sobs.

"So you can see again?" Mia asked after a while.

"Yes." She turned to look at the desolation that surrounded her. "Oh my God! Did I do this?"

"Not you. The people who channelled the energy through you."

Back at the foot of their little tree, they ate from the fruit and vegetables they'd found in the store buried under what once had been their shelter. Nala hadn't realised how hungry she was and their simple food was delicious.

"Nala," Mia asked as they lay back to rest and digest, "you said Connor was gone. What happened to him?"

"He sacrificed himself to save us and to get revenge against his uncle, I believe. It must have been his uncle that was behind that terrible energy they unleashed. He wanted to wipe out the Littl' People. I was connected to Connor at the end. For a short moment I saw the Black Castle as the wave of energy hit and the place crumbled in a smouldering heap."

Some time later, awakening from sleep, Nala stood and looked once more over the charred remains of the Lost Meadows.

"I wonder what Vee would have said about such desolation?" she said to herself.

"He would have said it would grow back more beautiful than ever," Vee replied.

"Vee!" she cried out in delight as she spun round trying to find where the voice had come from. But nobody was there. She sank to her knees, large tears rolling down over her cheeks.

"Why do you cry?" he asked. "I am still with you and I will always be with you."

She wanted to fling her arms around him, but how could you embrace a voice. She sobbed and laughed at the same time.

"Are you alright?" Mia asked, alarm in her voice.

"It's Vee," Nala replied. "He's here in me."

Mia didn't understand. How could she?

"D'rick told us this might happen. Vee is in me. He's a part of me. Like the Littl' People prophesied. I have two voices: one female and the other male."

"Exactly," Vee whispered in her head. "We are reunited as the legend foretold."

Nala wiped away her tears and turned to Mia.

"The only difficulty is that I can't hug him if he's in me," she said and burst out laughing.

"Then hug me instead," Mia suggested. "I badly need a hug," she added making a coy face.

"My man is far away."

And they both hugged and laughed together. And Vee laughed with them.

Shelter

"Withdraw deeper into the mountains," D'rick shouted.

Here and there small sections of the wall or roof of minor

tunnels had caved in and the Littl' People had a hard time clearing away the rubble and shoring up the tunnels.

"Leave the repairs! We'll see to 'em later."

A large number of the Littl' People had already retreated into the depths of the mountains. The team working with D'rick were ensuring that major passages remained accessible. Very few people had been hurt since the seismic waves began hitting the mountains, but D'rick was taking no chances. It was at that moment he saw El'na coming out of a side tunnel.

"All exits t' the Lost Meadows're tot'lly block'd," she announced.

Jake was perched on her shoulder, looking here and there anxiously.

"Get the bird t' saf'ty, g'rl." D'rick snapped and hurried off to ensure that his men were retreating safely.

"Greetings to you, too," El'na said sarcastically to his disappearing back.

"He's right," Jake screeched. "It's far too dangerous here."

"Men!" El'na muttered as she marched off down the main tunnel in the direction of the centre of the mountains.

Apparently tempers were fraying in the stress, Jake thought. He didn't blame them. There was nothing worse under ground than an earthquake, lest it be a pocket of gas. He made a deliberate effort to silence his fertile imagination as he stared into the tunnel they were taking.

Smoke from the fireplace was cunningly transported up and away by a series of pipes leaving the large cavern almost free of smoke. These Littl' People were really ingenious, he thought.

"Can I be of any 'elp?" El'na asked the woman in charge of cooking.

"No luv. You look after that bird," was all she got for answer as the women turned back to her pots and pans.

Jake was beginning to get used to being called the 'bird'. El'na seemed less happy with being stuck as his nursemaid. She moved away and sat at one of the long tables in the makeshift dining room to one end of the cavern, placing Jake on the table in front of her.

"Yer 'eavy," she said.

"It's not my fault." Jake replied.

"I know, I know," she said. "Times 're 'ard. I wanna 'elp."

Jake hopped away a few steps then turned to look at her. Give her something to chew on, he thought.

"How are we going to get out of here to reach the Lost Meadows?" he asked.

"The only thin' I can see is climb o'er the mountain. All the quick ways in 're blocked."

He realised he was as impatient as she was.

"I could fly over," he suggested.

"Sure. 'nd get lost and 'ave yer 'ead pecked off by an eagle."

Jake burst out laughing.

"Don't yer go laughin' at me!" she warned.

"I ain't laughin' at yer," he said imitating her way of talking.

"Men!" she said as if the word had four letters instead of three, and stomped off into a darker part of the cavern.

Jake took off from the table and soared into the upper reaches of the cavern looking for something to eat. After a none-too-tasty mouse that was more bones than flesh, he perched on a ridge far above the human activity and watched the Littl' People at work.

D'rick had just arrived and was making the rounds to see if everything was OK. His group of men were washing at a mountain stream while some of the women near the fireplace were laying the table. Suddenly a disturbance broke out. It couldn't be a fight. The Littl' People seemed so peaceful and good-natured.

"So where is 'e?" D'rick shouted.

"I dunno." El'na replied.

I'm causing her trouble again, Jake thought, as he launched off the ledge and glided down to land on El'na's shoulder.

"Is it me you are fighting about?" he twittered innocently. "It's not El'na's fault. I went off to get some food."

He extended his wings, hoping that would look impressive,

and continued, "Don't worry about Nala. She'll manage. She's a strong and resourceful woman."

Judging from the look on D'rick's face, his comment had hit the mark.

"As soon as the quakes stop, El'na is going to show me a way over the mountains... if you agree."

He felt El'na shift from one foot to the other and back again, but she didn't speak. All eyes were turned on D'rick.

"Sorry El'na. Go get somethin' to eat then show Jake the way. It looks like the quakes are over."

Guessing that D'rick would like to hug El'na but that he would not dare do it with an owl perched on her shoulder, Jake launched into the air for a tour of the cavern. When he came back, El'na was seated alone at table eating. Landing a bit further away, he waited for her to finish.

"Thanks," she said.

"Well maybe I should apologise too," Jake suggested.

After an hour's walk, El'na stepped out of the tunnel onto a ledge high above the valley. Fresh air, at last, Jake thought as he launched into the night air. It was a delight to be outside again. The air was so different. It was more alive. It spoke to him as it buoyed him up in its currents. However, aware of the dangers and mindful of El'na's concern for him, he curbed his desire to seek out the updrafts and landed back on her shoulder.

"The valley below is just across the mount'ins from ours," she explained. "Nobody lives there. And over there, behind that mount'in is the Cell'rini Castle. We should catch a glimpse of it from 'igher up."

She set off along a narrow path that snaked its way up the flank of the mountain. Jake flew just above, occasionally flying closer to warn her of what lay ahead. The moon was high and there was little wind. It was a pleasant night. Who would think that a catastrophe might be playing itself out nearby?

Several hours later they halted in a high pass for El'na to eat and rest. Jake flew higher trying to get a glimpse of the Lost Meadows, but they were still obscured by the mountains. As he turned to wing back to El'na he caught sight of a thick column of smoke rising over the mountains.

"There's smoke over there," he told El'na, worried it might mean a threat.

"That's where the Cell'rini Clan live," she said. "If we continue along this way we should see the Castl' from the next pass."

And sure enough, through a gap in the mountains they had a good view over the Cellerini estate from the next pass.

"I don't understand," El'na said, perplexed. "Where's the castl'? It should be there," pointing with her finger. "All I can see is a cloud."

"That's no cloud," Jake said, his owl eyes seeing much better than hers. "It's smoke and under the smoke there's an enormous heap of rubble. I think the castle has been destroyed."

Stunned, they both stared a long moment in silence.

"Cian'la must 'ave done that," El'na speculated.

Jake couldn't believe it. "Imagine the force you'd need to destroy such a castle!"

Turning their backs on the smoking ruins, they continued their way in silence. Jake wondered at the power that must have transited by Nala's body to destroy a whole castle and rock a chain of mountains. He feared what he would find when he finally arrived in the Lost Meadows.

Oh Nala, he thought, I pray you are OK. He shook his wings in a desperate effort to cast off the gloom that settled heavily over him.

El'na must have sensed his mood because she whispered, "She'll be all right..." and stroked his feathery head, something she'd never dared do before.

Dawn was breaking as they reached the final pass before the descent to the Lost Meadows. Jake couldn't resist flying ahead to see what could be seen. Filled with apprehension, he flew round the last bend and saw laid out in front of him a scene of utter desolation.

The whole valley had been completely reduced to cinders.

A wave of despair washed over him almost knocking him out of the sky. He sank to the ground, his wings hanging heavily about him, his breath coming with difficulty.

"Oh Nala! Was such a sacrifice really necessary."

El'na picked him up in her hands.

"Oh my God!" she said catching sight of the charred ruins for the first time. She burst out crying.

"It was such a beautiful place," she said. "How could anyone do this to us?"

She sank to the ground, still cradling the owl in her hands. She continued to caress his head and he cuddled up close, both seeking consolation.

Finally, El'na stood up.

"We must continue. We must go down and see wot's left. We owe that to Cian'la... and Mia, too," she said full of newfound determination.

Placing Jake on her shoulder anew, she strode off down the path towards the valley. Neither spoke. Jake felt numb. Everything was so pointless. His brain couldn't grasp what had happened. Both Nala and Mia gone. It was unimaginable. With eyes half closed, he let himself be carried by El'na. To his astonishment, the girl began to sing. He swivelled his head to look at her. He recognised her song: it was about the legend of Nala.

"It's to give us courage," she said interrupting her song for a moment, "... and to send strength to Cian'la. I am sure she's not dead." And she pursued her song.

It was true Elna's song made him feel much better. Straightening his back and spreading his wings, he opened wide his eyes. The valley was much closer now. He could see more details. Odd, he thought. What's that tiny splash of colour right in the middle of the blackened ruins? Letting out a wild screeched of hope and joy he beat his wings and rose into the air.

"Look," he called down to El'na who was startled by his behaviour and had stopped singing. "Can you see that tiny island of colour in the middle of all the blackness?"

Yes, she could, but she couldn't make it out.

"Join me down there," he called to her as he plunged towards the valley.

As he neared the valley floor, he let himself be carried up and around by a strong air current. Rising once more, he could see his goal more clearly: a small circle of green grass on top of a hill, a tiny oak tree and two dishevelled girls sleeping next to each other on the grass. It must be them. El'na was right to have faith. He hooted as no owl had ever hooted before. Joy and sadness mingled in his quavering voice.

He landed silently at a short distance from the girls and stood watching: Nala and Mia, very dirty but very much alive. As he watched, Nala opened her eyes and stared back at him. As their eyes locked he almost forgot himself and rushed to take her in his arms. But he was an owl now.

So pulling himself up to his full height he said: "Greetings Nala. You have succeeded."

It was a rather stupid thing to say, but he couldn't do what his whole body yearned to do: spin her round in a wild dance.

"Who are you, owl, that knows my name?"

He hopped a few steps forward.

"I am Jake. I've been looking for you for ages."

Nala sat up and examined him closely.

"Could you really be Jake? I wish I could believe you."

Jake hadn't imagined he'd have to prove who he was to Nala when they finally met. There were so many twists to this story.

"Hold on," he said. "I have one way to prove it to you. I know your other name."

She looked both alarmed and expectant. "Yes?"

"I love you Sally," he said, finally finding the right words.

Tears were streaming down her face as she leant even closer and whispered,

"I love you too, Brent."

"At last," Vee said in her head, making her smile. And she lent forward, cautiously stretching out her hand to caress his head and wings. Taking him bodily in her hands she stood and placed him on her shoulder.

"Let's go for a walk. I want to get some water at the well and you can tell me your story."

"... and the castle was a pile of ruins," Jake said, finishing his explanations from his vantage point perched on a rock by the well.

"Yes. I know. Tyrell sacrificed himself in the end to save me and all of us, but also to get revenge on his uncle. It was a terrible moment. I couldn't decide: trust him or not trust him; save myself or save him."

Both were silent for a while recalling memories of Tyrell and Connor.

"Now there's a thoughtful couple!" a voice interrupted their meditation.

Nala spun round to find El'na walking into the dip in the ground where their shelter had once been.

"I thought you'd have so much to say to each other."

"Well met, El'na," Nala greeted her.

The two embraced, at length and with pleasure ... to such an extent that Jake had to clear his throat to remind them he was there.

"Jake was telling me about the destruction of the Black Castle ..." and she went on to explain briefly to El'na what had happened on Oak Hill.

"And what about Mia and Vee?" El'na asked.

"Both are fine," she replied.

"Whose Vee?" Jake asked, a bit of an edge in his voice.

"Now we're in for fun," Vee whispered in her ear.

"Vee is a very close friend of mine. Someone I met on the road. Someone I hated at first. Someone I wanted to keep at a distance. Someone who remained faithful. Someone who saved my life and guided me painstakingly while I was blind. A dear friend who has gone now, who also sacrificed himself for me, but who will stay with me always."

"You did that rather well," Vee commented.

Jake looked perplexed Nala thought, although she'd never seen a perplexed owl before.

"So D'rick was right," El'na added. "You and Vee are one now."

"Yes," Nala said, a smile on her face. "I suppose he always was a part of me."

Nala had the impression Jake was in a huff because he said: "I'd like to go say hallo to Mia. I haven't seen her for ages."

"Silly man," Vee said. "He has nothing to be jealous of."

Nala turned to Jake and said: "Vee says you have nothing to be jealous of. I love you Brent."

Now it was El'na turn to be perplexed.

"Who's Brent?"

"This is Brent," Nala said indicating the owl. "Well in our world and in human form, that is his name."

"And wot's yer name in yer world?" El'na asked her.

"Sally."

"Wot a beautiful name."

"But I suggest we stick to Jake and Nala and Mia while we're in the Reaches." El'na nodded her approval.

"Jealousy or not," Jake said, "I think we should go back to Mia she'll worry if she wakes and finds herself alone."

Lost

Mia was nowhere to be found when they arrived back at Oak Hill. The contents of her bag lay scattered at the foot of the oak, large boot prints marking the ground around. Jake launched into the air. As he rose to get a better view an arrow whistled passed narrowly missing his wing.

He plunged to the ground screeching: "Take shelter. We're under attack."

The girls scurried down the hill, running passed the well and on towards the mountains.

"There's no way out," El'na panted. "We blocked the tunnels."

Reaching the cliff face they hid behind a large rock close to one of the obstructed entrances, Jake landing next to them. A band of thugs dressed in black leather carrying bows and arrows were approaching cautiously. Mia didn't seem to be with them. From time to time one shot off an arrow while others inched their way forward. The situation looked desperate. The immense beefy brutes were only thirty feet away and the two girls had nothing to retaliate with.

"Can't yer blast 'em?" El'na whispered.

"What if they're holding Mia?" Nala replied.

The men chose that moment to charge, breaking from cover and running heads down across the remaining short distance to where the girls were sheltered. None of them made their destination. Each stumbled and fell, an arrow sticking out of him. The surviving few that had hung back took to their heals and ran.

"You left that to the last minute," El'na said as she turned to see D'rick and his men push aside some rocks and step out of the tunnel entrance.

D'rick ignored her sarcasm and walked up to Nala to greet her and Jake who was now perched on her shoulder.

"We 'eard tell the Black Castl' was destroyed and a band of that Cell'rini mob were 'eading 'ere," he said by way of explanation.

"They've got Mia," El'na told him.

D'rick turned and gave orders to his men some of whom headed off across the charred valley in search of the fugitives and Mia.

"Looks like D'rick and El'na have something going between them," Vee commented, laughter in his voice.

Nala hadn't yet got used to talking to him in her head so she smiled instead.

Nala, Jake and El'na led D'rick to Oak Hill to show him where Mia had been taken from. All three stood silently around the tiny oak as Jake coasted above them.

"You need to do something about this place." Vee said.

"What can we possibly do?" Nala asked.

"Remember Oran Mor, the Great Song." Vee replied. "Didn't Naniu say: all things are shaped with music and movement."

"Ah!" Nala said out loud realising what he meant.

Her sudden exclamation surprised D'rick and El'na.

By way of explanation she said: "It's Vee. He's told me how to right things in the Lost Meadows."

Both looked questioningly at her.

"Can you bring all the Littl' People here, D'rick? And have them bring their instruments with them. We need to make some music."

D'rick loved music and was well aware of its power. Needing no further, he turned to one of his men and they discussed in hushed tones for quite a while.

"We'll gather the Littl' People 'ere just afore sunset t'night," he announced. "I go to make ready. But I leave a few men 'ere if ever Cellerini's thugs come back."

The Great Song

"What do you plan to do?" Jake asked as they sat at the foot of the tree eating some fruit El'na had fetched while they waited for the Littl' people to arrive.

"I don't rightly know," Nala replied. "Vee talked of Oran Mor."

Jake nodded his head. "I remember: The Great Song."

"Amongst the Littl' People we 'ave a legend that the world was created by song," El'na added. "Is that wot yer mean?"

Nala ran her fingers through her hair that was filthy with cinders. "Something like that. We need to sing the life back into this place. But first I need to wash. I can't recreate the world if I'm filthy!" she said laughing.

El'na stood to join her. "Then even if you are no longer blind, it would be my pride and privilege to wash you, Nala."

Nala glanced at Jake. "Then it is my pleasure to accept your offer. What about you Jake? How will you prepare?"

Jake hopped from one foot to another as if he were embarrassed. "I will prune my feathers and then I'll sit for a time in meditation." So saying he flew towards the mountains.

Clean and smelling of the herbal soap that El'na had produced from her bag, her clothes laid out to dry having been washed at the well, Nala sat shroud in a blanket that El'na had hauled from the tunnels. Her eyes closed, she listened to Vee who was recounting stories of Oran Mor. She hadn't realised what a rich source of knowledge he was. It was El'na that called her back to the present.

"The sun is about to set behind the mount'ins. I think yer'd do well to dress."

With El'na's help she donned the clothes the Littl' People had made for her and stood by the oak that reached to about the level of her breasts. A whoosh told her Jake had arrived and sure enough he landed on her shoulder as she turned to face the tunnel from which they expected the Littl' People to arrive.

They heard them before they saw them. Drums, rattles, strange string instruments, pipes and whistles, and their wonderful voices, of course. The music echoed from deep within the mountains and grew louder and closer as the sun finally sank behind the mountain peaks casting a rosy glow over the valley.

The first of the musicians stepped into the valley bearing torches and advanced towards Oak Hill. A steady procession of people wove its way along the path lit by a multitude of flickering torches, their song growing and swelling as they came. At the base of the Hill the procession split in two passing round both sides till Oak Hill was the centre of a massive choir and orchestra illuminated by hundreds of winking lights.

Nala felt the energy of the song bear her up and away as she stretched her arms above her head and began dancing with the music. Slowly, ever so slowly, she turned in circles round the oak, her hips swaying in sensuous curves. She could hear El'na singing nearby and D'rick who'd come to join her. Riding the music, she let herself flow out and up, feeling the sap of the earth rise through her making her shudder with pleasure.

Above she felt the stars twinkling into existence like so many tiny sources of energy that fell like sparkling flakes over her outstretched hands. Tears streamed down her face at the beauty of it. Widening her circles little by little she moved further away from the oak and closer to the singers and musicians. Music made the world, she thought, as myriad colours mingled with the notes, sparkling like a million rainbows in the notes themselves. Colour flowed out from her as she circled the base of the hill. She was vaguely aware that the Littl' People stepped aside to make way for her and then fell in behind her as her circles became ever larger.

Unable to contain herself any longer she began singing with them as she turned and turned, her arms outstretched like a Dervish. At some moment she lost all feeling of herself as separate from the rest of the world. She flowed in and out of everything. She was the all-knowing sap of the world that flowed between all things. She was the One. At that moment her turning came slowly to a halt and she opened wide her eyes. All around the Littl' People were kneeled in silence, their lights held high. All around, lush grass had sprouted with a multitude of wild flowers of all imaginable colours. She took a deep breath of the flower-scented air and wiped the tears from her eyes. Joy bubbled up and burst out of her as a laugh.

"Thank you," she said, finally. "Thank you from the depth of my heart."

Sinking to her knees and settling on the grass she was replete. Her task was done, she knew it for sure now. All that way for this, she thought. Soon she would go home. She would miss the Littl' People. But this was no time for regrets, the Littl' People had stood and were crowding round to touch her and thank her for all she'd done.

She didn't want to be the centre of their reverence. So as one of the men moved to thank her, she caught hold of his hands and swung him into a wild dance. D'rick immediately understood what was happening and grabbed El'na and began dancing with her. Musicians here and there began playing again and as there numbers swelled, more and more people began to dance.

Nala moved from group to group dancing with as many people as she could. Hours later, when she could dance no more, she found herself at the foot of Oak Hill that she slowly climbed seeking a familiar place to rest. To her surprise the oak was no longer tiny, but towered above her. She sat down and leaned against its massive trunk and closed her eyes.

When Nala awoke D'rick and El'na were sitting next to her in each other's arms.

"Where's Jake?" she asked.

"Nobody knows," El'na replied.

"Nobody's seen 'im." D'rick added.

"Where could he be?" Nala pursued.

"I think he's gone to find Mia," El'na said.

"Surely your men will find her," Nala said, trying to reassure herself.

"We've found no trace of 'em anywhere," D'rick had to admit.

"But this is terrible. Just when it is time to go home, both have left me."

El'na shifted closer and took Nala in her arms.

"Don't fret Cian'la. Maybe they 'ave other journeys to make. Think rather of the wonderful thin's yer 'ave done 'ere."

"It's almost dawn," D'rick added.

"We've prepared a feast to thank yer and to celebrate our legend."

Nala stood alone on top of Oak Hill. El'na had gone to supervise preparations for the feast that was to take place at the foot of the mountains near the entrance to the tunnels. D'rick was making the rounds of his men to gather news of the Cellerini gangs and possibly of Mia and Jake. As she watched the sun rise over the mountains a great wave of sadness rolled over Nala.

"Vee?" she said.

"Yes, Nala."

"I can't help feeling my whole mission has been a failure."

Vee waited in silence for her to say more.

"Tyrell is surely dead and probably many other people with him. He died trying to save me. Keira has been abducted because I wasn't there to watch over her. And now Jake has gone looking for her. I can't help feeling that he also left because he was jealous of me and El'na..."

Vee remained silent.

"Have you left me too, Vee?" she asked desperately.

"Nobody has left you, Cian'la," he said at last. "They are all still with you, after a fashion. And they always will be."

He paused for a long time during which Nala watched the colours of the peaks change from pink to red and then to orange and yellow as the sun rose slowly above the mountains.

"Yes," Vee pursued, "Tyrell has gone, it is true. Did you know how funny he was? A real clown! What he did was his choice. He finally decided for himself and we should honour him for his courage in doing so."

Now it was Nala's time to remain silent waiting for Vee to pursue.

"For whatever reasons Keira and Brent are no longer here now you can be sure it will make an interesting tale when they finally get back."

His laughter rang in Nala's head.

"Oh Vee. What would I do without you?"

"Now who's waxing sentimental," he chided mockingly. "You spent years unaware I was at your side and you got on very well all the same."

She had to laugh. He was right.

El'na arrived at that moment. "It's good to 'ear yer laughin', Cian'la," the girl said. "I was worried you'd be sad about yer lost friends."

"I was," she admitted. "But Vee made me laugh."

"Well done, Vee," El'na said taking Nala's arm and leading her down the hill towards to place were the celebrations were to take place.

"Vee says I should give you a kiss from him," she said stopping El'na and kissing her firmly on her lips.

"As if you needed Vee for excuse," El'na retorted.

The girls laughed together as they pursued their path.

Music could be heard coming from near the entrance to the tunnels as musicians warmed up. Fiddles, tambours and a harp. The music of the Littl' People was very much like that of the Celts, Nala thought.

A series of long tables had been laid out on a flat piece of ground with a cooking fire set in their middle. It reminded her of the open common room in the Littl' People's home valley. The tables were festooned with garlands of wild flowers gathered in the valley. Tureens smoked with piping hot soup. Large wooden platters overflowing with cuts of meat and chunks of cheeses lay here and there. Wicker baskets contained warm loaves of bread sprinkled with a variety of tiny seeds. Silver patens were piled high with all manner of fruits. Gold and silver pitchers encrusted with jewels bore beer and wine and water for the festivities.

As they approached, the musicians fell silent. A distinct sense of expectancy hung in the air. El'na led Nala to one of the tables where D'rick awaited her. The Littl' People filed silently out of the tunnels and took their places at the tables where they stood all heads turned towards her. When all were in place, D'rick turned to Nala and, taking something from his pocket, he bowed to her and placed a gold necklace around her neck that sparkled with a rich selection of precious stones. She recognised the delicate craftsmanship of the Littl' People with its intricate folds and twists.

"Thank yer, Cian'la," was all he said.

As if that were the signal, the Littl' People burst into song. It was the tale of the legend that she incarnated: the Princess come from under the mountains to save their lives. El'na had taught her the words and Nala sang along with them. She couldn't help herself, tears streamed down her cheeks as she place her right hand over her heart to feel the beautiful present she'd received.

When the music stopped, the Littl' People sat. But Nala remained standing.

"Friends," she began. "I will soon have to go back to where I come from, but know that you will always be in my heart. I will never forget you. In the name of Vee and Jake and Mia, I'd like to heartily thank you for the wonderful hospitality you've offered us. May you thrive and prosper. May your lives be filled with music and dance. Remember it is music that shaped and continues to shape the world."

And she sat down between El'na and D'rick to the sound of thunderous applause as all the Littl' People rose to salute her after their fashion.

'Goodbye my dear friends', she thought. 'May you be blessed.'

Chapter 14 - The Threads Unravel

Reunited

When Sally opened her eyes the first thing she saw was a slim, bald-headed girl in a blue tracksuit lying on the bed next to hers, her legs making cycling movements in the air above her. Sally wondered if she'd landed in a madhouse while she was away. Effectively, it looked like they were in a small hospital ward but without the typical hospital smell to it. Then a familiar figure stepped into view and tickled the girl's feet.

"How's your backache?" she asked.

"Better," the bald girl replied with a slight German accent.

"Jenny!" Sally called out, surprised. "What are you doing here?"

Jenny spun round at the sound of her name, a broad grin on her face.

"Welcome back Sally. I'm so happy you made it." Turning to the girl next to her, she said, "Meet Fran, a friend from Switzerland."

Fran rolled over and stood up, rubbing her back. She was not as tall as Jenny or herself but seemed full of energy.

"Fran, run and tell the others Sally is awake."

Sally sat up and pulled the electrodes from her head and arms. She was relieved to find she was properly dressed and not in one of those ugly hospital nightdresses.

"I wouldn't stand up if I were you," Jenny said. "They told me you might be a little shaky if you tried to stand the moment you woke."

Sally dangled her legs over the edge of the bed, scuffing her bare feet backwards and forwards on the parquet floor. She stretched out her arms to Jenny and said, "At least you can give me a hug," pretending to pout.

Once the two had hugged and kissed, Sally continued her questions: "How come you're here? Is Tom with you?"

"Yes, he is. Martin too. We came to see you. You can't imagine the adventures we've had."

"Great." Sally smiled. "You must tell me. I've been having such a boring time lying here in bed."

"What makes me think you're telling fibs, my friend?" Jenny countered.

At that moment Fran returned accompanied by Rafter, Tom and Martin.

"Am I glad to see you back," Rafter said, clasping her in a bear hug.

She'd forgotten how tall he was, but then he'd never given her such a hug before.

"You look so rested. Anyone would think you'd been asleep all this time."

Everybody laughed at his joke.

"Still as witty as ever, Professor." Sally said, surprised at how much more at ease she felt with the Professor now she'd had her adventures.

It was the sort of moment when Vee would have made a perspicacious comment but his voice was silent. Feeling a little hungry, she wondered how long she'd been away. She had the impression it had been for years.

"How long have I been away?" Rafter glanced at his gold watch.

"I saved you from the clutches of Leuchtli about three hours ago," he said dramatically.

This whole adventure had made him more playful, Sally thought.

"In the mean time your friends here arrived with some very

interesting news of Leuchtli and his company. But enough of that, you must be starving."

He helped her to her feet and she took a couple of hesitant steps. As she did something heavy swung from her chest, glittering in the sunlight flooding in through the window.

"Wow!" Jenny said. "What's that?"

Sally raised her hand to her heart placing it over the gold necklace.

"How did I manage to bring that back?" she wondered out loud. "It was a present from some very dear friends."

Rafter examined the necklace closely without actually touching it.

"We're going to have to hire a bodyguard if you insist on wearing that around the university," he joked.

Oh it was so good to be back, Sally thought.

"Seriously though," Rafter pursued, "I suggest you keep it well hidden. It could spark all sorts of questions."

Sally turned to look round the room for the first time. It was then that she saw the two other beds in which Brent and Keira lay sleeping. Her heart skipped a beat at the sight of them seemingly peacefully lying there. Walking over to Brent's bed she bent and kissed him on his forehead whispering: "Good luck my friend."

Hesitating a moment, she studied his placid face as she remembered the sharp features of the owl he'd become. Moving on, she kissed Keira too, saying: "I hope Brent and D'rick manage to rescue you."

During this time the others had discreetly stepped out into the corridor. "Come back to us soon," Sally concluded and, taking her leave, she followed the others barefoot out of the room.

News from Switzerland

Tom burst into the living room in Alo's country house. He looked like what Sally imagined to be the typical journalist in his faded jeans and chequered shirt. He even carried a notebook in his hand.

"You can't imagine what's just happened," he exclaimed.

Sally, Jenny, Martin and Fran sat comfortably in armchairs scattered around the room bringing each other up-to-date with some of what had happened.

"I just had a call from the banker in Switzerland."

At that moment, Rafter followed Tom into the room.

"So you are rich?" he quipped.

Tom laughed. "No. Nothing like that, unfortunately. A Swiss banker contacted us about Leuchtli, because they wanted to invest in ENERGOS but they had some doubts and they knew I was investigating the company. When we met Fran we had her tell the banker something of what she knew of Leuchtli's work. Since then we've had no news from them."

"So what did he have to say?" Jenny asked, impatient with the explanations.

"The police raided Energos yesterday. And rumour has it that they found several dead bodies concealed in the basement."

"Oh no!" Fran gasped.

"There's a warrant out for the arrest of Leuchtli. Apparently he can't be found anywhere."

Rafter settled in one of the armchairs "So we are likely to have a visit from the police sooner or later. People must have known we were working with him and that he was here until a very short while ago."

He took a cup of tea from Mrs. Martin who seemed to have an unending supply in her kitchen.

"I'll call Alo and Naniu. We need to talk about how to handle this. It could be rather complicated."

Mrs. Martin pulled a portable phone from the front pocket of her flowery pinafore. "Here, you are," she said, handing it to Rafter.

When Rafter left to phone, Tom related the rest of his conversation with the banker.

"One of Leuchtli's victims was a woman called Donna Martinez. They used the Machine on her and it drove her mad. We went to see her in the clinic where she was being treated. Well after raiding ENERGOS, the police wanted to question Donna. But they arrived too late. She'd managed to escape from the clinic. They found her later, hanging from a tree in the nearby forest."

Turning to Jenny he added: "Apparently she had your drawing of the tropical bird in her pocket."

Jenny burst into tears. "She was so frightened ... Why did this have to happen to her?" she said through her sobs.

Both Sally and Fran moved to console her. When she finally stopped crying, Jenny reached for her bag and pulled out her drawing block. Taking out the drawings Donna had made, she laid them out on the table explaining them to Sally.

"The poor woman," Sally said. "I hope they catch Leuchtli before he does any more damage."

Cataclysm

They sat around the brightly polished dinning room table in silence as Mrs. Martin brought in the scones she'd prepared. They smelt delicious, but few were hungry. Rafter had had no time to talk in private to either Naniu or Alo so he briefly recapitulated the situation before discussing what to do.

"The police will presumably want to know what Leuchtli was doing here," Tom said, jotting down a few words in his notebook. "The best thing would be to tell them the truth."

"I think you may be right, Tom," Rafter said. "We don't need to go into details. No mention of Brent and Keira ... or the involvement of Tyrell and his uncle. As for Sally's journey, all they need to know is that she was asleep."

Mrs. Martin stuck her head around the door. "There's a call for you, Professor."

Excusing himself, Rafter went to the study next door.

"Professor Rafter," he said picking up the phone. "No, sorry. I don't speak German."

He listened in silence as the person explained the situation.

"This is terrible," he finally said. "Of course. I will help you all I can."

And he hung up. Rather than return to the others, he sat quietly in meditation.

What a mess! he thought, wrapping his jacket tightly around himself as he felt cold all of a sudden. This was going to take some sorting out. He just hoped there wouldn't be any more victims.

Returning to the dining room, he sat in his place not wishing to talk immediately. The others were eating scones and butter and talking quietly in small groups.

"Are you alright?" Sally asked, noticing the pained look on his face.

"I am very sorry," he said gravely. "I have some bad news to announce. Tyrell is dead. As is his uncle and a large number of the staff from their castle. The German police are investigating what they think might have been a mass suicide."

Everybody looked shocked except Sally.

"Sally?" he asked.

"I knew," she admitted.

"It was me that killed him." She burst into tears, clasping her hands over her face.

"What do you mean it was you?" Alo asked, shocked.

Drying her eyes, Sally continued: "As the resonance increased, I couldn't handle the massive waves the Machine was channelling through me. They'd already reduced the whole valley to charred ruins."

"Unbelievable," Alo exclaimed.

"Tyrell, or rather Connor as he was called in the Reaches, reached out to me and told me to channel the energy to him at Cellerini castle. I hesitated but the force was too strong. I daren't wait a moment longer. So I did as he said. For a brief second I saw their castle crumble to ruins. Tyrell asked me to remember him. Those were his last words."

All looked aghast at Sally.

"What a terrible choice, " Jenny said, expressing an opinion shared by everybody.

"I thought something like this might happen," Rafter said.

"It was why I made sure you and Tyrell settled your feud. So you see, Sally, if anyone is to blame, it is me."

"For people who are supposed to be amongst the best brains in our world ..." Fran addressed them in a firm, determined voice standing as she did so, "... you really do get some things muddled up."

She began pacing slowly round the table. "Blame has nothing to do with this. There is no fault here, in a moral sense. If there are faults in our story then they are either geological or chaotic."

Everybody laughed. Rafter had the curious impression that the girl was getting taller and stronger as she walked round them.

"Sally, Tyrell, Brent, Keira, the Count, Rafter ... all of us, we made choices in an extremely complex situation. Who knows whether good or bad will come of them? What might have been is gone forever. What is now we have to learn to live with. It is time for us to turn our attention to what might be."

Running her hand over her baldhead, she looked at each of them in turn.

"So let's get on with it." And she sat down having reached her place.

There was a moment's silence then Rafter applauded vigorously. The others quickly joined in until all were applauding till their hands hurt. Rafter was glad the youngsters had arrived. He wondered how he would have handled this situation if they hadn't been there. Now that the air had cleared a little they could go on to talk about how to handle the police, Rafter thought.

Love and learning

Jenny and Sally, arm in arm, wandered thoughtfully along the path that led round Alo's house. Both had borrowed Alo's ponchos as the air outside was cold.

"We all got it wrong about Tyrell," Sally began. "You never met him did you? Vee told me he was very funny in fact; a real clown."

Jenny asked: "Who's Vee?"

"A very dear friend from the Reaches." Sally didn't want to say more. It would be rather complicated to explain, she thought. What's more, she wasn't sure if Vee was still with her. His voice had been silent since she got back. She thought of Vee's comment about D'rick and El'na and she said: "It looks like Martin and Fran have got something going together."

Jenny gave her a funny look as if not recognising her friend in what she said. "Matchmaking?" she asked with a nervous giggle and then added more seriously: "It does indeed. They go well together."

They turned off the main path and followed a narrow way that wound through large bushes of Rhododendrons.

"How about you Sally? Is there someone special in your life?"

Sally stopped to look at her friend, wondering what to say and what to keep to herself.

"There are lots of special people in my life, but two of them are particularly special: Brent and Keira. I love them both and they both love me..."

"And what about this Vee?"

"Ah. Vee. What would you answer Vee?" Not that she expected him to answer, but it was good to address him again.

"I would say we are so close it is sometimes hard to tell the difference," he replied.

Sally shrieked with delight at the sound of his voice in her head, startling Jenny.

"What's the matter? Are you alright?" Jenny asked, seeing Sally laughed till tears ran down her cheeks.

"I'm fine. It's Vee. He said we were so closer it was hard to tell us apart."

Jenny had a worried look on her face as if her friend had gone crazy.

"Don't worry so, Jenny. Let me explain." And so she told her the story of Vee with him putting in the occasional comment now and again. When she reached the end both were seated by a little fountain in a clearing. Jenny still looked perplexed.

"So Vee speaks in your head?"

"Yes, he does. He knows so much. And he sees things I haven't noticed."

"Let's not exaggerate," Vee commented.

Jenny stopped in front of Sally. She was more than a head smaller than Sally, but her intense green eyes were startling. Putting her hands on her friend's shoulders, she asked: "Do you think I could learn to travel like that? Maybe you could teach me. And I'm sure Fran would be game too."

It was Sally's turn to look serious. She remembered the blindness and the imprisonment in the Black Castle and her long and dangerous trip under the mountain.

"It's not all fun, you know. There are nightmares in the Dream Realm!"

But the idea of training a small group of people to go to the Dream Realm appealed to her. It opened all manner of exciting avenues. She would talk to Rafter and Alo about it. Maybe it could be part of her work as assistant now that the task for Leuchtli was over.

"I'll talk to Rafter about it. Let's see what he says," she concluded.

The necklace

Sally sat on Brent's bed, holding his hand. It felt strange to be hand in hand with someone who wasn't really there.

"They've been away too long, Vee. I want to go back to the Reaches and fetch them."

Vee remained silent for a moment.

"Maybe they have to make this journey by themselves. Perhaps you have other things to do," he finally said.

"It's odd," she replied as if thinking out loud. "I imagined us all coming back here and the adventure being over. Then we'd go on as before. Well with Brent as a new addition." She laughed at the expression. "But they're not here and so many things are still open that I can't see an end to it."

Alo knocked quietly at the door and stepped into the room.

"Sorry to disturb, Sally. Do you have that necklace with you? Rafter told me about it and I'd like to have a look."

She took a box out of her bag. Opening it she took out the necklace that was shroud in a black cloth to protect it. She went to hand it to Alo, but he refused to take it.

"Place it open on the bed over there, Sally, please. I don't think I should touch it," Alo explained.

"How do you think I managed to bring such a material object back from the Reaches, Alo?" She asked.

"That's what's troubling me," he mused. "You received it after you evoked Oran Mor?"

"Sort of. It was a present from the Littl' People for saving them and for restoring the Lost Meadows. For them, I am the incarnation of their legend."

Alo remained silent for a long while. Sally returned to studying Brent's face, wondering if his adventures might be reflected there. But if they were she couldn't read them.

"I think we need to take special care of this necklace," Alo said. "I suspect it has much more significance than it would at first seem. I'd like to talk to Rafter and Naniu about how best to protect it."

Placing his hand on her shoulder by way of farewell he left.

"Another thread unfolds before us," Vee said theatrically.

The Dream Class

Alo's country house was unusually quiet. Naniu had come to see Rafter and Alo but neither had arrived yet. In the sitting room she found Fran who was rubbing oil into her head.

"Would you like a short scalp massage?" Naniu asked.

"That would be wonderful," was Fran's surprised reply.

Naniu took some of the oil, rubbed it into her hands and then begin slow circular movements with her fingertips on the top of Fran's head. After a while Naniu asked, "Tell me Fran, why did you decide to shave your head?"

So Fran told her the story of her escape from Leuchtli until the time when Jenny suggested she shave her head as a defence against the Machine.

"Ingenious," Naniu commented as she continued the massage.

"The only problem is that I am condemned to continue shaving my head in case Leuchtli uses his Machine on me again."

"I think you should tell Rafter about that, he might be able to help."

At that moment Rafter and Alo walked into the room. Both were dressed elegantly, as if they were to attend an important meeting.

Greeting the two women, Rafter asked: "What am I supposed to know?"

"Why I have to keep my head shaved," Fran said and she went on to explain once again how she'd avoided Leuchtli's attack.

"I wouldn't worry too much about that Machine," Rafter said pulling a small cloth bag from his pocket. Opening it he showed Fran the Machine.

"I was unable to give it back to Dr. Leuchtli because he left suddenly without saying goodbye," he said with a wide grin.

"Then you will need this," Fran told him as she dug deep in her back pocket and pulled out a wad of toilet paper.

"I don't understand the joke," he said, perplexed.

"It is not a joke, Professor," she said, unwrapping the paper. "It's a sample of Leuchtli's hair!"

Alo burst out laughing.

"How did you manage to get that?" he asked, admiration in his voice.

"Soon you will know my whole story," Fran laughed.

So she told them of Leuchtli's charming tête-à-tête late one night in his office. They were both shocked and amused by her story.

"… so I took a pair of nail scissors and cut off a chunk of his greasy hair. I used the toilet paper to avoid touching it."

"You young people are far more resourceful and resilient than you look," Rafter commented.

Sally, who'd just arrived with Jenny, Tom and Martin, saw the occasion she'd been waiting for.

"That's why we have a suggestion to make."

Rafter turned to her, looking intrigued. "And what might that be?"

"I suggest I train our friends here to travel in the Dream World as part of my work for the Department."

From the glint in his eye, Sally knew he was in a playful mood.

"I suspect that might cause problems with the University if they are not matriculated. And how am I to explain that my new assistant was being paid to teach people how to sleep?"

Jenny looked crest fallen and Fran was about to complain when Sally put an end to their dismay.

"Don't take him seriously. He's joking."

Rafter put on a contrite face as if he were a naughty boy caught in the act.

"So do you agree?" Sally pursued.

"Of course! It's a wonderful idea." Rafter replied, smiling proudly at her.

"Anyone for tea and crumpets?" Mrs Martin said, balancing a heavy tray on her arm.

Everyone sat noisily at table. Jenny, Fran, Tom and Martin were congratulating Sally on getting their project accepted. Naniu and Alo were chatting with Rafter about lessons they could give the youngsters. Mrs. Martin dished out toasted crumpets all round, offering butter, cream and jam. Rafter got to his feet, raising his cup of tea in a toast: "To the Dream Class!" and the others echoed him: "To the Dream Class."

What with the cheering and clapping nobody heard the phone ring. It was Mrs. Martin that handed the phone to Rafter saying: "It's for you, Professor."

Rafter signalled for everybody to be quiet, but it took a while for people to calm down.

"Yes. Are you sure? This is alarming."

Everyone was impatient to hear the news, but Rafter was

still listening to the person at the other end.

"That's a very good idea. Thank you very much."

When he finally hung up, everybody crowded round. For once he didn't play with his audience, but got straight to the point.

"Brent and Keira have disappeared."

Sally broke the stupefied silence "Does that mean they've come back?"

"No. They were under constant surveillance. One minute they were there and the next they were gone."

Rafter looked at the worried faces around him and said, "Why don't we sit down and have some more of Mrs. Martin's excellent tea while we discuss what this could mean.

Annexes

332   Alan McCluskey

The author

Alan McCluskey lives amid the vineyards in a small Swiss village between three lakes and a range of mountains. Nearby, several thousands of years earlier, lakeside villages housed a thriving Celtic community. The ever-present heart-beat of that world continues to fuel his long-standing fascination for magic and fantasy.

All Alan McCluskey's books are about the self-empowerment of the young, girls in particular, in a world that tends to curtail their pportunities, belittle their abilities and discourage them from doing great things. His books also explore the difficulties of those whose gender and sexuality lies beyond the dominant binary divide between boy and girl. His goal in writing fiction is to imagine inspiring paths forward, despite the difficulties thrown in the way of these young people.

For more information:
Secret Paths: https://author.secret-paths.com
Facebook: https://www.facebook.com/Secret.Paths
Instagram: https://www.instagram.com/secretpathseditions/
Twitter: https://www.twitter.com/Almacme

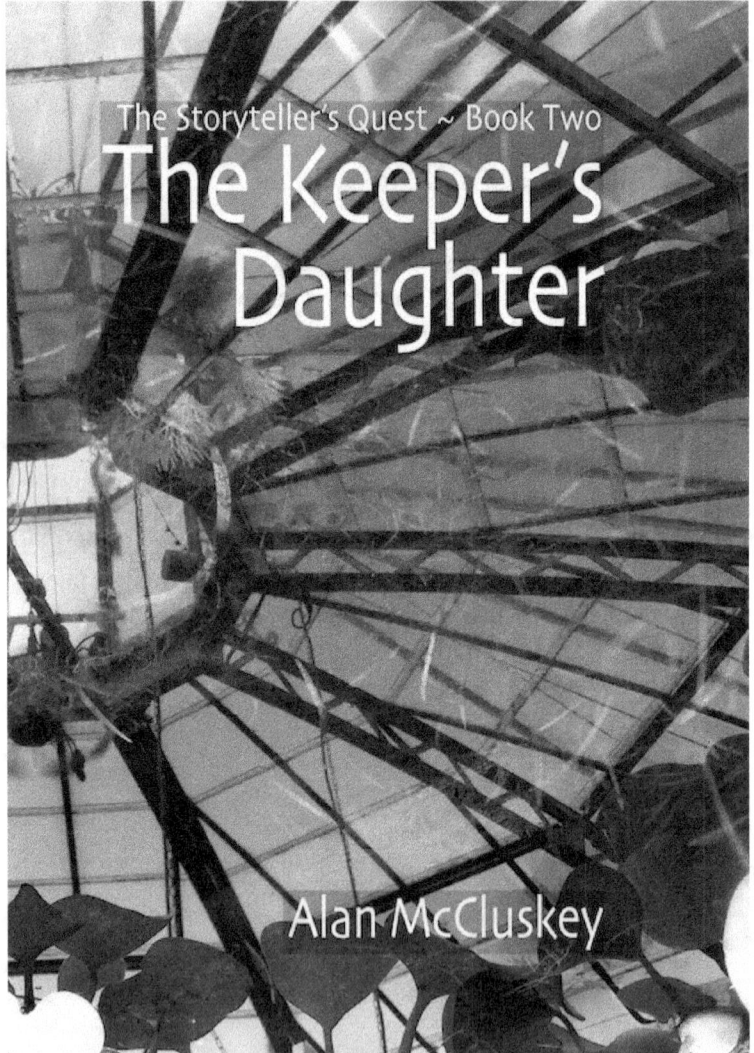

The Storyteller's Quest ~ Book Two

The Keeper's Daughter

Alan McCluskey

The Keeper's Daughter
The Storyteller's Quest - Book 2

It wasn't Brent's fault if he was stuck in the form of Jake the Owl, at least he didn't think it was as he sat on a branch preening despondently. The threads of all his stories had become inextricably muddled in his owlish head. To think that he'd once prided himself on being a storyteller. His stories had become adventures and some of those adventures had become nightmares, and now he was stuck with them. He'd flown in search of his friend and lover, Mia. She'd been dragged off by a band of thugs just when it was time for them all to return to their world. Only Sally, their mutual friend and lover, had made it back from the world of the Reaches to their hometown of Avan. Hearing her story, despite the dangers she'd had to face, her friends suggested Sally teach them to travel to the Dream Realm and beyond to the Reaches. The idea appealed to everybody. Not that Sally knew how to get back to the Reaches, but the idea of a 'dream class' as they called it pleased her and, above all, she wanted to return to the world where her newly-found half-sister lived and where her two friends had so abruptly disappeared.

The Storyteller's Quest ~ Book Three

The Starless Square

Alan McCluskey

The Starless Square
The Storyteller's Quest - Book 3

A weekend of joyous festivities! Such was the Theosophy department's response to a group of fanatics bent on destroying their reputation and having them shut down. Theosophy? Professor Rafter, head of the department, calls it "the study of our direct relationship with that which is beyond and above the normal range of human experience". He could just as well have been describing the adventures of a group of young friends who have been called back from their travels in another world to defend their department with their new-found abilities. But how could entrancing singing or breath-taking storytelling or exquisite cooking possibly stand a chance when pitted against the evil black cloud that threatens to obscure the Starless Square?

Boy & Girl Saga Book 1

Boy & Girl

2020 edition

Alan McCluskey

Boy & Girl
The Boy & Girl Saga - Book 1

When Peter awakes in the head of a girl, he is both delighted and alarmed that his secret yearnings have become reality. Very quickly, however, his error is apparent; this girl is not him. Kaitling –that's her name – is twelve years old, like Peter. She's the daughter of a magician, a prominent figure in another world. Boy and girl travel back and forth from each other's minds, but have little time to get acquainted before Kaitling's island is overrun by warrior priests and she has to flee. At home, a conflict erupts in Peter's family forcing him to take refuge at a friend's place. Meanwhile at school, a haughty new girl goads him about his girlishness and, spitting in his face, vows to rid the earth of people like him. The stage seems set for a desperate struggle to survive, but will ingenuity and youthful fervour be enough against folly and fanaticism?

Boy & Girl Saga Book 2

In Search of Lost Girls

2020 edition

Alan McCluskey

In Search of Lost Girls
The Boy & Girl Saga - Book 2

Listen carefully. You can just hear the mournful tolling of a bell over the shuffle of girls' feet as they traipse to Mass, nursing bruises and numb despair. No one cares. No one is there to stem the torrent of injustice and abuse. They are lost and forgotten. In another world, the cathedral still reverberates to the melody of angelic voices as the mourners file out, heads bowed, words hushed. If only they knew that the two girls whose music delights them so were really boys in disguise, sanctity would flee in the face of raging indignation. Then a gunshot threatens to put an end to the girls' lost cause. The scene is set. The author picks up his pen with trembling fingers and begins to write. Time to tear Kate and Peter apart. The thought of making her life hell has him dribbling in anticipation. Age is no excuse. He ought to know better. Things rarely turn out as an author expects.

Boy & Girl Saga Book 3

We Girls

2020 edition

Alan McCluskey

We Girls
The Boy & Girl Saga - Book 3

Peter is beset by an existential choice, retain his androgynous ambiguity or say goodbye to his girlish self. Circumstances, however, force both him and Kate to take up other challenges. By straddling the line between child and adult, between carefree creativity and weighty responsibility, between play and work, they find imaginative ways to confront far-reaching problems on which adults persistently turn a blind eye.

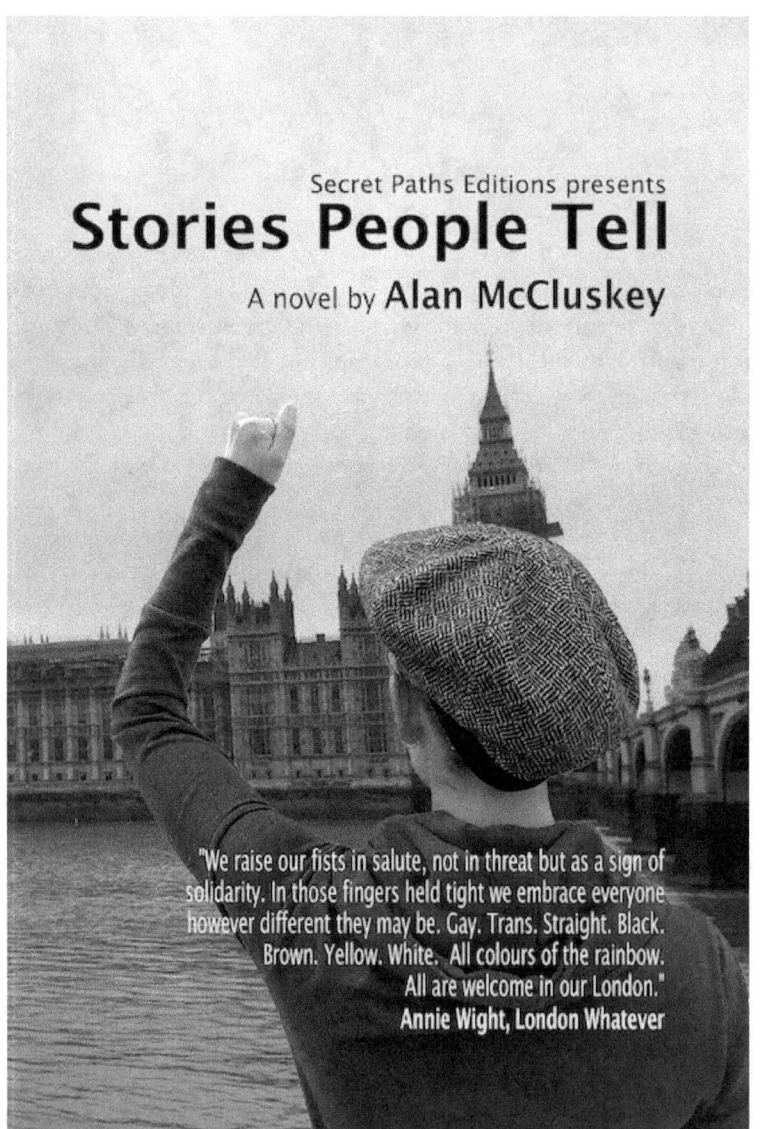

Secret Paths Editions presents

Stories People Tell

A novel by **Alan McCluskey**

"We raise our fists in salute, not in threat but as a sign of solidarity. In those fingers held tight we embrace everyone however different they may be. Gay. Trans. Straight. Black. Brown. Yellow. White. All colours of the rainbow. All are welcome in our London."
Annie Wight, London Whatever

Stories People Tell

Stories People Tell is a tale about Annie Wight, a shy school-girl who, despite sustained, cruel treatment and personal doubts, blossoms into a major voice in the grassroots movement 'London Whatever' celebrating gender diversity while struggling to end violence against women and care for the weak and marginalised.

Annie wasn't expecting to fall in love with a girl or to shoot to notoriety when she got swept up in 'London Whatever'. Nor could she have known that, right from the outset, she would become the number one target of Nolan Kard, the homophobic Lord Mayor of London. who was campaigning to 'Keep London Straight'. She bore the brunt of attacks from his rogue police, not to mention from a sinister gang of ghostwriters, the nightmare of all Kard's enemies.

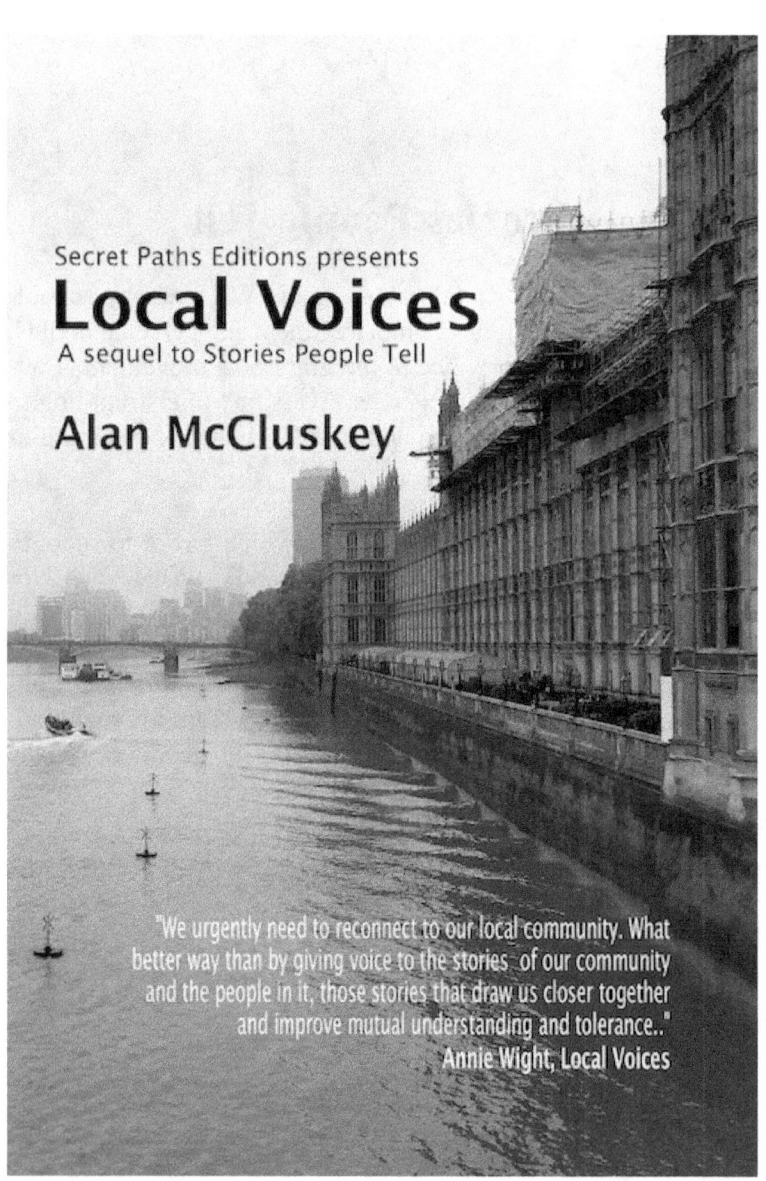

Secret Paths Editions presents

Local Voices
A sequel to Stories People Tell

Alan McCluskey

"We urgently need to reconnect to our local community. What
better way than by giving voice to the stories of our community
and the people in it, those stories that draw us closer together
and improve mutual understanding and tolerance.."
Annie Wight, Local Voices

Local Voices
A sequel to Stories People Tell

In her campaign to re-assert and strengthen the role of women at the heart of hearthside healthcare, seventeen-year-old Annie Wight finds herself pitted against Health England, a conservative think-tank backed by pharmaceutical giants and private healthcare providers. Pretexting the defence of the National Health Service, they stop at nothing to stamp out Annie's efforts. They target not just her but those close to her, wreaking havoc in friendships and affairs of the heart. As part of her response, Annie launches a project to share the stories of those that never figure in the spotlight. By celebrating local voices, the project fights against isolation and disempowerment.

Secret Paths Editions presents

Bursting with Life!

by Alan McCluskey

Bursting with Life!

Vint is bursting with life. So much so the world around him ripples with energy and takes on unexpected forms. His parents and carers have convinced him his hallucinations are a sign of madness. Repression is their sole remedy, seeking to rein in anything that can over stimulate and spark an attack. He is a willing prisoner in a grey world, stripped of friends, colour, movement and music…not to mention good food. Only when he escapes with Tara and meets her friends does he realise that what he sees may not be hallucinations but rather a gift to transform the world. In the light of this new perspective, he begins to lose his fear of being mad and discovers the richness of the world. All would be well, were it not for the greed and rapaciousness of his carers who seek to get him back and exploit his abilities.

Secret Paths Editions presents

The Cloud Catcher

by Alan McCluskey

The Cloud Catcher

Fran, an eighteen-year-old, has had a rough life and things seem set to continue that way, but a chance encounter leads with a ravishing girl her to discover potential in herself she couldn't have imagined... She's going to need it if she's to combat the sordid legacy of her father and build a new life for herself and her new-found friends.

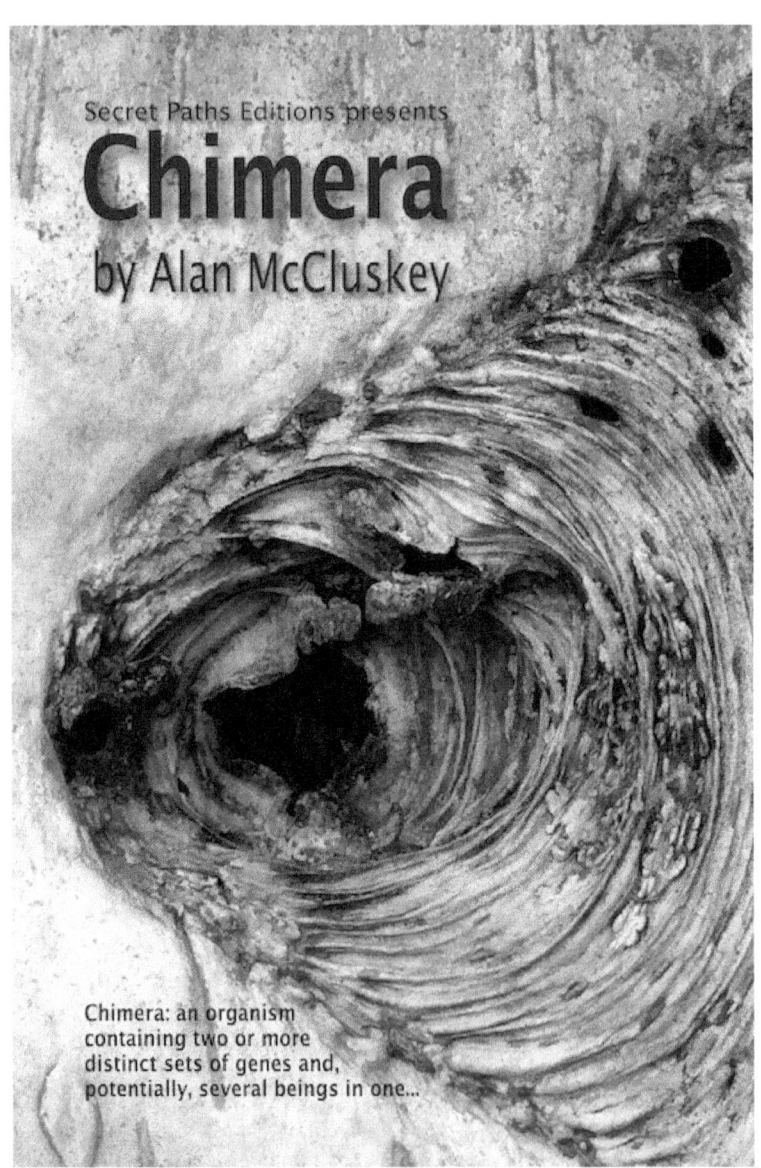

Secret Paths Editions presents

Chimera
by Alan McCluskey

Chimera: an organism
containing two or more
distinct sets of genes and,
potentially, several beings in one...

Chimera

A chimera is an organism containing two or more distinct sets of genes and, potentially, several beings in one. Sami and Sam are a chimera, two people in one, a girl and a boy, a leader and healer of people sharing a body with a brilliant but autistic child.

Sam talking to himself on discovering he is one half of a chimera...:
:: not being able to speak, to move - such was the price I had to pay - to cut out the chaos and confusion from a world run wild - a raw satisfaction - being barricaded in my head these past twelve years - all for nothing - that blasted girl has ruined everything - surging out of nowhere - pirating my body - bridging the gap between me and the others - letting chaos rush in - beguiling everyone with her codswallop - not me - I'm not impressed - some say she's destined to be our saviour - as if the block-head could save a fly - I just want her gone

Sami's first ever words to her teacher and her father...:
"I ... need ... to explain. Words come with ... difficulty. I must ... be brief. Sam and I are a ... chimera ... there are two of us... Sam is the boy you know. New things terrify him. He cannot speak ... out loud. He stumbles. He falls. I am new. I just awoke. I am a girl. I play piano I talk. I walk. As for that violence you just saw, that was Sam trying to kick me out"

www.ingramcontent.com/pod-product-compliance
Lightning Source LLC
Chambersburg PA
CBHW071847220626
47052CB00002B/6